First published by In My Lit Era Publishing LLC 2024

Copyright © 2024 by Stacey LP

All rights reserved. No part of this publication may be reproduced, stored, or transmitted in any form or by any means, electronic, mechanical, photocopying, recording, scanning, or otherwise, without written permission from the publisher. It is illegal to copy this book, post it to a website, or distribute it by any other means without permission.

No part of this book may be used to create, feed, or refine artificial intelligence models for any purpose without written permission from the author.

This novel is entirely a work of fiction. Any resemblance to actual persons, living or dead, events or localities is entirely coincidental.

The publishers and the book are not associated with any product or vendor mentioned in this book.

First edition

EPUB ISBN: 978-1-965557-00-6

PAPERBACK ISBN: 978-1-965557-01-3

Cover art by Stacey LP

Typeset and formatted by Stacey LP

Copy Editing by Hannah G. Scheffer-Wentz, English Proper Editing Services

AFTERGLOW: RISING FROM THE ASHES

AFTERGLOW RISING TRILOGY
BOOK 1

STACEY LP

COMMITMENT TO DIVERSE WORLDS IN SCI-FI AND FANTASY

Why is diversity important? Because *people* are diverse in experience, appearance, beliefs, sexuality, gender identity, and so much more. That is why I strive to include an array of characters in my work who represent the intersectionality of our real world.

As a bisexual female author, I know that representation is essential for readers to connect with and see themselves across all genres. And what better genre to embrace diversity than science fiction and fantasy—where new worlds can be anything we want them to be? Because leaders, heroes, and love come in many forms.

♡—Stacey

CONTENT AWARENESS

The *Afterglow Rising Trilogy* takes place in a post-apocalyptic setting and gets quite stressful. You can expect strong language/cursing throughout the text. Characters will experience and reflect on losing loved ones, coping with trauma, and there will be many heavy moments. Open-door love scenes are not off the table either, depending on what my characters feel like doing as the story evolves. For all of the above, the *Afterglow Rising Trilogy* is for adult readers 18+.

One last note before diving into what sensitive content is included: *Afterglow* tells multiple love stories, but *Afterglow* is not a romance novel. I want to set that expectation now, as happy endings are not guaranteed. What does that mean? I guess you'll have to stick around and find out, now.

Content:
- Aliens
- Medical equipment and procedures
- References to being abducted and experimented on
- Loss of memory
- Eight legged creatures
- Violence
- Injury
- Depictions of anxiety, panic attacks
- References to and experience of loss and death
- Cult-like depictions
- Open-door love scenes (eventually)

I apologize in advance for the myriad of emotions you are about to experience throughout this trilogy. Kind of.

Okay have fun, bye!

IMMERSIVE PLAYLIST

For an immersive playlist experience, check out the chapter-by-chapter playlist on Stacey's website!

To my mom,
Thank you for your endless support, amazing creative notes, and our mutual agreement to pretend any *romantic* scenes never happened when we talked about my book.
I love you.

PART ONE

ONE
ALINA

THE SOUND of a scream caught me off guard and I tripped back a step, looking over my shoulder in time to see a flash of red dart past me.

I whirled around to see Emma dive, legs disappearing over the edge of the dock and into the water. My best friend reemerged with a splash as she burst through the surface of the lake and pulled herself back up onto the pier. "Come on, don't tell me you haven't been looking forward to this all week." Emma smiled brightly as she shook out her short, red hair.

"Alright, Little Mermaid." I laughed, jogging the rest of the way over.

Emma scrunched her nose, tilting her head to look at me as her hands shielded her eyes from the sun. "Little Mermaid? Really?"

"I mean, red hair, water—it was the first thing that popped into my head. I'll do better next time." I shrugged, sitting down and dipping my toes into the water. Lounging on the dock, listening to the water gently lapping as the sun warmed my shoulders, I could feel the tension from the work week melting away already.

Emma and I always visited this lake with her older brother, Jason, when we were kids. As the years passed, our trips grew further apart, but no matter how much time went by, it always felt like it was still *our* place. "When was the last time we were here, anyway?" I asked.

Emma slipped her sunglasses on, laying back on the dock as she sighed. "Oh! I was just looking at pictures from that weekend. It was when Jason came home from the West Coast. You know, after his whole engagement fiasco? Your hair was blue, so it must have been around then." Emma tilted her sunglasses down to give me a *look*.

I cringed; though it had been years, the regret from my post-breakup impulse hair decision still haunted me. My hair had always been dark brown, just past my shoulders, and wavy. I'm not quite sure what made me pick blue, of all colors, at that point in time. Up until that moment, I'd only ever gotten subtle, natural-looking highlights. The blue thoroughly washed me out—even my hazel eyes dulled against the hue. I stubbornly stuck with it for several weeks before admitting I hated it. Safe to say, that was one choice I would not be repeating.

I looked at Emma lying beside me, her natural red hair shining in the sun. I could see a spot on her shoulder where she'd missed rubbing some sunscreen in, and without another thought, I reached over to blend it in for her. "Missed a spot."

"Thanks, friend!" Emma replied cheerily. "You know my pale ass needs all the protection it can get." She nailed me with a firm look. "You remembered your sunscreen, too, right?"

When we were kids, Emma had gotten a bad burn, landing her in the hospital with dehydration and heat stroke. She'd been militant about sunscreen ever since, going so far as to limit our time in direct sunlight during the height of summer. I was surprised she'd wanted to come to the lake today during peak UV hours.

I kicked a leg up, the SPF lotion I'd thrown on giving my tawny skin a soft glow in the sun. "SPF-30, baby."

"Good," Emma said, satisfied.

I lay back, closing my eyes as my mind drifted to our last lake visit just over five years ago. Jason had been living in California with his fiancée. A few weeks before their wedding date, he came home to find her in their bed with a coworker. Yet, somehow, Jason was the one who was kicked out of their apartment. Emma and I were still in Connecticut back then. I have to admit, I was more than overjoyed when Jason called Emma to tell her that he was moving back across the country to live near us again. When he finally arrived, before he even unpacked, he insisted on a lake camp-out to distract him from the dramatic breakup.

The three of us sat on this same dock, passing a bottle of vodka back and forth while Jason groaned about all the signs he'd missed, just a shade above self-deprecation. Eventually, Emma and I turned the conversation to reminiscing about our most embarrassing moments growing up, leaving our sides aching with laughter before long.

Tired from drinking and the late afternoon sun, Emma closed her eyes, *'just for a minute,'* which turned into several hours. Jason and I continued hanging out well into the sunset. As Emma's best friend since childhood, I'd also grown close to Jason over the years. No matter how much time passed between conversations, we could always pick up right where we'd left off.

The more vodka I drank, the more I couldn't stop staring at the way his blue eyes reflected the water from the lake as he, yet again, ran a hand through his tousled, ash-blond hair.

Whether it was the vodka or us both rebounding from recent breakups, there had been a moment where I *swore* there was something there. I remembered how the space seemed to spark with electricity as the distance closed between us, our body heat mingling as our skin almost touched. Of course, Emma had woken up before anything happened, and the night was uneventful from there on. Jason and I never mentioned the *almost* moment, but I had certainly thought about it over the years.

A gentle breeze picked up and I shivered as the memory slipped away. The air carried a sharp chill, breaking through the heat that radiated from the sun. I sat up and hugged my knees, staring out at the lake. I couldn't believe we didn't make the time to do this more often. The older we got, the quicker time seemed to drift away. Days grew into weeks, that dripped into months, and poured into years. I really needed to learn how to slow down, take more PTO, and make more memories like this. A pang squeezed in my chest, knowing that even this moment was fleeting.

The sun's rays danced across the water, shimmering with gentle ripples. At the water's edge, a shadow slowly rolled across the shore. I tilted my head, watching the shade bloom as it reached the lake.

The shadow grew, dimming the sun's reflected light. Silhouettes from trees that stretched across the once glittering surface faded into a dull gray as the darkness spread. I shivered again as goosebumps rose on my skin.

"Hey, is it supposed to rain? I didn't see—" A gasp escaped as I jolted upright.

The dock beside me was empty.

I was alone.

I scrambled for my flip-flops, calling out, "Emma? *Emma!*" My gaze darted across the tree line past the dock for any sign of my friend. The shadow covered the lake entirely now and I felt a pull calling me, begging to look up at the sky. I grit my teeth, shaking my head. *No. This wasn't right.* I forced myself to move, feeling like I was wading through quicksand as I tried to reach the end of the dock. My legs grew heavier with each step.

A mechanical groan echoed from the clouds and I fell to my knees, clutching my head. *Why is this happening? Where's Emma?* Nothing about the situation felt right.

My legs went numb as I scrambled to find my footing, only to fall back down to the ground. "*Emma!*" I yelled again, voice breaking. Shivers rolled across my skin as I stretched my arms out, clawing into the ground to try and pull myself forward. My heart pounded, every beat feeling like a punch to the chest. Eyes wide, hands still clawing for purchase, I finally turned my head to look up at the sky.

A bright white light flooded my vision, consuming everything around me before I plunged into darkness.

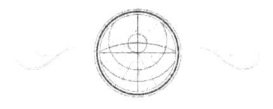

My head felt like it was being squeezed in a vice. Pounding—endless, relentless pounding. Groggily, I struggled to lift my eyelids; it felt like they were anchored shut. The leftover disorientation from my nightmare hung around my tired body like a mist as I pushed to bring myself back to full consciousness. *How long had I been asleep?* My eyes struggled to focus as my head swam and bile crept up my throat. *Was I hungover? Or did I have the flu?*

I wished I was still in my dream at the lake with Emma and almost started slipping back into sleep. A warm fuzziness wrapped around my brain. *Maybe we could go to the lake later today. Wait, no—* That lake was back in Connecticut, which would explain the nostalgic start of the dream sequence. We moved to Austin two years ago, so it truly had been a while since we'd visited the lake. I forced my mind the rest of the way back towards consciousness before the second half of my dream-turned-nightmare could creep back into my head.

Straining, I finally lifted my eyelids, blinking to try and regain focus. My heart stuttered as my eyesight finally adjusted—hard, curved sides surrounded me in a space no bigger than a coffin. Though it wasn't completely opaque, I couldn't see outside of the encasement. That's when I knew—I wasn't waking up from a typical night of rest. The root of my unconsciousness had to be something much deeper, more sinister.

Maybe I wasn't fully awake. Maybe I was still trapped in a nightmare. Nausea swirled in my stomach, heart rate rising as I struggled to lift my leaden arms. I couldn't move—*why couldn't I move?* Panic erupted from my chest, seeming to fill up the remaining space in the capsule as a soft blue light reflected throughout the small space. *Where the fuck was I?*

Sharp prickling pain crackled through my veins. The pins and needles stung like a wasp had been stabbing me repeatedly, all over. This wasn't a bad dream—I was in a waking nightmare. I squeezed my eyes shut as my heart pounded, the stinging still vibrating through my body.

"Please, please, please..." Shaky words rasped from my dry throat as I begged my lungs to hold oxygen. The tight space was starting to feel like it was caving in, and I couldn't tell if the air was actually thin or if my lungs were struggling from hyperventilation. My heart pounded as I closed my eyes, choking back sobs and counting slowly in my head to bring my heart rate down.

One.
Two.
Three.
Four...

My head swam as I tried to remember anything that could give me a clue as to where I was, but the memories were too far out of reach. After digging deep to pull up what remained of my courage, I forced myself to open my eyes again.

Though I couldn't move anything just yet, my eyes traced the outline of the encasement. As my sight adjusted, I realized it wasn't a solid tomb. The sides curved, almost in an egg shape. At the top, a deep groove carved an indent into the otherwise smooth surface. Maybe an opening? *I will find a way out. I* will *get out.*

Slowly, the prickling in my extremities dulled and I regained feeling in my fingers and toes. I cried out loud with relief as sensation trickled back into my arms and legs. After what felt like hours, I was finally able to lift a hand. I didn't hesitate before pounding my fists against the top of the encasement as hard as I could. The more that feeling returned, the harder I was able to shove at the top of my prison. I punched and pushed with my fists and once I could move my legs I started shallowly kicking, too. A click popped and a sliver of natural light leaked through a crack along the indentation. *It opened.*

I pushed against the lid while struggling to pull myself upright at the same time. Finally, I was able to shove the lid all the way open. It swung back on a hinge and I couldn't help feeling like I'd crawled back from the dead. Now that I could see the whole thing, it resembled a rounded nap pod more than the coffin I'd imagined. At least it didn't appear to be a final resting place. *Keep looking on the bright side, Lee,* I tried to encourage myself.

I wanted nothing more than to pull myself completely out of the pod, but my head was swirling with dizziness. Instead, I leaned against the opening, gripping the side like a life raft. My stomach churned with nausea as I lifted a hand to wipe away the tears, sweat, and probably snot that was running down my face. Wincing, I rubbed my eyes, feeling a slight pull on the back of my hand.

Oh, fuck.

Black, oily looking tubes trailed from where they sunk into the back of my hand, down my arm, and through a small opening at the bottom of the pod. Gasping, my hand shot away from my face as I jerked back. The sharp movement made my head spin, blurring my vision. I was so nauseous, I didn't know how much longer I could hold it back.

I swallowed hard, exhaling slowly to keep my breathing stable. The last thing I needed was to puke all over my...*What was I wearing?* The opaque, gauzy fabric initially looked like a loose, knee-length tunic, but the texture reminded me of shed snake skin.

With shaking hands, I gripped the tubes where they met the veins on my hand, taking a deep breath before yanking them from my skin. They let go with slurping sounds as the suction released. Circular indentations were left at the spots where they had been connected to my skin, reminding me of tiny teeth marks.

But that wasn't all. I struggled to fight off dizziness as I noticed suction-cup shells stuck to my chest, shoulders, and arms. "No, no, no, no, no," I moaned.

The discs throbbed every few seconds, swelling like sponges full of blood. With a whimper, I poked at one of the discs. *Please tell me this thing isn't alive.* Its surface caved with the depression of my fingertip, but it felt more like plastic—a mild relief. Frantically, I pulled at the adhesions that clung to my body like slugs, throwing them over the side of the capsule I was still sitting in.

As I tried to quell my shaking limbs, I looked around the room. It appeared to be an office conference room, or it used to be, at least. A whiteboard took up one whole wall and there were a few scattered desk chairs. Against an adjacent wall hung a lone screen that likely served as the former conference room's video monitor. The rest of the space was crammed with foreign, bulky metal devices that looked like they were painted with black oil. Given the tube and discs that had adorned my skin, I assumed the equipment was medical—though nothing resembled any of the machines or tools I was used to seeing in a doctor's office.

I tested my legs, bending them gently so I wouldn't trigger more vertigo when I noticed one more shiny tube leading down my leg, connected to a clear bag of yellow liquid that hung from the pod.

"Oh fuck, fuck, fuck!" I moaned, realizing exactly where it was attached. Slowly, so slowly, I reached my shaking hand between my legs and felt a thick, hard shell cupping me. I winced as I stuck a finger underneath the lip of the device, prying it from my body. As I threw the apparatus to the floor, I couldn't hold back the urge to vomit any longer.

I couldn't have imagined this, even in my worst nightmares. *What happened to me? How long have I been here? Did anyone even know I was gone?* I sobbed as I dry-heaved, unable to ignore the violation that coated me like a second skin.

Once I finished heaving and was able to gather some strength, I pulled myself up to lean over the open lip of the pod. I had to get out —get as far away as possible before whoever had done this came back.

I clung to the side of the container, struggling as I lifted a leg to straddle the opening and ease myself up and over. I hit the floor with a smack and groaned. Pushing upright, I panted as I took another look around the room.

"Okay. Okay, I got this," I whispered, gripping the side of the pod for balance as I stood with shaking legs.

Finally, in an upright position, I took inventory of my body. From what I could see so far, my skin was unmarred; even the indentations from the tube and discs seemed to be fading quickly without the devices attached. The jackhammer in my head had subdued to a dull throb and the nausea was easing a bit, as well.

Aside from the nausea and headache, only my nerves plagued me. I wasn't in pain otherwise. Still, my familiar curves, the soft swell of my hips and the fullness of my thighs, felt different somehow. The muscles beneath, stiff from being cramped in that pod for who knows how long, felt taut and firm as I stretched to awaken my limbs further.

I rubbed at my temples and tried to make sense of the images floating through my head. I knew that the lake was definitely a dream. That bright light, though…the fear that emerged with the nightmare felt too familiar. A wave of nausea hit me once more and I sank back to the floor to rest my head between my knees.

Emma and Jason...if I was here, where were they? I struggled to pull any memories forward, but it was still a jumbled mess.

Once again, I rose to my feet, pushing down panic and grasping tighter to the small thread of determination I was able to muster. The more I moved, the steadier my steps became. I made it out of the conference room and into the center of the office space when the soft padding of footsteps echoed from the adjacent hallway.

I froze in place, pulse pounding. I knew I wasn't fast enough to return to the other room and hide, but I couldn't stand out in the open, either.

"Move. *Move!*" I whispered, forcing my legs to carry me to a small mountain of office furniture stacked in the corner of the room. With aching knees, I lowered myself to the floor as a flash of memories sparked behind my eyes.

A shelter in place order. Emma's panicked voice on the phone. Something impossibly large blocking the sky over the city. Unidentified aircraft. Jason. Relief. Worry. Fear. We needed to get Emma.

I snapped back to the present as the sound from the hallway drew closer. A soft murmur echoed in the empty space, followed by a light sob and frantic whispers. People! They sounded scared. Maybe they'd been taken, just like me. I took a gamble, choked down my fear, and softly called, "Hello?"

A gasp echoed through the space, followed by shushing sounds. More whispers. Then, a male voice called out, "H-how many?"

Confusion blanketed my thoughts and I rubbed the side of my head, trying to understand the question. "How many *what*?"

"How many are there?" his voice snapped.

"It's just me," I answered. "I-I just woke up in a pod thing—there were tubes and, and, fuck!" I choked out, unable to keep the emotion from my words. I slowly stood, realizing there was no point in hiding any longer. Shuffling closer to the hallway, I saw three shadows on the wall. Three people. I let out a sob of relief when I saw they were dressed in identical gauze-like gowns, if only for the solidarity.

A young girl, maybe sixteen or seventeen, rushed towards me, grasping my forearms as tears streamed down her face. "We woke up a while ago and have been trying to find our way out since, but so many of the doors were locked. Where did you come from? Have you seen anyone else? Are *you* okay?" the teen rapid-fired.

I took in the sight of her. Limp, blonde hair draped over her shoulders and the gauzy gown hung over her small frame. The corners of her cracked lips trembled and I saw the same fear I felt reflected in her eyes. I glanced back to the room. "N-no—I mean, yeah, just me. My name is Alina, I—" The room started spinning and I swayed.

An older woman with deep mahogany skin jolted forward, wrapping an arm around my waist to brace my body with hers. "Let's get you out of here. Come on, we'll help you. I'm Jean." She gave me a tight-lipped smile, which was more than I could muster.

"I'm Gabriela." The young girl sniffed, raising a hand in greeting. "That's Ben out there."

I nodded, thanking Jean and stepping away once I regained some steadiness. The three of us quickly moved to the hallway where Ben waited. In the dim light, he looked to be older than Jean, maybe in his late sixties, with a pale, almost jaundiced complexion.

The four of us shuffled as fast as we could, passing more glass-walled conference rooms as we tried to find a clear way out. There was a staircase that connected the levels of the building internally, but any exit doors leading outside, even fire escapes, had been locked. We also couldn't turn on any lights—if it weren't for the giant windows, we'd be stuck in the dark. It seemed the power was cut entirely. Most of the other conference rooms held victims who were still contained in their pods. However, when we checked to see if they were alive, they weren't as lucky as we were. Jean informed me in a quiet voice that the other people they found before coming across me appeared to have passed away before anyone could find them. I thought of their families, how they might never get answers as to what happened to their loved ones. *What about my own family? What did they think happened to me?*

Just as we were about to turn another corner, I jolted to a halt, almost tripping Jean. "Wait—there are two pods in there." I bit my lip nervously.

Ben looked back, eyes darting between us. "Pods? You mean those giant test tubes? No one else was alive in the other rooms. Those probably just have more dead bodies. We should keep moving."

"I was alive," I replied, defensiveness growing in my chest. "And I don't know what I'd have done if you three hadn't found me. Waking up alone in there...We have to check, at least. I'm not going to leave another person behind."

Frustration carved deeper across Ben's face before I turned to the door, sliding it open.

Jean followed me in and together we lifted the lid of the first pod. A teenage boy who appeared no older than eighteen lay inside, too still. His skin had a dull, waxy sheen and my breath caught in my throat as Jean stepped closer. She reached into the open pod and placed two fingers at the pulse point on his neck. We waited in silence for a moment longer before she grimly shook her head.

"See," Ben scoffed, "I told y'all. Not worth it to waste—"

"There's still another one," I snapped.

The other pod sat in the back of the room. I rushed to the back, digging my fingers into the lid's groove. The hinge creaked as I opened this one. When I saw the person inside, I fell back a step, almost dropping the lid. Jean caught it and took over opening the pod before it could close again. A whimper left my lips as I fell to the ground. *How?* My breath came in short, choked gasps.

"What's wrong?" Gabriela called from the door; her brown eyes were wide as pools on her pale face as she watched us. Ben peered in from behind her, his bulky frame shadowing hers, but neither came closer.

"He's alive!" Jean yelled as she pulled the discs and tubes from his body. "Better to do this before he regains consciousness," she muttered.

Not a minute after she'd pulled the last suction disc from his chest, I heard a groan from inside the tinted encasement.

"He's—is he awake?" I gasped, scrambling to stand. I pushed past Jean to peer into the pod, still shaking. Tentatively, I reached down to grasp his limp palm in mine. He groaned again, eyes rolling underneath his closed lids; I imagined he was feeling the sharp tingle of sensation returning to his limbs just as I had.

He fought whatever sedation was still in his system, struggling to find his way back to consciousness. Ben was still complaining, but I could only focus on the face of the blond haired man in front of me. I clutched his hand, refusing to take my eyes off of him while Jean and Gabriela argued with Ben in the background.

Finally, those brilliant, blue eyes opened and met mine. I choked back another sob as I studied his pale face.

"Hi," I softly whispered, tears pouring down my cheeks as I brushed the hair from his sweaty forehead.

"Alina? Lee, it's really you?" he rasped.

"Yes, Jason, it's me. I'm here," I cried.

TWO
ALINA

JASON WAS STILL STRUGGLING as we stumbled through the building as fast as we could. I clung to his waist, helping him to stay upright with his arm draped across my shoulders. I wanted to stay in the room a bit longer so he could continue recovering, but like the others, Jason was desperate to get out and insisted we keep going.

We stopped in a few more rooms on the way out—partly to check the pods for anyone else who had woken up, partly so Jason could catch his breath and choke down the nausea he had yet to overcome. The others confirmed multiple times that they hadn't found any red-haired women in the other pods, which made it less likely that Emma was also here. Still, that information didn't bring relief and only led to darker possibilities intruding on my already panicked thoughts.

Straining, I tried again to grasp at memories just out of reach, desperate to understand how we all could have ended up here. I could practically feel the moments in time bubbling at the surface of my mind, waiting for me to pluck them out. All of the unknowns were more than overwhelming, but at least I wasn't alone. I glanced at Jason and the dazed expression he wore. Squeezing his side, I murmured, "I'm here. We can do this."

Jason pulled me closer in response.

"There," Jean yelled from ahead, "another exit!" Jean pushed hard against the door and this one burst open, letting the sunlight in.

We made it.

Holding the door, Jean ushered Gabriela, Ben, Jason, and me outside. My eyes darted up towards the sky, squinting to adjust to the brightness as pieces of memory flashed behind my eyes—

A dark hulking shadow covering the city. An emergency alert blaring from my phone. The news of unidentified aircraft. A shelter-in-place order. Emergency. Messages from Emma. Jason.

I squeezed my eyes shut as the memories jumbled again and tried instead to focus on identifying where we were. We stumbled across the pavement and I frantically looked around, squinting in the daylight for any landmarks to identify our location. Though our physical location was familiar, the details were just...wrong. It looked like a full-on war had taken place. Scorch marks stretched across the pavement and chunks of buildings had been blown to pieces, leaving giant holes in crumbling structures. The city's streets were littered with the remnants of what used to be storefronts, merchandise, beams from walls, and other unidentifiable rubble. The smell of rot and garbage wafted from the inside of the buildings and alleyways we passed. On the sidewalks, dark, rusty, brown stains were splattered across the cement and I tried not to think about what they could be from. The skeletons of what were once proud skyscrapers still lined the skyline, but as a broken urban forest. Finally, I realized we were in downtown Austin.

It was like we stepped through a portal and exited into some awful, alternative reality. Yet, even surrounded by destruction, seeing the city so empty was the most unsettling part. An eerie silence filled the air; it was like every other living thing had been blinked out of existence. And then...there was us.

My lungs screamed as we struggled to run. I didn't know how much longer I could keep moving or how far we had even managed to travel. The pounding in my chest from exertion mixed with anxiety was becoming unbearable. My feet felt like they were on fire against the hot pavement.

"I can't," Jean gasped. "I can't keep going."

"Turn here," Ben grunted as we stumbled onto a side street wrapped in shade.

We collapsed to the ground gasping for breath. I coughed as the dry air stuck to the back of my throat. *What I wouldn't do for some water.*

"Now what?" Gabriela whispered, nervously fidgeting with the ends of her hair.

Jean tried to smile and reassure the girl, but it looked more like a grimace. "Well," Jean panted, "we're free, I guess. I'm not convinced we didn't just walk into something worse, though."

"Let's take a second to think," Jason murmured, his voice still hoarse. He cleared his throat. "It doesn't seem like anyone's following us—or that anyone else is around, period. Let's try and figure out exactly where we are and where to go next."

"No. I'm done. Let's just get out of here," Ben interrupted, running a hand over his balding head and down his face. "I can't stay here. I don't want to waste more time."

"I want my dads," Gabriela quietly sobbed. Jean wrapped an arm around the girl in an attempt to comfort her.

Ben sneered and opened his mouth. Before he had a chance to speak again, I jumped in. "We're all in shock, but we won't be able to make smart decisions unless we can calm down, catch our breath, and think through our next steps."

My eyes met Ben's and he sneered back, "And why should we listen to you, girl?"

Wrapping a protective arm around my shoulders, Jason shot a venomous look in Ben's direction. "You might want to rethink your tone," he growled.

I closed my eyes and breathed deeply. "Let's just...chill. Fighting isn't going to help. No one is keeping you here, Ben. It was merely a suggestion."

"I can't—" Gabriela started. "I can't remember anything. I can't remember how I got to that building or what happened before."

"Neither can I," Jean murmured. "I keep trying to recall where I was before all this. My husband—what if he..." Her voice trailed off as she took a shaky breath.

I squeezed my eyes shut, pressing my fingers to my temples. It was right there; I knew if I concentrated a bit harder, I could force more memories to the surface.

"I remember some things," Jason said.

"What do you remember?" Gabriela sniffed.

"I think I was at the gym by your apartment, Lee," Jason said, turning to me. "I remember talking to you on the phone. And then people running, panicked. Mostly I remember this overwhelming urge to get to you. Then…ships in the sky." He shuddered.

I swallowed hard, closing my eyes as I pressed into his side, squeezing my arms around him tight.

Finally, a full memory burst free—

I was in my home office doing some reporting for work and almost dismissed the notification on my phone before seeing the preview. Confused, I clicked on the text to read more:

> [***EMERGENCY ALERT***]
> AUSTIN/TRAVIS COUNTY SHELTER IN PLACE ORDER
> 11/15/2024 10:55:00 AM
> UNIDENTIFIED AIRCRAFT ACTIVITY IN THE AREA. AN EMERGENCY HAS BEEN DECLARED THROUGHOUT THE STATE OF TEXAS. FOR YOUR SAFETY, PLEASE TAKE THE FOLLOWING ACTIONS IMMEDIATELY:
>
> - IF YOU ARE OUTSIDE, FIND SHELTER—DO NOT REMAIN IN YOUR VEHICLE
> - SECURE ALL DOORS AND WINDOWS
> - TURN OFF VENTILATION SYSTEMS (HEATING, AIR CONDITIONING, ETC.)
> - MOVE TO AN INTERIOR ROOM AWAY FROM WINDOWS, IF POSSIBLE
> - KEEP YOUR PHONE CHARGED AND ACCESSIBLE FOR FURTHER UPDATES
> - DO NOT LEAVE YOUR LOCATION UNTIL THE ALL-CLEAR IS GIVEN
>
> THIS ORDER IS IN EFFECT UNTIL FURTHER NOTICE.

My eyebrows knit in confusion. This had to be a joke. I mean, an unidentified aircraft? A literal U.F.O.? There was no way.

I picked up the TV remote while opening the Neighborhoods app to see what other people were saying. Clicking through the channels, I landed on the local news.

My mouth dropped open and I froze with my remote still aimed at the TV. The image was hard to make out at first. The downtown skyscrapers were no longer what dominated the skyline. Where I would expect to see bright blue skies, clouds rolling, and construction of new buildings in the distance, instead stood a darkened cityscape. Hovering just above the buildings, there was the metal underbelly of what could only be described as a giant ship casting the city in its shadow. A news reporter was talking, but I couldn't process their words.

I opened the Messages app on my phone to text Emma, but before I could type anything, a call notification rolled across the screen. Jason.

I barely had time to utter a hello before Jason blurted, voice sharp with urgency, "Oh, thank fuck. Lee, I'm at the gym a block away from your apartment. There's a huge fucking aircraft in the sky." I could hear commotion in the background, a flurry of voices and sound.

"Wha—" I started to answer as I received a notification from Emma. "Emma is texting me. I—Yeah, come over. I'll leave the door open for you."

"Coming now," Jason replied before hanging up the phone.

With shaking hands, I opened Emma's message. It was a picture of the downtown area from a different angle with the same colossal vessel defying gravity, suspended above our city. I stared at the image on the screen until another text from Emma came in.

EMMA

Lee. WTF. Do U see this?

ALINA

Im freaking out–WTF is going on?????
Terrorists? Govmnt test? Jason is coming to my apt from the gym.

EMMA

OMG at least U and Jayce will be together. I can't even leave work now–FUCK this WTF.

17

Clutching my phone, I crept to my apartment's balcony door. I took a deep breath before pulling the curtain aside to peek out. Lifting my gaze to the sky, there it was. Dark metal shining from above. Though its expanse didn't reach my apartment, I could clearly see the mammoth ship as it cloaked the city in a dark shadow. A whimper escaped my lips and I dropped my phone to the floor, narrowly missing my bare foot.

My front door burst open, and—

Nothing.

I couldn't remember what happened next—like the rest of the memory dissolved from my brain.

"Wait. Y'all know each other?" Gabriela asked, snapping me back to the present moment. Her questioning eyes darted back and forth between Jason and me.

Jean glanced over and Ben lifted his gaze as well.

"Yeah," I answered, looking at Jason. "We know each other."

"Since we were kids," Jason continued. "My younger sister, Emma, is best friends with Alina."

"So y'all were together when it happened? When the ships appeared in the sky?" Jean asked.

I nodded. "I think so. I remember seeing the news on TV about unidentified aircraft and getting the emergency alerts." I looked at Jason again. "And you called me. You said you were coming over, but I can't remember what happened after."

"So you're *together* together?" Gabriela tilted her head to the side curiously. "Wow. It's so lucky y'all didn't get separated," she breathed.

"*What*?" I choked as the words burst out of my mouth. "No. I mean, obviously, we must have been physically together. I mean—not physical like..." I shook my head, trying to regain some composure. "Physical, like, the same way we are here in front of you. But no. Not like—not like that," I sputtered, feeling my cheeks burn. I didn't know why Gabriela's statement affected me the way it did. Whether it was because of my dream with the memory of the lake, or if my brain was truly scrambled, or a mix of both—I had to regain focus. I shook my head to clear my mind. *What was wrong with me?*

I noticed the corner of Jason's mouth quirk upward, likely because he remembered all the other times I inserted my foot directly into my mouth. My shoulders relaxed as I realized that small flick of movement, the familiarity in his reaction, had done more for my mental state than any other reassurances so far. It was such a little thing, but it gave me hope. We would smile again. We would make it. We just had to keep going.

"Last I remember, I was reading a company email from my desk in the office when the alert came through. *Work,*" Ben stated gruffly. "I would have left right away, but everyone else was too nervous to make a move and I didn't want to be the only one."

"Where did you work? Maybe we were in the same area when we were all taken?" Jean asked. "I mean, I assume we were all captured somewhere. I don't think I would go to a place like that willingly."

"I don't think so, either," I responded.

"Well, I wasn't downtown," Ben replied. "Not anywhere near here."

Gabriela nodded. "Yeah, I live further north."

"Alina's apartment is on the south side," Jason added.

Gabriela suddenly jumped to her feet, eyes wide. "Wait, guys! Look!" She dashed across the street to tug down a large sign hanging off a lamppost, carrying the card stock back to us. I internally questioned where she got the energy until I saw what was written on the sign, perking right up along with her:

Austin/Downtown Area
11/18/2024
<u>Emergency Center Information:</u>

Please note: It's safest to stay inside and abide by the 'shelter in place' order. You are not required to find an emergency center if you are near another form of shelter.

If you need a safe place to stay, please find the Emergency Center location nearest to you from the list below.

<u>For the safety of all individuals:</u>
- No weapons of any kind
- Limit of 1 (one) bag per person to conserve space
- Leashed or contained pets permitted
- Please follow all instructions from Emergency personnel
- Do not engage with aircraft
- Do not travel by car, truck, or other motorized vehicles to avoid detection
- Do not wear bright clothing
- Keep all children and those needing assistance at your side at all times
- Move quietly, stay vigilant, keep safe

"Well, at least we know they had enough time to put up signs before it all went to shit," Ben muttered.

"Maybe we should try and find the emergency centers?" I thought out loud. "I mean, people probably went to one of those, right?"

Jean nodded. "I agree. That's probably the safest bet."

Jason pointed to a location on the sign. "Maybe we'll find someone who can fill in some of the blanks for us," he agreed.

"Yeah, why *haven't* we seen anyone else yet?" Gabriela wondered, nervously biting her lip. "Even when we were inside that building. We must have walked through almost the whole place. I thought we were the only ones left until we found you, Alina."

"It's like everything just...shut down. Maybe there was an evacuation?" Jean wondered.

The heat melted against my skin as I mentally calculated how far my apartment was from the area we were currently in. Then it struck me—*the heat*. Eyes wide, I grabbed Jason's arm. "It was autumn. Almost *winter*."

"What?" His brow furrowed.

"*November*. It was November." The words poured out of me. "I know global warming has made Austin literal hell on Earth with the heat, but it's never been this hot at the end of autumn."

"I don't know about that," Ben scoffed. *What was with this guy?*

"She's right." Gabriela nervously looked from Ben to me before straightening with a newfound confidence. "No way we are still in November."

"So, did we miss winter entirely?" Jean questioned.

Jason's frown deepened. I could practically see the wheels turning in his head as he tried to find the pieces to put together. "We'll figure it all out," he said. "Either way, I think we should start moving if we can. Is everyone okay to start walking again? If we head this way—"

"Wait!" Gabriela suddenly called out. She pointed towards the sun sinking lower in the sky. "There's a thrift store right down that way! I used to go there all the time. It's not far—a few more blocks. Maybe they have some water, or we can at least find some shoes before we have to walk much further?"

Jason's face brightened. "Yes! Great thinking, Gabriela."

Gabriela's cheeks turned pink at the acknowledgment and she shyly smiled back.

"A thrift store?" Ben scoffed. "Waste of time. We should just keep walking."

I snarled in the man's direction. "If you want to keep rocking a gown and bare feet, then by all means, you do you. But we need water. Food. Real clothes. Shoes. At least this place gives us a shot at getting two of those things taken care of right away." Whether it was because of dehydration or waking up in a makeshift lab straight from an *X-Files* episode, I had no more patience for Ben's rude condescension. I opened my mouth to tear into him again, but Jean interrupted.

"Yes!" Jean shot me a silent look to back down. "My feet are killing me. We will need some footwear to make it further than just a few more blocks."

Ben and I glared at each other once more before Jason took my hand and turned to follow Gabriela and Jean down the sidewalk.

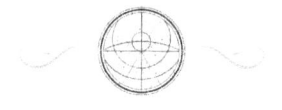

As we walked silently, the heat bore down like it was trying to crush us into the ground. A heavy quiet hung in the air with the streets absent of foot traffic and cars. I was so used to seeing green scooters whizzing down the sidewalks, people ducking into restaurants on lunch breaks, or rushing to the gym with yoga mats. Though I was seeing the state of the city with my own eyes, I still couldn't believe it was real.

My mind wandered to my family and a knot formed in my throat. They were so far away. I clenched my jaw to keep more tears from falling as I tried remembering if I heard anything about the East Coast where they lived. The more I tried to remember, the further away the memories seemed to slip.

Gabriela spoke, breaking the silence. "There! Up ahead."

Sweat trickled down my sides and I felt a spark of hope. "Maybe we'll luck out and the thrift store will have turned into an ice shop with wine, cheese, a nice comfy bed to watch Netflix in..."

Jason replied with a tired laugh, "Only the essentials, right?"

"A woman can dream," I answered with a sigh.

"Yes! We're here," Gabriela cheered and started jogging the rest of the way.

Already, I could feel the mood lighten, a shred of hope emerging as we approached the building. The storefront looked like it had taken a few sledgehammers to the face. Though the aisles were littered with items scattered across the floor, it looked like there was still a decent amount of stuff left to pick through—possibly a good sign. People surely wouldn't have left so many items untouched if things had gotten *that* bad. Maybe Jean was on to something and everyone had been evacuated. There could be a safe place just outside the city. Anything was possible.

Gabriela ran to a drink fridge next to the registers, swinging open the door to grab some off-brand sodas. I gratefully took a warm, flat drink, chugging half of it in one go. As everyone else followed suit and the sugar hit our systems, our small group started coming back to life.

We split up to search for the items we needed most. Gabriela and Jean followed me to the shoe section and lucked out with sneakers in their respective sizes while I found a pair of Docs. I would have preferred a cushy slip-on, but the boots would definitely be more practical, considering the destruction we had to walk through. Jean pulled open a bag of 'new' socks, though the bag itself looked like it had been sitting around for a few decades, and divided the socks among us. I immediately slipped them onto my sore feet and shoved on the Docs, almost sighing at the familiar feeling of soft fabric and worn-in leather hugging my feet. One step closer to normalcy.

"That's quite the look you have going on there," Jean said with a tired smile.

I smirked back at her, posing with my hands on my hips. "Didn't you hear? It's the latest in apocalypse fashion."

Gabriela ducked between the aisles to pull shorts on underneath her gown before throwing the creepy garment off in favor of an oversized t-shirt. "I never knew an old tee could feel so good." She sighed.

The action of 'shopping' even seemed to lighten Ben's mood as we each collected items across the store. I grabbed a backpack, shoving in extra clothes and anything else that appeared even remotely useful. Though I was hoping for the best, there was still a sinking feeling in my gut telling me we'd need to be prepared for anything. Jason and I met in the same aisle and he grabbed a few knives from the mish-mosh of cutlery on the shelf. We made eye contact as he shoved the knives into the front pocket of his backpack. "Just in case," he murmured before walking to the next aisle.

Great, I thought to myself, picking up a can opener and a few reusable water bottles to shove in my bag.

At the back of the building, I spotted a lone changing stall next to what was likely a door to the store's back room or storage area. I approached the door first, trying to turn the knob, but it was locked. Eager to finally change out of the gown and get a few seconds alone, I decided to slip inside the changing stall for some privacy.

I hesitantly looked into the dirty, floor-length mirror attached to the wall. This was the first opportunity I had to see my reflection since waking up. Holding my breath, I pulled my gown over my head, using the garment to wipe down the glass.

Surprisingly, my darker, tan skin still had a healthy sheen, even if it was a bit paler than usual from being locked in a box for who knows how long. I'd expected to wear the stress and exhaustion a bit heavier than the face I saw staring back at me in the mirror, so at least I didn't look as worn as I felt. My wavy, brown hair was a mess around my head, so I gathered the unruly strands into a ponytail, securing it with a scrunchie I'd found. Taking a step closer, I prodded my sides to look for anything unusual—operation marks, scars, cuts, or bruises. As I analyzed my reflection, realization dawned on me and I was suddenly taken aback.

The change wouldn't have been evident to anyone other than me. The curvier figure I was used to seeing in the mirror had lost some of its fullness. I pressed my fingers against my thick thighs, flexing the muscle as I remembered the unfamiliar firmness I felt earlier. I wasn't imagining things—my body felt different. Even my usual squishy stomach felt like it was hiding more muscle. I frowned, trying to shake away the unease as I tried to think of reasons this change could be possible. I could understand losing some weight if it had been a while—but gaining muscle?

A loud rumble echoed throughout the store as I threw on a pair of bike shorts and a tank top. *Thunder?* I scrambled to zip my backpack closed, shoving my arm through the strap as I opened the door and glanced around the store.

Dust motes still floated in the beams of light pouring in from the cracks in the ceiling and walls. "Hey, did you guys hear—" Another loud crash interrupted me before I could finish my question and I jumped. This time, I was confident it wasn't thunder.

I locked eyes with Jason and he yelled, "Run! Now!" before the next blast roared.

Ben, Jean, and Gabriela were closest to the entrance, not wasting any time as they scrambled towards the open door frame. "Go towards the Emergency Center," Jean called back to us as Ben shouldered past Gabriela and nearly knocked Jean over as he darted out onto the street. Another boom sounded, rattling the walls with reverberations.

Jason reached the front of the store and glanced over his shoulder as I tripped over the side of a shelf, my balance thrown off by the last rumble. I crashed to the ground, sprawled on my stomach as yet another wave of sound crashed through the streets. Jason yelled my name, barely audible over the echoes of the last blast still ringing in my ears. I pushed to my feet just as Jason reached me and grabbed my hand. "Come on. We have to—"

His last words were interrupted by the loudest sound yet.

And there it was—we could finally see it.

Explosions in the sky.

Jason dove between two aisles, holding me tight as the ceiling caved in.

THREE
ALINA

THE AISLE'S shelving fell at an angle that cast a protective cave over us. We crouched amongst shards of broken glass and ceramic, feeling the sting of shrapnel from the delicate objects that crashed around us. Blood mingled with the grit and dirt that coated our skin as the forgotten mementos and hand-me-down relics shattered on the floor. I clung to Jason, his arms tensing and tightening around me with each shock wave.

Finally, the explosions slowed. The trembling ground became an echo that resonated through every shiver of my panic-ridden body. We stayed under the cover of the shelves, frozen, anticipating more danger as the debris fell around us. Jason held me like an anchor, even after the roaring skies calmed to a creeping silence. I closed my eyes, focusing on the rise and fall of Jason's chest as he breathed.

When the galloping in my chest finally settled to a steady rhythm, I pulled back, locking eyes with Jason. He brought his hand to my face, wiping some dirt from my cheek. As he held his palm there a moment longer, his thumb gently stroked the side of my jaw. "Lee—" he half whispered, "We're okay."

I could feel the tears forming in my eyes, the burn threatening to set them free. I tried to hold it all back, knowing if I started crying now, I'd never stop.

"Hey," Jason murmured, tilting my chin to look up at him. "One step at a time, okay? We'll figure it out." He leaned back to get a better look at me as he asked, "Does anything hurt badly?"

"N-no. I don't think so," I whispered before falling into a coughing fit. Clearing my throat, I continued, "It feels like I just inhaled a sandbox, though."

"Yeah, we should probably find a safer spot," he thought out loud.

I braced myself, rising to a crouch as I held onto the side of the fallen shelf for balance. As I crept out, Jason was close behind me, coughing from the debris-ridden dust clouds that still surrounded us. We pushed broken objects, pieces of the building, and clothing remnants out of the way as we half crawled from the barrier of shelving. Looking around, I couldn't figure out how we managed to survive without anything worse than cuts and bruises. Something definitely crashed through the ceiling and into the store, but it was hard to tell exactly what caused the damage with the amount of rubble around us. I stared at the sky through the cavernous opening above us, watching the smoke trails for a moment. *What the fuck happened?* Outside the shop I could only see clouds of dust rolling down the street—hardly anything else was visible.

"How will we find the others?" I turned to look at Jason.

"Between the dust, debris, and smoke, I don't think it's safe to leave right now." Jason coughed roughly. "We don't know what we might be walking into with such limited visibility. The others were headed towards the emergency center, so maybe once we are able to start navigating things better..." His voice trailed off.

A cold chill ran down my spine and I felt a twinge of fear squeeze in my chest. We escaped one danger, only to run into another two seconds later. What would happen next?

I looked around the store and gasped in surprise, stifling another cough. "There! Look!" I pointed to the back of the building, where the store was more intact. "The door back there was locked before, but if we can open it, maybe the room inside isn't as bad? Maybe we can wait it out there?"

"Alright," Jason replied, reaching for my hand. "Anything to stop breathing this crap in."

We limped to the back of the store, navigating over thrift store remains as we coughed and stumbled. As we approached the door, I stopped, looking around. "Maybe there is something we can use to pick the lock. Do you think—"

A loud clang interrupted me. Gasping, I choked on a lungful of thrift store dust as my head jerked towards the sound.

"What?" Jason responded, lowering the metal bar he used to break the doorknob.

"Jason! You can't just—" I started before realizing how irrelevant the door knob was in the grand scheme of things. The entire store was destroyed, the city, and possibly the world—what's a broken door knob in the grand scheme of things? "Never mind. Will it open now?"

Sure enough, one more whack to the doorknob and we were able to pull the door open.

The room inside looked like a combination storage room and office. It was in decent enough condition, with only some broken shelving and fallen items—a stark difference from the space outside. We closed the door, stuffing grit-covered clothing in the gaps so the smoke and dust wouldn't continue seeping inside. There was a line of small rectangular windows near the top of the back wall, but hardly any light was able to shine through—likely because of the swirling clouds outside. Jason pressed the back of his hand against the emergency door on the other side of the room, feeling for signs of fire warming the door from outside.

"It isn't hot, but we should keep checking. We don't want to get caught off guard if any fires spread our way." He ensured the door was locked before crossing the room to stand at my side again.

We surveyed the room, taking everything in. The space was far from clean, but it was still an oasis compared to what we'd just crawled out of. We grabbed some more spare sodas from an open pack we found on the ground and I choked down a gag as I drank the warm, sugary liquid. At least it helped tame my cough.

As we explored the office, my lungs started to clear and I began breathing easier. We found some helpful items right away. Along with a first aid kit and some flashlights shoved in a desk drawer, we found a headlamp and snacks like beef jerky, trail mix, chips, and granola bars. There were also a few unopened water jugs for a top-loading water cooler next to the desk. The water cooler had fallen on its side and cracked, but we'd figure something out.

The space also had a tiny bathroom where we found a bunch of cleaning supplies. I tested the faucets only to discover that the pipes were completely dried up. Even the toilet tank was almost completely drained.

Jason set up the headlamp and flashlights to illuminate as much of the office space as possible. Though we didn't have a way to tell the time, judging by how low the sun hung in the sky before we arrived, it must have been close to sunset. The smoke and dust cloaking the sky quickly stole away the last rays of the sun, so the extra light was necessary to continue organizing our new shelter.

After determining the space was safe enough and collecting all of the useful items we could find, we decided to break into one of the water jugs. We were beyond thirsty at that point, having given up on the warm soda, and I was anxious to clean and assess our wounds—even if they were only as minor as they appeared.

It took us longer than expected to open one of the giant containers, fumbling in the mediocre light from the flashlights. The water jugs were heavy and hard to aim and pour without sloshing out too much water at once. We finally managed to fill the water bottles I snagged from the shelves earlier, leaving a small pool of water on the floor once the task was complete. Next, we heaved the container, pouring water into the stoppered bathroom sink so we could clean our wounds.

Though we wiped down the sink the best we could with the Lysol wipes we found, I wasn't too excited about touching an open wound in this environment. Still, it had to be done. We stood beside the sink, balancing the flashlights and headlamps on a decorative shelf on the opposite wall. It wasn't perfect, but it was enough to see what we were doing as we wiped down our skin and cleaned the minor cuts. The injuries weren't that bad and I breathed a sigh of relief once the part involving blood was done. Even my still-blooming bruises didn't look so angry once I cleaned off the dirt from the ceiling's collapse.

After putting away the first aid kit, we refilled the sink and continued cleaning off the rest of the grime that coated our skin. Each swipe of the paper towel came with a mental sigh of relief as the remnants of the collapse washed away. I was finally starting to feel human again.

Jason grabbed my attention just as I was about to leave the room. "Lee—there's still a smudge of something on your back, just between your shoulder blades."

"Aw, dammit," I muttered, twisting to try and see what Jason meant.

"You'll never get it like that." Jason chuckled. "Come here. I'll help."

I nodded as I took a step closer, my mouth suddenly dry. As I turned around, my nerves tingled just under my skin.

Growing up, Emma had always teased me for having a crush on her brother. I fully accepted that I'd never act on it, destined to remain his younger sister's awkward friend for the rest of my life; but the crush never completely faded as we got older. Even through adulthood, the feelings continued to linger just beneath the surface. Sometimes, I thought Jason might feel the same—like the almost-moment at the lake after his ex-fiancée's betrayal. Still, it was never something Jason and I ever spoke about.

Emma repeatedly told me she didn't care and that I should shoot my shot. Still, I knew her well enough to know she not-so-secretly hoped I'd continue to pine away with Jason none the wiser. Emma had a way of letting you know exactly how she felt about something, even when she didn't say it directly. Ultimately, I knew my friendship with Emma wasn't worth risking a relationship with someone who may or may not work out. As long-lived as my crush was, even with the chemistry I swore was there, it wasn't worth risking two friendships and a sibling's relationship over.

Jason's warm hand touched my shoulder as he gingerly wiped the paper towel down my spine to where the neckline of the tank top dipped low between my shoulder blades. I continued to repeat the 'just-friends' logic in my head.

Whoever wrote the 'best friends' handbook should have added an addendum to cover relationship best practices in post-apocalyptic dystopian survival situations. My heart squeezed as I thought of Emma, realizing her absence stung more than anything else. I shook thoughts of Jason from my head, reminding myself that letting my mind wander into 'what-ifs' was not a helpful way to work through trauma. I needed to focus on reality, not escape.

Jason paused, applying more pressure between my shoulder blades.

"Uh, everything okay back there?" I laughed nervously.

"Hold on," he said, reaching over my head to grab a flashlight from the shelf. "When did you get that tattoo?" he asked.

I frowned. "I've had my ankle and wrist tattoos since we were in our twenties. I think you were there when I got at least one of them."

"No, the one on your back."

I froze, twisting to look at him over my shoulder. "I don't *have* any back tattoos."

"Well, there is definitely something there," Jason murmured as he aimed the light at me. "I need a better look to be sure. Can I move your shirt?"

I pushed down the urge to nervously joke about taking me to dinner first and nodded silently, pulling my ponytail out of the way. I felt the gentle graze of his knuckles against my skin as he raised the hemline past my waist, exposing more of my back.

He dropped the paper towel and ran his thumb gently along what I assumed was the mark. Goosebumps rose where his finger trailed and my heart beat faster. I hoped the room was dark enough to hide the flicker of my pulse racing under my skin.

"There is a line of blue symbols, but it looks..." Jason dipped a new paper towel in the water as he trailed off, gently brushing down my spine again.

Little rivulets of water trickled down my back. "What kind of symbols?" I whispered, unable to stop the shiver that raced through my body. I reached over my shoulder, taking hold of my shirt so he could get a better look.

"It isn't any language I recognize." One of his hands rested gently on my bare waist as he leaned closer with the flashlight. "It starts right on your spine between your shoulder blades. The symbols stop about midway down from there. And, uh—" Jason pulled the shirt from my hand to lower it back down, straightening it where it fell at my hips. I turned to face him, trying to read the look on his face. "It's...glowing," he continued. "Not brightly, but there's definitely a kind of...aura to it."

I froze, waiting for him to tell me he was joking. When the worry never left his face, I tried to laugh away the fear churning in my stomach. "Kidnapping, waking up in an egg-shaped pod, lost memories, and now a surprise tattoo—I guess what happens in Austin stays in Austin, am I right?" I tried to smile through the tears that prickled in the corners of my eyes. My lips quivered as I wrapped my arms across my stomach, turning away from him again.

"Lee," Jason said, stepping around me so he was in front of me once again. He held my upper arms, gently rubbing soothing circles with his thumbs to keep my attention as he looked into my eyes. "Whatever is happening—whatever happened—I'm here. We'll figure it out together." His eyes searched mine as I slowly took in a deep breath, nodding.

"This is so fucked up," I whispered, biting the inside of my cheek so I wouldn't cry more. "We need to check you, too." As I said the words, I was unsure whether I was more worried about finding or not finding a brand on him, as well.

Jason turned around, pulling his shirt over his head as I grabbed another paper towel. Even before I picked up the flashlight to get a closer look, I knew there was no denying there were marks adorning his skin, as well. Still, I dabbed the paper towel against his spine, hoping I was hallucinating. Just as he said, an aura glowed around the symbols on his back. It wasn't bright enough to illuminate anything past his skin; rather, the glow seemed to hover just around the markings.

"You have it, too," I said, unable to stop the tremble in my voice.

Jason pulled his shirt back on and turned around, taking the paper towel from my hand. "Let's leave everything here; I think we need to sit down to process this," he said as he gently touched the small of my back, gesturing to the office area.

I shuffled over to where we placed our backpacks and sank to the floor, pulling my knees to my chest. Jason followed, sitting beside me as he started to rub my back. Exhaustion caught up with me and I released my knees so I could curl in closer to Jason's side. He wrapped an arm around my shoulders as I hugged his waist, resting my head in the space between his shoulder and clavicle.

"Jayce?" I whispered.

"Yeah?" he answered.

"What do we do now?"

FOUR
CARTER

I WOKE up to loud arguing. Again. Another great start to a new day in the hellscape our lives had become. Annoyed, I narrowed my eyes at the door as I stood to shove my boots on.

Before joining my current camp, I couldn't stick with any group for too long. Between dodging attacks from the invaders, getting separated, being left behind, or sneaking away of my own accord, there was no time to get to know anyone well enough to want to risk staying longer. Honestly, I preferred it that way, even before the invasion.

I wouldn't say I was 'always a loner' or some other romanticized bullshit. Over time, I just realized it wasn't worth pouring pieces of myself into others who would most likely screw me over, anyway. I had some people I kept close, though who knows what became of them since this whole thing went down. I tried not to think about it or I'd get stuck in a never-ending spiral of despair. Looking back, keeping my circle small was probably the only thing that helped me adjust to the invasion's aftermath. There isn't much to lose when you don't hold much to begin with.

I didn't believe it at first when I read the emergency text that first day back in mid-November. Then I looked out the goddamn window. There was no denying it—we were fucked.

According to the news, the unidentified aircraft invaded Earth's skies worldwide. Still, even after the shelter-in-place order, people tried to flee the city in hopes of finding a safer location. I spent the first two days trying to figure out how to get to my dad in Colorado before finally admitting there was just no viable option. Cars clogged the highways, which led to accidents and fear-inspired violence—at least from what I saw on social media and videos shared in group chats. There were moments in those first few days of isolation where I thought I must have finally snapped—that I was stuck in a nightmare that only existed in my head. Little did I know that things were about to get even worse.

First came the power surges, which led to flash fires. Cell towers went down and radio signals were blocked, cutting off our communications. Anything electronic, even battery-operated devices, started having trouble. Then, the attacks officially began.

I barely made it out of the city unscathed. Everywhere I turned, the invaders were rounding people up, stunning and capturing some, completely obliterating others. They marched through our streets with a sick confidence, almost a swagger, as they silently pointed their weapons at groups of people trying to escape. The invaders didn't seem to care about who or what they actually hit. I never once heard them try to communicate out loud, even when they acted out clearly coordinated attacks. At first, I tried to fight back, but I quickly realized that we were severely outmatched in terms of technology, even if we did have more numbers. The only options were to flee, get captured, or die—so I chose to run.

The invaders had to be over seven feet tall, and even with their hunched posture and stocky builds, they seemed to tower over the crowds they pursued. Though I never saw their faces through the blacked out visors on their full-body suits, I still remembered the way the sun glinted off their shiny, dark metallic helmets. Weapons were built into the sleeves of their suits, like a remote panel they controlled through some kind of track pad. The lazer that shot out could either render humans unconscious or completely dissolve victims into a fine mist—depending on how the invaders felt at any given moment. Larger groups didn't stand a chance when it came to staying undetected. I was convinced I only made it out of the city because I primarily tried to stay alone.

After escaping the city, I joined groups of people out of necessity. Combining resources was the only way to ensure you could get what you needed to survive—not just food and water, but also things like enough people for night-watch security shifts. There was nothing worse than only being able to sleep for minutes at a time because you had to stay alert constantly.

No matter how well we thought we'd concealed our camps, the invaders had a knack for tracking us down. That meant there was rarely any time to coordinate an escape that kept a group of people together. For months, I'd hide, scavenge, and run with different groups of people—barely able to catch my breath before having to make another split life-or-death decision.

After a while, the invaders' attacks slowed down. Word spread that it was safer being further away from the city, so many groups set their sights on the horizon, never looking back. I started running into new camps less and less, and it was getting increasingly more difficult to defend myself against the rogue gangs of humans that had turned violent, targeting smaller camps and people traveling alone. When I eventually stumbled into my current group's camp, I was so exhausted I would have done anything to eat a can of real food and sleep for more than a few minutes at a time. So, I stayed.

There were members within the camp who had experience foraging and surviving in the wild, and they invested their time in helping me learn. Others went out of their way to make sure I was adjusting alright, giving me space when I needed it while ensuring I was never forgotten. They had medical supplies, a decent group of leaders calling the shots, and generally treated each camp member with fairness as long as they did their part. I knew this was as good as it got.

There were still attacks from other humans and the invaders—we could never completely escape danger. Occasionally, someone would go missing without a trace. Still, we adapted to our new reality and I continued trying to keep my distance so I wouldn't get attached. What other choice was there?

And then, three days ago, the ships that had been lurking above Austin just...left.

There was no way to know if the ships would come back or if they were actually gone, but my camp was hopeful. As the hours ticked by, I couldn't shake the feeling that it wasn't over yet. If there was ever a time I wished the paranoia was just in my head, it was then. That afternoon, explosions from the city's center filled the sky with smoke. A few short hours later, our camp was destroyed, torn to pieces by new hell-creatures seemingly born from civilization's ashes.

Three days ago, there were twenty-two people in our group. Now, our camp was down to eight.

I trudged down the stairs of our safe house, making my way to the kitchen where I knew the others would be gathered. Upon entering the room, I realized I was the last to arrive. The Twenty-Somethings, Red, Cap, and Michelle stood around the kitchen and the air was thick with tension.

I looked at the pair at the center of it all, who were still glaring daggers at each other. "What the fuck is the problem now?" I asked.

Red's fierce, blue eyes met mine. "This asshole thinks I should start scouting and scavenging now. *Me*. Because apparently we can afford to risk the group's most valuable member." Red had been an emergency room RN before everything went down. Until now, she had been kept out of as many blatantly dangerous situations as possible. Still, the feisty thirty-three-year-old woman *was* the only person with enough knowledge to ensure we woke up to see another day after some of our worst injuries. She couldn't be risked, and she knew it.

"Be *so* fucking for real right now, Red!" Russell yelled, fists clenching and unclenching at his sides, muscles flexing. Somehow, Russell always managed to look like he just walked off the beach. He had what could only be described as 'California surfer in Texas' vibes —only without the chill. "Do you not see the number of people we have left? You've let everyone else do the heavy lifting for too fucking long. It's time to pick up the slack or leave. Even Sam has been pulling more than her own weight." Even though Sam was still technically nineteen, Russell and Sam were part of what had been dubbed the 'Twenty-Somethings' crew.

Russell had a point regarding Red's work ethic, but I could also see the burn it left on Sam as she fumed in her corner of the kitchen. Apparently, Russell had not yet learned to *never* compare women, especially when they were standing right next to each other. Sam narrowed her deep, brown eyes in Russell's direction.

Red threw her arms in the air with a frustrated growl. "I'm done with this bullshit." She turned and her wavy, auburn hair whipped dramatically behind her as she stormed out of the room.

Cap stepped to the middle of the kitchen, putting their hands up, palms out in a de-escalating position. "Enough. We've had a hell of a week and the last thing we need is another immature argument. We need to plan for our group's *survival*. Or did y'all forget what's waiting for us out there?" Cap turned their stormy gaze to focus on each person in the room one-by-one, shoulder muscles tensing as they crossed their arms in front of them.

Russell hesitated, running a hand through his light brown hair. Raising an eyebrow, he jerked a thumb in the direction Red had stormed off. His smirk grew as he said, "Well, with Red gone, I think we'll all get along just fine."

Cap let out an exasperated sigh, shaking their head.

"I'm out," Sam declared. "I need to separate myself before I say something deeply unproductive."

"Ah, fuck," Russell muttered, finally realizing the implications of what he'd said during the fight. He pushed his hair back from his face as his voice took on a pleading tone. "Sam, come on, babe. All I meant was, you're just a teenager and you've gone out of your way to help the group more than a thirty-year-old ever has."

Sam's eyes darkened in his direction, her rich, black skin flushing angrily. She kept her tone calm and cool as she replied, "Well, I'm going to go be 'just a teenager' upstairs then." Sam left the room without another look in Russell's direction.

"Sammy, come on!" Russell called after her, jogging to catch up with her. An awkward silence hung in the room as Russell's footsteps retreated after Sam.

Brian cleared his throat. "Well, on the bright side, who can miss reality TV with this entertainment each morning?"

I looked at Brian as he grinned, his almond-shaped, brown eyes shining from behind his black-rimmed glasses. He lounged against the counter as a ray of light from the window highlighted his bronze skin. It was fitting, as the guy might as well have been sunshine in human form. Brian always found ways to keep the peace and light up our darker days.

"Anyway—" Brian continued. "Good morning, Carter! Cap was just about to lead us through the plan for today when all of *that* happened." Brian emphasized with a gesture toward the hallway.

Dan crossed the room, hopping onto the counter Brian was leaning against, and the two smirked at each other. Dan, at twenty-three, was closer in age to Russell, while Brian was just a bit older at twenty-six. Dan and Russell were both tall with similar muscular builds, always looking like they just rolled out of a gym. That's about where their similarities ended, though. Where Russell was loud, never hesitating to blurt out the first thing that popped into his head with a smirk perpetually painted across his sun-kissed face—Dan had a softer, more thoughtful demeanor. Dan took his time soaking everything in, usually standing off to the side with his dark brown arms crossed over his chest as he analyzed the situation in front of him. Dan, Russell, Brian, and Sam completed the Twenty-Somethings, and for all their personality differences, they seemed to fit together perfectly as friends. A serious expression settled across Dan's face as he nudged Brian to pay attention to Cap.

"Well," Cap continued. "I just mentioned that things have been quiet the last few days. We've been able to collect ourselves, which is good, but we still have to figure out the next best move. With supplies running low, we need to decide on a plan by the end of the day today."

Michelle's face was scrunched with concern as she leaned into Cap. They instinctively wrapped an arm around their partner and a relieved smile warmed Michelle's fair cheeks, bringing light back to her blue eyes. Michelle and Cap were one of the few couples who managed to stay together since everything went down. They were the oldest in our group, both in their late forties.

Cap was short in stature with olive skin and shaggy light brown hair. They spent a lot of time working things out in their head, but when they spoke, everyone wanted to listen. They were a natural leader and their authority radiated with every word they spoke. Cap, raised by their survivalist father, conveniently had a panic shelter built under their house. Cap and Michelle were able to stay in the shelter for three months after the ships arrived before surfacing again. Eventually, they found this group. It's a good thing, too, because I was convinced Cap was the sole reason we made it this far.

"We have a few options as I see it," Cap continued. "We can keep moving further out from the city and hope to scavenge up enough supplies along the way. Or…" they paused, "we can finish the mission to check out the city first."

My eyebrows raised in surprise. I knew the city mission had been on Cap's mind, but I didn't realize they still considered it a viable option. Though it had been quiet in the days after the attack, we couldn't assume the city's condition would be any better after the ships, explosions, and attacks had seemingly passed.

"Red didn't like that idea," Brian stage-whispered from the counter. Dan nudged him to quiet down again, even as his light brown eyes glittered with amusement.

"Cap's right, though," Michelle said, shaking her head. "We have to decide our next move, and soon. Carter, you were with the group that tried going to the city that day. Tell us again what you saw?"

I sighed and leaned against the wall, crossing my arms. "The explosions seemed like they were centered in one spot, but it was still brutal. Buildings were collapsing, but it didn't look like more than a few could have been hit. My guess is that the others collapsed because of weak foundations from all of the other attacks. I'd bet anyone else would hesitate to go there, especially so soon after it all happened."

"Exactly." Cap nodded in agreement. "And since the area was occupied and dangerous for so long, we're more likely to find supplies that haven't been picked up—maybe even a working vehicle to get us in and out quickly. Because of the risk surrounding the area for so long, it's probably still largely untouched as far as supplies go. With the attacks starting that first week, there probably wasn't enough time for people to loot many supplies from stores."

A mission downtown was possibly suicide, but at this point, what wasn't? We were damned if we continued without enough supplies and would only end up having to take the risk in a more unfamiliar town down the line. We didn't know what waited beyond city limits for us, but at least we knew the downtown area well enough to hit the places we needed quickly.

I glanced around the room at those who remained. Cap and Michelle had moved to dole out rations to get us through the rest of the day while Brian and Dan spoke quietly against the counter, heads tilted close. Dan caught my eye and shifted back. "I'm going to go check on Russ," he muttered.

Brian eyed Dan briefly as mild annoyance crossed his face before he said, "If he's still with Sammy, she could probably use some rescuing by now. I'll come with."

The two walked towards the stairs and Brian called back, "Carter, that means Red is *all* yours! Have fun!" Their footsteps pounded up the stairs and I groaned, wiping a hand down my face. I was not ready for Red's attitude this early in the morning. Or ever.

As I left the room, Michelle said teasingly, "Good luck! Pro-tip: she doesn't bite as hard if you bring her snacks." She tossed me a granola bar while her blue eyes crinkled with laughter. Cap stifled a laugh and turned to give their partner a quick peck on the cheek, saying something that made Michelle burst into laughter all over again.

I took my time heading to the study Red had claimed as her room, half hoping she wouldn't answer her door once I arrived. Red wasn't always so bad, but I'd rather be anywhere else when she was in a mood. I sighed, exhausted before the conversation had a chance to begin, as I knocked.

The door yanked open so hard I could see the breeze from its swing ruffle Red's hair. Arms crossed against her chest and one hip popped, she glared from the door frame, clearly still in a bad mood.

Her shoulders relaxed just a bit as she realized it was me. Stepping to the side, she gestured to the room and smirked. "Finally deciding to come around?"

Red sauntered over to the chaise pushed up against the far wall, hips swaying. Her tank top clung to her body, showing just a bit of creamy, pale skin between its hem and the waistband of her shorts. Red was attractive; there was no denying it. Still, I rolled my eyes at her blatant persistence.

I wasn't against a casual hookup in less dystopian times and might have even entertained something before the invasion. Now? There was no way. Not when we were stuck in the same camp without an easy escape after. Yet, despite the standoffish vibes I knew I radiated, Red didn't care to read the memo. She seemed to revel in the challenge.

Leaving the door open, I leaned against the frame. "You really need to get over yourself."

"Ouch! Come on, lighten up, Mister Tall, Dark, and Gloomy! Or even better, I know what would relieve some tension." Red leaned back against the chaise and mockingly raised an eyebrow.

"We lost more than half of our group."

"Getting down to business, huh?"

"Your options are slim, Red. You need to accept that you have to do more now—not just hide away until you're needed to patch someone up."

"Slim options, indeed," she scoffed, looking me up and down dramatically.

Frown darkening, I clenched my fists at my side and took a deep breath to maintain my composure. "You're scared. I get it. We've all been through shit and it isn't over. All I'm saying is we don't know what else will be out there. Like it or not, this group is all we have right now and we all need to do our part."

"Like what? I can't fight!" Red yelled, bursting off the chaise. "I'm not fast. I'm not good at strategy. Every time we move somewhere new, I cling to the middle of the group, knowing that at least if we are attacked, those on the outside will be picked off first. And it's callous. It's cold. I know I'd be nowhere without this group." She threw her hands in the air and stormed across the room, kicking the wall as she muttered, "Half the time, I don't know why I'm trying so hard to survive anymore."

I let the weight of her words settle. Dark as it was, I couldn't deny I'd often had the same thought. We were working so hard to survive, but what for? Even if we managed to rebuild society—how could we truly return from the horrors we'd faced? The crushed morals? What even was there to come back to?

"I know I have to be a 'team player,'" Red continued, mockingly throwing up air quotes. "But I don't have to like it." She paused, closing her eyes and taking a breath. "I'll do what I have to. I'll go where the group goes." She narrowed her eyes. "But I won't take orders from that little shit, Russell. What was he before all of this, anyway? A personal trainer?" she all but spat out, shaking her head. "Yeah, right." She glanced at me, looking exhausted from the full range of emotions that just exploded from her. "Tell them I'll come back in a few. If I don't cool down, I'll end up in a yelling match again, which I *know* no one wants to deal with."

"Well," I smirked, "at least you're self-aware."

Red's mouth dropped open in mock outrage. "How rude!" She tossed a throw pillow from the chaise at the door, hitting my foot as it bounced to the ground. In return, I threw her the granola bar Michelle had passed on. Emma caught the bar with a smile, rolling her eyes as she said, "Get out of here. Go get back to your glowering or whatever it is you do."

"Yeah, yeah," I muttered as I stepped away from the room. I closed Red's door, pausing when I heard Sam's gentle laugh from upstairs. I took that as a sign she and Russell had also smoothed things over.

Over the next hour, everyone made their way back down to the kitchen. Cap had mapped out the basics of our plan to head towards the city, though they gave space for everyone else to share input before anything was made final. Everyone had a job to get us ready to leave in the morning, including securing this place. Nothing was for sure, but having the safe house to potentially return to wouldn't hurt.

Despite our small numbers, and the tension from this morning, the rest of the day went smoothly. All things considered, the group's spirits were in a good place. The only option we had was to keep moving forward. It's why Brian still joked, Red flirted and argued, and Cap kept planning. We all tried holding onto those small pieces of ourselves to sustain normalcy in any way we could.

Still, I couldn't shake the dark shadow wrapping around me like a damp cloak. I looked around the room at the others and their hopeful conversations. I knew better than to hope for much more than basic survival anymore, though.

Hope was a fine line—if you didn't hold onto enough, you'd always be one step away from the edge, at the mercy of the slightest breeze. Too much, though? Too much hope would only set you up for a more devastating plunge once you realized—the last thread holding your rope together? It was frayed and about to snap the whole damn time. The end's coming for us all; today, tomorrow, next week...it's just a matter of when.

When we turned in for the night, trying to get a final night's rest before setting out, I lay awake staring at the ceiling. I studied every crack, every bubble of paint that I could find. I counted time against the ticking of my pulse, knowing that each beat would bring me closer to a new day, new danger, and new uncertainty.

As darkness grew around the edges of my vision, I let my focus fade, still counting down.

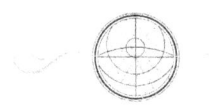

I woke with the sunrise and the house was quiet except for some doves cooing outside my window. It was a welcome change compared to yesterday.

I ran into Sam in the hall as she slipped out of the Twenty-Somethings' room. "Hey, kid," I greeted her.

Sam rolled her eyes and gave me a pointed look. "Hey, geezer."

"Ouch." I clutched my heart mockingly and scoffed. "Geezer? I have maybe seventeen years on you."

"I call it like I see it," she said with a grin before her face turned solemn again. "Do you think we're ready?"

Last night, before turning in, we'd extensively reviewed our plans, roles, and worst-case scenarios. Though I wasn't feeling too optimistic about our first mission as a group of eight, the others seemed to be looking on the bright side. I could be negative with everyone else, but I didn't have the heart to be as cold with Sam. She was a tough kid, but still too young to be jaded by all she'd been through. I wanted her to hold onto the last bit of light illuminating her from the inside out as long as possible.

"We're as ready as we're ever going to be," I muttered, patting her shoulder. "Come on, *kid,* let's get the good protein bars before the rest of the youngin's wake up."

Sam laughed in surprise at my joke and we headed down to the kitchen to see who else was up.

As we entered the kitchen, Michelle was the first person we saw. She was yawning as she reluctantly opened a protein bar.

"Morning, Chelle!" Sam chirped Michelle's nickname, giving her a warm smile.

"Morning, Sam. Morning, Carter," Michelle greeted us. "How are you feeling about everything?" she asked, looking at Sam, knowing she wouldn't get more than a grunt in response from me.

"I mean, hope for the best, but plan for the worst, right?" Sam responded, shrugging a shoulder. "Hopefully, it does end up being a quick in-and-out."

"Oh, are we talking about Dan's last date?" I heard Russell's voice boom as he made his presence known.

Brian snorted a laugh from behind him and Dan shot a glare Russell's way as they joined us.

"Funny," Sam deadpanned in Russell's direction.

"Joking, obviously." Russell gave Dan his biggest grin before casually throwing an arm around Sam's shoulders, whispering, "*Good morning,*" in her ear. I couldn't help noticing the smile she tried to hide as she pretended not to look at him through her lowered eyelashes. Meanwhile, I tried as hard as I could not to roll my eyes.

"Alright, alright, alright," Brian called out, clapping his hands. "Let's get serious. It's a big day." He looked around the room. "Where's

Cap? I thought they'd be in here going over plans for the eightieth time."

Michelle looked up from her protein bar. "Close. They're checking the packs."

"I heard that," Cap called from the other room.

"Not that it'll matter when the hell-creature comes back to finish the job," Dan said grimly. Dan was injured during the attack on our camp, just managing to escape with claw marks grazing his thigh. The wound was deep enough to cause a limp, but it could have been so much worse. I knew Dan accepted that he'd be joining Michelle and Red to hold down a temporary base at Town Lake; still, it was apparent he hated not being able to do more.

We determined the groups we'd split into and had a list of the most likely spots to find the supplies we needed. Though there hadn't been any sign of danger since the day of the explosions, we still packed knives. At least the smaller weapons could be easily carried. Ideally, we would have guns, but between running out of ammo and losing the rest in the rubble at our old camp, we were shit out of luck in the firearm department. Luckily, we were in Texas, so we hopefully wouldn't be unarmed for long.

The downtown area was about seventeen miles from where we were. Hot as it was, we could only walk for about an hour at a time. Frequent rests and hydration breaks were a must in the Texas heat. At least this time we would have the handheld fans.

By accident, the day after the attack on our old camp, we discovered that some of the battery-operated devices that had remained intact started working again. Whether it was coincidence or good luck that electronics started working once the ships left the sky, I decided to take it for the blessing it was. Being able to use the fans and Cap's long-range walkie-talkies was a significant win. Having a form of communication was a valuable resource, and any aid against the heat was a plus.

We hoped that meant we'd be able to get a car working, too. If we could manage it, our travel time would be cut significantly, giving us more room to make up for any hold-ups when it came to finding resources. All cars had been dormant for so long, and with everything that happened, who knew if we could even get one started? Still, it was tempting to think about what a car's air conditioning would feel like after so long.

I looked up as Red entered the room and Cap followed, smiling. "Well, we're all here now!" Something about starting a new mission always seemed to perk Cap right up. They thrived on planning and execution, and were well-known throughout our group for their survival knowledge. It was unanimous when we decided to vote them the unofficial-official leader of our smaller group.

"I'm having second thoughts," Red blurted out. "What if we can't get across the bridge at Ladybird Lake?"

"You mean Town Lake," Russell said, raising an eyebrow in Red's direction. "Only tourists and transplants call it Ladybird."

Red glared at him from across the room, but we didn't have time for another fight this morning. "If you want to get technical," I interrupted, "you should call it a Colorado River reservoir." Russell and Red both rolled their eyes, but neither tried to argue back.

"Listen, Red," I continued, "until you have a better plan, this is it. We can't waste any more time talking through the what-ifs. No plan is perfect; this is the best we've got."

Michelle scowled in my direction, likely because of my blunt response, before facing Red and grabbing her hands. "I know you're scared," Michelle said in a low voice. "I'm scared, too. We can do this, though. We have the easy job." Red forced a smile and squeezed Michelle's hands in return.

"And who knows," Brian chimed in. "Maybe we'll find a bottle of Tito's and the whole trip will be worth it."

"Ooh! I hope we find those little fruit cocktails in a can again!" Sam added.

"Forget Tito's—" Russell said. "Deadass, I'd low-key do anything for a bag of Hot Cheetos."

"Oh man," Dan groaned. "This is making me so hungry." Dan looked down at the protein bar in his hand, reluctantly taking a bite.

Cap laughed, shaking their head, and even Red cracked a smile. As much shit as I gave the Twenty-Somethings, they were good for lightening the mood.

"Alright," Cap said, raising their hands. "Let's grab our packs and get started before the day gets too hot."

"Cap, you say that like it isn't already a hundred degrees outside," Red said playfully.

"Well, let's get walking before it hits 105, then!" Michelle said, all but shooing us out the door.

I looked back at the house as we left. The secure walls and quietness of the neighborhood had been a relief after the absolute hell we'd walked through to get there. My heart raced as I stared at the open street. I took a deep breath, counting down from ten, and then followed my group into the next unknown.

FIVE
ALINA

Four days.

Four days ago, we woke up in the pods.

Once the adrenaline wore off from our escape and the explosions that followed, Jason and I realized we needed more time to regain our footing before taking another step. The first day and a half, we did little more than take turns sleeping, hydrating, and trying to rid ourselves of the pounding headaches that had returned with a vengeance.

As I slept, I was able to recall some more memories. Jason, too. Still, it was hard to tell whether a memory was real, or a piece of fiction my brain crafted to fit into the empty spaces I desperately wanted to fill. There were also nightmares, but I tried not to think about those. Jason and I spent most of our waking hours discussing how our memories connected to the timeline of events we knew of so far.

We knew that Jason made it to my apartment. We stayed there for at least a few days, talking to Emma on the phone whenever she could find a quiet space. Though Emma was adamant that Jason and I stay at my apartment, we were still trying to figure out how to get to her.

I remembered how the emergency centers started popping up,

too. Though we initially assumed it was a local government or civil service initiative, it was actually something started on social media before everything shut down. Neighborhoods started pooling together resources in school gyms, office buildings, or any other large space that could safely be filled. There were updates from the emergency alert system every few hours, but the system rarely told us anything new. We got most of our updates via text from what Emma heard through the grapevine until the power and cell services were cut. After that point? Everything was still hazy.

Still, I could almost feel the rest of the pieces buried in the back of my mind. Even when I slept—I knew there was more to the dreams and nightmares that scratched at the surface of my consciousness. It was only a matter of time before they fully resurfaced.

Once the pounding in our heads subsided and we regained some common sense, we realized waiting for a safer opportunity to leave would more likely lead to us burning with the rest of the city. So, we packed up some bags and laid out a plan.

"Can we talk through the plan one more time?" I begged, pulling the neckline of my sweaty t-shirt to try and stop it from sticking to my skin.

"Only one more time?" Jason asked with an amused look on his face. We'd been walking for a half hour and I might have asked more than once already.

"Yes. Just one more time," I replied. "The more I hear you say it, the more it sounds like we have a fully fleshed-out plan. You're very convincing."

"I'm pretty sure at this point, you could recite each step yourself, but sure." Jason laughed. "We are going to walk towards Ladybird Lake—"

"Town Lake," I interrupted.

Jason rolled his eyes. "Okay, we walk towards *Town Lake* because the smoke doesn't look like it reaches the water. By our logic, walking towards water is better than fire, right?"

"Right." I nodded, exhaling slowly. "Water is better than fire."

"Worst case scenario, we turn in another direction and walk that way instead."

"Solid plan," I confirmed. Okay, so 'plan' was a generous way to describe what we had going on.

"We'll figure it out," Jason said with a tired but reassuring smile.

It was impossible to feel anything but overwhelmed by the smoke and heat, and the humidity hung thickly in the air. Combined, it felt like we were walking through soup. Sweat poured down my sides, and my hair stuck to my face and neck like wet tendrils of seaweed before we'd gone more than a few blocks. I wondered if rain would at least come soon.

Still, we moved at a steady pace, keeping an eye out for any signs of danger. I wasn't quite sure what to expect, as we hadn't come across any other living thing since escaping—a fact that sat in the pit of my stomach like a rock.

"Hey, Jayce?" I asked, surprised I didn't sound as out of breath as expected. "What do we do if we come across other people? I mean, we have to find someone else eventually, right? How will we know they're someone safe?"

"Well..." Jason started. "Normally, I'd just flash a smile and hope my charm would do the rest, but I'm not sure if that will fly these days," he said with a light smile. "Seriously, though? I guess we'll just have to keep our guard up."

I rolled my eyes, then gasped. I hit his arm lightly as an idea popped into my head. "Oh! Or! You know how in *The Walking Dead* they had those three questions?" I lowered my voice and frowned deeply, doing my best Rick Grimes impression. "*How many walkers have you killed? How many people have you killed? Why?*' They'd ask outsiders those questions before letting anyone join up with them. We could do something like that."

Jason barked a laugh. "Of course, you'd bring that up. I mean, sure, that's one option. I doubt our situation involves 'walkers,' though."

"So..." My brow furrowed for real this time. We debated this question over the last few days, reluctant to define our assumed captors without ever having seen them. "Are we going with... aliens?" I cringed at the word. "I feel like that assumption isn't so off base anymore, right? Aliens?" I shook my head. "Every time I say it out loud, I feel like I've completely lost all hold on reality."

Jason thought for a second before responding. "From what we've seen? I keep coming back to aliens, as well. There were unidentified aircraft in the sky. The machines and tubes we were attached to seemed way too advanced to be human technology. Add in the glowing marks? If there was ever a time to use 'alien' to describe something, I feel like this might be it."

I paused, taking a deep breath of the thick, smoky air as I let the information sink in. As my mind wandered, I found myself cackling out loud.

"Lee, when you say you've completely lost reality...you good?" Jason asked.

"Yeah. No—no, I'm fine," I sputtered through my laughter. Okay, so I might have been just a bit delirious. Still, I turned to Jason, regaining some composure. "Basically—when you think about what was in those ships, you're not *saying* it was aliens...but..."

Jason stopped in his tracks. "Are you...quoting a meme right now?"

"Listen, all I'm saying is that Giorgio Tsoukalos from *Ancient Aliens* must be having the ultimate 'I told you so' moment."

Jason paused for a beat. "Wait, why do you know his full name?"

Another laugh bubbled out of my mouth and I snorted, causing Jason to break into laughter as well. Quoting a meme in the middle of a city burning to the ground was probably not the proper reaction for such a serious situation, but it felt good to laugh.

As my thoughts trailed on, the rumble of fire in the distance became white noise. The hypnotic rhythm blocked out everything else, even amidst the oppressive heat. Errant thoughts slipped away, leaving only the sensation of my Docs thumping against the pavement. I focused on the weight of each step as sweat trickled down my neck and pulled my water bottle from the outside pocket of my backpack. I was trying not to drink too much too quickly, but my throat felt impossibly dry. As I shoved the water back into its pocket, a prickling sensation danced along my spine and I shivered.

Jason suddenly grabbed my arm, pulling us against what used to be the outer wall of a bar. "What?" I yelped, stumbling backward as my back hit the building.

Jason put a finger to his lips, signaling the need for quiet. "Do you hear those scraping sounds?" Jason whispered, pulling me closer. I paused, trying to hear anything else over the hissing and crackling of the fire in the distance.

There—something metal hit the ground with a *clang* around the corner, followed by the snap of something breaking underfoot. I froze against the wall, staring back at Jason. My body was screaming to run and I wasn't sure how long I could fight the urge. Jason nodded towards a crumbling hole in the wall at our backs. The opening was just big enough for us to squeeze inside the dilapidated building. As we emerged on the other side, I looked over the room for immediate danger.

The place was wrecked. Not only did the ceiling cave in, the internal walls were crumbling, too. Scattered light leaked in from the cracks, just enough to be able to see while remaining cloaked in shadows. As we moved along the wall, I ran my hand along its rough surface until my fingers caught in one of the cracks. I looked closer, realizing I could see straight through to the sidewalk outside.

I touched Jason's arm to stop him from moving further, then pointed to the jagged opening. He caught on quickly as I mimed, pointing two fingers from my eyes to the crack in the wall, indicating I could see outside. We knelt on the ground and Jason held my shoulder, pulling me closer. He whispered so softly that if I didn't feel his breath against the shell of my ear, I might have missed it. "Unless something dangerous is trying to get in this building, we don't move."

I nodded, keeping my eye on the crevice. A rumble of a growl announced the creature's presence before I saw it and my breath caught in my throat. I braced a hand against the wall to keep myself steady as it stalked into view.

A long, brown leg with too many joints and prickly hairs bristling up its length crossed my line of sight. Then, another leg. And another. And another. I counted eight legs, each ending in claws with sharp, gnarled nails. My breath quickened as I blinked back the fear-induced tears pooling in my eyes. If the memory of ships in the sky hadn't already convinced me, this creature would be evidence enough—there was no way either came from our planet.

Its body was long and lean, with a hunched spine that jutted from its back. Blue-gray stripes stretched across its mottled brown, fleshy sides, and sparse, stiff hair prickled its skin. Muscles rippled and tensed as it moved, stalking close to the ground. Whatever it was, wherever it came from, it was unlike anything I'd ever seen before—a walking nightmare brought to life.

The beast froze in the middle of the street; its focus honed in on something we couldn't see. I held my breath as it reared on its back legs to examine the intersection. Standing upright, it had to be at least eight or nine feet tall. I brought a hand to my lips, afraid the whimper caught in my throat would escape without a physical barrier.

The terrifying beast surveyed the edges of the street as it made a low, wuffling sound. As it landed on its feet once more, the creature twisted its neck, tilting one large bat-like ear toward the ground. As it leaned closer, I could make out the almost feline shape of its head with four beady black eyes that sat at the center of its face. Another low, rumbling growl rolled from its chest and its whole body seemed to vibrate. I stared, barely breathing, as the short, stiff hairs on its body stuck straight up as if it were suddenly caught in a static storm. Then, the beast started changing color.

The brown deepened until it took on the same asphalt black of the pavement and the stripes on its back pulsed a bright, glowing blue. I stared in shock and horror as the blue flashed, remembering the glow of our tattoos. *Please tell me the glowing is a coincidence*; I prayed to whatever powers might be listening.

After the creature's new camouflage was complete, the glow radiating from its body faded back to its original, dull blue-gray markings that blended into its new hue seamlessly. It shook like a dog, stretching low before letting out a bone-chilling scream.

Scccccrrrrrrrrrrrreeeeeeeeeeeeccccccccchhhhhhhhhhhh

Jerking backward, I almost fell to the ground as the sound felt like it was tearing through me. Jason took my place at the wall and I heard his breath hitch when he saw the beast. Jason slowly leaned back, and as his eyes met mine, the creature outside let out another shriek.

The nightmare on legs wasn't breaking through the wall, so hopefully, it didn't know we were inside. My eyes darted around the room, scouting out all of the possible entrances and exit points. It looked like most of the cracks and openings were too small for the beast to get through easily. The windows were boarded over, but if the creature realized we were inside, I doubted pieces of plywood would stop it. Plus, there was a huge, gaping hole in the ceiling for it to climb through if it was feeling feisty.

I shifted, trying to crane my neck to get a better view of the opposite side of the bar, when I heard a bellowing growl in the distance. *No. Not more.* At the next screech, a chill ran through my body, even as I still tried to deny what that new sound meant.

Jason tapped my shoulder, pressing the handle of something into my palm. I quickly looked down to see he'd handed me one of the knives he'd taken from the thrift store. Not that it would do much against sharp claws and teeth.

A growl rumbled from outside and I pressed my eye harder against the opening, frantically trying to locate the second beast.

The first creature was still slowly moving along the street, stalking, and a clicking sound snapped over the low growls that still rolled from its throat. Slowly, it crept forward as the hairs on its body stood on end, then suddenly—it jerked up on its back legs as another beast, this one gray, barreled through the air, aiming to strike the first creature head-on.

The first creature was ready. As the gray nightmare was about to collide into the first one, Creature-One slammed its front legs forward, crashing its gray opponent to the pavement with an audible crack. They fought, legs jerking and wrapping around each other to try and claim dominance as claws tore through flesh. As they battled, the stripes on their backs flashed a brilliant, bright blue in time with their movements.

Creature-One opened its mouth and I gasped at the rows of sharp teeth as another screech poured from its unhinged jaws. The two monsters growled and shrieked as they wrestled on the ground, tearing and biting with a brutality I'd never witnessed in our animal kingdom. They were vicious. Ruthless. How could any human stand a chance?

The gray beast finally managed to pin Creature-One, opening its mouth wide as a series of clicks and screeches rattled from deep within its throat. The pinned creature grunted and I watched in shock as the gray beast released its hold, allowing the losing opponent an opportunity to right itself. They faced each other, growling, clicking, circling, and snapping before a crashing sound echoed farther away. Both creatures turned towards the sound, lowering into defensive stances, hesitating only a second before bounding down the street together, leaping across the parked cars and crushing the rubble in their path.

"They're leaving," I whispered, moving to the side so Jason could take another look. My heart pounded like it was trying to burst through my chest as I leaned against the wall.

Jason sank to the floor beside me and I took a shaky breath. "What the fuck, Jason?" I whispered, too scared to speak at a normal volume. "What the fuck was that?"

"I don't know," Jason murmured, wrapping an arm around my shoulders and pulling me closer to his side.

The pressure that built in my chest felt tight enough to snap. I tried to take a deep breath, but instead, the dam burst. I buried my face against Jason's shirt, desperate to stifle the gasping sounds that poured out of me. Jason ran his hands over my back, down my arms, trying to provide comfort as I shook with sobs. We were insane to think we'd leave this city alive.

I let myself cry freely for another minute before taking in deep breaths, forcing myself to regain control. Slowly, I released my hold on Jason as I lifted my head.

Jason kept his voice low as he said, "We'll find a way out. We have to."

I rested my head against Jason's shoulder and he just held me. I knew danger was out there. I wasn't naive. Still, until we witnessed the hellish creatures fighting right in front of us, I didn't realize just how dire the city's situation was. It made sense why we hadn't ran into anyone else.

"I saw something," I whispered, begging my voice not to break. "When the first creature was calling the other one and again when they were fighting—their markings were glowing, just like our tattoos."

Jason ran a hand down his face, letting out a long breath. "Well, fuck. That's something to process."

"Jason, how the hell are we going to get out of this?"

Jason stood, grabbing my hands and pulling me up along with him. His hands held my waist as if he were scared I would sink back down to the floor. "We'll make it. I know we will," he said.

Looking up at him, I could see the sincerity in his eyes. After everything, I couldn't understand how he was still able to believe we would survive. As if reading my mind, he added, "You don't have to believe me. I'm confident enough for the both of us."

As I stepped back from him, I grimly turned toward the room. "So, do we leave through the hole in the wall, or the door?"

SIX
CARTER

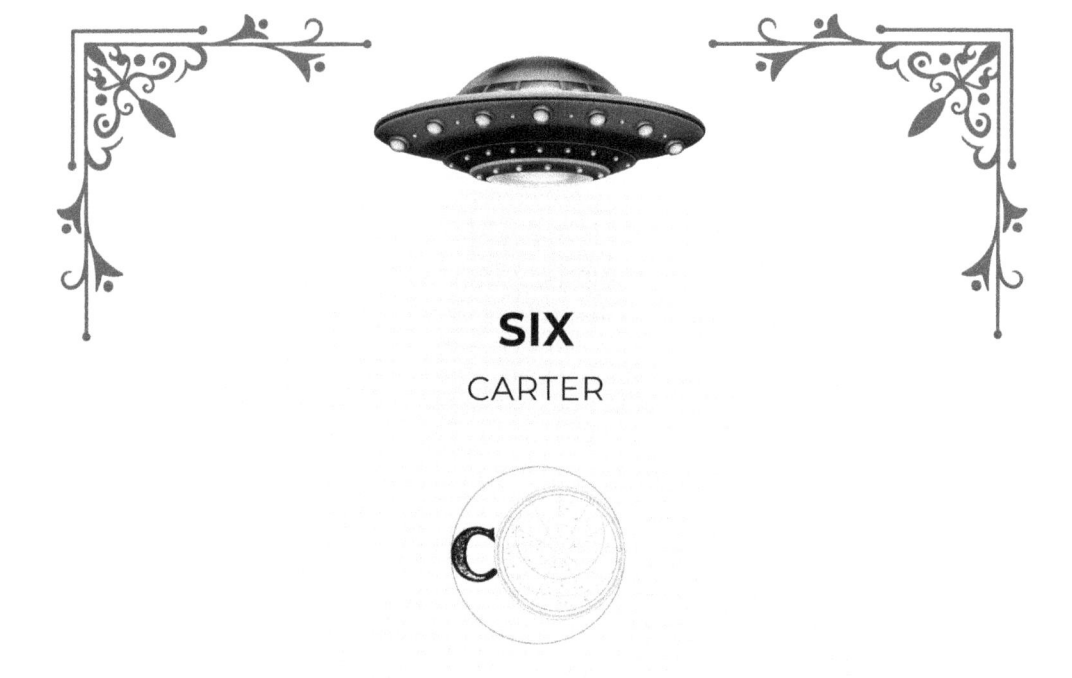

THE SUN WAS BRUTAL. We circulated the handheld fans, but they would never be enough to fully combat the summer heat.

Still, we walked on.

We planned to get a car working once we were out of the residential neighborhood. Of course, we passed all kinds of vehicles as we traveled, but the problem wasn't *finding* a car. The issue was getting one started. Whatever disruptors the invaders used to cut our power also interfered with battery-operated devices—but not all batteries were rendered useless, as the fans and walkie-talkies proved.

This was the first time we'd gone any significant distance since our group was attacked the day of the explosions. The memory weighed heavier with each step I took.

I wasn't there when the attack started on our camp.

I was part of a small group sent to check out the city after the ships left. Before we even got close to our destination, explosions filled the sky over the downtown area. We turned around immediately, but by the time we got back to camp, all we could hear were screams. Faces were missing among the dead, and I hoped those we couldn't find had at least escaped to a safe place. There was no feasible way even to begin looking for anyone presumed missing, either—especially when it wasn't guaranteed the people we were looking for were still alive. We just had to accept that they were gone.

Our group of eight may have been small, but we quickly became a well-oiled machine. We fell into a natural hierarchy and decision-making strategy when we voted for Cap to take the lead. For the most part, we'd decided on plans much quicker than when we were with the larger group. It made sense—there were fewer variables.

There was still tension, but we knew what had to be done and made sure it happened. The group was thankful to be alive, relieved to at least have each other. Still, everyone else couldn't help discussing the possibility of merging with another camp if we came across one. I kept quiet, but hoped we wouldn't have to worry about that for a long time. Adding in new people or joining an already established crew threw in all kinds of potential problems I didn't want to deal with.

Brian whistled from up ahead, signaling he'd spotted a location for our next break. As we got closer, I saw the roughed-up strip mall. I groaned internally, but we were due for some shade, food, and water if we didn't want anyone collapsing from heat stroke. These buildings were magnets for trouble, though. Rogue groups became more prevalent as time passed and people grew more desperate. Strip malls were perfect for hiding out and waiting for unsuspecting travelers to pass by.

Sam and I were voted to check out the building, so we broke from the others to head over to the row of stores. This wasn't my favorite type of task, but at least I knew Sam was thorough and I could trust her judgment. We often worked as a team, so I could almost anticipate what she'd do next as we scanned the location. We confirmed the stores were clear much quicker than expected—mainly because most shops were impossible to enter due to the destruction on the other side of the doors. The place was a mess, but it was acceptable for our purposes. I whistled to let the rest of the group know it was secure enough to follow us in, and Sam and I all but collapsed on the floor of one of the more intact former shops.

As soon as I felt the coolness of the tile, I sprawled out, not even caring how ridiculous I looked as I lay on the ground. Sam giggled and quickly followed suit. "Man, I needed this." She exclaimed dramatically.

I gave the kid a half-smile. "What, too hot? This is nothing."

Sam rolled her eyes. "Always with the tough-guy act."

"Act?" I exclaimed, rolling onto my side so I could face her. "Kid, this is anything but an act. I'm tough from the inside out."

Sam gently kicked my shin. "You don't have to keep it up, you know."

"Keep what up?" I replied, laying on my back again and draping an arm across my face.

"Pretending you don't care," she said quietly.

I moved my arm so I could see her face. She stared at me, a knowing look in her deep, brown eyes; her natural, curly, black hair spread around her head on the ground like a halo. "Try as you might to keep everyone at arm's length, I know you care. You're always looking out for everyone, even if you don't admit why you do the things you do. Like it or not, geezer, you're one of us." She paused. "Don't you think it's about time you let someone else in to care for you, too?"

I stared at Sam and the serious expression on her too-young face as she stared back, expectantly. Sam and I found our group around the same time, and since day one, she stuck close to my side. I assumed it was newbie solidarity and never paid her much attention back then.

We learned the ropes together and were often assigned to the same teams to work on tasks for our camp. She didn't talk much at first, but even then, I could see how she was busy observing everything around her. Sam wasn't shy; she was cautious, curious, learning everything she could before making choices and taking action. Before long, we were eating every meal together in addition to working on tasks as a team, and I found I'd come to rely on her presence without even realizing when it had happened.

I knew keeping someone close long-term in this environment wasn't realistic. Still, she snuck in and took hold of something inside me before I even realized she was there. I didn't have any siblings to compare our relationship to, but I imagined this was what it would have felt like. As much as I might have denied it out loud, she was the exception.

"Interesting character assessment, kid." I chuckled. "You know I keep my circle small."

"Sure." Sam rolled her eyes. "About eight people small, right?"

I rolled my eyes, getting ready with a comeback before accepting she wouldn't let this one go. Exhaling roughly, I responded, "Just don't go telling anyone else. I have a reputation to uphold."

Sam giggled, sitting upright again. "Oh no, wouldn't want to let people know you're anything more than a cantankerous, defensive asshole. Don't worry. Your secret's safe with me."

The others trickled in, making space on the floor to sit and escape the heat as best they could. Sam casually approached Russell and Dan, who started taking lunch out of their packs. As they sat down to eat, Brian quickly joined them and their laughter soon echoed across the room. Surprisingly, I found the noise to be almost soothing.

As I looked around, I found Red's focus was trained on me. She quickly glanced towards Michelle, who was talking quietly with Cap, then back at me. As she took a deep breath, I clearly saw her mutter, "Fuck it," under her breath without having to hear the actual words that left her mouth. *Oh, what fresh hell is this woman bringing me today?* I sat up, bracing myself for whatever was about to come.

Red approached and squatted down next to me, frowning in thought. It was a bit unusual, as Red never hesitated before speaking her mind before. After another awkward moment of silence, I decided to initiate the conversation. "What's up, Red?"

She frowned and I knew she was having an internal battle about whether she should say anything at all. We were definitely similar that way. She breathed deeply before speaking. "It's probably nothing—nerves or whatever. I feel stupid even saying anything, but if I don't get it out I know I won't be able to drop it.

"I have a bad feeling. It isn't rooted in anything tangible. It's not logical. I haven't seen anything weird to even make me feel this way. Still—I can't shake the feeling that something bad is going to happen."

I hummed in acknowledgment and debated whether I wanted to

continue entertaining the conversation. There were plenty of other people around for Red to vent to. I wasn't sure why she chose me, knowing I was far from empathetic on a good day. I caught Sam's eye from across the room and saw her glance at Red, then back to me, before subtly throwing me a thumbs-up. I didn't know what her sudden investment in my companionship with the others was about, but considering we had miles to go, I figured it wouldn't hurt to talk Red through what was on her mind. If anything, it would hopefully prevent a greater meltdown later on if the thoughts were left to fester.

Turning back to Red, I nodded. "Yeah? So what do you think is going to happen?"

"I can only describe it as Déjà vu, in every sense of the word. Being here, I just *know* something bad is going to happen."

I reflected on what she said for a moment before responding. "I mean, I guess it makes sense."

"It does?" Red answered, taken aback by my giving merit to her concerns.

"Yeah, it does. All of these places we're passing? You've probably been there before. It isn't like we are in a new city; we have history here. And bad things have happened. Look at the last time I tried going downtown—that trip ended in explosions and an attack on our camp. It makes sense why you're feeling the way you do."

Red blinked at me and let out a quick exhale of a laugh. "Well, that was certainly not the response I expected."

"And yet, you still came to *me*. What does that say?" I smirked back at her.

"Har har." Red rolled her eyes. "Seriously, though. Thanks."

"For what?"

"For not brushing me off. For listening." She shrugged and stood up. "Sometimes that's enough." She gave a tight smile and wandered back to the storefront, leaning against the shadowed edge of the door as she stared into the parking lot.

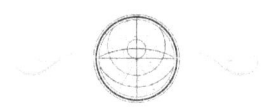

After we all ate our lunch, we met in the center of the room to discuss the next steps.

Once Cap was sure we were paying full attention, they asked, "Y'all doing okay so far?" Everyone either nodded or gave a thumbs-up, which was good enough for Cap to continue. "We are at the point in our trip that we talked about, where we have to make a decision. Now that we're essentially out of the quieter residential area, we're more likely to run into an auto shop or gas station carrying what we need to get a car running. We have a few options, depending on what we think is the most practical. Option one: We all keep continuing towards the city and stop at whatever place on our route looks like it might have what we need. Option two: We set up a temporary base here and send out a group to focus on finding something on this highway."

"So, what you're saying is, you want a longer break?" Red teased.

Cap laughed. "No, but I think if we can find a car sooner, we'd feel much better about continuing downtown. Especially as we get into the hotter points of the day."

"I think option two makes sense," Red said, shrugging. "Can I call 'not it' for the expedition, though?"

Russell groaned, but Brian elbowed him in the side before he could say something obnoxious. "I also vote for option two," Brian responded.

"Bet," Russell called out. "Also, I'm more than down for the *expedition*." He glared at Red, who gave him a snarky look in return.

"Honestly, I can go either way," Sam responded, with Michelle nodding in agreement.

"Considering I'm the weakest link, any option where I won't have to walk on this leg longer than I have to seems good to me," Dan added, a defeated look on his face. He'd been quieter than usual since he was injured. I assumed a lot of it was survivor's guilt—we all felt it to an extent.

"Hey!" Red snapped, frowning at Dan. "What did I say about talking like that? You're anything but weak, and what you're responsible for with Chelle and *me* is just as important as any physical task. Ability doesn't define worth. Don't make me repeat it again."

I blinked in surprise. That was probably one of the most supportive things I'd ever heard Red say to anyone else in the group. Dan's face softened and he gave Red a small smile as he nodded.

"Carter," Cap said, taking the attention off of Dan and Red. "What are your thoughts?"

I cleared my throat, thinking about what I wanted to say. "I think it comes down to what is the biggest priority? Do we want to focus on getting downtown? Or is finding a vehicle more important? If we go with option one, we'll still most likely find the supplies we need. The downside is we might not be able to transport as much. With option two, there is still no guarantee we can get a car to work, and a place like this isn't exactly the safest option the longer we have to stay. But, finding a car now would give us more flexibility with anything we do next."

"Damn, your logic." Russell shook his head. "Now I'm doubting my decision."

"That's exactly why we talk things out," Cap responded. "We want to consider all of our options thoroughly before deciding. It's good to pick the plan apart so we don't miss anything. It's why we waited until now to decide which option to go with."

"Well," Michelle tentatively started, "I think supplies might be the bigger priority, then—since we don't know if a car will work."

"I change my vote," Russell called out. "I vote for the city."

"So now we have two for the city, one neutral, three for the car, and I am still leaning towards the car, too," Red tallied out loud.

"I'm going to bet on the car," I added. "I don't want to stick around this area for too long, but if we are going to test out the car theory, I think now's the time."

"Same for me," Sam voted.

"So 'car' has the majority, six to two," Red called out.

"Unless there are any strong objections?" Cap looked around the room, taking the silence as agreement. "I'm thinking Russell, Carter, and Brian can go out. The rest of us can stay here and rest in shifts while we have two on watch at a time."

"Let me go," Sam said. "I used to work on cars with my dad."

I let the others debate logistics, and in the end, Russell and Sam were voted to go with me. We readied our packs and then set out.

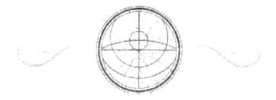

"Deadass, the car wash is going to be a waste. We're better off checking out the dealership a few miles down," Russell grumbled. We hit three gas stations so far, but still hadn't found what we needed.

"And I'm telling you, you're wrong," Sam bit back. "Car washes bank on people panic buying things they don't need at the register while they wait for their car. Plus, it's *right* there. Just a quick walk across the street and down a few storefronts. It'd be a *waste* not to check it out."

Russell groaned his reluctant resignation. At this point, it felt like he was arguing for the sake of arguing. I glared at him as I trailed behind them. I was keeping an eye out behind us to ensure nothing could sneak up as we crossed the street, but their conversation had become beyond distracting. Usually, Russell and Sam got along well —too well, if I was being honest. Maybe something else happened between them after his dumb comment the other day. *I should probably check with Sam to make sure—wait.* I ran a hand down my face to stop the thought before it could go any further. I knew Sam could handle herself. She was a smart kid and didn't need me butting in where it wasn't my business. Sam's talk earlier must have messed with my head or something.

Russell and Sam continued to speak quietly as we approached the car wash, and I stepped ahead of them to get to the store first. It was a small space, so I could see almost everything as I pointed my flashlight through the windows. I wasn't surprised the store was still in good condition. Most people probably assumed what Russell did —what good was a car wash when all the cars are dead?

My flashlight illuminated walls splattered with a rainbow of air fresheners. Bottles of windshield washer fluid and car cleaning products lined bottom shelves, while endcaps held an array of other car accessories. There were some other boxes in the back that I couldn't make out, but it was worth a shot to check.

I pulled a cloth from my pocket, wrapping it around my hand as I grabbed a rock from the ground. I lifted my arm, preparing to smash through the glass door, but before I could swing, Russell knocked my arm out of the way.

"Woah—hold up, bruh," he warned.

I glared at him. "Did you just call me 'bruh'?"

Russell rolled his eyes. "It's not that deep. The better question is why did you jump to smash first, ask questions later? The Hulk had more discrepancy."

"You mean, 'The Hulk was more discreet'?" Sam called from behind us.

Russell gave her a frustrated look before stepping in front of the door and leaning over to work at the lock. "You know what I meant. And I'm not tryna flex, but…" The door swung open with a click. "No smashing required."

I stared at the open door, knowing full-well confusion was written all over my face. Sam laughed as she bumped my shoulder and strolled inside. Russell started following her, but just as I was about to step through the door, he turned, blocking me from moving further with his arm. He smirked as he said one word, "Bump key."

"Bump key?" I repeated, squinting my eyes at him. "Where the fuck did you get a bump key?"

"Does it matter?" Russell replied. "If you were ever part of my scouting groups before now, you'd know that this is my specialty."

Was this kid a budget-version jewel thief in a past life?

Russell raised his eyebrows, stepping back with a mock bow as I entered the building. "How big is this thing we're looking for, again?" he asked.

"You mean, how big is the thing I just successfully found, even though you swore we wouldn't have any luck here?" Sam said, triumphantly holding up a container about the size of a shoe box.

Russell perked up, excitement crossing his face. "You found the jump starter?"

"Yep," Sam answered, popping the 'p' at the end of the word.

"Babe, you are the mother-fucking GOAT," Russell cheered, picking Sam up and swinging her around.

She let out a surprised yelp before demanding, "Put me down, dumbass."

"Let's not celebrate so soon," I interjected. "We still need to make sure it will actually work." I dug through the drawer underneath the register, narrowing my eyes in Russell's direction as his hands moved lower on Sam's hips while setting her down.

"Come on, Carter." Sam rolled her eyes. "This is a win, whether it works or not." She gave me a pointed look.

"Great job. We did it. Now let's go," I deadpanned.

Sam all but skipped to the front door and Russell paused to look at some of the car accessories on the walls. "Do you think we need any of this other stuff?"

"I mean, that largely depends on the condition of the car we get." Sam shrugged. "We don't want to be carrying stuff just for the hell of it. Once we get a car, we can come back and grab some of the fluids if we have to; but a lot of this is just vanity stuff."

"Bet." Russell nodded.

We left the store and made our way to the lone truck in the parking lot. It was a small pick-up, but if we used the truck's bed, everyone would technically be able to fit. It wasn't the safest, but it would get the job done. *If it starts,* I reminded myself.

"Okay," Sam said, clapping her hands and whirling around to face us once we reached the truck. "Make sure you listen to each step and don't interrupt. Here's how this is going to work. The truck has to be off, first, which, duh—we're already there. We'll pop the hood and connect the jumper cables." Sam held up the red and black clamps. "We don't want this black piece to touch anything metal or it'll spark. Understand?"

Russell nodded thoughtfully and I chuckled, nodding as well. I knew all of this already, but figured I'd let her have her moment.

"Don't turn on the car until I say so," Sam said pointedly. "Once everything is connected, we'll turn on the jump starter and then we should be able to try and start the truck."

"If the jump starter has enough juice to get it started," I added.

"We're going for positive manifestation here, Carter," Sam said, giving me a stern look.

"Should we, like, say a prayer?" Russell asked, his face completely serious.

"I can't tell if you're mocking me or not. Let's do this," Sam answered before turning to pull open the truck's driver-side door. She pulled the handle again before turning back around with a huff, "It's locked."

"Of course it is." I smirked. "The truck is in a public parking lot. Would you have left your car unlocked in a public place?"

Sam pouted. "Okay. Fine. Point made. What do we do now?"

I pulled out the key chain I found under the register. "We use the key."

Sam threw her hands in the air in exasperation. "Why are you just revealing this now?"

"You told us not to interrupt," I answered.

Sam growled in frustration as she grabbed the keys from my hands, stopping to narrow her eyes at me before turning to open the car door for real this time. Then we got to work.

We still weren't sure what would happen when we tried to charge the car's battery. In theory, giving it a jump start would work, but *actually* doing so assumed the battery would be able to receive a charge in the first place.

When Cap and I returned to our old camp the day after the attack to look for survivors, we tried powering on other devices we'd found as we picked through what remained of our camp. After realizing that electronics weren't working, most people didn't bother carrying their devices anymore. Still, enough was held onto for us to test the theory out. Some things, like the walkie-talkies, worked; others wouldn't power on, even with replacement batteries.

"Alright, the moment of truth," Sam murmured as we all stared at the jump starter. She bent down to flick the power switch and then screamed at the top of her lungs.

Russell and I lunged forward to grab her, but Russell was faster. Pulling her upright and into his arms, he frantically searched her for any sign of injury. "Fuck, Sammy—are you okay? Are you hurt? What happened?"

Sam burst out laughing and crying simultaneously. "It turned on! It works!"

With my heart still racing, I knelt next to the jump starter to see a tiny, green, blinking light. The screen had a power level indicator as well. "It's on one bar. Hopefully, that's all we need." Even as my heart pounded with anticipation, a sliver of hope began slicing its way through. I turned to see Sam still in Russell's arms, her back to his chest as his arms circled her waist. She was still laughing and crying, and Russell grinned even wider.

"This is it! Let's get that bag!" Russell cheered, giving Sam another squeeze and kissing her cheek.

I jumped into the driver's side of the truck, stepped on the brake, and twisted the key in the ignition. The engine turned over, struggling and sputtering, as I silently begged it to start.

After a second, the truck roared to life as static blasted from the stereo. "Yes!" I roared.

Russell and Sam excitedly started jumping up and down. "We have a fucking car!" Russell yelled.

As I stepped down from the truck, Sam ran over and wrapped her arms around my neck in a giant hug, and Russell wasn't far behind. I wasn't even mad as they squeezed me in their group hug, celebrating our win.

This would change everything.

SEVEN
CARTER

We rolled up to the abandoned strip mall, tires bumping over the rough pavement as I tried to avoid any obstacles that could seriously damage the car. As we got closer, Russell and Sam started belting out the lyrics to *We Are the Champions* by Queen at the top of their lungs.

For months, we had been in a state of constant damage control. Every day we woke up was another day of figuring out how to survive —where to get food, where to sleep, who to trust. Sure, short respites along the way gave us a chance to catch our breath, but this was the first solid win that felt like we were approaching smoother shores instead of endlessly treading water.

As we drove closer, the rest of the group dashed from the shelter, staring at the truck with varying looks of awe. Michelle was the first to break the silence, letting out a wild cheer and grabbing Cap into a suffocating hug. Brian sprinted towards us with Dan limping behind him, and Red brought her hands to her mouth, stifling the smile breaking through her tears of happiness and relief.

I couldn't stop my own grin from spreading wider across my face. We needed this.

I slowed the truck to a stop as Brian jumped into the back, punching the air with another whooping celebration call. Russell and Sam barreled out of the cab, jumping into the truck's bed with Brian before they all helped Dan climb up to join them. They wrapped their arms around each other in a giant group hug, laughing and crying as they continued yelling the Queen song together—they almost got all the words right, too.

Red climbed into the passenger seat with a sigh, groaning as she felt the air conditioning hit her skin. "This has to be heaven."

I chuckled as Cap and Michelle climbed into the cab. "We are claiming our seats before the others remember cars have AC." Michelle laughed.

"I never thought I'd feel this again." Cap leaned back, placing an arm around Michelle's shoulders. "We needed this win, Carter." Their sparkling gray eyes met mine in the rearview mirror. "Great work. Seriously."

"I almost don't want to turn it off in case it doesn't turn back on." I chuckled.

I felt a swat on my shoulder and looked to the back seat in shock. "I won't have any negative talk in my truck," Michelle scolded.

"Oh, it's your truck now?" Cap teased.

"Yes. And her name is Nancy," Michelle stated matter-of-factly, folding her arms as she got comfortable in the back seat.

"I don't care what her name is or who she belongs to as long as I can live here for the rest of my life." Red sighed.

I smirked, looking in the side-view mirror at the rest of our crew, who were now lounging in the truck bed. "Hey," I called through the open window. "What do you think? Should we take a drive? Find another one of these bad boys?"

"Bad girl," Michelle reminded me without missing a beat.

"Excuse me." I chuckled. "My mistake. Let's find another one of these *bad girls* and figure out how to stock up on some fuel while we're at it."

"Let's do it!" Dan cheered from the back. "Russell and Brian can load our packs into the back."

"I'm so happy we don't have to walk the rest of the way; I'm not even mad that you just gave us an order," Brian said, grabbing the sides of Dan's head and planting a kiss right on his forehead before leaping out of the truck bed with Russell.

We set off down the road once Brian and Russell were back in the truck with our packs. The road was in pretty rough condition, so I made sure to mind our speed as I listed potential risks in my head—animals, rogue groups, debris, potholes…the hell-creature responsible for our group's attack…the ships that might come back while we're on the highway with no chance of reaching cover. You know, the usual.

Though it had been days since the ships disappeared, I wasn't convinced it was the last we'd see of the invaders. I wouldn't let myself forget they could return as quickly as they seemingly left. Same with the creature. We hadn't seen any sign of the hell-beast since it attacked our camp, but I knew it must still be out there somewhere.

I didn't get a good look at it that night, but Dan was able to give us a first-hand account describing in detail what the fucker looked like before it sliced his leg. He said it had eight legs and a long torso with angles in all the wrong places. Though its skin was tinted with a rotting kind of gray, there were blue stripes lining its body. As it attacked, the stripes pulsed with some kind of otherworldly, bioluminescent glow. With jaws like a shark's and claws sharp enough to match in ferocity, it's a miracle Dan wasn't more injured. If Brian and Russ hadn't distracted it at just the right time, who knew if he'd have made it. Though we had a few good days since then, I had no doubt it was only a matter of time before we ran into that hell-beast or the invaders again.

I wondered how many other camps were destroyed like ours. On our travel days, we used to see at least one other group per day, but even as far as we ventured today, we still didn't run into anyone. Maybe I shouldn't have been surprised. For a while now, we'd been hearing from groups in passing that camps were moving further from the city. The hope was to find a more isolated spot to set up longer-term shelters. Still, there could be others like us who chose to stay and recover from their losses before making any moves.

I didn't mind the lack of run-ins. The less outside influence there was to worry about, the better. Once we got settled somewhere, that would be a different story. Still, I doubted the rest of my people could avoid taking someone else in, should we cross them.

I frowned, trying to push the intrusive thoughts back as I drove.

"You okay, Carter?" Red asked, jolting my focus to those in the car with me.

I turned briefly to see her staring, a curious look on her face. "Yeah."

"You sure? Because you're brooding again," Red teased. "Come on. This is supposed to be our celebration lap. What's bugging you?"

"Who's saying I'm not celebrating?" I answered in a gruff voice. When Red didn't reply, I glanced in her direction and caught her glaring.

"Is it even possible for you to not be a downer?" she snarked.

"Are you seriously starting an argument right now?" I threw back.

Red rolled her eyes, angrily shaking her head in disagreement.

"Hey now, come on. Let's calm down," Michelle said from the back seat.

"I am calm," I grunted, clenching my hands on the steering wheel.

"Oh yes. Look at you, the perfect picture of calmness and relaxation," Red snapped. "You sit there, glowering at the road, practically grinding your teeth to dust, then bite anyone who reaches out a hand to help."

"Are you serious right now?" I exploded. "You're mad at me because what? My answer wasn't deep enough for you? Just because I let you vent for a minute during our break to avoid another 'Red Meltdown' doesn't mean we are suddenly best friends. I don't owe you anything. Stop pushing me."

"Fuck you, Carter," Red spat. "I just—"

"Enough!" Cap shouted from the backseat, silencing Red before she could continue. "What we're not going to do is fall back into petty arguments. We aren't out of danger and I need y'all to focus on something that *actually* fucking matters." Cap paused. "Take a breath. Apologize to each other. And drop it."

It was rare for Cap to raise their voice, so Red and I must have been pushing more than just each other's buttons. Red and I muttered half-assed apologies to each other, and Michelle gently eased Red into a conversation about what they should set up once we got to Town Lake.

I let the chatter fade into the background as I drove on, easing my grip on the wheel.

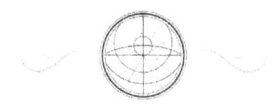

While we figured out how to siphon gas reasonably quickly, finding two more working vehicles took longer than expected. The same battery issues we'd faced with some of our smaller devices also seemed to have affected many of the larger car batteries. We'd anticipated as much, but it was still annoying to deal with. We had to try a few different cars before we found one with a battery capable of holding a charge. Luckily, 'Nancy' held strong, and we eventually found a sedan and an SUV to complete our caravan.

After finding the third car, we reviewed our plan for Town Lake again. This 'plan, reassess, move forward' tactic was a decision-making strategy Cap implemented with our smaller group. Cap would talk us through the basics of their idea, give space for everyone to voice their opinions, ask questions, and fully explore the strategy to see if there were any holes. They never insulted or judged anyone for bringing up concerns. Sometimes, I even forgot Cap was steering our ship because of how open and transparent they were. They were nothing like previous group leaders, which was absolutely for the better.

Power was tempting no matter the situation, and the pressure to maintain that claimed power could lead a group to its ruin. Hell, I'd experienced it multiple times in other groups I'd been a part of since this all started. Too many people felt challenged by questions—afraid that their authority would be diminished when all anyone usually wanted was reassurance. In these last four days, tensions aside, it felt like we were making progress towards something more stable. However, the relief I felt could have had something to do with no longer being in the same car as Red.

Red, Michelle, and Dan took the SUV to set up a base by Town Lake. They were in charge of keeping time with the clock on the walkie-talkies and monitoring everyone's locations on one of our maps. Cap was in the truck with Russell and Sam, set to scour the city's west side for supplies. Brian and I took the sedan and were in charge of the east. Each group took a walkie-talkie so we could keep in contact throughout the mission and have a way to make sure we didn't spend too much time in one place. We decided the best way to stay in touch without over-communicating was to share updates as we traveled from one location to the next.

When the lake appeared in the distance, Brian let out a sharp exhale, shaking me back into reality as he softly murmured, "Man, we made it."

"Made good time, too. Even with the detour to find cars, we still arrived earlier than planned," I responded.

Brian nodded. "They better find a good place out of sight to set up camp," Brian thought out loud.

"They know what they're doing," I reassured him.

"It's different this time." Brian shifted in his seat, unable to sit still. "Granted, the cars are a game changer, but still—we have to re-learn how to survive in another new environment, even though we're still in the same place we were before."

I paused, thinking about what Brian said. "Still, some things remain the same."

"How do you figure?"

"It's still all about survival, just as it was before all of this happened." I gave Brian a pointed look. "The dangers and our motivations may have changed, but the subconscious drive to fight through it all and survive is still the same."

Brian nodded grimly. "Honestly, I'm mostly worried about Dan right now. He's still hurt. If they have to run—"

"He's tough," I interrupted. "Don't forget—he made it through a lot before he found our group. If he got this far, I can't see him stopping anytime soon."

"I guess." Brian sighed. "I just hate not being together."

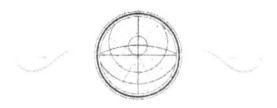

Navigating around stopped cars became more challenging as we crossed the South Congress Bridge. We debated trying to jump a few of the abandoned vehicles to move them off our path, but decided it would be too time-consuming. Still, there was enough space to clear a path if we could maneuver some of the cars out of our way. We decided to put the most obstructive cars in neutral and push them. It ate through some time, but if the mission succeeded, we would have to leave this way, anyway.

The skyline was clouded in smoke from the fire still raging in the city's center. I thought back to the early days of the invasion and wondered what could have gone differently if only the fates tipped in a different direction. Even if the invaders were really gone for good, I wasn't convinced society would ever be able to return from the destruction and trauma—at least not to the way things were.

"What's first on our list?" Brian panted, one hand on the steering wheel, the other braced against the car's frame as we pushed the last vehicle to the side, clearing a path across.

"From the look of that fire, we probably won't be able to get anywhere near the capital. If they're still intact, our best bet will probably be the hotels off of San Jacinto. We should stick to searching the ground floors, though."

"Right." Brian nodded. "Hopefully, those little hotel lobby stores will have stuff we can use. If we can make it to 3rd Street, there are a few smaller markets we can try to hit, too."

With the rest of the path clear enough to weave through, we returned to the car to drive across the bridge. We found the streets on the other side weren't as bad as we expected. There was still a good amount of debris and rubble to navigate, but it was manageable in the small sedan. Brian reported our status back to the others as we approached the hotel.

"You know," Brian said as we left the car and walked towards the hotel entrance. "Not that it's been *incredibly* easy to get here—but I'm surprised we haven't hit anything too crazy yet."

"Goddammit," I muttered, glaring in his direction. "You do realize you just jinxed us?"

Brian snorted a laugh as we made our way into the first building.

Whichever way our luck would turn, there was no backing out now.

EIGHT
CARTER

EVIDENCE OF A FIGHT long lost greeted us as we walked through the hotel lobby. There were dark spots on the carpet marking where the invaders' guns had disintegrated their victims. I couldn't push the imagery from my head.

We started going through the luggage that was left in the main lobby. Brian emptied one of the larger suitcases to hold any items we planned on taking. Of course, we still had our backpacks, but the more we could bring back to recover what the camp lost, the better.

"Should we grab any clothing?" Brian called over. "I'm not sure what size everyone is, but there are shirts I can totally see Sam or Red wearing."

"Has anyone mentioned being low on clothes?" I replied, not looking up from the bag I was digging through.

"I mean, Red, but she always wants more clothes, whether she needs them or not. It's like, her comfort thing."

"We should probably grab extras of everything if we can—never know what we'll need. Plus, if it makes Red happy, might as well."

"Carter!" Brian placed a hand over his heart. "Doing something for Red's happiness? There's a warm squishy heart in there, after all!" he teased.

"If anyone asks, it was your idea," I mumbled.

Brian laughed, tossing rejected items into our discard pile. "It *was* my idea, so I will take all the credit *regardless*—" Brian switched subjects, interrupting himself as he was distracted by a new find. "Sam likes to read, right?"

I glanced at Brian holding a few books. "Yeah, Sam likes books. She is always talking about some fantasy novel or other." I couldn't help chuckling as I recalled one of her rants about the differences between dragons and why-verns—whatever a 'why-vern' was.

"Think she'd like this?" Brian tossed a red paperback my way.

"*A Court of Thorns and Roses*? Probably." I stuffed the book in my backpack. Even if it wasn't an old favorite, she'd probably be happy enough to have a physical book.

"There are two more 'Court' books." Brian looked back and forth between the teal and purple covers in his hands. I noticed they had the same font on their covers as the one I'd just stuffed in my backpack.

I nodded. "Give 'em here. We'll take them back and let her decide if she wants to keep all three."

"Hey, while we're keeping an eye out for things everyone likes, if you find any candy, let me know. Dan has been whining about his stash running out."

I chuckled and told Brian I'd help, remembering the dramatic way Dan dumped out the entire contents of his pack a few days ago to look for one last piece of candy. I wouldn't usually get caught up in something so frivolous, but Brian's excitement was contagious. With the extra space we had, thanks to the cars, I figured we might as well.

We managed to collect a decent amount of travel-sized toiletries, mini first-aid kits with Band-Aids, Neosporin, and over-the-counter medication. We even found some prescription painkillers and antibiotics. There were a bunch of pills we weren't familiar with in the medication pile, as well; Red could decide if they were worth keeping. It was always better to take something and not need it, than to need it later on and regret not grabbing it.

We found some snack foods and a few packs of unopened candies that hadn't completely melted, too. Brian was overjoyed at the discovery, and the feeling carried him through the rest of our search.

After picking through everything we could, Brian and I walked the rest of the ground floor—what we had access to, anyway. Most rooms were shut with electronic locks we couldn't figure out how to open. There was a mini-mart in the hotel with snacks and drinks, but it was locked behind a thick, metal gate.

We debated searching the check-in counter for a master key, but ultimately decided our time would be better spent getting to the next place. Part of our mission was to see how the city had been affected. If we wanted to survey more than a few streets, we couldn't stay in one spot for too long. Aside from timing, the smoke and dust were already getting to us. It was hard to keep from coughing and sneezing, and my eyes started getting irritated.

Brian got on the walkie-talkie to update the others. "Bri-Bri comin' at you on the Wi-Fi," he crooned into the walkie. "Carter and I found toiletries and medicine at the first hotel. The store inside the hotel is locked, so I think we're done here. Over."

"Wi-Fi, my guy?" Dan retorted over the radio. "*You wish. Over.*"

"I do, in fact, wish for Wi-Fi daily, on every shooting star and little dandelion puff I find. Anyway. Before I take up too much time—we're heading to the next location." Brian rattled off the name of the crossroads we were aiming for and lowered the volume on the walkie-talkie before shoving it into the outside pocket of his backpack. He grinned as he turned towards me. "Ready, C-Dawg?"

"Always with the fucking nicknames," I grumbled.

Brian snorted, replying, "Like you don't call the others 'kid' on a regular basis?"

"That's different," I said. "It isn't a nickname if I'm just calling them what they are. Let's get back to the car."

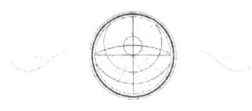

At the next hotel, we found much of the same—except the hotel store was actually accessible. We were able to score some unopened toiletries and sanitary products. The usual over-the-counter medications like Advil, Pepto, and some cold medicines were stocked well enough. Not to mention, we managed to fill a whole suitcase with snacks and drinks. Brian full-on crowed when he found mini-bar bottles of Tito's and an unopened pallet of snack-sized chips—Hot Cheetos included. After only two locations, our trunk was just over half-full. Depending on what the following places held, there was a chance we'd have to leave some of the less critical stuff behind to make space. Overall, it was a good problem to have.

After Brian and I loaded the car again, we debated where to go next. There was another hotel up the block, but if we went a bit further, we could check out one of the small corner markets. Ultimately, we decided to try our luck at a market so we could hopefully have more variety to choose from.

Brian slid into the passenger seat as Russell's voice broke through the crackle of our walkie-talkie. "*Heyyyyyyy fam, DJ Russ here, ready to get littyyyyyy with today's 'slays' and 'nays.' The convenience store was a complete flop. Trashed and uninhabitable.*"

"What does 'uninhabitable' have to do with anything? We weren't going to live there," Sam corrected in the background, and Brian and I exchanged an amused look.

"*Sam, don't kill the vibe! Anyway...*" Russell rambled on, sharing more details about what the group had been able to find and where they were going next.

Brian smirked, lowering the walkie's volume. "So, how crazy do you think Russell is driving Cap by now?"

"*Stop monopolizing the airwaves, Russell.*" Dan's voice crackled through the walkie-talkie before I could answer Brian.

"Cap knows how to keep Russell on track. Plus, they have the patience of a saint. I'm more concerned about Sam. She and Russell have been arguing lately."

"Nah, they're fine," Brian replied, brushing it off. "Russ is like, totally in love with her. They'll be golden once he gets over himself and admits his real feelings." He folded his arms behind his head, leaning back in his seat.

I grimaced. "And Sam's really into all of...that?"

Brian laughed. "What's wrong with Russ?"

Russell had followed Sam around like a lost puppy from the

moment he met her. If he wasn't with the Twenty-Somethings, he was trying to strike up a conversation with Sam, find reasons to bring her things, or make her laugh. Because of Russell, Sam also started hanging out with the other Twenty-Somethings. After the few months she'd known him, she was definitely aware of who Russell was as a person, even if he wasn't always the sharpest tool in the shed. I always thought Sam had good judgment with everything else, so why should this be any different? When I really thought about it, Russell didn't have any dangerous red flags—annoying flags, but not dangerous ones. Sam had every right to make her own decisions and mistakes. Life was too short for it all to matter, anyway.

I rolled my eyes, trying to dismiss the question. "Half the time, I can't figure out what the kid is saying."

"I mean, he lays it on a little thick with the Gen-Z slang, but ultimately, he's loyal, trustworthy, and has a big heart. Name one time he didn't come through when we needed him to. Not to mention, I've totally seen you laugh at his jokes—don't deny it!" He pointed a finger at me as I opened my mouth to retort. "Russ is a good guy."

"If you say so. Now, can we please talk about anything other than who is in love with who? I didn't sign up for fucking *Love Island* or whatever reality show we've fallen into."

Brian's jaw dropped and I groaned inwardly, anticipating his next words. "Carter. Are you a *Love Island* fan?"

"I give up," I groaned, gripping the steering wheel tighter. We were close to the market now, but there was too much rubble to continue driving safely. Turning off the ignition, I looked at Brian, who was still grinning like a Cheshire Cat. "This is as close as we can get without risking a flat. Remember, once we are out of the car, we have to be quiet to avoid unwanted attention."

"Are you using danger as an excuse to end our conversation?" Brian accused before noticing my glare. His mouth twitched as he stifled a laugh. "Well, it's a good thing I'm done talking, then." He reached for the car door handle, then paused. "One last thing—you need a new default setting or that scowl will freeze on your face permanently. You don't want to get wrinkles, what with skincare being so hard to find these days." He patted my cheek before yanking open the door. *"Quiet time, now,"* he mouthed, bringing a finger to his lips.

I ran a hand down my face in exasperation before following Brian towards the store. The smoke was more prevalent here, along with the stench of something rotten. I looked around warily as I surveyed the area. The street was a map of destruction—nearly all of the buildings had blown-out windows and smashed sidewalks. I carefully approached a car with a crushed roof and shattered windshield, inspecting the damage.

Scratches gouged through the paint, deep into the car's metal. Getting closer, I noticed claw marks lined the edges of each dent like the vehicle was used as a landing pad. Only one thing could have done that damage. Fucking hell.

I jogged towards the market's storefront to catch up with Brian. As quietly as I could, I informed him, "Hell-creature was in this area at some point. Keep your eyes open."

Brian nodded, a grim expression crossing his face.

We didn't know when the car was damaged. The destructive beast probably ran through the area and was long gone by now. Still, it was a good reminder of why we shouldn't assume anything. I cursed under my breath. We were careless, barely vetting our surroundings because of the false sense of safety and reassurance our luck brought. We needed to be more vigilant.

As we approached the store, the reek of rotting meat and produce wafted toward us, mixing with the smell of smoke like a wave of burning trash. We pulled pieces of cloth from our packs to cover our noses and mouths, trying to block out the putrid stench. Brian frantically tapped my arm, and I turned in time to see him brace his hands on his knees while he dry-heaved on the sidewalk. I slipped the pack from his shoulders, hoping it would take some pressure off of him while he regained his composure. When Brian stood up straight again, I showed him a thumbs-up, raising my eyebrow in question. He grimaced, nodding slightly as he hooked his backpack around his arm again.

We crept through the doorway, taking care not to step too heavily on the glass at our feet. Brian caught my eye and gestured to the left side of the store. I nodded, indicating I'd take the right. Though we generally tried to stay together in situations like this, the store was small enough. It made more sense to split up and cover ground quicker, especially with how hard it was trying to breathe without gagging. *Just like a game of Supermarket Sweep*, I thought to myself—quickly grab whatever looks remotely useful, then get the hell out.

Opening my backpack in front of me, I quickly walked down the aisles, grabbing anything still in good condition. The canned goods aisle was where I hit the jackpot, though. There were beans, mixed vegetables, various fruits, soups, Chef Boyardee, tuna, and chicken—hell, I probably even took a can or two of Spam.

I grabbed a few boxes of garbage bags and plastic utensils in the next aisle before my stomach started roiling. The smell was beyond overpowering at this point. Brian jogged around the corner, and we briefly looked at each other before he grabbed a few things off the shelves and threw me a thumbs-up. I pointed towards the previous aisle and darted back to fill up the rest of my pack with more canned goods, then met Brian at the front of the store. He looked like he was itching to jump over the threshold and race back to the car, and honestly, I felt the same.

We stepped through the doorway, pausing just long enough to scan the street and listen for any foreign sounds before quickly walking back towards the intersection where we left the car. "I still feel like I'm going to puke," Brian muttered under his breath as we clung to the wall of buildings next to us, stopping just before the corner. I barely registered the sound of heavy footsteps rushing towards us before we were almost knocked flat on our backs.

NINE
CARTER

A WOMAN with wild hazel eyes charged straight into my chest as she barreled around the corner. Brian gasped as a tall, white man with tousled, blond hair followed behind her, nearly knocking into him. The woman shot a look behind her, eyes wide with fear as she grabbed my hand and whirled me around, tugging me back in the direction Brian and I just came from.

"What the fuck?!" I hissed, yanking my hand back, causing the woman to stumble. Those hazel eyes met mine as she panted from exertion, and I quickly took her in. Beads of sweat collected on her darker, tan skin as she ran shaking hands through her wild, wavy, brown hair. Her almond-shaped eyes were wide, darting over the street in panic before her gaze fell to her companion again.

"Jayce!" she yelled before clapping a hand over her mouth, muttering a curse under her breath. 'Jayce,' I guess, was stiffly staring at Brian, who'd taken a defensive stance, fists raised.

"We have to run. Find a place to hide," she sputtered. "It's coming!"

A crash echoed around the corner, which was all the confirmation I needed. I turned, locking eyes with Brian as I jerked my head back towards the market, and we took off in a sprint.

"We can't go back in there, man," he panted as he ran next to me, the strangers on our heels.

"End of the street, around the corner." I glanced behind us; the crunch of metal and shattering glass the next street over was too close for comfort.

Brian dipped his chin in agreement and we pushed to run faster.

Goddammit, I thought. *God. Fucking. Dammit.*

TEN
ALINA

My lungs were screaming and a sharp stitch felt like it was stabbing the side of my stomach as I pushed my body to keep up with the men we literally just ran into. I didn't dare look behind us; instead, I focused on the direction in which they were heading. Hopefully, they were leading us someplace safer.

The two men quickly turned a corner, only slowing down as they approached an upcoming storefront. I just caught the end of the bigger one saying the building was a 'no-go' as we closed the gap between us. Jason raced past them to the next one. "Here!" he hissed.

I sprinted towards him as he pulled open the door. After we barreled inside, Jason started pushing a bench across the foyer; the metal legs loudly scraped against the tiled floor and I cringed at the noise.

"You've gotta be fucking kidding me," the man I'd run into growled, shooting a poisonous look Jason's way as he picked up one end of the bench to help Jason carry it to the door to use as a blockade. It wouldn't be enough to stop that thing from getting inside, but it was something.

"Get to the back," the man hissed at his companion.

"Come on, it's okay," the other man said gently, extending a hand to me. Behind his glasses, he had warm, brown eyes, and I could tell he was trying to gain my trust with the gesture. Though I could see lines worn with tension etched across his forehead, his features were still softer than his friend's. I let him take my hand as we quickly walked to the back of the building.

Jason and the angry one were moving some more furniture to block the door, and it still looked tense between them.

"I'm Alina," I whispered.

"Brian," he offered with a strained smile. "Don't worry—we got this."

We went through a door in the back of the building and found ourselves in a large kitchen. I finally registered where we were—a restaurant. I was about to wonder why it didn't smell as rank as some of the other places we passed, until I saw a handwritten sign on a walk-in freezer warning, *"Food Defrosted - Trash Hold Only."* Though the smell hovered around the door, thankfully, it didn't permeate the rest of the space.

Brian led me to the back of the kitchen and we cautiously peered out the small window at the top of the door, overlooking the alley. The door was still latched shut with a deadbolt, but we could easily unlock it and get through if necessary. "Looks quiet," he murmured. "Stay here, I'm going to check on them."

I sunk to the floor, clutching my knees as Brian returned to the kitchen door, stifling a cough. He cracked it open just enough to peer through, giving a low whistle to catch his friend's attention. Shortly after Brian's signal, Jason and the other man swept into the kitchen. After pushing the door closed and bolting the lock, the angry one tested its strength with a pull.

Brian stayed at the door, whispering with his partner while Jason briskly walked towards me.

Kneeling at my level, Jason asked, "Are you okay?" He pushed back a strand of hair that fell across my cheek.

I nodded. "I guess so? Are you okay?"

Jason nodded, glancing over his shoulder at our new companions. "What do you think of them?"

I sarcastically replied, "I think, 'Wow, so there *are* still people left out here!' It seems like they've been around for a while." My voice grew softer as I added, "Brian seems nice."

"Yeah..." Jason trailed off, studying them as they spoke.

I also looked over, noticing Brian's frustrated expression as the other man spoke in low, intense tones. My mouth suddenly felt dry and I cleared my throat. "Do you think they've been staying in the city? Maybe they have a safe place nearby?"

"Maybe," Jason answered.

Brian caught me staring and gave me a small wave before falling into a coughing fit. As his friend noticed the gesture, he turned, locking eyes with me. His sharp jaw twitched as he stared. Everything about him was as cold and solid as stone, including the way he stood. The muscles in his arms tensed as he clenched and unclenched his fists. His brows pinched together in a perpetual frown, darkening his brown eyes as he stared with such intensity it was hard to match his gaze. Black and gray tattoos covered his dark, bronze skin, though I couldn't make out the designs from this far away.

Brian waved a hand in front of the man's face after drinking some water from the pack he still wore on his back, murmuring something to break his attention. The man rolled his eyes with an exasperated sigh before muttering something and stalking off to the other side of the kitchen.

"Lee?" Jason gently pulled back my attention, and I realized I didn't hear a word he said.

"I can't figure that guy out." I frowned.

"Not much to figure out. Seems like a dick," Jason muttered.

Brian's voice caught me off guard as he asked, "Talking about Carter? I'm sure he's grumbling the same things about y'all right now." I jumped, not realizing Brian had approached us. Though he sounded calm, I could read the defensiveness in his expression. "Let's hold off judging the book until we've read a few more pages, alright?" Brian added, giving each of us a long look to gauge our responses.

So, the man had a name. Carter.

As Jason opened his mouth to retort, the muffled sound of radio static cut through the quiet room.

"Oh, shit," Brian muttered, pulling a walkie-talkie from his backpack and turning up the volume. He pressed a button, speaking low, "Ran into trouble—fucking hell-creature. It didn't see us, though. We found two other people and we're waiting it out in a restaurant. Over."

"Fuck, Bri. What can we do?" a deep, nervous voice replied.

"Are you and Carter safe?" asked a younger, softer, feminine voice. *"You're okay, right? Over."*

Brian coughed again, making sure his throat was clear before responding, "Yeah, Sammy, we're alright. I'm not sure there's anything to do right now except wait. Try not to worry. We'll figure out a way back soon." He hesitated before continuing. "It might be a good idea for both of your groups to head back to the safe house…decrease the risks for everyone else. Over."

"I hate this, Bri, but fine. Over," the younger voice answered.

"Come back to us as soon as you can," the first person said, ending with, *"Don't do anything stupid. Over."*

Brian lowered the volume and put the walkie-talkie back in its pocket as Carter stalked over.

"Was that the others?" he asked.

"Yeah," Brian answered, lowering to the ground to sit across from Jason and me. "Dan and Sam. I told them they should get back to the safe house."

Carter nodded, processing the information before quietly responding, "Good."

Brian turned to Jason and extended a hand. "I'm Brian, by the way. That's Carter. I already had the pleasure of introducing myself to Alina, what's your name?"

Jason looked at his hand tentatively before reciprocating the handshake, replying, "Jason."

Carter chose that moment to sit next to Brian, tossing a pile of knives into the center of our circle.

I stared at the utensils meant to be weapons. "So, that's where we're at?" I tried to joke. "And I thought we were getting along so well until now."

Carter stared at me blankly for a moment before addressing us as a group. "Take your pick. It won't do much against those things, but it's better than nothing."

Jason nodded and slid two knives my way, keeping a meat cleaver for himself. I noted how he didn't reveal that we already had our own knives. Brian took a longer chef's knife as Carter sat back, sharpening the last knife with a hand-held sharpener.

After a few moments, Jason tentatively asked, "So, have you been staying downtown?"

"Here?" Brian asked, raising his eyebrows. "No way. Only someone with a death wish would set up camp downtown. We are just trying to find supplies. Why? Where have y'all been staying?"

Jason and I exchanged glances, and I opened my mouth to explain, "Well—"

"Not too far," Jason interrupted, giving me a pointed look.

Well, alrighty, then, I thought.

"How many people are in your group?" Carter asked bluntly, taking Brian's knife from his hands and trading it for the newly sharpened one. He didn't look at us as he started sharpening the other knife.

"When we woke up, there were a few others, three," I said before Jason could step in. "But now it's just us."

"When you woke up? Like, this morning?" Brian asked, confusion crossing his face.

"No, when we all woke up four days ago," I clarified.

Carter halted his work and leveled a sharp look in my direction. "What do you mean, when you woke up 'four days ago'?"

"She means we were a group of five then. Now we're two," Jason said sternly, sitting up straighter and squaring his shoulders. "We were separated during the explosion."

"Why are you avoiding directly answering the questions?" Carter said, his voice dangerously low as his eyes narrowed in Jason's direction.

"I answered well enough," Jason replied just as firmly.

"Okay," Brian interjected. "I get the defensiveness, but y'all need to chill."

Carter grunted his acquiescence, but kept Jason targeted with a glare.

"We've all had a rough week, I'm sure." Brian's voice softened. "There were twenty-two people in our group before the explosions. Then, a creature, probably like the one y'all are running from, attacked our camp. Now we are down to a group of eight. We lost a lot, so I think some of us are just a bit more protective than usual at the moment." Brian not so subtly jerked his head towards Carter on the last statement.

I pursed my lips, gently resting my hand on Jason's thigh to draw his attention away from the glaring contest he was in with Carter. Jason's eyes softened as they met mine, and he put his arm around me protectively.

"So...what do we do now?" I asked tentatively.

"We hope that thing ran past this street and didn't notice where we went. Wait until nightfall to make sure it doesn't come back, then get back to the car and get out of here," Carter answered, his attention now turned back to sharpening the knife he took from Brian.

"You have a car?" I perked up with the realization. "So, you can bring us to the nearest emergency center? I think that's where—"

"Emergency center?" Brian frowned in confusion. "Why would y'all go to one of those? It's been months since any have been active, let alone intact."

"Where exactly were the two of you when the explosions hit?" Carter questioned, slowly standing up from his place on the floor. The knife glinted in his hand and Jason gripped me tighter.

"*Carter*," Brian warned.

"No," Carter growled. "No more games. They tell the truth or they leave."

Leave? I narrowed my eyes in his direction and jumped to my feet, almost stepping towards Carter before remembering he held a knife. I raised my hands to show I wasn't a threat. "We *can't* leave. We aren't going back out there until it's *safe*."

"And I'm not going to let two liars stay here and manipulate us," Carter bit back.

"Liars?!" I exclaimed, my voice raising. I stepped forward until I was just inches from Carter's chest, a move he was not expecting. He reflexively raised the knife and my anger-fueled confidence wavered. I glanced at the weapon in his hand, wishing it wasn't too late to take back my impulsive power-move.

Carter's eyes darted between my face and my open hands. With a rough exhale, he tossed the weapon to the floor and stepped back, folding his arms.

Jason jerked my arm, pulling me back as he stepped in front of me.

Brian moved in front of Carter, creating a barrier of his own. "Need I remind everyone—we have to chill the fuck out and keep quiet. We're all on edge, clearly, but I think we have the same goal right now, yeah?" Brian looked at us before glancing over his shoulder at Carter. "So why don't we just accept that we will be stuck in this room for a while and start being honest with one another." Brian fixed his gaze on me again with a calm, but firm expression. "Now, Alina, can we please start over? What happened four days ago?"

Jason opened his mouth to interject, but I was too wound up to let him dig us further into a hole. The words exploded from my mouth like a waterfall. "Alright. Fine. Four days ago, I woke up in what I *thought* was a coffin, but nope! *Surprise*! It was an egg-shaped pod thing. Oh, but it doesn't stop there! There were these creepy-ass tubes connected to my body that I had to *pull. Off. Myself*. After I realized I was in some makeshift medical facility, I ran into three other people who were also trying to find a way out. They helped me. And then we found Jason. We escaped together and then the explosion happened. We were separated from the others, so Jason and I stayed in a thrift store to wait things out until we realized it probably wouldn't get much safer around here. We left this morning and have been dodging those...those...*monsters* all fucking day. So *sorry* if we are a bit on edge. It's been a lot to process in a very short period of time." I choked down tears of anger and folded my arms, avoiding eye-contact with the others.

"Okay," Brian said slowly, "that is...a lot to digest."

"You're fucking telling me," I replied, throwing my hands in the air.

"I...have some questions," Brian added.

"Us first," Jason jumped in. "You heard our story. Now, what's yours?"

"Alright," Brian said, easing back down to the floor.

I followed his lead. Jason stared at Carter a moment before lowering to the ground beside me. Carter fell into a coughing attack and used the opportunity to face the back door. Even after the coughing passed, he remained standing with his arms folded, the muscle in his jaw twitching.

"Carter and I weren't together when this started," Brian explained. "When the ships appeared, I was on UT Campus. Once the power went out and the invaders started attacking, we did what we had to do to survive. For me, that meant a lot of running and hiding, trying to save people and failing miserably—just trying to make it to the next day. All of us have been with a bunch of different groups since then, but eventually, we found ours. That's the short version."

I nodded, absorbing Brian's recap of their situation before one part hit me hard. "So..." I bit my lip, reluctant to ask. "When you say, 'this whole time,' exactly how long are we talking?"

Brian stared at me, blinking as realization hit him. "It's been just over eight months, eight and a half, maybe?"

I let the information sink in...eight months. Based on the weather, I knew a significant amount of time must have passed. The confirmation of how much time we lost didn't do much to put me more at ease, though.

"So," Brian said, "Y'all really don't have any idea what's been happening?"

I shook my head. "I told you—we literally just woke up four days ago. The last thing I remember is seeing the ships in the sky and Jason coming to my apartment as the shelter-in-place order went out. Maybe a day or two after."

"Damn." Brian brought a hand to the back of his neck. "Well, welcome back to the world, I guess. Sorry, it's a bit of a shit-show. Y'all were taken together, then?"

"I guess so," I said, shrugging.

"Our memories are still kinda hazy. Bits and pieces have started coming back, but slowly. We still don't remember *how* we were taken or what was done to us…" Jason trailed off.

"So, are the ships gone now? For real? And what about the things chasing us? Those creatures can't be the same as the aliens that took us, can they? They are aliens, right? I just assumed, but—does that mean there's more than one type of alien here?" The questions poured out of my mouth one after the other, and I immediately regretted my lack of decorum. I could only imagine how I sounded at the moment.

Carter stared at me with a curious look before he spoke. "The ships did leave, but we don't know if they'll stay gone." Carter returned to our circle, taking his place next to Brian again. His voice was gruff and he still wore that same frustrated look on his face, but at least he talked to us more neutrally instead of growling every word. I gave him an encouraging smile, but his scowl only deepened.

"We haven't seen any signs of the invaders since. The fucking hell-creature is new, though. After the ships left, I tried to get to the city with some others. Our group wanted to see if we could find anything helpful and see whether the city was safe enough to come back to. The explosion happened before we could get downtown, so we turned around. By the time we got back to camp, hardly anyone was left. Fuckers tore them apart. Destroyed a lot of our supplies. We took a big hit."

"I'm so sorry," I murmured as my heart twinged. I couldn't even imagine what their experiences must have been like. Carter nodded in acknowledgment before looking away.

"I have another question, if you don't mind," Carter said, still not looking back at me.

"Okay," I replied.

"It sounds like you've seen more than one of the hell-beasts?" Carter asked.

"We've come across at least three since we left this morning," Jason responded.

"Three?" Brian gasped, eyes wide. "And you made it this far? I mean—no offense, but one of those things took out almost our entire camp. How did you...how?"

I shrugged. "We just kept hiding and running. I don't know; we were doing alright until that last one spotted us."

Brian and Carter didn't seem to know much more about the creatures than we did, aside from the fact that the monsters were destructive and killed indiscriminately. Brian filled us in a bit more about what their group's experiences were like until now. It sounded like they'd relied on the food they scrounged from abandoned stores, houses, or overgrown backyard gardens, hunting when they could. From how they talked about the rest of their crew, it sounded like the group was closely knit, too.

Carter explained how people divided into factions based on their circumstances, and as survival got harder, groups started adapting in different ways—some more questionable than others. Carter, in particular, sounded like he had bad experiences with some of the rougher groups. Though I wanted to know more, I didn't think it was the time to push for that information just yet. I thought that knowing more would help me to adjust to everything, but the more I learned, the less I knew what to do with the information.

Brian was telling us how he'd been forced to catch koi fish from a backyard pond once, when we heard static crackle from the radio. Someone named Cap confirmed that they arrived back at the 'safe house.' Carter and Brian took the walkie-talkie to the far side of the kitchen. It seemed they needed to discuss some things with Cap privately. I could still hear some of what they were saying, but not enough to fully understand what they were talking about.

Once they returned, we started discussing a plan to get back to Carter and Brian's car as safely as possible. I realized it was probably a good thing we ran into those two after all. They had more experience when it came to moving carefully, including a bunch of hand signals I prayed I would be able to remember. Hopefully, we'd be ready to face whatever was out there come nightfall.

I tried to push back the anxiety curling through my chest—one step at a time, right?

ELEVEN
CARTER

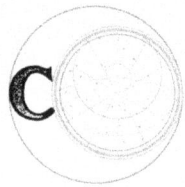

THE LATE EVENING sky melted from orange into dark reds that deepened as the night sky spread. It was almost time to go.

The two people we were stuck with confirmed what I'd feared—the hell-creature that attacked our camp wasn't the only one. Misdirection seemed to work when it came to escaping the last one, at least. As far as we could tell, there hadn't been any sign of that hell-beast or others since. Though, who knew what would happen once we left the confines of the restaurant? As long as our two newcomers could follow directions, we'd hopefully be able to get back to the car without incident.

I didn't want to take them with us—not to our safe house. Hell, I didn't even want them sharing the car, but the majority of our group already voted in favor of bringing the newbies back to camp before Cap checked in on the walkie-talkie. With Brian also in favor, my opinion was outnumbered, no matter how strongly I felt about it.

From talking to Alina and Jason over the past few hours, it was clear how clueless they were. Honestly, I was surprised they made it *this* far without getting killed. When they crashed into us, the creature they were running from was the *third* they'd encountered in one day. They'd been scrambling from building to building as they tried to escape the city when the last one saw them through a storefront reflection. Lucky for them, we were there to help throw the fucker off track; unlucky for us, we were now involved in their mess.

There were still pieces of their story that didn't sit right with me. I could accept the fact that they kept themselves alive the past four days, but why would the invaders leave them behind without another thought after eight months? How did they survive the explosion when they were so close to the building that went up in flames? After four days, why didn't the smoke seem to bother them, when Brian and I kept falling into coughing fits? It didn't add up—not enough for me to fully believe them.

Alina was huddled by the back door with Jason, who couldn't keep his hands off her. We'd only been in this room for a few hours, and he constantly had his arm around her shoulders or was touching her lower back. Whenever he pulled her close, I fought the urge to cringe.

Alina must have felt my stare. As she turned her head in my direction, we locked eyes, and a curious expression crossed her face. How different the last eight months had been for us. The two of them had no idea how lucky they were to have missed the worst of it.

Jason noticed her focus shifted. His brow furrowed, eyes narrowing in my direction momentarily before he murmured something in her ear. A small smile crossed her face as she looked back at him.

"What do you think, C?" Brian asked, approaching me with his bag hooked over one shoulder.

"Now's as good a time as any," I answered. "Sun's down; it should be easy to stick to the shadows."

Brian nodded. "I'll tell them to get their stuff."

"Wait—" I grabbed Brian's elbow before he could walk off and pulled him around one of the counters so we'd be just out of view. "We need to talk about what we'll do if they start acting in any questionable sort of way."

"Carter, come on." Brian sighed. "We've been stuck in this room with them for hours now. If they were going to do something sketchy, they've had every opportunity to stab us and run away with our shit. Also—need I remind you—*you* are the one who gave them knives."

"Their story doesn't add up," I retorted.

"I mean, doesn't it, though? If anyone were to escape the situation they said they were in, wouldn't the day the ships left be the most opportune time? We can't expect them to have all the answers when there's so much we don't know ourselves."

Exasperated, I tried once more, "But do we really want to bring two strangers back to our group? Risk what we have left?"

"You were a stranger once," Brian said softly. "So was I. We all were. We took a chance because that's who we are. How can humanity be restored if we aren't willing to do our part, as well?"

"Fuck," I relented, running a hand over my face. "How the hell am I supposed to argue against that?"

"You can't," Brian answered, clapping me on the shoulder. "That's the point. Let's get going."

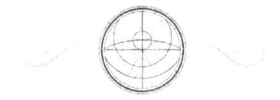

We gathered at the back door and went over the plan once more. We were only a block and a half from the car, so we didn't have too far to go. Our strategy was simple enough—stick to the shadows, don't make a sound. I'd take the lead, and Brian would watch our backs while the two newbies stayed in the middle. Once we finished reviewing everything, I opened the door to step outside.

I scanned the alleyway to make sure it was clear before gesturing to the others to follow. The moon was shining bright, which helped illuminate our path. I tried not to think about the hell-beasts as more smoke from the fire slipped into my lungs. The urge to cough was strong, but I'd be damned if a cough was the reason I finally got taken out.

We moved slowly, stopping after each storefront to listen and scan the area. It was harder to avoid the debris here, but with how slow we were moving, we hoped to prevent any accidental missteps. As we grew closer to the market, the familiar reek of rotting food wafted toward us and I heard Brian gag. I paused, snapping around to make sure he was okay. He threw me a thumbs-up with one hand while clasping a cloth over his nose and mouth with the other. Alina was behind me, using what looked like a tank top as a mask. Jason pressed a similar item of clothing to his face.

Alina took a tentative step forward, placing a hand delicately on my arm as she held out a bandana for me to take. I stared at it for a moment, feeling the warmth of her hand against my skin. With a slight shake of my head, I dismissed her offer. Her hand fell back to her side, but even after, I could still feel the imprint where she'd touched me. Any extra contact seemed to stick in this heat, but the brush of Alina's hand left a particularly uncomfortable pulling in the pit of my stomach. I rubbed my arm to rid myself of the lingering feeling.

We reached the corner of the intersection and the car was waiting for us right where we left it. This was the most critical stretch, as we wouldn't have the cover of the buildings once we hit the street. I knew the sedan was unlocked, so we just needed to make it to the other side of the intersection and we'd be home-free.

A soft clang echoed, stopping me in my tracks. I held up the signal to wait, listening intently for any other telling sounds. Alina inhaled sharply and I whipped around, immediately searching for Brian's eye contact. I pointed to my ear, yet Brian shook his head in confusion. My eyes darted back to the street ahead as my heart pounded. Could I have imagined it? Alina's breath hitched again as if she were holding back a gasp before a crash rang from down the block.

"*Go*," I hissed.

We raced across the street. A muffled growl followed the sound of something being overturned in an alleyway. I hoped it was far enough away to give us the head start we needed.

Yanking open the door to the car, I threw my backpack in the backseat and started the engine, waiting just long enough for the others to pile inside before stomping on the gas. Jason's door barely closed before the car lurched forward. Brian took a shaking breath beside me, which only made him cough more as he scrambled to buckle his seat belt. I heard a low whimper from Alina in the backseat and I looked in the rearview mirror to see she sank low in her seat, curling in on herself. Jason was twisted around, watching behind us. The street was dark and I couldn't make out any movement.

"The bridge," Brian exclaimed. "Just head for the bridge. We can lose it if we can get to the other side."

"Shouldn't we find somewhere closer and hide?" Jason asked in a low voice.

"No," I answered. "We were out all day and didn't see any of those things on the way downtown. Roads are clearer that way too."

With the headlights off, there was low visibility and the car kept hitting debris. We just couldn't risk any extra light that would help to pinpoint where we were. The front wheel hit a deep pothole, and I cursed under my breath as the car shook with a loud thunk.

Though I didn't see anything following us, the growls and shrieks that carried through the streets were warning enough to keep going as fast as we could. "Bri, do you remember seeing any cars on the hill we passed right before we hit the bridge?"

"Uhm—" Brian's voice shook as he monitored the sideview mirror. "I think so. Why?"

"We need them for a distraction," I answered.

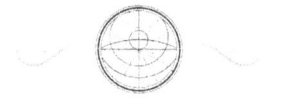

We sped over the bridge directly towards the hill as I quickly explained my half-assed plan. I had no idea if it would work, but we had to try. The sedan was pushed to its limit as it climbed the steep hill on the other side of the bridge. A few cars were abandoned along the side of the road, but we needed vehicles closer to the top.

I stopped at the crest of the hill, leaving just enough of an angle for us to make a quick getaway. Launching out the door, I gestured for Jason to follow me while Brian slipped into the driver's seat. At least if I didn't make it, Brian would still be able to get back with the car.

Jason and I sprinted to opposite sides of the road and took our places, making sure everything was ready to go. There was only one chance to get this right. One wrong move, a single delay, and it would be the end for us. My pulse raced in my ears as adrenaline buzzed in my veins. I knew the creature couldn't be too far behind. At least if I didn't make it, Brian would be able to get the supplies back to the group.

Growls rumbled up the hill and the sound chilled me to the bone. I caught Jason's eye and held up a hand. Timing would be everything. We needed to trust each other and be perfectly coordinated for this to work. He nodded and I set my sights at the base of the hill as the fucker skidded into view.

It crept low to the ground, tilting its head as it clicked and rumbled. It was searching for us, which meant we still had a chance to catch it off-guard before we were spotted. Slowly, it raised to its full height, opening its jaws with a bone-shattering cry. The creature fixed its gaze on the top of the hill, taking another step forward. Whether it saw us or not, it was time.

I swung my hand down to signal 'go' before diving across the driver's seat of the parked car to shift it into neutral. Hopefully, Jason caught the signal in time. Cranking the wheel, I angled it as best as I could before pushing it down the hill. Once it started rolling, I sprinted over to Jason's car.

He'd gotten it into position and I ripped open the passenger door to help him the last few steps, pushing with all the strength I could summon. I didn't wait to see whether the cars would hit their mark before I started running to our sedan.

Jason slid across the hood of the car to reach the other side, opening the passenger door to jump into the car. Alina pushed open the back door for me to barrel inside and then Brian stomped on the gas.

The car lurched forward, and I whipped around to look out of the back window. The first vehicle picked up speed as it rolled down the hill, but it was about to collide with another parked car at the bottom. The hell-beast arched its back and shrieked at the quickly approaching vehicle. *Come on, come on...don't miss the mark.*

The monster stalked the rolling projectile, closing in on it like the predator it was. Until this point, it likely hadn't seen a car move, and I hoped the bigger 'prey' would keep the beast's attention long enough for our escape. A gut-wrenching screech streamed from the creature's mouth as the first car bounced off another with a crash, propelling it back towards the beast. The last thing I saw was the creature launching itself into the air, landing on the car's roof as the second vehicle hit both straight-on.

The sound of crunching metal and high-pitched shrieks filled the air as our engine roared, taking us further away.

TWELVE
ALINA

I SHOOK with residual nerves as I stared out the back window. I expected to see the creature streaking behind us, realizing its mistake. The shrieks and growls grew quieter as we put distance between us, until the only sound I heard was the pounding of my pulse in my head. The city grew smaller with each passing second and I finally took a quivering breath. *It worked. Thank goodness, it worked.*

Jason's muffled voice brought me back to reality and I realized he'd been trying to grab my attention. I blinked, turning to see him leaning over the center console. The rushing in my ears faded to a dull ringing as his voice became clearer. "Lee? Talk to me."

"Give her a minute, for fuck's sake," Carter growled.

I shook my head and rubbed my temples, finally feeling the goosebumps on my arms starting to fade.

"You know what, fuck you, man!" Jason yelled, slamming his fist on the center console.

"Stop!" I burst out. "Both of you, just stop!"

The car went silent and Carter sat back, folding his arms and glaring out his window. Jason eyed him for a moment longer before turning back to me. "You say the word, and we will figure out somewhere else to go," he murmured low enough so only I could hear him.

"It's fine," I replied, a bit too harsh. I softened my tone before continuing, "I'm...processing."

Brian cleared his throat. "Well, ah, job well done. We're all still alive. Carter, would you mind checking in with the others to let them know we haven't been eaten?" He glanced towards Jason. "If you wouldn't mind, Jason, my pack is at your feet with the walkie."

Jason nodded, rummaging through the side pockets until he found the device. Carter held out his hand expectantly as Jason shoved the walkie-talkie at him.

Carter pressed a button on the side. "Base—come in. Over."

"Carter?" a woman's voice frantically responded. *"Are you alright? Where are you? Is Brian okay?"*

"Hey, hey," a muffled voice spoke in the background. *"Let him get a word in."*

"Oh! Right," the woman replied. *"Over."*

To my surprise, the corners of Carter's mouth perked up in a slight smile as he responded, "We're all okay, Michelle. Brian's driving. Over."

"And the others you found? Are they still with you? Are they okay? Over." Michelle questioned.

"Yeah—"

"Say hi, guys!" Brian interrupted, shouting from the driver's seat.

Jason muttered a weak hello and I leaned over to get closer to the speaker. "Hi, Michelle, was it? I'm Alina. Over."

Michelle's warm voice hummed over the radio, *"Hi Nina, I am very excited to meet you and your friend. Over."*

I breathed a laugh and opened my mouth to correct her, but Carter took over before I could say another word. "Going to save battery now. See you in fifteen to twenty minutes, tops. Over."

"Please stay safe. Over."

Carter looked down at the walkie-talkie in his hand, his scowl less severe. He tapped the device on his leg as he looked out the window, his shoulders finally losing some pent-up tension.

I rested my head against the seat, watching the world pass by. As I closed my eyes, stray hairs gently tickled my face and I realized —"Wait, do I feel air conditioning?"

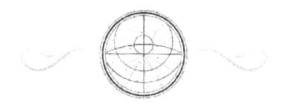

We pulled up to a small house set further back from the road at the end of a long driveway. My leg bounced and my stomach twisted as we grew closer—with nerves or excitement, I wasn't quite sure. It was probably a bit of both.

I couldn't remember how many people were a part of their group. Was it eight? I inwardly cursed myself for not asking for everyone else's names as the car shifted into park at the end of the drive. I didn't know how to act or what would be expected of us. Were there rules I should know about? A set of dystopian social expectations?

Brian turned off the ignition and slapped his hands on the steering wheel. "Alright, we're here!"

"I'm nervous," I blurted out, cringing as the words tumbled from my mouth. Oh well, they wanted honesty, right?

Brian grinned. "Ah, don't worry. Carter's the only intimidating one, and you already aced your first mission together. Before you know it, you'll be best of friends with everyone."

"'Aced' is a bit generous," Carter mumbled.

"Anything we should know before going inside?" Jason asked.

Brian shrugged, opening his door. "As long as you don't take Dan's snacks, you'll be fine."

A smile quirked on my lips as we climbed out of the car. I appreciated Brian's efforts to make us feel comfortable. After everything they'd been through, I knew it couldn't be easy to welcome two new strangers into their circle. It was honestly a relief to know we'd be able to learn from people who had been dealing with everything from the start.

We climbed out of the car, grabbing our backpacks before helping Carter and Brian with the heavier bags and suitcases from the trunk. I shifted nervously as we reached the door, stepping to the side. "Do you have like, a secret knock? Or code word so they know it's us?" I asked.

The walkie-talkie clicked, static rumbling for a second before Carter said, "Open the door. We're here. Over."

Ah, yes. That would be the most logical thing to do, wouldn't it? I shifted behind the others as we listened to the clicking of locks and heavy shuffling on the other side of the door. No sooner did the door open before a tall, younger-looking man with dark brown skin and short, dark hair dove over the threshold towards Brian.

Brian dropped his bags, a broad smile stretching across his face as he embraced his friend. With a squeal, a shorter girl with black skin and gorgeous, curly hair joined their embrace, followed by a tall, white guy with floppy brown hair who carried an emergency lantern. Shadows danced behind the foursome as they hugged, shapes bouncing in the light as they laughed and celebrated Brian and Carter's return. I glanced at Carter, whose shoulders had finally relaxed fully, and his expression softened as he watched the group. I swear I almost saw a smile starting at the corner of his mouth as the girl squeezed out of the circle and threw her arms around Carter for a quick hug.

After Carter awkwardly patted her shoulder in return, the girl turned to us with a welcoming smile. "Hi, I'm Sam."

"I'm Alina," I replied, trying to match her friendliness. "And this is Jason."

"Awesome! Great to meet you! Come on inside." Sam turned, beckoning us to follow. Sam and the floppy-haired guy picked up the extra bags we brought over from the trunk as the other young man threw his arm around Brian's shoulders, leading us inside with a slight limp.

As floppy hair stepped over the threshold, he turned to call over his shoulder, "Welcome back, Carter. I'd hug you, but I value my life." He shot a cheesy grin Carter's way before disappearing beyond the threshold.

A half-smile crossed Carter's face as he chuckled, quietly following the group inside, pulling two suitcases behind him.

I followed Carter into the foyer of the two-story house, immediately greeted by a wide staircase. The house wasn't small by any means, nor was it overly large. A slight musty smell wafted off of the worn-in furniture, but overall there was a cozy hominess to the place. I let out a deep breath I didn't realize I'd been holding.

A gentle hand touched my shoulder and Sam said, "You can put your backpack by the staircase. We always keep things close to the door in case, well, you know..." She trailed off as the first guy from outside walked over with a lantern. Sam grabbed his arm, pulling him closer. "This is Dan," she said, giving him a look.

Dan gave an awkward wave as he pulled out of Sam's grasp, setting the lantern on the staircase. His eyes quickly darted to Brian and the other guy before settling on us again. "Hey," he said. I waited for him to say more, but it seemed like that was the end of his greeting.

Jason stepped forward, extending his hand. "Hi, I'm Jason and that's Alina."

Dan gave us a tight smile, shaking Jason's hand before making his way back to Brian and the other one.

Sam sighed. "Clearly, not everyone remembered to bring their apocalypse manners tonight." She rolled her eyes and continued, "That's Russell over there."

"Yoooo, what's good?" Russell called over, shaking longer pieces of hair out of his face as he grinned an award-winning smile. Russell walked over, extending his fist to Jason to bump. He turned to me next, holding up his hand for a high-five.

I wasn't quite sure what to make of him and laughed nervously as I tapped his hand in the weakest high-five I'd ever given in my life. He winked, flashing me an amused smile before moving next to Sam and throwing an arm over her shoulders.

"Come on in, get comfortable," Russell said, leading us further into the house.

Jason and I were ushered into what I assumed was a living room, and I saw Carter eyeing us with a wary look similar to the one Dan occasionally shot our way as he talked quietly with Brian. Sam looked over my shoulder, waving to someone on the stairs. "Red, come meet the new people."

I turned around to see who she was talking to. The hair on the back of my neck stood on end as I saw the auburn-haired woman step from silhouette into full view.

"Alina?! Holy fuck, Jason? What—how—" she stuttered as she rushed closer, tears pooling in her wide, light blue eyes.

I couldn't move. I had to be dreaming—

"Emma?!" Jason gasped, closing the distance and pulling his sister into a hug. "I didn't know—Fuck, it's really you? You're okay?" He gripped Emma tightly as she broke down sobbing.

Emma—it was Emma. This wasn't a dream and she was here—*we* were here. Her hair was longer and her skin was blooming with freckles. A bit of pink kissed her shoulders, nose, chest, and cheeks from sun exposure, and I couldn't help but choke on a laugh as my own tears poured down my cheeks.

I finally recovered enough to remember how to move, wrapping my arms around Emma and Jason, joining their embrace. Emma's arm slipped out to pull me deeper into the hug as her body shook with heaving sobs.

"How are you here? *How* are you *here*?" she repeated, voice barely above a whisper through her tears.

All of my words remained caught in my chest.

We were together and that meant everything had to be okay.

THIRTEEN
CARTER

The newbies and Red clutched each other tight, sobbing and laughing simultaneously. Cap and Michelle finally arrived downstairs and stood across the way, staring at the trio with equal looks of confusion. Finally, the three pulled their limbs free just enough to get a good look at each other.

"I can't believe you're here," Red sobbed. She brought Alina and Jason's hands to her lips as if she had to acknowledge their presence with all her senses. "How—"

Cap finally cleared their throat, stepping toward the group. "I hate to interrupt…"

Red pulled away and turned her watery gaze to Cap. "Cap, this is my brother, Jason. And this, this is Alina. She's been my best friend my entire life." Red turned to Jason and Alina again, her voice breaking as she exclaimed, "And you're here. You're alive. How are you alive? Where have you been? Why did it take so long to—" Red's questions were interrupted by another bout of sobbing that shook her thin frame.

The rest of us seemed to be frozen where we were, exchanging equal looks of confusion, shock, and awe at the bizarre reunion happening in front of us.

"Talk about twisting the plot." Brian took his glasses off and rubbed at his eyes, wiping away tears of his own.

Sam approached them, gently leading Red and the other two over to the lumpy, worn couch shoved in the corner. Red sunk to the cushion, pulling Jason and Alina to settle on either side of her, clutching a hand from each of them in her fists. I stole a look at Alina's face as she blinked, her mouth opening and closing as if she couldn't find words anymore.

Jason hadn't taken his eyes off of his sister—his *sister*. As they sat next to each other, I noticed their resemblance and wondered how I didn't clock it sooner. Red's hair was a deep auburn, while Jason's was dark blond, but they had the same light blue eyes. I could see it so clearly now from the shape of their faces, slope of their noses, and sharp jawlines.

Michelle and Cap stepped closer to the trio, Cap lowering to their knees so they were on equal ground. "Emma?" they asked.

Red laughed through her tears as she confirmed, "Yeah, that's me. Emma. Surprise?"

"So, your name isn't Red? This is all next fucking level," Russell responded. "I feel like I've been living a lie—or...well, I guess you've been living a lie, Red...Do we still call you Red?"

Red—no, *Emma*—rolled her eyes. "I figured 'Red' would be easier for people to remember. You know how it was in the early days—bigger groups and new faces to learn so frequently. It was better than people shouting, 'nurse' when they needed me, anyway. So, 'Red,' 'Emma'—either is fine."

"Well, I guess getting back to official introductions—I'm Cap." Cap extended a hand, shaking Alina's hand first before replicating the gesture with Jason.

"*They're* our leader," Russell called from across the room, his posture stiffening. "Cap, that is." It was hard to miss the way he'd worked in Cap's pronouns. We never knew who we would encounter, and there were more than a few times some jackass tried to start some bigoted shit. It was one of the reasons I'd become even more wary of interacting with strangers. However, we usually took a more subtle approach to gauge someone's safety. Cap didn't need us to stand up for them and was perfectly capable of defending themself. Clearly, we were *all* still feeling particularly protective, though.

"We all work together," Cap interjected. "Everyone has a voice. We make our decisions as a group. I might give us direction, but we all play our parts."

"Don't be so modest, Cap," Emma teased, turning to Alina. "They are literally the reason we are all still alive. Ask anyone."

"Hello!" Michelle interrupted with an awkward little wave. "I'm Michelle."

Alina perked up as she recognized Michelle's name. "We met on the radio! I think you misheard my name and thought I was Nina, though—which, I mean, I'm used to. It's not the most common name, I guess—but, it's Alina. I'm Alina. Hi," she rambled nervously.

"Got it! Alina, not Nina." Michelle gave Alina one of her classic warm smiles and nodded. Alina relaxed, gifting Michelle a small smile in return.

"Well, I'm pretty sure everyone knows by now, but I feel like it's still rude not to introduce myself officially. I'm Jason," Jason said, waving to the room and wearing a friendly expression the whole damn time.

Emma laughed, her tears finally trickling to a stop. "We just spent the last half an hour prepping a room for you both, but I don't think I can let either of you out of my sight. I have so many questions that need answers like—*eight months ago*. I'll have to drag my stuff in there with you two. By the way, Carter, that means you're in the study now."

I snapped to attention at Emma's declaration. "No. No way."

A look of confusion spread across Emma's face. "Um. I didn't know you were so attached to your room?"

"No—I mean no way you are going to lock yourself in a room alone with them."

A cold fire ignited in Emma's icy blue eyes. "You did *not* just try to forbid me from being in the same room as my brother and best friend. Are you *fucking* serious?"

Michelle visibly cringed and the room went silent. My frown darkened as my heart rate increased and I clenched my jaw. *Yeah, I'm the asshole, again.* Before anyone else could interject, I continued, "We don't know what *exactly* has happened to them over the last eight months. They said they escaped some makeshift medical facility downtown near where the explosions started. For all we know, they could have ticking time bombs inside their bodies, too."

"Woah—wait, back up, medical facility?" Emma questioned, squinting at me.

Russell's eyes went wide. "Or they could be, like, body snatchers?"

Dan smacked his arm. "For real, Russ?" he hissed, glaring at his friend.

Jason rose, his tone beyond livid as he said, "There is no way you are keeping my sister from me."

Cap subtly moved between us. "Let's slow down, alright? I see there is a *lot* the rest of us need to catch up on. Why don't we have something to eat, sit down, and get to know each other a bit before jumping to any conclusions." Cap matched Jason's gaze until he finally backed down. Jason brought his hand up to rub his neck as he nodded in agreement.

My gaze shifted just behind him, where Alina was staring back at me with a look that could rival Emma's in ferocity. I understood the anger. I probably would have reacted exactly the same if someone tried to suggest someone I cared for couldn't be trusted. The truth of the matter was—we didn't know enough. Red, or rather, Emma, vouched for them, sure. That didn't change the fact that they were still strangers to the rest of us. Newcomers always went through a trial period with strict rules before they received full access to our group—I didn't see why these two should be any different.

Sam broke the silence, stating, "I agree with Cap. Food's a good plan. We will get some snacks ready or...something." Sam gestured toward the kitchen as she grabbed Russell's hand, shooting me a look I couldn't decipher as she left the room. Brian and Dan quickly followed them.

Cap watched the Twenty-Somethings leave the room, waiting a moment before turning their attention to me. "Carter, I understand why you're feeling protective and I agree that we need to be cautious."

Emma bristled at their statement. As she opened her mouth to retort, Michelle cautiously grasped her shoulder, shaking her head slightly.

Cap continued, "But, we have someone here who has spent her whole life with these folks—someone we trust. I think we ought to give her judgment the benefit of the doubt."

How could I be the only one saying anything? Frustrated, I fought back. "But we don't know—"

"That's right," Alina said, bursting up from the couch and storming my way. She stood less than a foot away as she continued, "You *don't* know. You don't know the first thing about us, and frankly, you've been a complete *asshole* since we ran into each other."

"You mean since *you* ran into *me*," I shot back. Tension squeezed my chest like a band about to snap.

"What the fuck ever!" Alina yelled. "You know what, I don't care what *you* think," she said, jabbing a finger towards me. "I won't even *have* to prove I have good intentions because that's just *who. I. Am.* And I can't wait to make you eat your words." The golden flecks in her hazel eyes were practically burning with fire by the end of her short speech as she held my stare, daring me to fight back.

"You should probably take a walk, now," Emma snarled in my direction, joining her friend.

I kept my eyes on Alina as I responded, refusing to be the one to break eye contact first. "Believe it or not, I'm only trying to prioritize my group's safety—which *includes* your best friend, by the way. You're forgetting one important part in your argument, though—there's a lot *you* don't know as well. You *don't know* the kind of people left out there. You *don't know* what we have been dealing with, Alina. You *don't know,* because you weren't *around* for any of the shit we went through. I've seen even the most pious people drop their morals and 'good intentions' when pressed into a corner. So yeah, I might be an asshole. But I'd rather be an asshole than take a risk trusting the wrong people again."

Alina's expression faltered just for a second, allowing a flash of something softer to break through the fiery look she was trying to maintain. I didn't want to be the one to back down first, but the extended eye contact was too overwhelming to continue any longer. I turned away from her, scrubbing a hand down my face in exasperation. "What the hell happened to common fucking sense? Assessing a situation before inviting in more unknowns?" I said to no one in particular as the feeling in my chest tightened. Directing my attention back to Emma, I tried to even out my tone as I said, "I'm not saying throw them out on their asses. I'm saying we should be *careful* until we know the invaders haven't messed with them in a way that could hurt *us*. We lost too many people. Too fucking many. I'm not doing it again."

The edges of my vision were buzzing with static by the time I finished talking. I couldn't do this anymore.

A soft hand grazed my arm and I jerked at the touch. My attention snapped back as I realized it was Alina who stepped closer, the tips of her fingers still touching my arm. "I get it, Carter, I do," she said in a soft voice. Her eyes met mine again, all flame gone this time. "You care about your people. I care about mine, too. Considering the fact that one of my people is also one of yours, I think we can agree that we are trying to work towards the same goal, here. Jason and I will do what we have to and prove to you that we're safe—even if we have to sleep outside."

"Well, I wouldn't go that far," I mumbled, and we fell silent.

Michelle cleared her throat. "So, are we done arguing, now?"

Alina realized her fingers were still just touching my arm and she pulled back sheepishly, pursing her lips into a tight smile. I crossed my arms, stepping back to allow the rest of them to walk ahead.

Emma wrapped an arm around Alina's shoulders, gesturing to Jason with her other hand to follow.

I stared at their backs as they walked towards the kitchen. The mental pressure of the day started sinking in and I suddenly felt exhausted.

As I turned to leave the room, Cap grabbed my attention. "Carter. A moment?"

I paused, allowing Cap and Michelle to approach. "That can't happen again," they said. "You are allowed to be concerned. You're even allowed to be angry. But next time, Carter, just fucking step away. I get why you've been on the edge. We are all still grieving. But these explosive fights need to stop. That goes for everyone."

I took a deep breath, letting Cap's words sink in, nodding and rubbing the back of my head with a hand. "Yeah. Yeah, you're right."

Michelle took my elbow, clutching my arm in a half-hug. "Next time, just say you need to go chop some firewood. I'll go outside with you and we can take turns throwing an axe at a tree."

I barked a laugh, completely caught off guard. "You want to take up axe-throwing, Michelle?"

"Why not? It seems like a good way to release stress," she answered

Cap wrapped their arm around Michelle's shoulders and kissed her head. "You are an absolute treasure, my love."

Michelle beamed back at them. "I know."

I shook my head with a soft chuckle and the three of us walked towards the kitchen.

FOURTEEN
ALINA

I PINCHED the skin on my wrist until I felt a bead of blood burst onto my fingers.

This was real.

We escaped the city and the monsters. We found a safe place. We found Emma.

I stared at my childhood friend as she and the other members of her group laughed and joked with a familiarity Emma reserved for her closest friends. Every few seconds, she'd look back at Jason and me, shooting us a smile in an attempt to include us as she poked through the snacks and drinks Carter and Brian brought back. I couldn't process a single word that was said as we awkwardly stood behind her.

Just earlier today, we weren't sure we would survive. We didn't know whether we were the last people left alive in the city or whether those creatures had taken over. And then...Emma. The day's events crashed in my head like stormy waves at the sides of a sinking ship.

Jason tapped my shoulder and I nearly jumped out of my skin. "Need a break?"

I nodded as my hands started to shake, suddenly feeling lightheaded.

Jason got Emma's attention, whispering something about getting some air. Her jaw stiffened for a moment, and I could tell she was getting ready to push back. Before she could, Jason looped his arm around my waist and pulled me along, directing me out of the room. We walked swiftly past Cap, Michelle, and Carter, the latter curiously turning his head as we aimed for the front door.

As soon as we were outside, I fell to my knees. The tension built up and was ready to explode. All of the oxygen I gasped felt like it was sucked away just before hitting my lungs. Jason knelt down, pulling me against his chest.

Emma burst outside and her breath hitched. "What the fuck?! Lee, are you okay? What's wrong? Are you hurt?"

"She's having a panic attack—they started happening after we escaped," Jason murmured, his attention still fully focused on me as he gently pulled me closer against him. "Can you get her some water?"

"Wait—Jason, I need more than that. What do you mean 'escaped'? What happened to you guys? I'm a fucking nurse, tell me what happened so I can help," Emma exclaimed.

"Em, I love you and I promise we will tell you everything, but I need your help with Lee right now," Jason pleaded. "Please—water?"

Emma hesitated and I squeezed my eyes shut, not knowing how to navigate the situation. "Fine," Emma said. Before she left, she knelt down next to me, squeezing my shoulder. "I'll be right back, babe. I'll take care of you." She kissed my forehead before I heard her footsteps quickly retreat back inside.

All of the emotions I'd been pushing down seemed to have burst to the surface at once and I couldn't figure out which to deal with first —the terror, relief, anger, grief, and shock all hit me simultaneously. Everything felt too surreal.

I pulled oxygen into my lungs in shallow gasps, trying to match the rhythm of Jason's chest rising and falling. His fingertips tickled as they traced patterns on my arm, whispering a trail across my skin. As a warm breeze wrapped around us, I felt the rough stubble of his chin lightly scratching against my temple as he leaned his cheek to the top of my head.

"I'm here, Lee," Jason murmured. "I've got you." Throughout everything, he continued to be my anchor.

The door banged open again and Emma hissed at someone inside, telling them to give us space. Emma's footsteps slowly approached as if she were scared I'd run off like a deer. A faint throbbing pulsed across my forehead as I registered each step.

I knew I should open my eyes. I should talk to her—I just couldn't force myself to pry my fingers from Jason's shirt and face her.

"Alina, babe, come on, you're scaring me," Emma said.

"It's okay, I got her," Jason murmured.

A faint rustling next to us indicated Emma was sitting by our side, confirmed by the gentle touch of her hand on my knee. I breathed in through my nose, holding the air in for a second before slowly blowing out through pursed lips.

"That's it," Jason said. "Just breathe slowly. I'm here."

"Jason, what happened to you guys?" Emma asked, tension filling her voice.

"Later, Em," he answered.

I opened my eyes and caught Emma eyeing her brother as if trying to figure out the answer to a question that hadn't been asked.

I reached a shaking hand to rest on top of Emma's. "I'm...I'm okay. I'm so sorry," I said, unable to keep the tremble from my voice.

Emma's gaze snapped to mine and she cupped my face in her hands. "You have nothing to apologize for. Tell me what you're feeling right now."

"I, um, I—" I tried to find the words, still feeling dizzy. "Heart... beating fast...breathing..." My eyes filled up with tears before I could say anything else.

"Does anything hurt you right now?" she asked, her tone clinical.

"N...no. I mean...my head," I responded.

Emma opened the water bottle and held it to my lips. With a shaking hand, I took the bottle from her and Jason helped me sit upright so I could take a sip. Emma's eyes never left me as I drank; she studied me, her expression unreadable.

"How about now?" she asked.

"Em, come on," Jason said, frustration creeping into his tone.

"I'm a fucking nurse, Jason, or did you forget in the last eight fucking months? I'm helping my friend. Let me do my job," Emma snapped.

She returned her focus to me, grabbing my hands, rubbing the tops with her thumbs. "We're going to breathe together now, okay? Watch me and follow along." One of Emma's fingers crept to my wrist and I knew she was trying to monitor my pulse. I needed to calm down.

I nodded, taking a shaky breath in before it abruptly burst into an exhale.

"Again," she said, and I continued through the motions. I followed her instruction for a few more minutes until my breathing evened out enough for her to be satisfied. She finally stood up, extending a hand to me.

I took Emma's hand and stood on shaky legs.

"You're looking better already," Emma said with a smile that didn't quite meet her eyes. "Why don't we go up to our room with some food? We can talk, get that blood sugar back up? I'll tell the others to lay off for the night and that we can do a more in depth intro tomorrow."

Weakly, I returned her smile. "Yeah...yeah, that sounds good."

"I'll take her up," Jason said, "just tell me which door. You get the other stuff. I feel like Lee and I should make ourselves scarce anyway with everything that asshole was yelling."

Emma studied Jason for a moment, eyes narrowed slightly before she nodded, turning to walk back inside. "First on the left up the stairs. Take a lantern," she called without looking back.

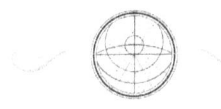

Jason grabbed our backpacks and a lantern from where they sat in the foyer, and I let him lead me up the stairs into the room we were to share with Emma. Once we dropped our packs, I pulled out a new pair of shorts and a big t-shirt, eager to get out of my sweaty, grimy clothes. Jason followed suit and we turned our backs to each other to get changed, as had become the norm.

Once we were more comfortable, I took in the space. A queen-sized bed took up most of the room, with blank, white walls on all sides. There was a dresser, a night stand, and a closet, but that was about all of the personality in the room. I was tempted to pull open the closet to see what was inside when Emma shouldered her way past the partially closed door.

"Oh! Let me help," I sputtered, grabbing the backpack from her arm as she juggled another bag and an armful of candles in the other.

"Thanks," Emma answered with a tight smile. Her tone wasn't unfamiliar; I'd heard it many times over the years when she was less than satisfied. My stomach flipped.

"So," Emma said, her tone still flat as she entered the room. "You two, start talking. Where have you been? Have you really been together this whole time? What the fuck was Carter talking about with medical shit?"

I dropped the backpack at the foot of the bed and watched as Emma carefully placed and lit the candles around the room. Exhausted, I sat on the bed, scootching up to lean against the headboard. Jason sat at the edge of the bed on the other side, eyeing his sister as she moved around the room.

"Em, the room is fine. Come sit so we can talk," Jason said cautiously.

Emma's lips pressed into a flat line as she walked past Jason to sit next to me at the headboard. "Okay—talk," she said, staring at her brother.

"We woke up four days ago in one of the office buildings downtown. It was filled with medical equipment and we were being kept in these...we've been describing them as 'pods.'" Jason paused, swallowing hard. "I guess we were unconscious the whole time because we have no memory of anything that happened before we woke up. There are a lot of pieces still missing," Jason summarized.

"Well, fuck," Emma said, choking up. "I don't even know what to say." We sat in silence for a few minutes until Emma spoke again. "So obviously you two were taken together, then? The last time I spoke with you, you both were at Alina's apartment."

"I guess so," I said quietly. "Neither of us remember how we were captured, though. I do remember talking to you. It's one of the only clear memories I've had." My voice broke.

Jason and I took turns recounting the events of the last four days—waking up, the medical facility, meeting the others, the explosion, the thrift store, and the creatures. As Jason was explaining how we'd crept from one crumbled building to the next to evade the creatures hunting us, Emma interrupted—

"Wait, back up—there were *multiple* of those creepy fucks hunting you? And you *escaped*?" Her face paled as she shivered. "It only took one to destroy our entire camp."

"I guess we were just lucky—well, until the last one," I replied. "That's when I literally ran into Carter, and Jason nearly collided with Brian."

"Yeah, what's with that guy?" Jason asked, not even bothering to hide the disdain in his voice.

Emma laughed, sarcastic as she said, "Oh, your first meeting with our resident grump didn't go so well? Shocker; I'd have never guessed."

"Fucking prick is what he is," Jason said bitterly, his jaw clenching.

"He did get us out though—Carter and Brian did, I mean," I quickly interjected. "I don't know how we'd have escaped without them."

Jason nodded, losing some of his venom as he added, "Yeah, his plan with the hill was pretty damn smart."

"Hill?" Emma questioned, raising an eyebrow.

Emma listened with rapt attention as we finished retelling the rest of the day's story. As we talked, the tension seemed to ease off of her just a bit; her shoulders relaxed, and her tone softened.

Still, I couldn't help noticing how Emma always made sure to create a physical boundary between Jason and me. Every so often, I'd catch her staring. With the way her eyes darted between us, studying us, I couldn't help feeling like I was under a microscope.

I knew something about my interactions with Jason were bothering her, but a selfish piece of me just needed to be near him. It was because of Jason that I'd gotten this far to begin with. I'd sought comfort from Jason's closeness without hesitation. Given how protective Jason had become with me, I imagined Emma translated our trauma bond into validation that she'd been replaced. As happy as I knew she was to see us, I could imagine it must have stung to realize we still had each other when she'd been alone. Jason and I hadn't just gotten closer due to circumstance, we'd been physically clinging to each other for support, and I could only imagine how that looked to Emma.

I needed to figure out a way to show her how much we still cared for her…that we'd never willingly abandon her. I just didn't have the energy to start thinking about how to accomplish that at the moment.

Jason was in the middle of talking to Emma about their parents when a knock startled me out of my thoughts. I grabbed a thick candle on my way to the door, thankful for the interruption and a chance to break from my thoughts.

Opening the door a crack, I was greeted by an armful of blankets that towered over Michelle's head. "I brought these up for you!" she said, her voice muffled in the fabric.

I couldn't help the soft laugh that escaped my lips as I put down the candle and took the pile from Michelle's arms. Her cheeks were pink from hauling everything upstairs at once as she pushed her blonde hair from her face.

Emma joined my side, taking half of the stack. "Thanks, Chelle, I don't know if we'll need so many blankets in the dead of summer, though."

"They will be perfect for giving whoever sleeps on the floor some extra cushioning, though," I said, not wanting to seem ungrateful. "This was really thoughtful. Thank you."

"Oh, we take care of our own here. Right, Re—I mean, Emma?" Michelle laughed. "It will take me a while to get used to your real name."

Emma gave Michelle a soft smile. "Red, Emma—it's all the same to me now. Like I said earlier, call me whichever you'd like."

Michelle nodded, her gaze shifting from one of us to the other before clapping her hands together. "Well! I'll be heading back down now. Take your time in the morning—I think everyone needs some decompression time before we have to talk shop. I'll see you all tomorrow."

"Thank you for everything, Michelle," Jason called. "Tell the others goodnight for us, too."

I shut the door, turning back to the bed where I saw Emma reclaimed her spot at the headboard. I padded over to the other side, crawling up next to her with a sigh. Jason still sat on the edge of the bed and a silence fell upon the room.

I looked at Emma from the corner of my eye, noticing how she picked at her cuticles, "Hey, Em?" I asked.

"Mmhmm?" she replied, not bothering to look up.

"I know this is a lot for you." I paused. "For Jason and me, it almost feels like it's just a continuation of that first week, still. For you, though? You've had to go through all this alone for so long."

"Yeah, well, not completely alone," she said softly. "I looked for you, you know—asked every group I met. When we were forced out of the hospital, I specifically went south so I could attempt to track you guys down. But then, so much time went by—I assumed the worst."

Jason moved closer to his sister's side, pulling her into a hug. "It's a goddamn miracle we found each other again," he mumbled into her hair.

"You know how I was stuck at the hospital?" She hesitated for just a moment as we nodded in confirmation. She took a deep breath and continued, "I couldn't leave, not with so many patients who couldn't be moved. Then more people started pouring in, trying to seek shelter or medical attention. So many people needed help.

"In our last text, you told me you two were going to come to the hospital since I couldn't leave. No matter how hard I pushed you both to just stay where you were, you didn't want to listen. The number of times you told me, *'Best friends face hell together,'* Alina." Emma

125

breathed a laugh at the memory before turning somber again. "We didn't see hell yet."

Emma paused for a moment before continuing, "The ER was overwhelmed, and everyone was freaking out trying to figure out how to manage all of the patients and visitors. When word got out about the emergency centers, we made the remaining hospital security guards escort groups of kids and adults to what we thought was safety. We basically sent anyone who could move without collapsing. We hoped they wouldn't be seen in the dark, and at least we could get some people to a safer area, what with the ship directly above us and all. The other problem was we couldn't maintain so many people. We had no choice but to lock our doors, turning people away unless they were seriously injured." Emma took a shaky breath. "Many of our doctors and nursing staff committed to staying, but we still didn't have enough hands to help everyone who needed it. We had been running on maybe an hour of sleep each day, if we could even find a moment to rest. And then when the power cut?"

I grabbed Emma's hand, squeezing. "I have no doubt you did everything you could. Staying? Tackling all of that? You were so brave." I was trying so hard to keep from crying again, not wanting to take away from what Emma was feeling.

"I was chicken-shit." Emma rolled her eyes, scoffing. "I feel like I spent half my time breaking down in a supply closet so I wouldn't freak patients out."

"What happened after you left the hospital?" Jason asked.

Emma took a deep breath. "After the power cut and those...*things* came down from their ships to attack...We took as many supplies as we could carry and tried to lead people south. There were patients in wheelchairs, gurneys, but it wasn't enough. We had to leave *so many* patients behind after fighting for so long to help them because they just couldn't move. So many patients were in and out of our care for months—years. Every single one told us to go, to save whoever actually stood a chance—that they understood. I still get sick over it.

"We still managed to get a lot of people out, but we were sitting ducks. We had to split up before long. Run. Hide. That's the way it was for a long time." Emma shuddered, wrapping her arms around herself.

I bit my lip, unable to keep more tears from escaping as I took a shaky breath. "Well, it doesn't make up for the fact that we weren't together before, but we are here now," I told her.

"And nothing will separate us again," Jason finished.

FIFTEEN
CARTER

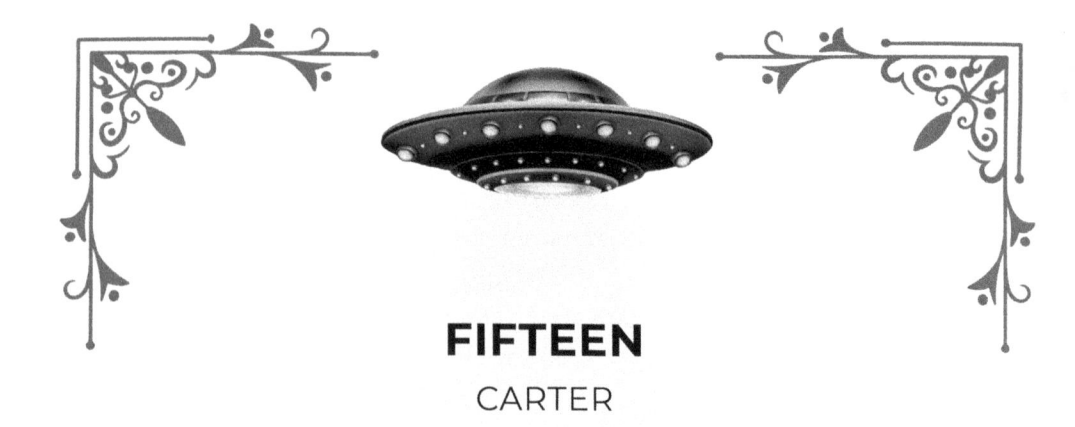

IT WAS LATE.

After Cap and Michelle turned in, I spent the rest of the night drinking vodka with the Twenty-Somethings and actually had a decent time. If I learned one thing after all we faced—sometimes the only choice was to embrace the small reprieves between chaos. The kids were good at finding unique ways to bring some normalcy back into their lives, and it felt good to tear down the walls and join them for a while.

Maybe this was what Sam was talking about; letting people in—or getting closer to it. I surveyed the room, watching Russell play with Sam's curls as she lay her head on his lap. His fingers crept to caress her cheek, and she grinned up at him as she twined her fingers through his. I would never understand how two people so different could end up together, but they looked happy—when they weren't fighting over stupid shit, at least.

Brian and Dan were sprawled on the floor, flipping through the books we brought back for Sam, reading passages out loud and cackling at the more...explicit scenes when they managed to find them. Sam actually screamed when she saw the books, clutching them to her chest as if we'd given her the Heart of the Ocean. Every once in a while, when the conversation would waver, she'd bring up another plot point, her excitement still as high as when Brian revealed the gift—even as Dan teased her for the 'faerie porn.'

I'd kept a steady buzz going, but after a few hours, I decided it was about time to turn in. Though we humored the idea of getting drunk, going as far as to make mixed drinks with warm sodas, no one actually made it past tipsy. I wasn't too eager to face a hangover in tomorrow's summer heat, especially when I knew we'd have work to do. Then there was the point no one wanted to say out loud—the threats were still out there and we needed to keep our wits about us.

Before I could sink too deeply into my thoughts, I waved to the room. "Alright. I'm out. See you in the morning." Their chorus of goodnights followed as I retreated upstairs.

At the top of the steps, I turned left before remembering I was supposed to sleep downstairs in the study. Instead of correcting my misdirection, I stood outside my old room facing the door. I hesitated, squeezing my fists as I listened to Emma, Alina, and Jason's muffled voices inside. Whether habit or curiosity led me there, I couldn't walk away. I knocked on the door before rational thought could stop me.

There was some rustling and the soft sound of footsteps on carpet before the door opened. Alina stood before me, her face illuminated in soft candlelight. Her wavy hair was piled up on top of her head and I could see the tired expression on her face, even in the dim light of the small fluttering flame. She sniffed and I noticed her eyes were red and watery as she asked, "Can I help you?"

Her voice wavered like she'd been crying and I was about to ask why—barely able to hold the question back in my loosened state.

Instead, I said, "I was a dick."

Alina blinked and I heard a frustrated huff behind her. Even though the faint light cast them in shadows, it wasn't dark enough to hide Jason and Emma's identical looks of disdain. Their pale, blue eyes practically shot daggers at me.

I directed the next part to them. "I overstepped. As much as I stand by my logic, I could have delivered it in a less confrontational way." I paused. "I was a dick."

Turning back to Alina, I matched her gaze. Remnants of the tears she shed glimmered in her eyes—a sad, serene kind of tranquility that flickered in the candlelight. My mouth went dry and I swallowed before softly saying, "I'm sorry."

"Coming to our door to apologize? Who are you and what did you do with the stubborn asshole we have come to know and reluctantly love?" Emma replied as she swept to Alina's side, quirking an eyebrow.

I snorted. "Brian gave me vodka."

"Ah," Emma answered, "that'll do it."

Jason was still glaring, choosing not to respond from his spot across the room. *Whatever. I did my part*, I thought.

I leaned against the door frame while my head buzzed from the alcohol, realizing after the fact that I'd also leaned into Alina's space. She didn't move, though.

Wordlessly, I let my gaze meet hers once more. Even in the candlelight, I could see the rosy flush dusting across the apples of her cheeks before melting back into the smooth skin of her tawny complexion.

She nervously smoothed a piece of hair back against the mess on top of her head. "Thank you, for apologizing." She shifted on her feet. "We have some of those little bottles of alcohol, too, but haven't opened any yet. Do you want to come in for a 'truce' shot?" She stepped back as Emma opened the door further and gestured inside.

Though I'd only spent a handful of days in this room, it was still strange to see how quickly they'd taken over. Clothes and shoes were strewn next to the bed and empty snack bags decorated the top of the nightstand.

I stepped closer, my arm almost grazing Alina's, before my sober brain checked back in. I gave the trio a crooked smile, raising my hand to rub the back of my neck. "I think I've had my share tonight. Better get some rest now." I'd already let the conversation run for too long.

"Your loss," Emma replied, her usual sass back in full force. "See you in the morning?"

"Yeah." I let my arm fall, feeling my fingers twitch as they lightly made contact against Alina's hand on their way down. I backed up a step. "Night."

"Goodnight," Alina answered.

I turned and walked back downstairs towards my new room.

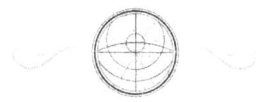

I was surprised when I woke up feeling rested. After being plagued by insomnia and nightmares all week, it was nice to have a night of solid dreamless sleep. The chaise was too small for me to sleep on comfortably, so I crashed on top of some blankets on the floor instead. With how tired I was, I probably could have slept anywhere, though.

The house was still quiet, so I peered through a crack in the blinds to get an idea of what time it could be. Golden streaks painted the sky as the sun slowly climbed higher. *Still early, then.*

I looked back at the blankets on the floor and briefly considered trying to get some more rest. There were only so many days where I could take advantage of a slower start. The more I thought about it, the more I realized settling back down would be next to impossible; my body itched to move. It was as good a time as any to start the day.

I thumped down the stairs and out the front door to take a piss just off the property before finding a quiet spot in the front yard to wake up the rest of my body. It was the perfect time of day when the air still felt light and the morning sun's warmth was welcoming. Beads of dew still adorned the grass, not yet dried.

I took my time running through stretches, adding some extra push-ups, crunches, and burpees. With my increased heart rate, I already felt the endorphins flooding my system. I could almost fully give in to the distraction from real life with a morning like this.

Feeling a boost of energy from the exercise, I jogged back inside to find Michelle. She had been scheduled to take watch after the Twenty-Somethings turned in for the night and was probably eager to be relieved of her duty. We all took shifts, alternating so no one would go for too long without getting enough rest. I probably should have stopped to say hi to her before I ran outside, but she would understand.

The living room was empty and thankfully clean from the night before; probably Dan's doing. The sun's rays poured in through the blinds and I could still practically smell the grass, even from inside. I took a deep breath, soaking it all in before making my way to the kitchen area.

I was surprised to find an empty room there as well.

Frowning, I called out, "Michelle? Hello?"

There was no way she'd just abandon her shift, so where could she have gone?

A quiet humming traveled through a crack in the back door, so I followed the sound outside.

I lifted my hand to shield my eyes as I scanned the backyard. A figure sat perched on the arm of a low, plastic lawn chair, backlit by the sunrise. As I moved closer, she turned around, freezing for a second before slowly standing and walking towards me.

To my surprise, it wasn't Michelle I found, but Alina. She was still wearing the baggy t-shirt and shorts from last night, but with the addition of her Doc Martens covering her feet. The laces from her boots looped lazily, untied with the ends tucked under the tongue.

I frowned. "Where's Michelle?"

Alina frowned back. "Good morning to you, too."

"Yeah, morning. Where is she? She was on watch last night."

"I woke up early. Couldn't sleep." Alina shrugged. "I came downstairs just before the sun started to rise and Michelle looked dead on her feet. I told her I'd take over so she could get some rest."

I nodded, processing what she said. Michelle just…left her. Pressure built as unease coiled in my chest. Alina was helping. She wanted to do her part. Still, letting someone new take over our safety so quickly felt…

I shifted, recognizing the way my chest tightened. Breathing in slowly through my nose, I turned away from Alina. As I exhaled through my mouth, I rolled my shoulders to shake off the growing tension.

There was a gentle brush against my arm and I jerked at the touch.

"I'm just trying to help," Alina said in a quiet voice.

I forced myself to relax, shaking out my arms. "Yeah....yeah. Thanks," I mumbled.

I tried to ignore the shift I felt when Alina was around, but in the quiet morning without any other distractions, it was harder to ignore the way she affected me. Something about her made me feel so out of my element. At first, I thought it was because she and Jason were new to us. Though, over the last twenty-four hours, I realized that if I wasn't arguing with the other man, he didn't even cross my mind. It was just her.

I avoided her eye contact as I cleared my throat. "So, why couldn't you sleep?"

She hesitated a moment before answering, "Well, I guess I got used to only sleeping for a few hours at a time when it was just Jayce and I." She breathed a laugh, shaking her head. "I think I am still on guard from the time we spent in the city..." She trailed off.

"Four days, yeah?" I glanced at Alina from the corner of my eye, noticing she was resting against the lawn chair once more, kicking her foot against a rock lodged in the ground.

She nodded, still staring at her feet. We stood silently for a moment longer until a morning dove cooed somewhere close-by, chirping a song. A small smile curved across her lips as she noticed and she looked towards the direction of the sound.

"Do you remember anything new?" I asked, crossing my arms.

"From before? I mean—" Alina paused. "There are pieces...like, a collage of moments crossing over each other instead of just one linear series of memories. I think that's also why I can't sleep. It's hard to separate what an actual memory is versus what my brain's made up to fill in the blanks. And then, of course, there are the nightmares."

"Nightmares?" I asked, my curiosity genuinely peaked.

"Well..." She bit her lip, shifting uncomfortably.

"You don't have to." I shook my head. "Sorry, that was overstepping."

"No," Alina said quickly. "No, it's okay." She took a deep breath before continuing, her chest slowly rising as the air hit her lungs. Clasping her hands in front of her, she continued, "Before I woke up in the pod, I was having this dream. It wasn't even anything crazy. I was at this lake I used to go to with Emma, and we were talking about our last *real* lake trip. In real life, Emma and I hadn't been there in over five years, not since Jason's—" She paused. "Not since Jason moved back with his parents for a bit...The memory inside of the dream was real, but the rest of it was made up in my head."

"That does sound confusing."

"So..." Alina said and I looked up to catch her gaze.

"So?" I replied.

"How does everyone—" She shifted again, fidgeting with the hem of her shorts. "How does everyone shower? Jason and I used some large water jugs for a sponge bath-type situation when we were in the thrift store, but..."

I stifled a laugh, caught off guard from the sudden change in subject. "Yeah, we have something similar going on here. We make use of water collection bins, but we have to prioritize drinking water first. We always try to be closer to some kind of water source so we can still clean, but it isn't always accessible. We have a smaller group now, though, so—" I cut myself off before finishing the statement. I braced myself, feeling the tension digging into my muscles again, taking root.

"Yeah," Alina jumped in. "Yeah, I was a bit worried about that."

"Baths?"

"No!" She flushed as she stammered. "I mean, yes, but mostly what the water situation was in general."

The corner of my mouth twitched up in amusement as I answered her questions about how we'd been collecting or traveling to water for drinking and cleaning purposes. It took a while in the beginning to figure out how to accomplish the task, especially when a body of water wasn't close by. Most of the time, we had to filter, boil, and fill what bottles we could carry and wait for rain to do the rest. It was a learning curve that took longer to perfect than I'd care to admit.

Alina asked a few more questions about rations, chores, scouting, and travel. As I told her about our methods with Cap compared to other groups I'd been a part of, I realized just how far we'd come in figuring out how to survive without electricity, government, or technology. I couldn't help but feel a pinch of envy, knowing she wouldn't have to deal with that struggle—not to the extent we did, anyway. She had us to teach her. Talk about lucking out.

I looked back at the house, thinking about what would come next. The unsettling feeling that crept into my chest every time Alina was near had dulled and I almost felt at ease next to her now. I breathed out, taking care to unclench my jaw as I rolled my neck. Maybe it *was* just fear of the unknown manifesting through anxiety. It made sense the more I thought about it—all of the heightened energy I'd felt crashed down on me after the collision that introduced us. No wonder my brain associated her with panic. This was something I could work with. A quiet laugh escaped as I shook my head.

Turning back to Alina, I noticed her eyes were already on me. My stomach flipped, but I shook it off this time.

"What's so funny?" she asked.

"Everything," I replied with a crooked grin before walking back towards the house.

SIXTEEN
ALINA

FEELING DAZED, I watched Carter's retreating form as he walked back into the house. It felt like I was talking to an entirely different person compared to our interactions from the day before. It was...nice. I hadn't been prepared for the comfortable conversation we'd fallen into, but I was really glad it happened. Smiling to myself, I followed Carter.

Sam greeted us with a yawn as we stepped inside. "How is it morning again?"

Carter answered with a chuckle, "Great to see you too, kid."

"Is it nice out?" she asked.

"Incredible." I sighed, leaning across the counter. "It isn't too hot yet and there's a super nice breeze. I wish this weather could last all day."

"Makes me wish I had a cup of coffee to take out there." Carter added, the corner of his lip almost curving into a half-smile.

An amused smirk pulled at the corners of Sam's lips. "Why, that *does* sound lovely."

Sam moved to a stack of cans on the counter and began sorting them into piles. I sat back as she worked, content to watch the mundane activity. She started humming a familiar tune I couldn't place, and I pulled out a chair to relax at the small table in the kitchen.

A thought popped into my head and I couldn't help asking, "I have another question about what happened in the early days after the power went out."

Sam tilted her head as Carter responded, "Shoot."

"You said the electricity and cell towers were cut, and I can see how that could happen…but I don't understand why batteries would stop working, too," I thought out loud.

"And your question is?" Carter raised an eyebrow as he leaned against the back door.

"Well, how?" I asked.

"How?" Sam repeated.

"Yeah—*how*?" I emphasized. "I can understand how they can use some kind of signal to interfere with electricity and radio waves, or whatever—but that's not how batteries work. Batteries use a chemical reaction to convert energy."

"Okay…" Carter replied.

"Well, how could an *electrical* disruption stop a battery's *chemical* reaction?" I asked.

Carter and Sam stared at me for a moment before Sam spoke, "Huh. Yeah…how does that work?"

We both looked at Carter expectantly.

"I mean, I don't know. Do I look like I invented the alien technology?" he responded.

"No, but it's a really good question, right?" Sam responded, folding her arms. "How did it happen? And then! Also! Why didn't it affect *all* batteries?"

"It's alien," Carter replied in exasperation. "Does it have to make sense? Hell, before all of this, the entire human race regularly debated whether aliens existed in the first place. Is it so outlandish after finding out that they *do* exist, that they could also have a technology that could accomplish what it did? Technology we wouldn't understand?"

"I just don't get it," I replied.

"What is there to get?" Carter's voice rose as he grew frustrated with our questioning. "It's alien technology. If we understood it, we wouldn't be in this spot because we could have stopped it!"

"I'm just saying—" I started as Russell walked in.

"What's going on?" Russell asked, rubbing his eyes.

"Why did batteries stop working when the aliens cut our power?" Sam pointed the question his way as Carter groaned, wiping a palm down his face.

"I don't know," Russell yawned, draping an arm across Sam's shoulders as he kissed the side of her head. "It's aliens. Do you need more of an answer than that?"

"That's what I said!" Carter yelled.

The debate lasted longer than I expected. Every time someone new woke up and joined us in the kitchen, they were presented with the question. By the time the last person, Brian, arrived, our sides ached with laughter and we were too incoherent to ask him which side he stood on. Team: Don't Question It...It's Aliens vs. Team: But Why!? would have to wait for a tie-breaker, it seemed.

"How about this," Cap finally said, a sly smile crossing their face. "As soon as we track down some scientists, we demand *they* find the answer."

They used the temporary truce to ease us into a planning conversation. Though everyone relaxed, casually sitting at the kitchen table or against the counter, all eyes were glued to Cap in rapt attention, while Michelle wrote to-dos and assignments on a yellow legal pad. The stark difference between how Jason and I had been winging it the last few days and the order that Emma's group commanded was astonishing—another reminder of how unprepared Jason and I had truly been for this world.

I tried to focus on the planning conversation, but as the heat of the morning settled in, I couldn't keep my mind from drifting. Everything happened so fast over the last handful of days and the emotional whiplash of everything still had me spinning.

Jason had become quieter since we arrived at the house. I looked at him out of the corner of my eye, studying him. He was standing with his arms crossed, back straight, and the tight, white t-shirt he wore clung to his skin, emphasizing his strong chest and shoulders.

Even though it had been less than twenty-four hours, the sudden absence of our constant conversation and contact pulled like an invisible string. With Emma centered in our orbit once again, I found myself cringing with pangs of aching guilt for not finding her sooner. I knew it was illogical. Still. Some dynamics just don't change, I guess.

Jason's jaw twitched, as he realized he'd been clenching his teeth, and he rolled his neck to loosen the tension he so visibly carried. Jason caught me staring as he shifted and an amused smile crept across his lips. I looked down quickly, embarrassed that he caught me staring, before awkwardly glancing back over with a sheepish smile. His grin grew as a glint in his blue eyes sparkled.

A bony elbow jutted into my ribs and I inhaled sharply.

"Pay attention," Emma hissed, nodding towards Cap and throwing her brother a reprimanding glare.

I scowled, reaching across my stomach to rub my side. *Okay. Fine.* She had a point.

The rest of the meeting wrapped up quickly and the tasks for the day seemed simple enough. Cap and Carter were on map duty, whatever that meant. Jason and Emma were to take inventory of our supplies and reorganize all of the bags, while Sam and Michelle checked weapons. I was assigned to join Russell, Brian, and Dan on water collection.

I was about to head out the front door to help the guys pack the truck when Jason grabbed my elbow. "Hey, got a sec?"

I glanced at the guys as they hefted galvanized tubs into the truck's bed. They seemed to have things under control for the time being. I nodded back at Jason.

"It feels like we haven't had time to talk about anything—which, I know, sounds nuts considering we were trapped together the past few days—" He winced. "Not trapped. Man, this is not coming out right." Jason sighed.

A confused smile tipped the corners of my lips. "Yeah, want to try that again?" I teased.

"I guess—" he started.

"Jayce, come on!" Emma's voice interrupted as she called from within the house.

"I...guess I'll finish that thought later." He pressed his lips together. "Stay safe out there, okay? Let's find each other later and catch up." He touched my elbow again as if he were about to pull me closer, but instead, he stifled the movement, lowering his hand as he took a step back.

"Yeah, totally," I replied. "Have fun with inventory."

I made my way to the parked truck as Dan finished securing our supplies in the truck's bed. Brian explained that they found the four galvanized tubs in neighboring yards over the last few days, and that we'd be taking them with us to try and find a decent water source. Backyard gardens were popular around here, and with the droughts Texas kept running into, water collection bins also became more common. Apparently, before the group got cars, they had to take shifts traveling to water sources for their needs. Maintaining a water supply was a near-daily activity, with drinkable water taking priority. Any bottled drinks they'd save for times when water was more scarce. Looking back, I really took the water jugs in the thrift store's office for granted.

"It was rough in the beginning," Dan explained as he drove. "Before my first group figured out how to filter and sterilize the water correctly, a lot of people got sick."

"With the invaders rounding people up, we ran with whatever was on our backs. It was hard to maintain basic hydration, nutrition, and sleep," Brian added. "It was one of the reasons a lot of people didn't make it in the earlier days."

I nodded, sitting with that information for a moment. "So," I asked slowly, "Dan, you said 'your' first group—you all didn't start off together?"

"Nah," Dan answered, looking at me in the rearview mirror. "I think Brian and I found the same group about three months in, but it was another month before we wound up with our current crew."

"Yeah, I joined about the same time," Russell added. "I was with a few people when we came across them. Everyone seemed chill so we stuck around. Best choice I made."

I sat with that information for a moment. With the way the three of them interacted, you'd think they knew each other for years, not months. Though, with the amount of time everyone spent together, I could see how it might not take long to form a strong bond. From observing the group and how they interacted this morning, it was clear they all looked out for and cared about each other, almost like a family would.

"Think we can convince the others to stay at the safe house for a while?" Dan asked, changing the subject. I saw him glance at Brian, a look of worry clearly stamped on his face as he gripped the steering wheel.

"Doubt it," Russell answered from next to me in the back seat. "Always gotta keep moving, fam, you know that."

"Why, though?" I asked. "I would think if you had a good thing going, you'd want to stay, right?"

"Well, yeah," Brian picked up the answer. "Of course we *want* to. Something always happens, though. In the early days, the invaders would target larger groups so we really couldn't stay in one spot for long. Other times, a rogue group of human assholes would steal our supplies or threaten us, and we'd have to leave. There's always something. We're hoping we can find a more rural spot where we can stay for a while, next. Hopefully once we are further from major cities it will be easier."

"How did you end up at the house we're all at now?" I asked.

There was a moment of silence before Brian cleared his throat. "Well, we were a few miles away, closer to downtown. We hadn't been at the last camp long and really weren't planning on staying, either. We were just passing through. Other groups we encountered mentioned moving to the more rural areas; supposedly it was safer. Our group's plan was to keep heading south until we got somewhere quieter, I guess." He paused, glancing at Dan next to him. "The day the ships disappeared, we were attacked, as you know. The eight of us managed to escape, and then we ran until we couldn't anymore. We were actually staying in a different place at first, but it was too close to the other spot to really feel comfortable. Then we found the one we're in now."

"Wow," I breathed. "And Carter said the day the ships left was the first time you saw those...things?"

"Yeah," Dan answered, clenching his jaw. "We never saw any before then. Because of course, the invaders would hit us with a trash consolation prize when they got sick of us and left."

Brian reached across the console to grasp Dan's shoulder supportively, squeezing once before letting go.

"There," Russell called. "Up ahead—pond."

We pulled up to the sidewalk in front of the man-made pond with a fountain in the center. I imagined it would have been a pretty cute fixture in the community with the fountain turned on. Trees lined an overgrown bike path that weaved around the fountain, and I could see a hiking trail leading into the greenspace just past some wooden picnic tables.

"Alright, so this is the boring part." Brian turned around in his seat to face me. "Basically, we are going to set up a small fire, collect water from the pond, pour the water over a cloth and into the camping pots to filter out any sediment or solid stuff, then wait for the water to boil. Once it's done boiling, we will pour it into the bins in the back of the truck. Then...we repeat until the bins are full enough to take back."

"Well, at least that seems simple enough," I said, trying to be optimistic.

"Simple, yes. It's also mad boring," Russell grumbled. "Deadass, I'd rather be stuck with Red."

I shot a look his way when he mentioned Emma. "What's wrong with Em?"

Russell cringed. "We just...don't vibe. I'm pretty sure we are one argument away from her cutting off my balls to keep in a jar when she isn't using them for voodoo torture revenge shit."

I stifled a laugh as I responded, "To be fair, it doesn't take much to get on Emma's ball-chopping list. She's a good friend once you get past the prickly surface and get to know her, though."

"Yeah, like I've been telling you," Dan interjected, glaring at Russell. "It's because you instigate. Red's chill once you stop coming for her."

"Of course you'd say that." Russell smirked at Dan. "You've been her perfect little patient the last few days."

"Uncalled for, man," Brian said, giving Russell a warning look.

"Oh, come on. I didn't mean it like—" Russell paused, seeming to collect himself before looking back at Dan with a more serious expression on his face. "Shit, my bad. That was a dick thing to say; I'm sorry. Sam's been telling me I need to think before I speak. Impulse control and all that."

Brian threw a cheeky smile Russell's way. "See? I told you, if you actually *listen* to Sam, you'll put yourself in a much better spot—not just in your situation."

"I swear, I don't know what you did to convince Sam to be your girl, but you better not fuck that shit up," Dan added, a slight smile pulling at the corner of his mouth.

Russell grinned back at Dan in the front seat and it seemed like they came to an understanding.

"Alright," Brian said. "Let's get this started so we're not out here all day."

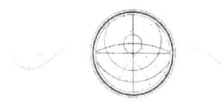

By the time we collapsed into the car after collecting enough water, I was slick with sweat and ready for a good nap. I pulled my own water bottle open, sipping slowly as we sat silently in the air conditioning, panting.

"Hey," I said suddenly, sitting up straight. "Are we planning on using these water bins for everything? Like, drinking, bathing, cleaning, laundry...all that?"

"Yeah, that's usually how it goes," Dan answered.

"So, what if we keep these bins at the house for drinking water and dishes, but everyone bathes and does laundry here? It'll make the water in the bins last longer," I said.

A thoughtful expression crossed Dan's face. "Yeah, that should work."

"Let's go back and talk to the others." Brian shrugged.

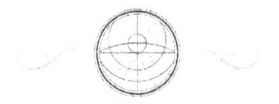

Russell and Dan sang some pop punk song the whole ride home, and though I found the trio to be funny and their banter was endearing, I didn't mind having some quieter space once we separated at the house. Brian told us he'd check in with Cap, while Russell and Dan wandered off to find Sam. I made my way to the kitchen, where Jason and Emma were still working on their task.

"Hey, friends," I said as I entered the room.

The siblings sat in the middle of the floor with pens and scraps of paper, and Jason eagerly hopped up to greet me, dropping his pen to the floor as he stepped through the piles of supplies to wrap an arm around my shoulder in a brief half hug. Emma rolled her eyes at the discarded notes before standing up to acknowledge me with a tight smile.

The light that sifted through the blinds softly played across the cans, toiletries, cleaning supplies, and other various items on the floor. It was late-afternoon, nearing the hottest point of the day.

"It looks like you two have been busy here," I said, nodding towards the carefully sorted supplies.

"Yeah." Emma sighed and stretched. "Honestly, it went fast. It's easy just to turn off, sort, and count."

"Turn off?" Jason raised an eyebrow in her direction. "Is that what you call snapping at me every time I put something in a pile you disapproved of while huffing and puffing for the last few hours?"

I stifled a laugh as Emma stuck out her tongue and scowled at Jason before turning back to me. "We have a very specific system. It isn't that hard to follow. How was water collection?"

"Good—great, actually. We have four full bins now, minus what spilled because of bumps and rough roads on the ride back. I actually had a resource-saving idea on the way home, too."

"Oh yeah?" Emma asked, twisting open her water bottle. "Do tell."

"Well, I figured since we have the cars, we can drive out there to bathe and do laundry. This way we can keep more water at the house for cleaning dishes and stuff. It'll last longer." I looked hopefully at Emma.

She nodded. "Yeah, that's a good idea. Look at the newbie bringing up obvious ideas we should have thought of in the first place!"

I laughed nervously. "Thanks, I think?"

Jason rolled his eyes and grabbed his sister's attention. "So, do we just put this stuff back in bags? What do we do now?"

"Now that it's sorted, we will separate out eight—well, ten, now—sets of travel rations. Basically, two days' worth of food per person. I'll do that part. The rest will be sorted in a similar way, balanced by weight so it'll be easy to carry."

Emma got to work, separating the items into the appropriate piles. Jason and I were pretty useless for that part, so we mostly watched and tried to absorb the process. Once everything was sorted, we helped pack the items into all of the appropriate bags.

"That was kinda fun!" I exclaimed.

Jason laughed. "Of course, you'd think organization is fun."

"What? It's satisfying to see everything all sorted and neatly put away," I replied.

"You and Cap are going to be best friends," Emma snorted.

"Who is my new best friend?" Cap asked as they leaned against the entryway.

"Alina," Emma said as I waved to Cap. "You Type A weirdos are going to get along swimmingly."

Cap chuckled, a smirk peeking at the corner of their lips. "At least I won't be the only one yelling at your disorganized asses, now."

Emma's mouth dropped open in mock offence. "You say to the person who beautifully organized our entire inventory?" Emma's lips pursed into a pout.

"Um. You had some help, remember?" Jason muttered.

"Alright—" Cap laughed. "Let's get into the living room so we can all talk about what's next."

SEVENTEEN
CARTER

"So, basically, I thought it would make more sense for us to take the cars back to the pond tonight before the sun starts setting. We can even bring one of the bins with us if we can empty the water into some of the other smaller containers we have. Then, we can bathe at the pond and bring back another full bin of water after." Alina dropped her hands to her sides after she finished her pitch and rocked back on her heels. "So, now what? Do we vote?"

Cap stood up and lightly touched her arm, gesturing to the spot on the couch where they'd been sitting. "Now, we talk about it. Have a seat."

Alina took Cap's seat on the couch next to Michelle who squeezed Alina's knee in a show of support. "Thank you for sharing your idea, Alina. Anything that helps save time and resources is a good idea to explore in my book," Michelle said, exchanging a smile with a relieved looking Alina.

"Who wants to share thoughts on Alina's idea?" Cap asked us, surveying the room. "Jason, how about you start us off?"

Jason sat up straighter, caught off guard. "Oh, yeah, sure." He shifted in his seat. "I think it makes sense. It would be a time-saver and water-saver in the grand scheme of things. I think we should do it."

"And safety?" Cap asked, crossing their arms as they leaned against a wall. "Does it make sense for safety?"

Jason hesitated before asking, "What do you mean?"

"Is it safe if we take a car to a pond out in the open?" they asked, looking at the rest of the group. "What are some potential risks? Do those risks outweigh the benefits?"

Jason sat back in his seat and I had to hold back a smirk.

"It's been quiet around here. We haven't seen any hell-creatures or even other people," Sam said thoughtfully. "Of course, that doesn't mean they're not around."

"We do everything in shifts anyway, and there's more than enough people to stand on watch. If we split into two groups it'll be quick." Russell shrugged. "I think it makes sense to go there for bathing, then if it works well we can try laundry tomorrow.

Cap nodded. "All good points. Alina, what are you thinking now?"

Alina shifted in her seat. "I'm thinking that I probably should have thought this through more." She breathed a nervous laugh, rubbing her hands against her thighs.

"Hey," Cap said, their voice growing softer as they directed their words towards Alina. "Every idea starts somewhere and grows as you explore it from all sides." Cap smiled, waiting for Alina to make eye contact with them again. "We're here to help flesh out the details as a team. You brought us the vision, and now we are planning together. It was a good start; don't question yourself."

Alina smiled more genuinely this time, though she still bit her lip nervously as she nodded. "I guess that's the perfectionist in me—wanting to get an A the first time I present to the group."

"Oh stop, Lee," Emma called from across the room in an exasperated tone. "There are no teacher's-pets here."

I thought I saw Alina bristle at that statement—a slight tensing of her shoulders. Jason shot an annoyed look in his sister's direction.

Interesting.

Alina licked her lips and took a breath before speaking again. "I was joking, Em."

Emma laughed suddenly and rolled her eyes. "So was I. Geeze."

"*Moving on.*" Cap raised their voice, giving Emma a warning look as they shifted back into planning mode. "No matter what we do, there will be a risk. As I said, it's about determining what the risk threshold is and whether the reward makes the risk worth the effort."

Brian leaned against the back of the couch, crossing a foot over one knee. "We have a bunch of dishes and laundry to clean. If we all travel together, we also have safety in numbers. Russel's idea of going in shifts also ensures that we always have someone on watch and that no one is ever alone. It isn't far, either, so I'm for it."

Even before our planning session started, I knew that we all would decide to go. I mean, it wasn't like the idea was a brilliant stroke of genius—Cap and I already started talking about using the cars for the same thing if the water crew was able to find a good enough spot. When Brian gave us the cliff notes for Alina's idea and we made plans to talk it out, I asked Cap why they didn't mention how we'd already started discussing the same thing.

Cap responded with, *"It'll be good for her to share her idea and build confidence—help the newcomers feel part of the group. We can use the opportunity to show how we talk through plans and see how they take criticism, too."*

Basically, a nice way of saying the newbies were getting their first test.

Cap specifically asked that I didn't contribute to the conversation, though we didn't tell the others that's what was happening.

When everyone allowed Alina and Jason to stay, I worried that we would blindly accept them without question. Honestly, it was a relief that Cap was still vetting them, even if it was a bit more subtle. I shouldn't have doubted their methods; I knew better than to question Cap's judgment.

It wasn't a terrible introduction so far. Alina and Jason seemed quick to volunteer for tasks, and Brian said that Alina especially kept her group on track today. Maybe everyone's instincts to grow our group *were* right. Even just having two extra people today, we got everything taken care of sooner than expected. Maybe I *was* being too paranoid. I wasn't exactly ready to cast my doubt aside, but I did try and push it down a bit more to give them a fair shot.

After our meeting ended, I made my way to the study to gather a change of clothes and my every-day backpack. Though it was only going to be a quick trip to the pond and back, we still needed to prepare as if we'd have to run at a moment's notice. It only took learning the hard way once to know it was necessary to bring your essentials with you wherever you go, no matter how short the excursion.

As I was about to leave the room, I heard voices from the hallway just outside the study—

"I don't know what crawled up your ass, but you need to stop being such a bitch to Alina. If you want to take your anger out on someone, be mad at me—but she doesn't deserve it," Jason said, his voice low but sharp.

Emma scoffed audibly, "Wow, Jason. Overprotective much?"

"Overprotective?" he sputtered. "Really, Em, what's going on?"

"I can see it, you know. You two think you're sneaky, acting like nothing is happening—but I see it. You have each other, now. You've been together this whole time and it's clear you both *finally* got what you wanted. So, why don't you go run back to your girlfriend and get off my case."

"Emma, what the fuck?" Jason hissed. "Are you serious right now?"

"So, you're admitting it," Emma spat.

"Admitting what? I have no idea what you are even angry about in the first place! Alina is your best friend. And yeah, I'm protective over her; why wouldn't I be? We've known each other forever. She was the first thing I saw when I woke up, and she's been what's kept me going since. If we hadn't been together, who knows if we would have even made it back to you? And yeah, sure, maybe we're closer because of it. I'd think you would understand the—"

"I'd *understand*?" Emma yelled. "As if I haven't been dealing with my own nightmares—and *alone!*"

There was a tense pause before I heard Jason speak again, his voice softer. "And here I was, thinking you found yourself a pretty solid group of people to have your back. Yeah, you've been through hell. But you aren't alone, Em. And I'm *here* now. So is Alina, if you don't keep pushing her away."

"Fuck," Emma choked on a sob. "Jayce, I just don't want to be left behind."

Their voices lowered, and I shifted awkwardly behind my door as Jason continued to whisper words of comfort to his sister. It was past the point of awkwardness now. If I left the room, they'd absolutely know I'd heard their whole argument, and this was not something I wanted to get in the middle of.

Finally, I heard footsteps retreating down the hall. I left the room, and as I turned to head towards the front door, I almost ran straight into Alina. Again.

"You know, Carter, we have to stop running into each other like this," Alina joked. "One of us is going to break a leg or something."

"I still maintain that it's you who keeps running into me."

Alina paused, nervously looking behind her. "Hey, Emma just rushed outside. She looked upset. I was going to follow, but Jason told me not to go after her. Did you see anything...happen?"

"Yeah—sibling argument," I responded, moving past her to grab the handle to the front door.

"What do you mean?" Alina asked, blocking my path.

I regretted saying anything the moment I saw her worried look. "Stupid shit. They'll get over it. Can I go now?"

"O...kay," Alina responded. "Hey, if you see Jason, tell him I'll be down in a sec. I think I forgot something in our room."

"Not your messenger," I muttered as I pulled the door open.

Sure enough, there was Jason just a foot away from the front door, glaring at the horizon like it insulted him. I groaned internally and started walking past him.

"Hey, is Lee—" Jason started.

"Figure it out yourself," I muttered as I brushed past.

Almost everyone else was already waiting by the truck. Dan and Sam were lounging in the grass and Cap was leaning against the truck bed, talking quietly with Michelle. Russell and Brian emerged from the backyard carrying an empty galvanized tub, and Emma was already in the truck—probably still fuming. Her temper could take some time to burn out, and I was fine ignoring it and letting her simmer.

Just as I'd caught up to the others, I heard the front door open and shut behind me. Alina's quiet laugh drifted across the short distance, and I glanced over my shoulder to see her and Jason walking, his arm thrown around her shoulder, as usual. My jaw clenched involuntarily and I turned away, ignoring their approach.

Once Russell and Brian loaded the water bin into the truck bed, Michelle, Cap, Alina, and Sam piled into the cab with Emma. The rest of us packed in with the galvanized tub in the back, and I tuned everything else out, focusing on the warm breeze as we drove.

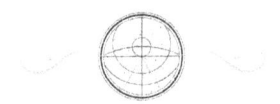

Brian, Russell, Dan, Cap, and I went first. There wasn't much we could do in terms of privacy, but we were used to keeping our underwear on and bathing around the clothing by now.

The extra clothes we brought back from the hotels were more necessary than we initially anticipated. As it turned out, we were all running low on clean clothing. We'd been utilizing sun sterilization to refresh most of our clothes, but by this point, everyone had items that needed a proper washing down.

The sun was hanging low in the sky, covering the pond with its golden light. We still had another hour or two before sundown and our group finished washing up quickly. It's amazing how one small change can make the most basic task ten times easier. It was nice to be able to take care of at least one thing easily.

Sam, Alina, Michelle, Jason, and Emma were up next. Just as I slipped a new shirt over my head, I heard Emma's shrill voice yell, *"What the fuck is that?!"*

I jerked around, jumping down from the truck as the others moved into defensive stances, eyes open to catch any potential threats. I just managed to catch the back of Russell's shirt as he tried to run past me.

Panicked, he pulled against my grasp and hissed, "Sam."

"Assess the situation first," I responded sternly.

I closed my eyes, but could still hear her fidgeting beside me.

Sitting up, I pulled a pack from the pile behind us, relieved to find it was Brian's. There was no way either of us would be able to get any rest if she couldn't stop moving around. I dug through the bag until I found a t-shirt and a hoodie.

"Here," I said as I tossed the hoodie to Alina before rolling the t-shirt into a makeshift pillow.

"Oh, you didn't have to," Alina replied as she sat up, carefully folding the hoodie.

"It's fine. It's Brian's. He'd be mad if you *didn't* take it."

With the thin cushion for my head, I settled back down, clasping my hands on my chest as I stared at the sky above us. After a moment, Alina bunched up the hoodie and lay back down.

Alina turned her head to face me as she asked, "You sure Brian won't mind?"

I turned my head and noticed the nervous look on her face.

"Trust me," I answered. "Brian will be happy to know he helped in his sleep."

She dipped her chin, nodding slightly before turning her gaze upwards.

"The stars are so bright," she whispered.

I studied her profile as she looked up at the night sky. Though her words were casual enough, a sort of melancholy lingered in the expression she wore.

"What's really on your mind?" I asked her before I could stop myself.

She froze, bringing her hands up to scrub down her face before rolling to her side to match my eye contact. She propped her head up with her hand as she rested on an elbow.

"I'm not sure you really want to start that conversation," she answered, cocking an eyebrow.

"Yeah, you're right. I'm sure the rate at which light travels from burning balls of gas in the sky is much easier to digest at this time of night," I deadpanned.

Alina's face scrunched as she processed my words before a soft laugh escaped her lips. "Oh, so we joke now?"

He shot me a scathing look before quickly scanning the area, pulling free of my grasp, and running to Sam.

As Russell reached the others by the pond, we realized Emma's yelling wasn't due to any external threat. Jason was trying to mediate between his sister and Alina, who was pulling her shirt back on over her sports bra and shorts.

"Carter, Brian, get them back up here before they can make more noise," Cap said, their voice growing frosty. "Dan, get ready to start the truck in case something heard her yelling. Keep your eyes open."

Brian and I ran towards the group as Emma jabbed an accusing finger at Alina, nearly making contact before Jason knocked Emma's hand away.

Russell cautiously stepped between them, hands out to show he was not a threat. "Woah, okay, let's just chill for a second. Red, stop attacking your friend. Whatever it is, we can figure it out," he said, surprisingly calm.

"You didn't see it!" Emma shrieked, turning back to Alina. "And I even asked you yesterday, Jason too, if there was anything else I should know. Why would you keep it a secret unless it was something bad?"

Sam's eyes met mine, pleading. *"Do something,"* she mouthed, jerking her chin towards Emma. Alina's eyes were wide and she seemed frozen.

Jason slowly approached his sister, holding out a hand. "Em, this reaction is a bit extreme. You're freaking me out."

Emma laughed incredulously. "Oh, I'm freaking you out? I'm freaking *you* out?!"

"She's lost it," Russell said quietly as he grabbed Alina's arm, pulling her towards him and Sam. He wore a hardened expression I'd never seen on his face before.

Brian and I exchanged looks as Emma continued to rant. "Carter was right," she said, her finger shaking as she pointed around Jason towards Alina. Her face twisted into a look of betrayal. "He was fucking right. They did something to you and you were trying to hide it."

"Emma," Alina cried from behind Russell. "It's not like that, please just let me talk."

I clapped my hands, the sound cracking across the space as everyone's attention turned my way. "Everyone needs to shut the fuck up and go back to the truck," I hissed. "We need to make sure nothing else heard this bullshit."

Russell and Jason started leading Sam and Alina back to the truck while Brian and I approached Emma.

"Red," Brian said gently, reaching a hand towards the woman. "Walk with me. Whatever it is, we'll figure it out. But right now, we need to make sure nothing heard us."

Emma pushed away Brian's hand, ice in her eyes as she stalked back towards the truck.

"Things can never just be easy, can they?" Brian muttered before sighing and trudging back towards the others.

Emma stopped a few feet from the group, glaring at her friend standing beside her brother.

"Not one word until I say so," Cap hissed. We circled the truck, everyone facing outwards to watch and listen for any signs of something approaching. When Cap was satisfied that nothing had been lured in from the noise, they faced us again with a chilling glare in their stormy eyes.

"What. Was. That?" Cap said, their voice quiet but commanding as they stared down Emma.

"Her." Emma jerked her head towards Alina. "She has a mark on her back. I saw it. Blue and glowing, just like those things that attacked us."

I blinked, not sure I was hearing her correctly.

"This is about our tattoos?" Jason asked, squinting at his sister.

"You have one, too?" Sam asked, her voice low.

"Yeah." Jason turned around and pulled his shirt over his head as Alina seemed to curl in on herself beside him.

"I see blue marks, yes. I don't see glowing," Cap responded. "Was there anything else, Emma? Did she threaten you? Hurt you?"

"It. Was. Glowing!" she said through gritted teeth. "It was fucking glowing. Like a tracker or something. Probably leading those space fuckers right back to us."

Jason stepped toward his sister, gritting his teeth. "That doesn't answer the question. Did Alina actually do anything to you? Because from what I saw, she slipped, almost fell, and then you fucking attacked her."

Emma's jaw stiffened, gaze darkening as she stared at her brother. Reluctantly, she finally shook her head no.

Jason took a deep breath, gritting his teeth, and his whole body tensed as he stiffly commanded, "Emma, this has to stop."

"Oh shit," Russell said, pointing at Jason's back. "It *is* glowing."

I stepped towards Jason, nudging him to turn around so I could look at the marks on his back up close. Sure enough, a bioluminescent blue glow was pulsing from the markings on his spine. I took a cautious step back.

"Well, fuck," Dan muttered. "Just when you think things can't get weirder."

"Weird, yes, but is it cause for alarm?" Brian asked, looking at each of us one by one. "Alina and Jason have been with Carter and me for nearly twenty-four hours now. They were on their own in the city for four days before that. If it was a tracker, wouldn't they have been found by now? We still don't know anything for sure. For all we know, it could just be how the invaders labeled their experiments or something."

Alina choked on a cry, bringing her hands to her mouth and squeezing her eyes shut. "Please," she said, opening her eyes, tears trickling down her cheeks. "Don't call us experiments," she whimpered, voice breaking.

Brian stepped closer to Alina, his face full of regret as he tentatively placed his hands on her shoulders to take her attention off the others before speaking. "Alina, I am so, so sorry. No—you're absolutely not an experiment. You're a person who had her agency taken away and can't help what has been done. You've been one of us from the moment we voted you in, and you're still one of us now." He lowered his hands, turning around to face the group again with a firm look on his face. "This changes nothing."

Jason pulled Alina back into his side as Brian continued talking, "This is *not* how we handle things. This isn't how we treat each other."

"Brian's right," Cap said, holding us in their steely gaze one by one until we were all focused on them. "We will continue talking once we are back at the house. Second group, finish up quick and then get back to the truck."

"What about the water bin?" Dan asked, gesturing towards the truck bed where the tub still sat in the back.

"We'll figure that out later. The priority right now is to get clean and return to the safe house. Quickly," Cap directed.

The second group walked back down to the pond to finish up.

I held myself back from saying anything during the confrontation and the entire ride back, partly because I wasn't sure what to think anymore. The way Emma switched perspectives so quickly should have validated everything I said the night before about our newcomers. Instead, the words sat like a rock in the pit of my stomach.

EIGHTEEN
ALINA

My best friend. My *best* friend—the words repeated in my head as I sat tucked into Jason's side on the living room couch. A conversation was happening around me, but all I could think about was how she looked at me at the pond and how she refused to match my gaze now.

The pure anger and fear that coated her words.

Sam's gasp as she stepped back.

The way Jason and Russell felt they had to step between us.

Everything just kept replaying over and over again in my head.

It didn't escape me that Emma's comments were directed specifically at me. Jason did not receive the same vitriol; not even when he showed the others he bore the same marks. How did things change so quickly in the last twenty-four hours? The emotional whiplash cut deep and I felt sick.

Jason and I were back to being a safety concern and I couldn't even dispute those fears. My skin crawled at the reminder that I still had no idea what happened to my body. What if Emma was right and we were being tracked? What if Carter was right all along and we were just ticking time bombs? With Emma changing her mind, the rest of the group might quickly follow. The only reason they had to trust us was Emma, and now? What if they should have listened to

Carter from the start when he fought to keep us from joining the group? What if we brought the threat with us?

Cap was still speaking in the middle of the room when I realized their eyes were trained on me.

"Alina?" Cap asked tentatively. "Are you alright?"

"I—I'm sorry. I'm just—I'm having a really hard time focusing right now," I practically gasped as I tried to hold back tears and keep my breathing even.

Cap stared back at me for a moment, their face unreadable. I inhaled deeply and slowly exhaled, feeling my chest stiffen as I controlled my breath's release. Once all of the air cleared my lungs, I tried to focus on relaxing my tense muscles. I couldn't look like a basket case. I needed to find a way to come back down. Squeezing my eyes closed, I took another deep breath. A hand grasped my own, a familiar, comforting squeeze letting me know I wasn't alone. Jason.

I glanced at him out of the corner of my eye and saw the muscle in his jaw twitching. His other hand was curled in a fist. It was clear that Jason was trying just as hard as I was to keep his composure.

After what seemed like ages, Cap started speaking again, "Okay, here is what we are going to do. Emotions are high right now. We could all use some separation to decompress before talking this through further. Emma." They turned towards her. "You and Michelle can go outside. I'll be there in a moment."

"Fine," Emma muttered. She stood without saying another word and walked to the back door. The room was so quiet I could hear the hinges squeak as she stepped outside, followed by the slam of the door. Michelle exchanged a look with Cap before leaving the room and following Emma's retreat.

Cap turned back to the rest of us.

"Alina, Jason," they paused, calculating their next words, "since you are new, I want to make sure you're aware of how we handle situations like this. With conflict, we need to sort things out as quickly as possible. Our group relies on us being a cohesive unit for our survival. Respect is a must, and you were not treated with respect today."

I blinked, sitting up straighter at their words. It was...not what I expected to hear. I was so convinced that we were about to be given an ultimatum, or at least a warning, because of the unknown threat attached to our skin. Though everyone sat or stood quietly in the room; as I studied their faces, I didn't see the animosity I was anticipating. No one looked at us differently—aside from Carter, who was back to not looking at us at all. He seemed to be lost in thought; a frown etched across his forehead as he stared off.

"Full transparency, that isn't to say I'm not concerned. I want to make sure we have a chance to talk more about this so I can have a full understanding of everything. I'm going to head out back to talk with Emma. You don't have to sit here and wait, but don't go far. We should connect again before everyone turns in for the night," Cap finished.

As soon as Cap left through the back door, Carter pushed away from his spot against the wall and walked towards the study without another word.

"Try not to stress it too much. Red can be quick to react—" Sam paused, wincing as she realized who she was talking to. "But I guess you know that. You probably know...Emma better than we do. Sorry, I don't know why—" Sam stammered.

Jason gave her a melancholy smile as he stood up from the couch. "I get what you're trying to say. She's always been kinda hot-headed. It's why we love her, but it's also how she drives us insane."

Sam's expression relaxed as a small smile pulled at her lips. "I think it's just been a lot for her, you know?"

"Still doesn't make it right," Russell said bluntly, shrugging his shoulders. "You can't help what happened to you any more than we can. You're still chill in my book."

Russell threw his arm around Sam's shoulders and flashed us a sympathetic smile as they left the room, Dan following close behind.

Only Brian, Jason, and I were left now. Jason crossed his arms, looking down at the floor. I didn't have to ask to know what was on his mind—the hurt was written all over his face.

Though we'd witnessed Emma's intense reactions over the years, it was rare that either of us were ever on the receiving end. Being reunited was a confusing adjustment for all of us, no matter how happy we were to be together again. I'd been brushing off her shortness and sarcasm, chalking it up to just dealing with change and general stress. In reality, there was a cavern between us and I didn't know how to close the divide.

"So, are y'all doing alright?" Brian asked, sitting on the arm of the couch.

Jason sank down to his spot beside me once again before answering. "Honestly? I feel like shit."

"I just don't know what I did to make her so angry," I whispered.

"I don't think it's you," Brian answered.

I looked up at him on his elevated position on the couch arm. "Then…why?"

"Only Emma can answer that one," Jason added. "But regardless of whether there's an underlying reason, it doesn't excuse the fact that she has been incredibly harsh with you. It isn't right."

There was a moment of silence before Brian asked Jason, "Were you and Red close growing up?"

"Yeah, always. Actually, I was usually her voice of reason." Jason laughed.

"Well, I can certainly see that." Brian chuckled. "Yeah, Red definitely benefits from having someone around to ground her. Michelle has kinda been her person for that, but I try my best to look out for her, too." He waited a moment before adding, "She struggles more than she lets on."

We talked for a bit longer, easing into casual conversation. By the time Cap, Michelle, and Emma came back inside, the pressure that squeezed inside my chest had nearly subsided.

Cap and Michelle returned to the living room and exchanged awkward greetings. Though Cap kept their expression unreadable, Michelle was visibly exhausted. I waited for Emma to join, but there was no sign of her. I assumed she must have taken a moment to be by herself.

I got up to meet them in the center of the room. "I just want to say I'm so sorry for causing so much…I don't even know. I'm just sorry."

Michelle grabbed my hand. "We're working through it. Yes, things got heated, but you can't control how someone else reacts. We knew taking you in came with unknowns. Emma certainly has an extra layer to process on top of that. We all have our limits; just give her some space for now and let her come to you."

I swallowed. "Thank you."

"Now, if you don't mind, I don't think I'm needed for this portion of the conversation. I'm going to go rest." Michelle yawned. "I'll see everyone in the morning."

Michelle and Cap kissed goodnight, and Michelle waved to the rest of us as she left the room.

"So," Jason started. "Do we talk here? Or should we go outside, too?"

"Whatever is more comfortable for y'all," Cap answered.

Jason looked to me in question and I shrugged. At this point, all I wanted was to curl up in our room and forget that today ever happened.

"We can stay here," Jason replied.

"I'll stay for moral support," Brian stated, looking between Jason and I.

I blinked, not expecting the support. In the past twenty-four hours, Brian repeatedly surprised me with his trust and kindness. Since he introduced himself in the restaurant, he continuously checked in to make sure we were alright.

"Sure." Cap nodded. "Brian, why don't you go and grab two chairs from the kitchen and we can get more comfortable in here."

Cap gestured for us to sit on the couch and, once Brian returned, took one of the chairs from him.

"It can be a lot to adjust to a new group," Cap started, relaxing against the chair. "Honestly, I was planning on having this conversation with y'all at the end of the day, anyway. It's important to me that we get to know each other. After the day we had, though, I mostly want to see how y'all are holding up."

"So...we aren't getting kicked out?" I asked.

"No," Cap said without hesitation.

"Like I said," Brian added. "You can't help what was done to you."

Cap nodded in agreement. "I still want to be cautious. You'll need to tell us everything you currently know about those marks and what happened in the...facility." They paused. "Being informed is important to me, to all of us, and while I know it will feel awkward, it is necessary for all of our safety, including yours. Let's circle back on this in the morning after everyone's had some rest and time to cool down, yeah? In the meantime, if y'all start to feel anything abnormal or even just slightly off, please come tell me, first. Remember, this is as much about keeping *you* safe as it is the rest of the group."

I nodded and felt Jason shift beside me.

"No offense, but how do we know that you won't just kick us out after *that* conversation?" Jason asked.

"You don't," Cap answered, shrugging their shoulders. "I have to earn your trust just as much as you have to earn the rest of the group's. It starts with honesty, though."

I nodded slowly, absorbing everything Cap said. "Thank you—" I finally said, "for checking in. I have to admit that I'm mostly just feeling overwhelmed. I feel guilty for saying it, since I know we've probably turned your world upside down."

"Nah, don't worry. After a few hell-creatures, it will take a lot more than a glowing tattoo to scare us off," Brian joked.

NINETEEN
CARTER

As soon as Cap left the room, I retreated to the study. I couldn't care anymore. The amount of unnecessary angst and fighting that occurred in the last twenty-four hours alone was exactly what I wanted to avoid with newcomers joining the group. And those marks...I couldn't even begin to process what the glowing could mean.

I was surprised when Emma flipped out the way she did—especially after the emotional reunion with her best friend and brother last night. Maybe the reunion wasn't as happy as she thought it would be. What happened at the pond could have ended so much worse.

Whatever. It was done.

I shut the door to the study and lay on the floor, clasping my hands behind my head. Footsteps pounded up the stairs adjacent to my room and I could just make out Sam, Russell, and Dan's voices as they stomped upstairs.

Alina, Jason, and Brian were likely still in the living room. I wouldn't be surprised if Brian opted to stay with them. Brian was always the peacemaker of our group—always the first to provide a warm welcome or ask about your day. He had a way of showing support in the exact way you needed it without overstepping. No doubt, even though Alina and Jason were new, he was likely showing them the same kind of camaraderie.

I closed my eyes and tried to block everything else out. It had been so long since I'd had solid rest without keeping one eye open that I didn't even know if it was possible anymore. What I wouldn't give to lock myself in my old apartment, turn off all the lights, and listen to a podcast as I fell asleep on the couch. The small comforts that were once taken for granted had quickly turned into impossibilities. The steady ache in my chest pulled up remnants of a time that might as well not have existed in the first place.

After deep breathing, meditation, and staring at the ceiling, I accepted the fact that rest would not come easily. No sooner had I sat up than there was a quiet knock on the door.

"Yeah?" I called.

The door opened and Emma slipped in, quietly shutting the door behind her. She stared at me and her ice-blue eyes flickered, a hint of flame underneath.

"What do you need?" I asked, still not getting up from the floor.

"No talking," Emma said, shaking her head as she crept closer. "I don't want to talk. I don't want to feel. I want to pretend to be anywhere but here."

Emma sank to the floor, and before there was time to react, her lips crashed against mine.

Her tongue trailed my bottom lip before the sharp pinch of her teeth seemed to steal my breath. *Fuck.* A quick exhale left my lungs as the heat from her mouth traveled down my throat to swirl in my stomach. Her small hands pressed against my chest, sliding over my shoulders to grip the back of my neck as I fell back against the floor. As her light frame collided with mine and she rolled her hips against me, a soft moan tumbled from her lips. I couldn't help grabbing the curve where her hips met her thighs, pulling her closer.

She trailed kisses down my jaw, biting at my neck with an insatiable hunger. The press of her body, the drag of her hips, the way her nails clawed into my shoulders—I couldn't think. She moved against me with desperation and my hands slipped under her shirt to feel the heat of her skin. The kissing grew frantic, panting, and I grabbed her ass, pulling her against me harder, aching for the friction.

Another soft moan escaped her mouth as she pulled back for a minute and my blood froze in my veins.

Fuck. *Fuck*. What was I doing?

I all but pushed her off of me, scrambling to my feet and pacing the room as I panted, trying to regain composure.

"What the fuck, Carter?" she growled from the floor.

"What the fuck? What the *fuck*, Red?" I sputtered. "What are you doing? You can't just—"

She pushed to her feet and her hands clenched into fists at her sides. Her cheeks were still flushed as strands of disheveled auburn hair fluttered across her face. "Can't just what? It's the end of the fucking world, Carter. Who really gives a shit anymore?"

"I need you to leave," I said, gesturing to the door.

"No." Red crossed her arms and walked over to sit on the chaise, making a show of getting comfortable.

"Fine," I said, grabbing my backpack and leaving the room without another word. I didn't need this—not tonight, not ever.

I burst out the front door, not caring as it banged back against the hinges. Storming over to the truck, I heaved my backpack over the side. It tumbled into the vehicle, and I heard a gasp as someone scrambled to sit up in the truck bed. *Fuck, what now.*

Alina's eyes widened as they met mine and she froze. I could only imagine how rough I looked, still fuming from the series of events that drove me outside. I groaned, frustrated, as I ran a hand through my short hair.

"Sorry," I muttered. "Didn't expect anyone to be out here."

"Oh, sorry. I can go. I just—"

"No, you're fine. Stay. I'll go." I hopped into the bed to grab my bag. Alina stood as she picked up the backpack.

Confusion crossed her face as she looked from the bag back to me. "Are you...going somewhere?"

"No, just needed some air."

"Then why the—you know what," Alina caught herself. "It's none of my business. Sorry. Again." She held the backpack towards me, pressing her lips into a stiff smile.

I hesitated before grabbing the bag, responding gruffly, "As I said, you're fine. I just got kicked out of my room and needed some quiet." The words were out of my mouth before I could stop them.

"Kicked out of your room?" she asked, her brow furrowing with the question.

"Yep." I hopped down from the truck, turning to face Alina as she stared down at me. With the moon shining behind her, it almost looked like she was part of the soft, ethereal light.

Alina lowered into a seated position, crossing one ankle over the other as her legs dangled off the tailgate. She stared at me curiously.

"Don't ask," I muttered, letting the backpack drop to my feet.

"Wasn't going to," she answered as the corner of her lip twitched upward. I'd come out here wanting to be alone, but something about the way she held back her words piqued my curiosity.

"What are *you* doing out here?" I asked, changing the subject.

"Needed some air," she answered quietly, staring at her hands in her lap.

"Did the conversation not go well in there?"

"No, actually—" Alina said. "I was convinced we were going to be asked to leave, but Cap basically just said they wanted us to have a bigger conversation about what we know. They said they wanted to be cautious, but informed, and to let them know if we start to feel 'off' so we could figure it out together. They also said Emma shouldn't have…" Her voice trailed off.

"Yeah, Red 'shouldn't have' a lot of things," I said bitterly.

Alina frowned, but thankfully didn't ask questions. I leaned against the truck next to where Alina sat, resting an elbow on the tailgate.

It was significantly cooler than it was earlier. Aside from crickets chirping and a barely-there breeze rustling through the trees in the green-space next to the house, the night was quiet and still.

After a few moments, Alina spoke again, her voice soft. "We weren't trying to keep the marks a secret. I just didn't think—I assumed it was kind of a given that stuff happened to us and I didn't think to mention the tattoos outside of that. I feel like some kind of freak not even being able to explain what's going on with my own body."

I glanced over, noticing how she wrung her hands in her lap. Her hair started coming undone and a halo of fly-aways broke free from her loose ponytail.

I thought back to the early days when I was still trying to figure out what was going on. At the time, there was solidarity in not knowing what was happening and fighting against the same enemy. Alina and Jason were outsiders in more than one sense of the word. They were new to the group, sure, but they also bore a connection to the same enemies we'd been fighting for the last eight months. The marks on their skin weren't just evidence that something had happened to them—those glowing, blue tattoos would forever link them to their captors, a constant reminder of who took away their freedom and autonomy. Those symbols separated them from potential allies and alienated them from those who they were once closest to.

Alina caught me staring as her hazel eyes connected with my gaze. There it was again—that questioning look that would be so easy to miss if her expressive eyes didn't betray her. I knew there must be so much more she needed to know. I opened my mouth, ready to extend the invitation for her to ask questions, but another voice interrupted before the words could form.

"Hey, what's going on?" Jason's voice was calm and casual, but I could still hear the tension. Hell, even I couldn't hold that against him anymore.

"Just getting some air." Alina threw me a conspiratorial smile like we now had an inside joke or something, before turning towards Jason. "It's a nice night."

He visibly relaxed as he made eye contact with her. "I went to our room to look for Em, but she wasn't there. I was hoping you were with her."

"Oh, no. I haven't seen her." She turned to look back at the house as if she could see through the walls and find Red's location.

"She's fine," I interrupted. "She's back in the study." It was a half-truth, but I wasn't about to call Red out in front of the two people she needed most—whether she'd admit she needed them or not.

"Oh." Jason's brow furrowed. "Isn't that where you are staying?"

"Yeah, looks like she took it back, though," I replied. "It's fine. I'm not too picky about where I sleep as long as I have my space."

Jason nodded, hopping into the back of the truck beside Alina before laying back to look up at the sky. We fell into a comfortable silence and I was surprised at how easy it felt. I let down my guard, a bit, as I scanned the yard.

The stars were out and I couldn't help thinking of other times I'd sat outside staring at the sky, wondering what was out there. The tiny pinpricks of light in the distance still held the same awe-inspiring mystery, but now they were also laced with reminders of fear and loss. Gray clouds drifted in from the east, wisping across the scattered light. I watched as clusters of stars seemed to blink out of existence in the clouds' path and the night grew darker.

"Think that's rain coming?" Jason asked, the first of us to break the silence.

Alina laughed. "Resorting to talk about the weather, now? What, have we run out of things to say, already?" She shivered as she spoke the last word.

I laughed under my breath, shaking my head as I turned to face them. At the very least, I expected to see an amused expression on Jason's face. He was propped up on his elbows, a concerned look on his face as he stared at Alina's back. I hopped up without a second thought, gently shifting in between them and tapping Alina's shoulder.

"Can I?" I asked Alina.

A worried expression crossed her face, but she nodded, pulling her ponytail over her shoulder so I could look. The bioluminescent glow from her mark pulsed faintly, just peeking out the top of the tank top she now wore.

I glanced at Jason, who knelt at my side. "Yours?" I asked.

"I don't know," Jason said as he pulled his shirt over his head and turned around. His was glowing, too.

Alina looked over my shoulder. "What does it mean?" she asked.

"Do you feel," I paused, "different?"

"I'm not sure," Jason answered, pulling his shirt back on.

The glow behind Alina pulsed brighter and there was a look of fear in her eyes. I thought back to the pond when Jason's mark illuminated before us. Could it be fear that causes it to glow? Anger?

"I kinda feel like…" Alina paused, shaking her head.

"What is it, Lee?" Jason asked, looking at her expectantly, grabbing her hand.

Always with the touching. I clenched my jaw.

She continued, "You know that feeling at the top of a roller coaster when you know the drop is coming?"

I nodded.

"That," she said. "It feels like a warning. I felt it yesterday, too, in the city. At first, I thought it was just anxiety, but I was feeling pretty calm just before this, so…"

"I think I get what you mean," Jason answered, holding out his arm. Goosebumps prickled along his skin, the hair standing on end.

Alina raised her arm to reveal the same and they both looked at me.

I held out my arm as well, extending it between theirs—only my skin was still smooth.

Alina swallowed. "Do you think it's—"

"Quiet," I hissed, holding out a hand as I scanned the area. There was movement amidst the trees. While it could have been the wind, I knew better than to assume.

I gestured to Alina and Jason, silently asking them to follow my lead as I slowly got down from the truck. I extended my hand to Alina to help her down as Jason softly landed beside us. We crouched low to blend in with the shadows of the vehicle as we looked around the yard.

There—snapping branches, rustling, and I realized even the crickets silenced their song.

TWENTY
ALINA

JASON and I followed Carter's lead as we crouched behind the truck, obscuring ourselves from view. Something was moving in the trees next to the house, stalking under the cover of the green-space. Carter's eyes darted between Jason and me and he swiftly pulled his shirt over his head, tossing it to me. I looked at it for a second before realizing he meant for me to use it to cover my mark—Jason's was already covered by his dark t-shirt. I pulled it on over my thin tank top, hoping it would be enough to dim my tattoo's glow.

There was a crunch, something snapping near the middle of the driveway. I stared, breathing shallowly in an attempt to keep as still as possible. My heart was pounding so hard that I wouldn't have been surprised if its beating gave our hiding spot away.

The creature emerged from the shadow of the trees, a gruff, wuffling sound coming from its jaws. It prowled low to the ground; eight legs moving with a slow, stalking stretch. Its head turned and its large ears tilted like a satellite, trying to catch the sounds of potential prey. Even from here, I could see its four glittering eyes in the moonlight.

A clatter sounded from inside the house and the creature's head jerked in that direction as a low growl rumbled from its chest. The stripes lining its sides flashed, dancing brighter against the dark gray of its mottled flesh as it continued to click, hum, and growl. It bared its claws, all eight sets digging into the ground, kneading, almost like a cat, before it began stalking towards the house.

Cold fear flooded my system as I realized we had no way to warn the others. My eyes darted between the creature and the house. "They don't know," I whispered.

"Don't move," Carter whispered back, barely making a sound. My gaze frantically darted from the expanse of the yard to the winding driveway. We needed something to cause a distraction—to warn the others.

There was nothing. And that beast was only drawing closer. With each step, it was like there was a magnetic charge pushing against me. My nerves were practically sizzling and I couldn't focus on anything but the creature's movement.

I braced my hand against the truck, shifting weight to my front foot.

The creature stood upright on its back legs, tilting its head from side to side as it looked for any movement in the house. It most definitely heard the sound coming from inside. It snapped its jaws as drool oozed between its sharp teeth.

I took a deep breath.

The creature stomped its front legs down to the ground as a gut-wrenching shriek ripped from its jaws. It stretched down low, getting ready to bound forward on its long, bent legs.

At least the others would have heard *that*. I couldn't let it get closer to the house. Not if the others were going to escape.

Without turning around, I whispered to Jason and Carter, "Get the others and go."

Before they could react, I was up and running.

"*Hey!*" I screamed at the top of my lungs, sprinting in the opposite direction of the house towards the neighbor's yard. "*This way!*"

I didn't dare turn around and risk my speed to confirm, but I heard its claws skitter across the driveway as its large body whipped around, a blood-curdling shriek ripping from its lungs. The goosebumps on my skin prickled so intensely it almost hurt. Still—I had to keep moving. If the others were going to have a chance, I needed to lead it far enough away.

So I ran, and I didn't turn back.

TWENTY-ONE
CARTER

No.

As soon as she took off I grabbed Jason, pinning his arms to his sides in a bear hug to stop him from running after her. My heart pounded in my chest like it was trying to punch a hole and escape. *What was she thinking?* I watched Alina sprinting towards the neighboring property as the hell-beast gained on her. *Where was she leading it?* I doubted she had more of a plan, but that didn't stop her from sprinting a straight shot across the yards.

I pulled Jason back against my chest so I could quickly give him orders—we didn't have much time if we were going to have a shot at getting everyone out alive. "I know you want to go after her, but please for the sake of all of us, I need you to get your *sister* and the others into the SUV and truck. Tell Cap to head towards the west state park—they will know what that means. I'll get Alina."

He froze for a second, looking towards Alina before cursing under his breath. "I'll tell the others, but I'm not leaving without her," he said as he turned and raced to the house.

TWENTY-TWO
ALINA

I RACED towards the neighboring yard, pushing myself to keep moving. *Just make it far enough. Just far enough so the others can get away. Just make it far enough,* I repeated over and over and over in my head. I could give them that much.

My calves were burning and I was breathing hard. I was never a fast runner, but I didn't have to escape completely—I just needed to run far enough.

The beast grunted behind me as it galloped and I realized just how close it was. My heart sank. I turned my head and missed seeing a rock jutting out of the ground. I flew forward, hitting the dirt hard before rolling to a stop.

This was it.

This was it.

It growled, dangerously close; a hulking mass creeping closer and closer. I fought the urge to squeeze my eyes shut as I scrambled to get upright, scooting backwards on my butt. But the beast wasn't attacking—yet.

It prowled forward, flexing its claws into the dry ground. With its jaws open, I could see double rows of razor sharp teeth. Drool oozed between each knife-like edge as its low rumbling growl reverberated through me. I was numb with fear, like my blood froze in my veins.

Still, I scuttled backwards in the dirt with the last piece of self-preservation I could muster. Puffs of dust clouded around me on the dry ground with each jerky movement.

The monstrous beast clicked, a chirping sound twittering from its throat like a deranged bird of prey. The creature was taking its time, the hot, wet heat from its breath hitting my shins, now.

It lowered its head and drops of saliva hit my legs as it snuffled at my shoe, investigating. I cringed, whimpering as I felt the ooze drip down my shins.

Maybe it was like a bear and I could play dead—cover my neck with my hands and curl into a ball. Maybe it would get sick of me if I just sat there, not moving. Maybe it was all just a game, the prowl, the chase, the hunt and it would get bored and move on—

Maybe...

Maybe...

Maybe...

A long, dark tongue rolled from between its open jaws as its head lowered, sniffing once, twice before the damn creature lapped at my boot. I tried to keep from whimpering as it licked up my shin to my knee, tilting its head as if it were judging the taste.

Please don't hurt me. Please don't hurt me. Please don't hurt me. Please don't hurt me, I begged in my mind. I repeated the mantra, hoping there was even a speck of luck left for me. The beast hovered over me, its face lowering down towards mine, glittering black eyes narrowing, when—

BWEEEEEEEEEEEEEEEEEEEEEEEEEEEE
BEEPBEEPBEEPBEEPBEEP

The sound of a horn blaring, beaten with a fist, snapped the spell and the beast jerked backwards, screeching. It whipped around, setting its sights on the sedan in the street, and took off like a shot.

There was no time to make another choice, so I turned and ran back towards the safe house.

TWENTY-THREE
ALINA

The SUV and the truck were slowly rolling down the driveway as I finally reached the safe house's property once again. Jason jumped down from the back of the truck, racing over.

"Are you hurt?" he asked, catching me in his arms. His voice was urgent, even as he tried to stay quiet. I shook my head no, unable to speak as he grabbed my hand and we sprinted back towards the slow-moving vehicles. The truck stopped, just for a moment, as we jumped into the back and I nearly fell into the empty water collection bin still sitting there from earlier this afternoon.

The truck continued rolling again and Brian opened the small window between the cab and the bed. "Keep low, stay quiet so we don't grab its attention back," he ordered. I nodded, the movement jerky as I still shook with terror.

My face was inches from Brian's as he looked back at me from inside.

"Carter?" I asked.

Brian shook his head with a grim expression. "Who do you think is driving the sedan?" Brian answered.

I sunk down further as Jason wrapped me in his arms. "Fuck, don't ever do that again, Lee," Jason said, his voice breaking as he gripped me tighter. "I can't fucking lose you." He pressed his lips to the top of my head as he held me close.

I didn't say a word, knowing I'd make the same choice again if it meant the others would have a chance.

Come on, Carter.

The SUV started accelerating and Dan's voice crackled through the walkie-talkie. "*Cap says it's time to move.*"

"Go. We can see Carter running back," Brian lied, speaking into his walkie. "We'll catch up."

There was a pause before Dan responded, "*Promise?*"

Brian swallowed hard before answering, "Promise."

The crackling faded as the SUV picked up speed, moving further away from our truck that still idled in place.

A loud crash rang from the next street over, followed by the screeching wail of the beast's cry. My heart stopped in my chest. *No.*

I scrambled to the edge of the truck, searching for any sign of Carter.

"Fuck!" Brian cursed, punching the back of his seat.

"We're running out of time," Russell said through gritted teeth. I could see his expression in the side view mirror, cold defeat already written on his face as his eyes scanned his side of the road.

"Wait—just a little longer, please," Sam begged, frantic.

"As long as I can, Sammy," Russell answered. His reflection was pale as a ghost's.

I squinted into the darkness, looking for any sign that Carter was making his way back to us.

Finally, I saw movement in the shadows. I might have missed him without the moonlight glinting off the sweat coating his bare torso.

"It's him," I said, voice breaking. "Back there!"

"I can't see shit," Russell said in a low voice, growing frustrated.

"I swear, it's him. Back up the driveway—he's cutting through the yard!" I pleaded.

Russell groaned, "I'm trusting you on this, Lee."

The truck lurched as Russell pushed the gear into reverse, stomping on the gas.

I knocked into the side of the bed as the truck sped backward towards Carter. As soon as we started moving, Carter pushed himself to run even faster, racing towards us.

"Stop—stopstopstop," Jason called through the back window as we grew dangerously close.

I gripped the side of the truck as it slammed to a halt, but I still fell forward, bashing my shoulder against the truck bed. Ignoring the searing pain radiating down my arm, I scrambled to unlatch the tailgate with shaking hands.

"Come on, C!" Russell called out the window as he shifted the car back into drive. He clenched the steering wheel in his grip and I saw his eyes in the side-view mirror, begging Carter to run faster.

No sooner did Carter launch himself into the bed than Russell stomped on the gas, pushing the truck to its limits.

The engine roared along with the sound of crunching metal and beastly shrieks from the next street over as we raced down the dark street.

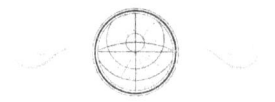

Jason's arm wrapped around my waist where we sat in the truck bed pressed against the outside of the cab, and Carter was just as close on my other side. We sat shoulder to shoulder, bracing against each bump in the road as Russell drove on into the night. Brian assured us that everyone else was able to get away in the SUV, so at least that was one worry I could scratch off the list.

It must have been at least an hour before Russell pulled into a parking lot, stopping next to a group of abandoned cars. We all exited the truck and convened in a small circle beside the vehicle.

"Everyone okay?" Russell asked.

His serious expression took me aback as he looked over all of us with concern—including Jason and me. Russell had been full of light humor since we first interacted, and while I could see his dedication to the group, I didn't expect to be included—at least not so soon. It was a warm realization I was more than thankful for.

"Yeah," Jason answered. "Overall, I think we're okay."

Carter's bare arm touched mine as he stood beside me and I automatically looked in his direction. My cheeks warmed as I realized I was still wearing his shirt. Though I tried not to stare, I noticed that the black and gray tattoos on his arms spread across his shoulders as well; there was more ink on his ribs, too.

Fumbling, I pulled the t-shirt over my head. "Sorry, I forgot," I muttered, pushing the shirt into his hands.

He accepted the shirt back with a stiff nod, pulling it on over his head before folding his arms across his chest in his usual closed-off stance.

"So, we need gas," Brian said, grabbing our attention. "This is as good a place as any to take a break and get the bags and supplies better situated. Then we can get you three back inside the truck with us."

The adrenaline wore off and exhaustion was starting to heavily weigh on every muscle as I nodded in agreement along with the others. Whether for lack of words or still coming down from heightened nerves, we silently stood in a circle for a few moments longer.

Sam was the first to break the tension. "How did it find us?"

Russell wrapped his arms around her waist, pulling her against his chest as he buried his face in her neck. "I'm getting really fucking tired of those shitheads crashing our camp," he said, voice muffled.

"It's not like we moved that far from where our last camp was located; I'm not surprised another one found us. They were bound to start branching out from the city area eventually," Carter answered. "I think it's time we accepted that this might be a regular occurrence we need to prepare for."

Carter and Jason updated the others on what they missed, including the way our tattoos illuminated as the creature grew closer. We debated what might have triggered the glow, but there was one thing I knew for certain—there was more to the connection between the marks and the beasts than we all initially thought.

"Damn," Russell said, raising his eyebrows at me after we finished recapping. "Bold move distracting it on your own, Lee, for real."

"Stupid move," Carter growled. "That thing all but had you. You could have been killed."

I narrowed my eyes at him. "You're one to talk. Drawing the creature away with *another* car trick instead of running with everyone else?"

"Yeah...that was too close for comfort," Brian said. "Also, Carter, we might need to rethink your weapons strategy, or we will quickly run out of working vehicles."

Russell snorted, failing to hold back an exhausted laugh. "I mean, Cap did say we should always use all of our resources, right?"

Carter rolled his eyes, but I saw the hint of a smirk.

"What happened once you turned the corner, Carter?" Jason questioned. "I heard the crash and…"

Carter stiffened, and I saw his Adam's apple bob in his throat. "Short version is, I used a brick from the driveway on the gas pedal to keep the car moving as I jumped out. Fucker must have some shitty eyesight—it ran right past me to keep pursuing the car. I didn't see what happened after that because I just ran."

"Damn," Jason replied. "Well, thank you for what you did. You put yourself at risk to give us all a chance to escape, including Alina. You didn't have to do that, but you did. That means a lot."

Carter shrugged. "Couldn't let it win that easily." His eyes flicked to mine before he turned to face the others again as we worked out logistics for the few tasks at hand.

We decided to divide the work between all of us. Russell and Brian worked together to siphon gas from vehicles while Carter and Jason reorganized the truck to make room for everyone in the cab. It would be a tight squeeze, but ultimately safer than having some of us continue riding in the back.

I worked with Sam to go through any unlocked cars in close proximity, and she told me about the books Carter and Brian brought back for her from the city. I could tell talking about the books was both a comfort and distraction for her, so I listened intently.

"Please tell me to stop at any time, but I really hope you don't," Sam said. "Okay, so my favorite book is the fifth book in the series—fourth if you don't count the novella. Considering the novella is over like, two hundred pages, I still count it. So in the fifth book, we get a story from Nesta's perspective," Sam enthusiastically explained. "She's this badass, take-no-shit kind of girl, but she also has to learn to cope with some pretty significant trauma. Her book is really about how she finds herself again and becomes her own source of strength. I just love her character arc," Sam gushed as we made it back to the others.

"And Nesta is..." I questioned, trying to keep up.

"Nesta is Feyre's bitchy sister," Russell jumped in.

"Hey! I won't have any Nesta slander in this group!" Sam lectured. "Especially from someone who has yet to read the first book. Not that Nesta's actions in the first book would *help* my argument—but still."

"Babe." Russell gave her an incredulous look. "I'm pretty sure I could tell Lee the full plot of the entire series by now. Probably better than you could."

His casual smile broke its way through as he laughed and pulled her closer, kissing her cheek. Try as she might to roll her eyes, she couldn't keep a straight face, either.

"I'm beginning to regret bringing back those books," Carter mumbled.

Sam punched Carter's shoulder and Carter threw his arms in the air, exclaiming, "Why do I get punched?" He gently pushed Sam back as she giggled.

"Because she doesn't want to risk any damage to my manly, God-like form," Russell answered, flexing his arms.

Before long, their petty banter had us all laughing. I sighed, relishing the tired ache in my stomach and the flood of endorphins that laughter brought.

Talking about something so inane after experiencing a life-threatening situation was completely bizarre, but for the first time that entire day, I finally felt like I could breathe.

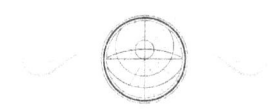

We drove through the night with Brian and Carter in the front seats while Russell, Sam, Jason, and I squished into the back. Jason had to sit at an angle to squeeze behind Brian's driver's seat in the small space, so I was practically in his lap. Sam was fully and unabashedly in Russell's lap, completely tangled in his embrace. Russell's muscular frame wrapped around her smaller body as they cuddled against the car's passenger side door. Every once in a while I heard a light snore from Russell, which was actually quite endearing.

I glanced down at Jason's arms clutched around me and realized how we must have looked with his head resting against the back of my shoulder. It didn't escape my attention how there was hardly a moment he wasn't checking in with me, catching my line of sight, or physically touching me when we were around each other. Aside from some innocent flirting as teens, friendly hugs, or an occasional kiss on the cheek, the lake incident had been the only time over the course of our entire friendship where we'd almost crossed that invisible, unspoken line.

Now, I wasn't even sure where we stood. After everything we'd gone through together, it was evident that everything changed, but into what? This had to be at least part of the reason why Emma turned so cold. Her fear of abandonment was all-consuming even before the invasion happened. I could only imagine how she'd see our interactions and interpret the implications. Jason stirred, holding me tighter in his sleep, and my heart leaped into my throat.

It appeared Carter had fallen asleep, as well. His arms were crossed over his chest as his head rested against the window. Even in sleep, he looked like he still had his guard up.

I caught Sam's eye contact as my gaze hopped from one of our companions to another, and she smiled.

"How are you holding up?" I asked quietly. Jason didn't even stir when I spoke, his breathing steady and slow.

Sam shrugged. "Is there a point past trauma? Honestly, I try not to think about any of it for too long. There's no point, you know? We can't help what will happen and when, so why dwell on it? We just have to find a way to keep going."

Russell stirred in his sleep, pulling Sam even closer as he nuzzled into the crook of her neck. I looked at the girl wondering what her life was like before. She had to be just out of high school. She should be going to college, getting tacos with friends, and curling up on a couch with her favorite books. My heart sank for the younger generations who would miss the rest of their childhoods and enter straight into an adulthood they never asked for, never getting to experience any of what they dreamed their life could be.

"How long have you two..." I trailed off, gesturing to Russell behind her.

A shy smile spread across her face. "I don't really know. It's one of those things that just kinda happened. We hadn't given a name to it—"

"It's called 'love', Sam," Brian interrupted from the driver's seat, flashing us a cheeky smile in the rearview mirror.

Sam rolled her eyes, but the smile didn't leave her face. "Well, whatever it is, we just decided to make it official as of..." she paused before saying, "yesterday."

"Oh!" I said, surprised.

"I mean, things started a while ago and have been building up since. We just figured it was time to call it what it was, what with life being short and all."

To hear Sam speaking with such finality struck me like a knife through the chest.

"You okay?" Sam asked as her warm, brown eyes studied me.

"I...yeah. It's just—you've been through so much and you're so young. All of you."

"I mean, it can be argued that so are you," Brian said, raising an eyebrow in the rearview mirror and giving me a pointed look. "I can't be that much younger than you."

"Why? How old are you?" I asked, amused.

"Twenty-six, turning twenty-seven by the end of this year. What are you, like thirty? I think Red said she was in her early thirties."

"Yeah, Emma and I are thirty-three."

"See, still young," Brian replied with a wink in the rearview mirror. "Those two next to you are the babies, though."

"Oh, give it up, already." Sam rolled her eyes, groaning. "I'm nineteen, closer to twenty. Russell is twenty-two."

A comfortable silence fell over the car for a few minutes until Sam shifted to lean closer to me. With her voice lower than before, she caught my attention. "And you two? What's the deal there?"

"Jason and I? We've been friends since we were kids, through Emma."

"Okay, yeah, I already heard that part. What's the real tea?" she asked with a raised eyebrow.

"No tea—just friends," I answered, knowing exactly how convincing I looked with Jason's arms wrapped around me.

Sam hesitated a moment before asking, "Can I give you some unsolicited advice?"

The corner of my mouth tilted upwards. "Sure."

"If you find happiness, don't hesitate." Sam looked at me knowingly. "We have such little control over everything else. Don't let anything, or anyone, stop you from taking happiness wherever you can find it."

I breathed a nervous laugh. "Are you sure you're nineteen?"

Sam settled back against Russell, smirking. "Just think about what I said."

TWENTY-FOUR
CARTER

"Just think about what I said."

Sam's words replayed inside my head long after she'd spoken them to Alina. If there was one thing Sam was good at, it was telling people exactly what they needed to hear without pushing an agenda. I should know; she'd done the exact same thing to me just the day before.

Sam warmed up to Alina particularly fast and I could understand why. In the short time since we met, Alina proved herself to be selfless (even if it resulted in recklessness), kind (almost to a fault), and patient (anyone who could last an afternoon with Russell, Brian, and Dan without losing it deserved a medal). I guessed it also helped to have a more approachable woman around who was closer to her in age.

Realizing the others had been silent for a while, I looked in the rearview mirror to check the backseat. Alina and Sam had finally fallen asleep, and a peaceful expression settled on Sam's face as she slowly breathed in and out.

Alina looked a bit more restless. She winced in her sleep and small whimpers escaped her lips. Nightmares were common for all of us, but it didn't make it any easier to witness someone else going through one. I remembered what she said earlier about nightmares and debated whether I should wake her. Usually, we tried to get whatever sleep we could, nightmares and all.

Not that it was my place to decide.

Still.

"Ah, so you're done pretending to sleep now?" Brian joked without taking his eyes off the road.

"Pretending? More like trying and failing," I answered, briefly looking over at him.

A crooked grin crossed Brian's face. "Sure, whatever you need to tell yourself."

I rolled my eyes and couldn't help checking the rearview mirror once more.

"So...Alina and Jason aren't together after all," Brian mused. "That's kind of a shocker."

My eyes darted back over to him. "And why are we talking about this?" I replied, quickly looking in the mirror once again to make sure they were still asleep back there.

"I mean, you were the one looking."

"What's that supposed to mean?" I growled.

"Chill, chill. It was just a joke," Brian said before a sly smile crept back onto his face, "Unless it wasn't..."

I glared at Brian, rolling my eyes as I faced the window. Of course, I couldn't help thinking about them once he'd brought up their situation. The conversation I'd overheard between Jason and Red this morning replayed in my head. It seemed the tension was rooted in jealousy on Red's part, but I didn't see what there was to be jealous about if Alina wasn't with Jason to begin with. Though right now, if I had to pick who I'd rather spend time with, I'd probably pick Jason over Red, as well.

Either way—that mystery would just have to unfold on its own.

There was a state park just over three hours west of Austin that Cap and I had been looking at as a potential location for our next campsite. It wasn't huge, but could be remote enough to provide some good cover and natural resources. Even if we didn't stay too long, it'd be a good spot to determine the next steps.

I didn't mind the fact that we would be camping outside, either.

When we were in abandoned neighborhoods or even the more urban areas closer to downtown, I couldn't help feeling suffocated by the empty buildings that loomed on the horizon. At least when I was surrounded by trees, I could temporarily forget about our lost city and embrace the nature that never left. It was comforting, like coming home.

Once we reached what we guessed was the halfway mark, I swapped driving responsibilities with Brian. Brian quickly fell asleep along with the others, leaving me alone with my thoughts. Though, as I drove, I found the quiet wasn't exactly what I wanted.

I checked on the four in the back once more before my focus fell fully to the road.

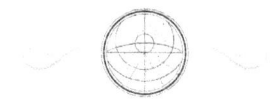

As we pulled into the state park, driving along the winding road through the campsites, the others started waking up.

"Are we there?" Sam yawned.

"Just about," I answered.

"Man, waking up when it's dark out is so disorienting," Russell groaned.

"At least we're still able to wake up," Jason answered.

"Alright, Carter 2.0," Russell retorted.

I rolled my eyes.

"What's that supposed to mean?" Jason asked, a mix of confusion and offense coating his words.

"Sheesh, you're grumpy when you wake up." Russell laughed. "It just means Carter is like, Mayor Gloom and Doom of our little Misfit Island. It's totally something he would say. That's all."

"Is it 'gloom and doom?' Or is it simply being realistic?" I asked, looking in the rearview mirror.

I caught Alina's eye as she stifled a laugh and heard Sam groan. I couldn't help the smirk that crossed my own lips.

"Alright—everyone quiet for a minute, I'm going to check in with the others," Brian said, digging out the walkie-talkie.

"Come in, this is Brian, over," he spoke into the device.

The walkie-talkie on the other end hissed static until a voice answered, *"Yeah—where are you?"* Red's voice buzzed through.

"Just turned into the park, do you know which campsite number you're at? Over."

"I think sixty-one. Over."

Brian paused, and I could hear annoyance creeping into his tone as he asked, "You think, Red?"

"Yeah. Just look for the SUV. It's by the lake. There's a dock. Can't miss it. Over."

"Thanks," Brian muttered as he lowered the walkie-talkie's volume and put it away.

I drove slowly with the brights on as we followed the winding road through the trees. The headlights bounced off the wooden signs, casting menacing shadows that faded into the darkness of the wooded trails. Our tires crunched over the dirt road and everyone kept quiet as we looked for signs indicating we were on the right path.

Finally, Brian spotted a sign for the lake and we arrived at campsite sixty-one. I parked the truck alongside the SUV and stored the keys in the sun visor, before walking around the truck to join everyone who had gathered.

"How'd it go?" Cap asked Brian as we all joined the circle. Michelle and Dan were standing beside Cap. Red stood a bit further back to the side, leaning against the SUV.

"Well, we got Carter back!" Brian gestured to me before continuing, "So, good, I guess."

"Good. What about the sedan?" Cap asked.

"Totaled," I answered, "Had to use it as a distraction."

Cap nodded stiffly and an awkward silence followed.

"Did any of you sleep yet?" Brian asked.

Dan shook his head before responding. "Too freaked out waiting for you guys. We were just discussing how we could probably just sleep in the cars, though."

Michelle continued, "We arrived about forty minutes before you did, but since there wasn't enough light to fully scope out the area, we decided against unpacking and setting up a separate sleep area. We managed to make some decent space in the SUV, though."

"We'll want to keep two people on guard at a time until sunrise," Cap jumped in. "That gives us eight people sleeping and two awake at a time if we do two-hour shifts."

"Well, I know Russell fell asleep first in our car. I was probably out soon after. Since we got the most sleep, we can take the first shift," Jason volunteered.

"I mean, I wasn't going to say anything, but since the cat's out of the bag." Russell shrugged in agreement.

"Sam and I can go after," Brian said. "Carter and Alina can take us through to sunrise."

"Well, that was easy enough," Cap said, sounding relieved.

Exhaustion was written all over their face and I could tell they needed a break. Brian and I took action to get the rest of the supplies situated in order to optimize sleep space. At the end, we were left with enough space for two people to fit in the truck bed, with three inside each vehicle. It wouldn't be the most comfortable, but at least it would fit eight people.

No one mentioned the unspoken part—the arrangement would also keep us conveniently close together if we ended up needing another quick getaway.

As soon as we finished organizing, Red opened the door to the SUV and claimed the back seat for herself. Everyone else trailed off one by one until only Russell, Jason, Alina, and I were left.

"Where should we watch from? Do you guys light a fire or use flashlights?" Jason asked, looking around.

Russell shook his head. "Nah, man. No lights. It would be like shining a big 'abduct me' sign over our heads."

"You should still hold onto two flashlights, just in case. If anything, you can use them as weapons." I handed Russell and Jason each a tactical flashlight. "But, to Russell's point, keep them off unless you have no choice. The bright light could temporarily blind you to the darkness your eyes are already adjusted to, just as much as it can illuminate the area. Don't go too far—nowhere near those trees, got it? Make sure you rotate around the perimeter, too, don't just stay in one spot."

"Don't worry, C, I can fill him in on the rest." Russell flashed a grin my way as he grabbed the flashlights, handing one to Jason.

"Are you sure you're going to be okay?" Alina asked Jason, hugging her arms across her stomach.

"Yeah, Lee. I'll be fine. I'm sure Russell is a pro," Jason answered, the corner of his mouth quirking upwards into a tired smile.

"Facts," Russell answered, holding out his fist for Jason to bump. "Alright. Sleep well, dudes," Russell said, tipping his flashlight in a salute as he and Jason walked away.

"I guess let's see what's open," I said. Alina nodded, following me as we checked the SUV first, then the truck.

Of course, as luck would have it, the only spot open was the truck's bed. We stood in front of the tailgate just a moment too long for it to be anything but awkward. Though I was used to sleeping beside random members of the camp at this point, I wasn't so sure Alina would be as comfortable.

"I can, ah, make Dan or Brian switch with you if you want?" I offered, rubbing the back of my neck.

"No," Alina hesitated. "No, everyone is exhausted; I don't want to cause more trouble." She gestured to the truck bed. "It's fine; there's enough space for both of us. Unless you don't want—"

"No, no, it's fine," I answered, realizing just how badly I needed sleep. It was getting harder to keep my head on straight and I was overthinking things that didn't warrant the extra time. I gestured for Alina to climb up first before jumping in myself.

We adjusted some of the bags before laying back. I made sure to keep a respectable amount of space between us as we tried to get comfortable.

I lay on my back, bending an arm behind my head to cushion against the hard surface.

Alina shifted, curling on her side facing the truck bed's wall, and using her folded arm as a pillow. Before long, she rolled onto her back, bending her knees up and stretching an arm underneath her head.

"Oh no, that was a completely serious statement," I replied, trying to hold back the hint of a smile.

Alina rolled her eyes mockingly, but an amused smile teased at her lips.

"Sure," she said before rolling to her back again, bending her knees and resting her hands lightly on her ribs, looking more relaxed than before.

"Really, though," I continued. "I'm too restless to sleep, so if you want to take advantage of a captive audience who won't interject..."

"Oh, I see your angle. You want me to bore you to sleep? Is that it?"

Caught off guard by her response, it was my turn to laugh. I saw her grin out of the corner of my eye, but kept facing the vast expanse of the sky. After a few beats, Alina started speaking again. "It feels like I've lived ten different lives in one week."

I didn't respond, letting her find the words.

"I was so relieved that Jason and I had each other after waking up. I kept thinking, 'At least we're together still. If nothing else, we aren't alone.' But I also felt so guilty.

"I worried about Emma. I still worry about my mom, brother, nephews, other friends—" Alina's voice broke as she took a breath. "Not that I think any amount of time could allow for someone to fully process...any of it. But the back-and-forth of being so incredibly thankful to not be alone, and the extreme guilt over feeling any relief at all...I still feel it pulling me in two different directions and I don't know how to make it stop," she finished.

I turned slightly to face her as she stared at the sky. I could practically feel the weight of the guilt she carried, pulling like gravity.

"And then we found you and Brian, and you brought us back to Emma. I can't even begin to explain what it felt like seeing her. I mean, what are the odds? I thought it for sure had to be a sign that we found our way. But now..." Alina paused. "I feel like I've ruined whatever solace she'd managed to find. Not to mention whatever mess these marks are causing. It's my fault—"

"It's not," I interrupted her starlit confession, shifting to my side so I could face her fully. I propped myself up on an elbow so I could steadily look down at her, catching her hazel eyes.

"It isn't your fault those things came back. How Red processes trauma isn't your fault, either. We've all been there, and you can't hold yourself responsible for how someone else deals with their own shit. I don't think the way Red reacted today was right, even if I understand where it came from. It doesn't mean you deserve to be the one she takes it out on," I said. The last part was for myself just as much as it was for Alina.

She studied my face for a moment before a slow smile spread across her face. "I thought you said no interjections?"

"Yeah, I did, didn't I?" I answered.

"So, my word vomit of woe *was* more engaging than burning balls of gas in the sky, then?"

"I think that's still up for debate," I replied.

Sinking back down to the truck's bed, I raised an arm behind my head. My limbs felt heavy in anticipation of sleep, but for once, the weight that had long pressed against my chest was lighter. I took a deep breath, feeling extra tension dissipate with an exhale.

After a few more moments of silence, I opened my eyes, turning my head to look at Alina. She was curled on her side facing me, half hugging the hoodie under her cheek. Her head rested in the cradle of her bent arm as she steadily breathed in and out. I watched her for a moment longer, remembering the way she was plagued by nightmares in the car, but any tension in her face had melted into a blissful calm.

The quiet was absorbed into the warmth of the summer night, and soon, I drifted off to sleep to the sound of her soft breathing.

TWENTY-FIVE
ALINA

The pain was all-consuming.

A sharp pinch bit into the middle of my spine as a long, thin instrument shoved between the vertebrae. Bright white light flickered around me, causing static spots to dance across my vision. I was blinded to any hint of what was happening in the room.

Hands.

Voices.

Something holding down my wrists and ankles.

Another sharp pinch. Pressure. An impossible pressure.

I desperately tried to see through the light, but the more I tried, the more my vision spotted.

A flood of unnervingly cool liquid pushed through the biting pain in my back and splashed down my spine, spreading throughout my body as paralysis took over. A fuzziness filled my head, and as darkness took my vision, my mouth opened in a silent scream.

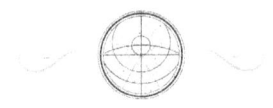

Alina, a voice murmured quietly, as something encased my hand in a protective warmth.

Alina, the voice said again, and a gentle flutter rolled from my chest to curl around my spine before wrapping around me like a warm blanket.

As I settled, shaking breaths broke, returning as soft sighs.

My muscles relaxed into the warmth, and I drifted into a quiet unconsciousness—still as a lake.

TWENTY-SIX
CARTER

"Alina?" I quietly said her name again, tentatively placing my hand over her tightly clutched fist. The blue from her tattoo reflected off the side of the truck and I swore it was even brighter than earlier. She tensed, all muscle movement seeming to freeze as another whimper escaped her lips. I felt her hand subconsciously squeeze mine back and the tension started slowly draining from her body. Her fingers loosened underneath my mine as her shaking softened into quiet trembles. Though her fists clenched every so often as aftershocks of panic rolled through her in her sleep, she seemed to be calming down. The reflected glow faded into nothing more than an afterimage and I almost questioned whether I truly saw it to begin with.

I lifted my hand slowly to avoid disturbing her, but as soon as I let go, her shaking intensified once again. She whimpered softly, only settling after I placed my hand back over hers.

Okay, no moving.

I inched closer so I could lie down more comfortably. The pull of sleep was calling, desperate for every second, but I didn't want to risk waking her by moving my hand again. I tried to maintain some space between us as I settled back onto my makeshift pillow, but we were noticeably closer than before.

If I wasn't so tired, I might have tried to find another solution, but I was past the point of overthinking.

My eyes closed and I fell asleep to the soft, rhythmic whispers of her breath on my fingers.

TWENTY-SEVEN

ALINA

I WOKE up to a gentle hand shaking my ankle.

I slowly blinked my eyes open and was surprised to see Carter's sleeping face just inches from mine. He held my hand cupped in his and his lips grazed my knuckles with each exhale. I felt my heart jump as I stared at how our hands were entwined before remembering that something else had woken me up.

I sat up slowly, gently unwinding my hand from Carter's and sliding further away. As I finally looked up, I saw Sam and Brian's grinning faces at the edge of the truck.

"Good morning," Sam whispered, batting her dark eyelashes.

I felt my cheeks heat as I threw them a quick smile.

"Morning," I murmured. "Is it our turn already?"

"We were actually going to let Carter stay asleep, but if you need more rest, too…" Sam replied casually.

"No!" I blurted. "I mean, no," I responded, lowering my voice. "Not necessary. I slept the whole time, so I'm good."

Brian held back a laugh, extending a hand to help me jump down from the truck. As I landed on my feet, I turned to look back and make sure Carter was still asleep. His arm stretched over where I'd been lying and I felt my cheeks heat again.

"So, am I on watch alone?" I asked, keeping my voice low, trying to hide my apprehension at the thought.

"No, you and I will be together," Brian clarified as we walked away from the truck. "Jason and Russell went kinda rogue with the schedule. They took three hours on the first watch together to give everyone else an extra hour of sleep. Russ stayed on another half-hour once Sam swapped out with Jason, too."

"I forced Russell to grab some sleep and tag Brian in about an hour and a half ago," Sam finished.

"O...kay," I said slowly, yawning. "I think I followed that."

"Alright, so you two are good?" Sam asked, holding back a yawn of her own.

"Yes." Brian pulled her in for a hug and kissed the top of her head. "Go get some more rest."

"Wait, before you go—where are the ladies..." I hesitated, not sure why the question felt embarrassing. Sucking it up, I finished my question, "Where are we peeing?"

"Oh! It's not too far, but I'll go with you. I know it feels awkward with the buddy system at first, but you'll get used to it," Sam answered.

After Sam escorted me and I did my business as privately as I was able, we joined Brian back near the cars.

"Shout if you need anything." Sam waved as she walked back towards the truck.

We watched as she pulled open the front passenger door, where I presumed Russell was already resting. I didn't bother thinking about the logistics of them both squeezing into one seat; they'd find a way.

Seeing the two of them together on the ride here, along with what I'd seen of Cap and Michelle's relationship, inspired more hope than anything else in the past few days. Call me a romantic at heart, but seeing love like that survive did more for my soul than I ever thought possible.

"Ah, young love," Brian joked, removing his glasses to rub the lenses clean against his shirt.

"I must admit, they are very cute together," I said as we started walking again.

"You say that now," Brian said through a laugh.

A smile crept across my face. "What? They're sweet."

"If you say so," Brian joked. A sly smile pulled at the corner of his mouth. "I'd rather talk about you and Carter."

My eyes went wide as I stopped in my tracks. "I swear, nothing happened. We must have gotten closer in our sleep and—"

"It's okay, I'm just teasing. There's nothing to defend." Brian laughed. "It was nice to see him relaxed for once, though. I swear, that man even scowls in his sleep."

Brian and I walked in silence for a while. As the sunrise grew closer, the dark shadows melted away, allowing the vibrancy of green trees to replace the tall, gray shadows that loomed over us at night. Streaks of deep red started mixing with the dark navy sky and clouds illuminated with bright oranges, hinting that morning would come soon. As we walked, I noticed wildflowers poking through the tall grass right up to the edge of the lake that stood still at the foot of the campsite. Every once in a while, the water's surface would break as a fish caught its breakfast.

The cars sat quietly in the middle of it all, reminding me of the many trips Emma, Jason, and I had taken to our lake throughout our youth. A pang of nostalgia stabbed at my chest as I longed for just one more carefree day—one more day to appreciate a quiet sunrise without terror and apprehension hanging in the background as a constant reminder that the peace wouldn't last.

We stopped walking as we approached the lake, sitting on the grass to the side of the dock.

"So," Brian said, breaking the silence.

"So," I answered. "What do we do now?"

"Well, we keep our eyes and ears open. We'll do a walk around the perimeter every fifteen minutes or so, which is really a guestimation since we don't have a watch or the walkie-talkies right now. Hopefully, we won't see anything and will just get to chill until the others wake up."

"Oh...I have to admit, I'm a bit nervous about that last part," I said quietly.

"Hey, listen, I don't presume to know Jason better than you do, but I can't see him getting mad about your sleeping arrangement."

"Wait, what? I meant I was nervous about seeing Emma," I responded, frowning. "As I said in the car, nothing is happening with Jason. We're friends. Only friends. Always have been, always will be." I raised an eyebrow at him. "You really need to get another fixation, dude."

"I don't know, Alina," Brian replied, his face growing more serious. "I've seen the way he looks at you."

"The way he looks at me?" I bristled. "Brian, I'm sorry to be the one to break it to you, but there's nothing there to gossip about. We almost died, like, fifty times—of course he's looking at me; he wants to make sure I'm okay. Plus, come on, we are adults—too old for 'he likes me, he likes me not' games, especially during an apocalypse."

Brian gave me an apologetic smile. "Sorry, I really wasn't trying to push. I guess my boundaries have kinda blurred when it comes to what's appropriate conversation these days. I really didn't mean to make you uncomfortable."

"Well, okay." I relaxed a bit.

We sat silently for a few moments before I started feeling guilty. While I knew it was valid to be frustrated, Brian was likely just trying to bond in some way. He'd been kind since we met and had been on our side since Jason and I joined the group.

"I'm sorry for overreacting," I said.

"Alina, please don't apologize," Brian responded.

"You aren't completely wrong, by the way—" I said softly. "About there being feelings when it comes to Jason. I'm pretty sure I've had a thing for him as long as I've known him. Emma knows it, too. It isn't like I've kept it from her. At the end of the day, though, we're friends. I wouldn't act on it. Not when I know how it would make Emma feel."

"Alina," Brian interjected. "You're adults. It's the end of the world. If there were ever a time to change up the way things have always been, this is it."

I nodded, letting the words sink in.

"Honestly, I'm not even sure what those feelings are anymore. Everything is..." I shook my head.

"Well, I won't say I'm the expert on *those* conversations, but if you want a sounding board, I'm here. I might be nosy, but I'm a good listener."

I stood up, brushing stray pieces of grass from the back of my shorts. "Well, enough talking about me; tell me more about you and the rest of the group."

I extended a hand towards Brian and he grasped it as he pulled himself up from the ground.

"Well, I think it's fairly apparent we are all a bit off our rockers in our own ways, some more than others. We argue. We joke. We have regular mental breakdowns. But overall, there's a lot of respect and care, too. We might not have all started together, but we've become a weird little family somewhere along the way. I love these folks to the end of the world." He said, waiting a moment before adding, "Hopefully, the actual end of said world won't be coming for a long, long time, though."

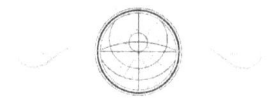

Brian and I continued talking for a while as we walked the perimeter. It was a cool morning, by Texas summer standards, and the sun was low in the sky, still climbing the horizon. Brian and I sat a few yards away from the cars while he explained in great detail how they usually went about catching fish.

As he continued his instruction, Dan walked over and plopped down next to us, laying his head in Brian's lap.

"Well, good morning to you, too." Brian laughed, resting an arm on Dan and gently squeezing his shoulder.

Dan grumbled, "I hate sleeping in cars."

"Well, you had a whole seat to yourself; that was nice, wasn't it?" Brian asked.

"Maybe if I actually got some sleep. You were snoring the whole time you were in there. Then, when Russell came back and passed out, he started talking in his sleep. I'm not sure what kind of heavy breathing sounds were coming out of Jason's mouth, but I legit almost checked his pulse before I got out of the car. Sam, as usual, was an angel, though. A quiet, peaceful angel y'all should take a lesson from."

I burst out laughing and Dan pushed back up to a sitting position as he said, "See, you get it, Lee."

He shot a grin my way, one that crinkled the corners of his eyes. Dan had been fairly quiet until this point, but I was beginning to see why he, Brian, and Russell were so close.

"You guys are something else," I said as my laughter died down.

"Well, since I'm up, Alina, I don't mind taking over your spot if you want to get some more rest?" Dan offered.

"Oh, that's sweet! Thank you, but the sun is already halfway up. I figure I might as well stay awake at this point. I'm actually feeling pretty alright. Brian and I had a nice therapy session earlier so—" My lips quirked in a half-smile as I glanced back over at Brian, who gave me a warm smile in return. "Brian, do you want the break?" I asked him.

"Nah, I'm good," he said, glancing at Dan.

"So, when do we start fishing?" I asked Brian.

"No," Dan said without hesitation. "Nope. Too early to talk about doing things. We are going to sit here until that sun is all the way up."

"Not a morning person, I take it?" I laughed.

"Nope," Dan replied. He stretched out in the grass, clasping his hands behind his head as he closed his eyes again.

My eyes shifted towards Brian, who was still contentedly looking at Dan sprawled in the grass beside him. Without saying another word, Brian lay down as well, a deep exhale leaving his lungs as he lounged on the grass.

We stayed there in silence as the golden glow of morning spread across the campsite. Even with how intense the previous night had gotten, I found that I felt more relaxed in that moment than I had in a long time.

I smiled, setting my sights on the horizon.

TWENTY-EIGHT
CARTER

I WOKE up to a sharp pain radiating down my shin, where a sneakered foot had struck me.

Groaning, I rolled over, arm knocking into the side of the truck before I remembered where I was. My eyes snapped open and I sat up, looking to my side to find that Alina had already gotten up.

"Over here, asshole," Red said, a scowl on her face. Her arms were crossed over her chest defensively and her red hair looked even more fiery with the rising sun behind her.

I groaned again, "What do you want?"

Red let out a frustrated huff as if I were inconveniencing her instead of the other way around.

"Well?" I asked, knowing fully well that my tone was less than friendly.

Red dropped her hands to her sides, annoyed already. "Can we talk? Seriously? Before you say no—it's because I want to apologize and I'd rather not do it where everyone else can hear."

I sat for a moment, feeling the muscles in my jaw tense. This was not how I imagined starting this morning.

"Yeah," I said. "Just give me a minute to take a piss."

As I walked to a spot by the trees, I noticed Alina leaning back in the grass with Brian and Dan. At least someone seemed to be having a better start to the morning.

Once I was done, I reluctantly made my way over to where Red was sitting on the dock. She didn't look up, even when the thudding of my boots reached her side. I stood, waiting for her to speak before she finally patted the spot beside her.

"Might as well have a seat before this gets even more awkward," she said.

I sat down, looking at her with a bored expression on my face.

Red made eye contact before quickly looking away and cursing, "Fucking, ugh, I'm so bad at this." She took a breath. "Fuck it—Carter, I'm sorry."

Red made eye contact with me and her expression softened.

"What I did wasn't right," she continued. "No matter how I was feeling, I shouldn't have assumed that I could use you to make myself feel...whatever it was I wanted to feel. More than that, I'm sorry I didn't ask you first. I didn't give you a chance to consent before I jumped you, and that also wasn't right. You've been a good friend the last few days. It really wasn't fair for me to do."

"Yeah, it was kinda fucked up," I said.

"Please, don't rub it in," she muttered. We made awkward eye contact again and laughed as the tension finally broke.

"Listen, Red, I'm only going to say this once, and then let's forget the whole situation ever happened. You're an attractive woman. You're smart, you're funny, you're a pain in the ass, and you're a good person underneath it all. I just don't want...that."

"I mean, you're not exactly my usual type either." She laughed. "You're hot and all, but honestly, I usually prefer women. If I'm being completely honest, you were the only *single* candidate around here who *actually* lived through most of the 90's, so..."

"Is that why you're so pissed at your brother and Alina?" I regretted the question immediately after it left my mouth.

"What?" She barked a laugh. "No. Not at all. I love Alina, but never like that. We've always been best friends, nothing more."

"But you *are* pissed at them?" I asked.

Red hesitated. "Yes? No? I don't know. My head is a mess. I swear, even Michelle is about to kick me to the curb, and she's, like, the most patient person I've ever met." She forced a stiff smile.

Before everything went down, Michelle had been a psychologist. She often got people talking before anyone else even knew there was something wrong. Looking back, it should have been obvious that Red was struggling; I just hadn't realized how much.

"I'm sure Michelle has had more difficult patients than you." I paused. "Though they were probably paying."

"Ugh, you are such a dick." Emma swatted my arm. "Michelle is my friend. I wouldn't force her to be my personal therapist. But, sweet, compassionate, stubborn angel she is—once she fights me into talking, I can't stop."

"Oh, so you've just been keeping everything bottled up otherwise? Very healthy. I can relate," I teased.

Red's face grew serious and she hesitated before speaking again. "Are you...okay? I mean, I know Sam has always been your person, your *only* person. You did a good job keeping your distance from anyone else—but that doesn't mean there weren't other people you cared about who might not...be with us anymore. How have you been holding up?"

"I try not to think about it," I answered, looking down. "That day was the most terrifying one I've experienced so far, mainly because I had something I was terrified of losing." I felt myself start to get choked up, but fought the feeling back down.

"Kid grew on me. She was practically my shadow when we first met the group and I just kind of got used to her being around. Then suddenly, I had this younger sibling I never wanted. Don't tell her I said that, though. She'll never let me live it down." I laughed. "But no, I didn't really get close to anyone else. Not that I didn't care—if anything, I learned just how much I *do* care about the rest of you fuckers. I guess what scares me is the fact that even though I tried so hard to keep my distance, it didn't matter anyway. If anything else were to happen..." I trailed off.

"I get that," Emma said as a sympathetic look ghosted across her face.

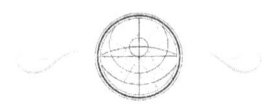

Surprisingly, the conversation with Emma put me in a better mood. By the time we joined the rest of the group, they were circulating a box of protein bars for breakfast.

"Oh man, I thought we could at least take a break from the bars," Dan groaned.

"Easiest way to start the day with some protein without dipping too much into the food supply. All the more incentive to try our best at foraging and fishing today," Michelle replied with a sympathetic smile.

"So, that's the plan for today?" Emma asked, putting her hands on her hips.

"Part of it," Cap answered, nodding. They were all business this morning. "This will be a good opportunity to help Alina and Jason learn some bushcraft basics. The goal will be to set us up with shelter and food for the next few days. Don't get too comfortable, though. If last night showed us anything, it's that we have to be ready to go at a moment's notice."

We discussed contingency plans, ensuring everyone knew what to do if we needed a quick escape, including where to meet up if we got separated. Once the most important processes were established, we started dividing up the tasks for the day.

The goal was to set a perimeter, get enough food for the day, filter and boil water, do some broader cleaning, and take stock of the weapons that were left. It was a low-stress plan, one where it would be easy to just turn off and work.

"Brian and Dan—y'all can set up the minnow traps. Take the mesh net out to see if you can catch some fish in the shallows, too. Don't forget about edible plants like cattails and watercress, either. I want at least three people to confirm identification before anyone eats any wild vegetation," Cap instructed.

"Aye, Cap." Dan saluted.

"Still not funny," Cap said, though we all saw the smile teasing at the corner of their mouth. "Russell and Sam—you will take care of weapons. Make sure all of the blades are sharp, that no handles are loose, and just general inventory of everything else."

"On it," Sam said.

"Jason and Emma, you're in charge of water for cleaning and water for drinking. We have that one galvanized tub in the back of the truck that was never unloaded yesterday. You'll want to set up the tarp, as well. Emma, make sure you take your time showing Jason each step."

"Yep," Emma confirmed as Jason nodded.

Cap turned to me. "Carter, take Alina with you to forage. I trust your plant knowledge, but expect you to follow the same rule as the others. We want to save our non-perishables as long as we can and take advantage of what we can find in nature."

I dipped my chin, acknowledging the task. Cap explained how they would establish the perimeter with Michelle, and I allowed myself a moment of distraction to glance at Alina and gauge her response. She nervously fidgeted with the belt loops on her jean shorts. Still, when Cap asked if there were any concerns, she shook her head along with the others, committing to her assigned task.

As the group broke up to start getting ready, I made my way towards Alina. Before I could grab her attention, Jason was there, tapping her on the shoulder.

"Hey, we didn't get a chance to talk last night. Can I grab you for a few minutes now?"

"Now? Um, Sure, I just—" Alina was interrupted when Emma burst into their bubble, grabbing Alina's hand.

"I need to talk to Lee first. Sorry, Jayce—best friend privileges," Emma said as she pulled Alina away from the group.

Jason watched them walk towards the dock, shaking his head. As he turned around, he wore a look of frustration across his face.

"Everything alright?" I asked.

He sighed. "Yeah, just Emma being Emma."

The corner of my mouth twitched upwards. "I'm guessing she's always been a tornado, then?"

He let out a quick breath of a laugh. "Don't I know it. I swear, she was born with a mission all her own and hasn't stopped pursuing it, since—no matter how wide the path of destruction gets."

Though his mood temporarily lightened, as he stared toward Emma and Alina on the dock, the muscle in his jaw ticked and his shoulders stiffened again.

I watched him for a moment before realizing that it wasn't frustration written all over his face—it was nerves. I searched for the right words before speaking again.

"I know it's hard to trust they'll be okay," I said. "Especially when it's been one disaster after another. From what I've seen, they're both strong, smart, capable—they'll be alright."

Jason looked at the ground, kicking his shoe at a clump of grass.

"Guess I'm that transparent, huh?" he replied. "I swear I've spent most of my life looking out for them, usually to stop Emma from getting them into too much trouble. After the last few days with Alina, though, I don't know, I realized it goes deeper than that."

I froze, eyes fixed on him as he continued talking.

"I really love her," he said quietly. "What a time for that realization, huh?"

His statement hung in the air around us as I watched him stare towards the two women on the dock.

Except, I realized I was wrong.

He wasn't watching over them.

He was only looking at her.

TWENTY-NINE
ALINA

"I'm just going to come out and say it—I've been awful, Lee," Emma said as soon as we hit the dock.

I opened my mouth to reply, but she held up a hand, stopping me before any words could come out.

"No—you're going to say that you understand and that *you* should or shouldn't have done something or other. None of it's you, Lee," Emma said, worry lines etching into her forehead. "You know I get so caught up in my spiraling. I was so happy when I saw you and Jason in that room—so relieved. It's like I got a piece of my old self back again. But then, I realized how different everything was. I remembered all the time that had passed and how alone I felt. I was so *mean*—I should have just been happy that my two favorite people were together this whole time. But I was jealous. And as always, that stupid green bitch got in my ear and I just spun out.

"I shouldn't have flipped out on you, though—full stop, no excuses. Most of all, I shouldn't have put any blame on you for what happened *to* you. And if that mark on your back *does* turn out to be a tracker, I'll stab those motherfuckers in the face before they can even think about taking you and Jason from me again."

Emma let out a giant sigh when she finished her speech, clearly relieved to have gotten it all out. She rarely apologized, mainly because she hated these moments, so I knew she truly meant it. I couldn't help smiling through the tears running down my face.

"*Damn*, I missed you, Em," I said as I wrapped my arms around her neck.

"I missed you too, bitch," she replied, squeezing me tight.

She breathed deeply, and when we pulled apart, she seemed to be standing taller, like a weight had finally lifted.

"Brand new start. Starting now. Fuck, after talking to you and Carter, I feel the need to officially declare today the start of Emma's Apology Tour '24. There's one more heavy hitter I have to speak to." She nodded in Jason's direction. "Jayce has been staring daggers at me since I pulled you away. At least his apology should be easier," she thought out loud.

"Wait, wait, back up. What happened with Carter?"

Emma groaned, "Basically, I burst into his room and started dry-humping him like a horny teenager with a mission to fuck myself out of my own head."

"Oh!" My eyebrows shot to my hairline. "And why would…that… require an apology?"

"Long story short—it wasn't what he signed up for. At all. Sure, he's a hot distraction, and I'm sure it would have been a good time, but he's also a friend, so—boundaries, I guess." She shrugged.

"Oh, girl." I shook my head. "I know we've always wondered what you'd do without me—but let's *never* allow the opportunity for Emma's 'burn the world to the ground' intrusive thoughts to take the wheel ever again."

Emma laughed, hugging me once more before wrapping an arm around my waist and leading me back to where Jason and Carter were standing.

Jason immediately perked up once he saw us walking back and his mouth curved into a slow smile. As my eyes shifted to Carter, I noticed his scowl had returned; a dark contrast to Jason's bright energy.

Damn. Just when I thought we'd turned a corner.

Jason started walking to meet us halfway, but Carter stood firmly in place.

"So, do I finally get to talk with Lee now?" Jason asked.

Emma rolled her eyes, but before she could answer, I shook my head, "I'm so sorry, Jayce. I know you wanted a proper check-in, but I really don't want to be the cause of a delay in our tasks for today. Plus, after last night…"

"Hey, it's fine," Jason said, tilting my chin so I could look up into his sky-blue eyes. "Later works, too."

Relieved, I replied, "Well then, I'm all yours once we get a break. Promise."

A soft smile curved his lips and his blue eyes stared into mine for a moment longer. He stepped back, running his fingers through his hair as he replied, "It's a date."

"Okay, you've staked your claim," Emma interjected, rolling her eyes. "Now, let's get to work. Oh! Before that—" Emma grabbed her brother's hands, turning him to face her. "I'm sorry. I've been a dick. I love you. Forgive me?"

Jason rolled his eyes and pulled Emma into a hug. "Yeah, I guess." He sighed. When they pulled apart, a genuine smile was on his face. He could never stay mad at Emma long, and she knew it.

"Alright. Bye, Lee!" Emma waved and started pulling her brother away.

Jason turned around once more to flash a smile at me before following Emma's lead.

I watched them walk away for a moment longer before finally turning towards Carter.

"Sorry for the delay," I apologized as I approached him. "Ready?"

"Yep," Carter mumbled with a complete lack of interest as he handed me a backpack. "Let's get started."

The bag felt light, but I heard a metal canteen clink against another solid object inside as I swung it over my shoulder.

Carter was a few paces ahead, and when I realized he wasn't slowing down for me to catch up, I jogged a few steps to meet his side.

"So, is there anything important I should know before we start?" I asked.

"It's more of a 'learn by doing' type of task," he replied.

"Oh, okay. Well, it's a good thing I'm a 'learn by doing' type of gal." I cast a smile his way, but his eyes remained fixed forward.

When I realized he wasn't going to say anything more, I nodded, gripping the straps of my backpack, silently following him into the trees.

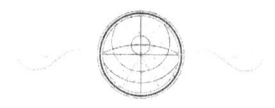

The hiking trails were exploding with overgrowth, but we wouldn't be relying on trails for our foraging expedition anyway. Experiencing another new environment was a bit overwhelming, but I was excited to learn something useful. Hopefully, learning would be the extent of the excitement for the day. If the past week had taught me anything, nothing stays calm for long, though.

The state park wasn't huge, but Carter still marked trees along our path to track our route. As Carter said at the beginning of the forest, *"Better safe than sorry."* Any extra efforts to ensure our safety were worth it.

As invigorating as it was to be immersed in undisturbed nature, the further into the greenery we ventured, the more tense I became. Carter barely spoke to me as we walked through the forest and I'd be lying if I said it didn't sting. No matter how often I caught up to his side while we walked, he always ended up a few paces ahead before long. After a while, I gave up trying to keep pace, trailing just behind him as he cautiously weaved through the trees.

When we spoke the night before, it felt like the ice was breaking, warming up to at least casual friendliness. The memory of entwined fingers and the gentle whisper of his breath on my hand bubbled up to the surface of my mind, and the back of my neck heated. Was that the reason he grew standoffish again? The moment was awkward, yes, but completely innocent. Still, I wasn't about to bring it up. For all I knew, something entirely different was on his mind—like what Emma told me earlier. Though, based on what I'd heard from the others, I suspected this hot and cold back-and-forth was something I should expect with Carter.

I sighed, shrugging away the thoughts as I tried to focus on the 'learning' part of the day. Carter patiently talked me through the identifying characteristics of each plant we found and what edible parts could be harvested. We'd already discovered a decent variety of vegetation that, until this point, I had written off as mere weeds. Who knew those garden suckers would one day be our next four-course meal?

After the first few demonstrations, Carter let me take the lead when it came to harvesting. I felt more at ease once immersed in the activity and found I actually really enjoyed the whole process. At least when I was distracted by leaves, roots, stems, and the occasional fruit, I didn't have to wonder why he was so avoidant outside of his instruction.

Still, I couldn't help weaving narratives in my head, constructing precisely what I wanted to say to him once he gave me the opening. New friends, teammates, or whatever label best fit our current situation—at least some baseline expectations needed to be set if we were to continue working together.

As we hiked through the trees, I noticed the forest growing denser with foliage. As a little kid, I'd often run through the garden in our backyard as I pretended to be Alice discovering Wonderland. I'm pretty sure my mom ran out of ways to dole out consequences for trampling so many flowers before I was even close to growing out of my Alice phase. It had been so long since I'd felt that warm spark of wonder that burst inside my chest. I took a deep breath, soaking in the moment.

After clearing a particularly low branch, I looked up, realizing Carter stopped moving. He froze, staring at something just out of my line of sight. My stomach flipped as I met Carter's side.

He placed a finger to his lips and gently pressed a hand between my shoulder blades, signaling me to lower to the ground. We crept through the brush until we found a cluster of bushes large enough to conceal us from immediate sight.

Every nerve buzzed with anxiety as I ran through the options of what he could have seen and the fact that I felt so far out of the loop. I strained to see farther, shifting to catch different views of the clearing in front of us through the branches, desperate to complete the picture. As we peered through the leaves, frustration and apprehension squeezed tighter with each breath and I finally realized it wasn't what Carter had seen that gave him pause—it was what he heard.

A twig snapped as brush crackled underfoot, followed by a soft dragging sound. The steps scuttled forward, stopping occasionally before starting right up again. It seemed so close, but I still couldn't see the source of the unnerving sound.

When it sounded like the creature should have been directly in front of us, Carter stood up, slowly creeping towards a break in the bush to get a better look. *What was he doing? Do I follow? Do I stay? Should I get ready to fight something?* I squeezed my hands, digging my nails into my palm to keep myself grounded while I waited for Carter to give me any indication of what the plan was.

He froze momentarily before his stance loosened. A crooked smile crossed his face as he chuckled under his breath. "Fucking armadillo."

An armadillo. An armadillo? I stood up just in time to see the animal scuttle off into the bushes, and the pressure of keeping my thoughts to myself finally burst.

"Awesome. Thank you for sharing that insight. It's nice to finally be looped in." Sarcasm oozed from my words as I glared at him.

Carter blinked. His head tilted to the side as he tried to process my sudden change in tone. "Uh, you're welcome? What's wrong? Are you disappointed we didn't run into another eight-legged monstrosity?" he tried to joke.

"Obviously not, Carter. I was *hoping* you'd have gotten past whatever grudge you held against me by now and would start looping me into what's happening—what I'm directly a part of right now! After last night—"

"Wait, what?" he interrupted, a look of pure confusion crossing his face.

I threw my arms up in exasperation before the rest poured out, "You refuse to wait for me. I've been trailing behind you this whole time like a lost puppy. You haven't spoken one word except to instruct me on how to do something—not even when there's potential danger! Seriously? I'm just supposed to *know* what you're thinking and guess what to do next? I mean, come on."

"Woah, slow down." Carter's expression shifted in surprise as he responded, "First off—there's no grudge to be held."

After pausing for a beat, I asked, "Then...why?"

Carter scrubbed a hand down his face, shifting on his feet as he tried to find the words.

"Well, we're in the woods, for one. I walked ahead to make sure we wouldn't run into any surprises. Since we were navigating through unknown territory, I thought being quiet was a given. I didn't realize..." Carter winced. "Shit, yeah, that must have looked bad."

My cheeks burned as heat crept up the back of my neck. Of course, there was a normal, logical, *necessary* reason for the silence and distance.

"Of course, it makes sense now," I muttered. "No, I'm sorry. I don't know why I was being so sensitive. That was dumb. I should have asked you sooner instead of stewing like an angsty teen."

"No, you're right to be upset. I fucked up," Carter replied, crossing his arms. "You specifically asked me if there was anything you should know before we went in. I didn't give you all the details. That's on me."

We stood across from each other, avoiding eye contact for a moment longer until Carter spoke again.

"For the record," he started, "right now, I'm only not talking to you because this is awkward, and I don't know what to do next."

I finally met his eyes, only to be met with a deer in the headlights. The lost look was so uncharacteristic of him that I couldn't help the laugh that exploded from my chest. After registering the change in mood, the corners of his eyes crinkled and a genuine grin spread across his face.

"Does this mean I'm forgiven and we can move on now?" he asked.

"Yes," I answered, wiping tears from my eyes, still feeling the squeeze of laughter hugging my ribs. "New plan, though. Let's review communication protocol, make a *verbal* list of our next focuses, and finish up so we can bring our haul back to camp."

"Good plan," Carter agreed, and I was relieved when his smile didn't fade.

THIRTY
CARTER

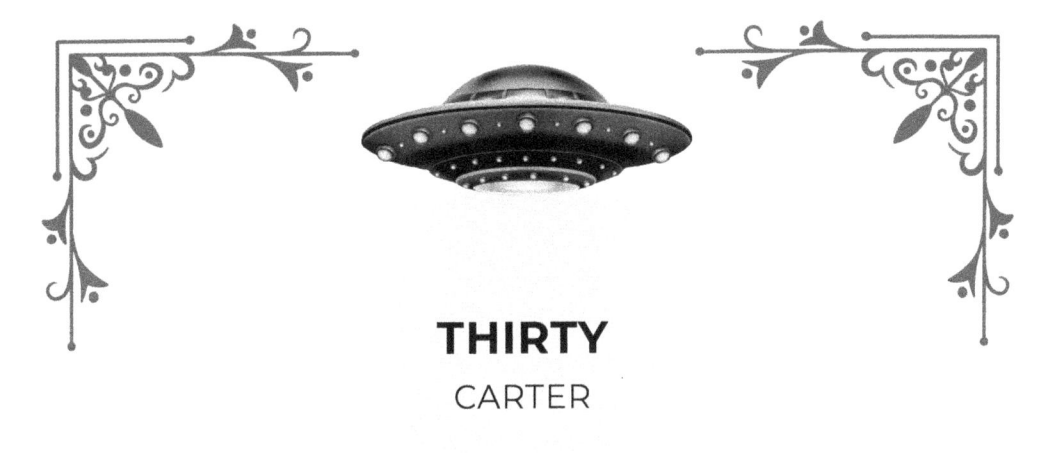

I couldn't believe I'd slipped up on something so vital. Nothing should have distracted me from properly preparing us, and I'd put us both at risk. At least Alina had good intuition and could follow someone else's lead—still. I needed to get my head back on straight.

Once we cleared up the confusion, Alina's mood noticeably brightened. I made more effort to loop her in, pointing out what to listen for when the woods grew quieter, explaining why we went in some directions and not others, and why certain plants needed specific areas to thrive.

"You know a lot about plants," Alina said as we made our way back to camp.

Our last find of the day was a patch of prickly pear cacti—a nice high note to end on.

"Yeah, I learned a lot from Cap. Back when the group was larger, Sam and I would go foraging with them a lot."

"Okay, I feel like Cap knows everything, somehow," Alina said.

I laughed. "I mean, kind of, yeah they do. At least when it comes to anything outdoors or survival related."

"Were they in the army or something?"

"No, they learned from their dad. He was some sort of survival enthusiast."

I thought back to the conversations I had with Cap when we were still getting to know each other. When Cap talked about their father, it sounded a lot like my childhood—the only way my dad knew how to bond was through teaching or making something with his hands. As a kid, I spent a lot of time shadowing my dad when he would let me, absorbing whatever knowledge and skills I could. I think that's one of the reasons why, right from the start, Cap and I were able to work together so well. We'd both been trained from a young age to observe, absorb, learn, do.

"Where'd you go just then?" Alina broke my train of thought, looking at me expectantly.

I shifted the bag on my back. "Just remembering some of the conversations Cap and I used to have."

"Used to?"

"In the earlier days, when we were still getting to know one another—I worked with Cap a lot."

"Everyone seems really close now," Alina added.

I nodded. "Yeah, seems that way."

"Is that not true?"

"No, it is."

"You are really good at answering questions," Alina teased.

I chuckled. "Let me try again. Yes, the group has gotten closer. It really didn't start until recently, though. Since Michelle and Cap are partners, I got to know Michelle through Cap. The Twenty-Somethings were always together, so when Sam gravitated towards them, I guess they just got used to me as part of the package deal. I didn't talk to Emma much, that is a more recent...Do I even call it a 'friendship?'" I thought out loud.

Alina laughed. "If Emma makes it a point to regularly interact with you, then yes. She probably counts you as a friend."

"Got it."

"It sounds like you all at least had some connections to each other throughout the larger group, though." Alina cringed. "Sorry, that wound is probably still raw. I didn't mean to pry."

"No, you're not prying," I replied. "Loss isn't really something that you can avoid talking about these days."

Alina nodded. She quietly glanced over at me as we walked. I waited, letting her think through whatever she was turning over in her mind, not minding the quiet breaks in conversation.

Finally, she opened her mouth to ask, "Did you lose anyone you were really close to?"

I let the question sink in before answering.

"Not from that group. It feels wrong to say out loud, but I'm glad I didn't know anyone else too well. It stung, losing so many at once. There were so many good people...but it could have hurt so much more. My family doesn't live around here, and after we lost power and cell service, I couldn't keep track of the friends I had in the area either. I don't know *who* I've actually lost."

"Yeah," Alina agreed softly. "I've been wondering about my mom, my brother, and his family. But once I start wondering, it's a slippery slope until I end up thinking about everyone I've ever met throughout the course of my life, and then it's just one big doom spiral."

I stopped walking, and Alina turned to face me.

"Listen, I'm really bad at this," I said, lifting a hand to rub the back of my neck, not exactly sure why I thought this would be a good idea. Still, I shoved down the hesitation and continued, "If you need to talk to someone who won't place expectations, judge you, or whatever—even if you just want to sit in silence. I'm...yeah."

Alina's face melted into a soft expression as her lips curved into a smile. "Thanks, Carter. And same goes for you. If you need me, I'm... *'yeah,'* too."

She couldn't hold back a soft laugh at her own joke and a half-smile spread across my face as any lingering awkwardness lifted.

"Deal," I responded.

Alina stuck out her pinky finger. "I mean, if you say it's a deal, you gotta seal it."

She raised an eyebrow, challenging me, and I shook my head, chuckling. *Fuck it*, I thought. Giving in, I looped my finger around hers and shook our joined hands.

"What...are you doing?" Alina asked as she shook my hand back.

"I'm shaking on it," I responded, letting go of her hand.

"Have you never made a pinky promise before?" she asked, her eyes glittering in amusement.

"I think the last one was when I was like, ten, so...it's been a while."

Alina rolled her eyes, grabbing my pinky with hers again. "For a regular pinky promises, you just link fingers. You don't *shake* it, though. For the really serious ones—" She stopped talking and brought her thumb to her lips with our fingers still joined, placing a small kiss on the back of her finger. "For the *really* serious pinky promises, you seal them with a kiss." Her eyes met mine and her cheeks flushed as she unlinked our fingers. "It might be legally binding at that point, though. Did you know that back in the day a pinky promise meant that if the promise was broken, you could cut off the other person's finger? Dark, huh?" she said, laughing nervously as she quickly turned around to start walking again.

"I'll...keep that in mind for next time," I replied before following.

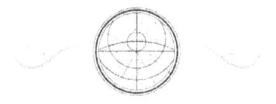

When we got back to camp, Jason and Emma strolled over to greet us.

"Here, let me get that," Jason said, extending a hand to Alina to grab the pack from her shoulders.

"Oh, thanks," she replied, shaking out her arms and cracking her neck.

"Where's my bag service?" I jokingly raised an eyebrow at Emma.

"Ah, no," she replied, batting her eyelashes before grabbing Alina's elbow and the three of them walked away.

Alina turned around to mouth, "*Later!*" as she flashed a peace sign.

I laughed quietly as she turned back around, and the three of them meandered over to drop the pack off with the other food supplies.

The sun was high in the sky and it must have been just after noon. All-in-all, it had been a pretty decent morning. I found myself smiling as I thought about it all. Before I could fall too deep into thought, my stomach growled. It had definitely been a while since that morning's protein bar.

I spotted Dan and Brian cooking over a fire and decided to head their way. As I approached, the scent of smoked fish wafted towards me. Minnows and crickets sizzled in a pan while cattails, watercress, and some duckweed bubbled between two pots. I stopped overthinking our meal combinations a while ago, but this concoction didn't seem so bad as far as soups go. Plus, thanks to finding the patch of prickly pear cacti, we'd have nopales, too.

Brian pulled a round, almost blue-tinted egg from a carefully wrapped bag, cracking it over the soup.

"Duck egg?" I asked. "Isn't it a bit late in the season for those?"

Brian shrugged. "I'm not questioning it. There are thirteen! We're gonna eat good this afternoon!"

"Don't tell Michelle there were thirteen, though," Dan added.

I chuckled. "Why not?"

"She has a thing with thirteen. Says it's bad luck." Dan shrugged.

"Taylor Swift would say otherwise," Brian added nonchalantly as he stirred the soup. After a moment of silence, his brow wrinkled in thought. He looked up at us and asked, "What do you think happened to all of the celebrities, anyway?"

Dan stood up, ignoring Brian's question, asking, "How did the plant hunt go?"

"Good. Found the usuals—lots of purslane. We were also able to grab some wild grapes and low-hanging persimmons. We'll definitely have to go back and climb for some more fruit tomorrow. We brought back some nopales, too."

"Hopefully with less stabbing compared to last time?" Brian teased, looking up from the soup.

"Yeah, I learned my lesson. Between the tongs to hold the cactus and my lighter to burn off the smaller spines, I think they're in good shape. They still need to be peeled, so don't stick your hand in the bag yet; just in case," I answered.

"How did the fruit look?" Dan asked, glancing down at my bag.

I opened the top of my pack, tilting it so the wine-red, prickly pears were visible.

"Nice," Dan said with appreciation.

Brian set the pot of soup on the ground so it could cool down away from the fire and the three of us got to work skinning the nopales.

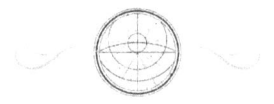

The rest of the day went by quickly. With the end-of-day activities quickly taken care of, we found ourselves with some extra time on our hands.

Sam and Alina read while Russell, Dan, Brian, and Jason trailed off to the water's edge to look for crawfish. It was pretty late in the season, so I doubted they'd find any. Something told me they didn't really care one way or another. The sound of their intense debating carried across the warm evening breeze. I caught the names, "Taylor Swift…Beyoncé…Nick Offerman," and assumed they were likely circling back to Brian's question about celebrities from earlier.

Michelle and Cap laughed as they chatted with Emma, all three of them seeming lighter than they had in days. I watched each of the members of our group, a feeling of contentment slipping over me as I shifted my gaze from one cluster of people to another. I debated leaning back and closing my eyes, when Sam threw a pebble at my foot.

I looked at her, raising an eyebrow.

"Put those hawk eyes away and come chill, geezer," she teased.

Alina looked up from her book. "Hawk eyes?"

"Yep. Can't stay off guard duty for even ten minutes, that one," she responded, a look of challenge forming on her face.

A sly smile pulled at the corner of my mouth as I got up, closing the small distance that separated us. Neither woman moved, choosing to peer up at me from where they sat, books still in hand. Before they could react, I snatched the red book from Alina.

"Hey, I was reading that!" She laughed, jumping up and reaching for the book.

"You barely made a dent in it," I said, holding it higher in the air. "I promise, you won't even notice it's gone."

Alina jumped for the book again, crashing straight into me.

"Again? Really?" I laughed as I stumbled backward, dropping the book as I caught her waist to steady us both before we could topple over.

"What can I say, Carter? You have a knack for sweeping me off my feet," she retorted, sarcastically sweet. She caught Sam's eye and the two dissolved into laughter again.

Chuckling, I let my hand slip from her waist. "Smooth," I joked back, rolling my eyes, still wearing an amused grin.

"What...did I just witness?" I heard Russell's voice before I saw him. He was standing just behind Sam, who was still recovering from her laughing fit. He grasped at his heart in mock astonishment. "Was Carter actually...having fun? If the end of the world didn't already happen, this would for sure be a sign of the apocalypse." Nerves crept into his voice as he asked, "Could there be more than one apocalypse?"

"Listen, Carter, if you wanted to read about faeries, all you had to do was ask," Sam said, a smug look plastered on her face as her remaining giggles died down.

"You know what? Maybe I do," I said, sitting down across from her. "I've always wanted to be part of a book club. You've talked about these books nonstop, so maybe I *am* curious. I think it's about time we all discovered what this *'Avatar'* is all about."

"One, it's *'ACOTAR'*, as in, *A Court of Thorns and Roses*. Two, I'm calling your bluff. You want a book club? You're reading first." Sam nodded towards the book on the ground, a challenge in her eyes.

I snatched the book from where it lay, declaring, "I accept your challenge, kid."

Sam leaned back against Russell, who had joined her on the ground. She folded her arms and snarkily replied, "Good luck."

"Why would I need luck?" I muttered as I opened the book. Flipping through the pages, I landed on a map. "Pry-*thigh*-an?" I muttered, sounding out the word as Sam burst into laughter again.

"Oh, this is going to be good." She snickered.

THIRTY-ONE
ALINA

"So, there I was, wasted and stuck in a tree, and I couldn't for the life of me remember how to get back down. The bars had all closed a few hours prior and it was nearing four in the morning. Now, you have to remember that it was almost a decade before everyone was practically born with a cell phone in their hand. Thanks to my overprotective parents, I was one of the privileged few who had a cellphone bestowed upon me. I beat that little Motorola flip phone into the ground, too! It wasn't until I completely snapped it in half that it stopped working.

"Well, I just started calling down the list of names in my phone book until finally, my dialogue partner for Spanish class answered." Michelle paused her story to smile adoringly at Cap, squeezing their hand. "It was a Wednesday, so like any other *normal* person, they were at home and sober." She paused again, thinking. "Well, technically, by that point, I guess it was already Thursday...Anyway—they hopped right in their car, drove on over, and climbed up that tree to help me back down. It was history from there."

Cap tilted Michelle's chin from where she rested against their shoulder and kissed her softly. Michelle turned back to us, glowing in the firelight.

"Honestly, I should have sent my ex a thank you card after all that," she continued. "If he hadn't cheated on me, I wouldn't have been drinking alone in the park. Nor would I have decided that the answer to all of life's problems was to climb a tree."

Though we planned on turning in for the night once the sun went down, instead, we found ourselves around a small campfire sharing stories from The Before—as our past had officially been dubbed.

"Fuck him," Cap said, eyes still on Michelle as if she were the most valuable jewel.

"I'd really rather not," Michelle deadpanned before chuckling at her own joke, the rest of us quickly dissolving into laughter alongside her.

The way they looked at each other, they were absolutely the two luckiest people on the planet.

"Well, alright, kids," Cap said, wiping tears of laughter from their eyes. "We should get some rest before it gets too late."

"Cap! Don't you go starting with the 'kids' thing, too!" Russell groaned from across the circle.

"Yeah—" Carter smirked. "That's my thing."

"Because you're like an eighty-year-old grump stuck in a mid-thirty-year-old man's body," Sam snarked right back, holding up her hand for Russell to high-five.

Everyone was in a light mood as we cleaned up the campfire area and started getting ready to turn in for the night. Michelle read out our night-watch times and partners. When she called Jason's and my name together, I realized the two of us still hadn't talked. Once the plan for the night was set, I grabbed Jason's arm.

"Hey," I said. "Should we..." I gestured towards the dock.

"Yeah, better go now before someone steals you away again." Jason winked, a casual smile gracing his face.

I rolled my eyes, laughing. "Alright, come on."

We didn't speak as we approached the water. When we reached the dock, I sat against one of the posts. As I waited for Jason to sit across from me, butterflies awakened in my stomach with a frantic fluttering of wings. I shifted, biting my bottom lip.

"Nervous? I swear it's nothing bad," Jason said. "Probably should have led with that."

"No, it's just—it kind of feels..." I exhaled sharply. "It's stupid. Forget it."

"Whatever it is, you know I don't judge," Jason replied, his blue eyes reflecting the moon's silver light.

"Does this feel like déjà vu to you, too?" I finally admitted, punctuated with a nervous laugh.

Jason stilled for a moment before a grin crossed his face. He pushed a hand through his hair as he rested back against the post on the opposite side of the dock. Subtle sounds from the rest of the group getting ready to turn in for the night carried across the short distance and I tried not to get too distracted.

"The lake?" he asked.

The back of my neck grew warm as I nodded.

"Yeah..." Jason stared out at the lake, his grin relaxing into a soft smile. "Yeah, it really does."

"A lot's happened since then, hasn't it?" I murmured.

"You know, looking back, I realized—" Jason paused. "...Do you remember when my engagement to Sarah ended?"

The light flutters in my stomach graduated to galloping in my chest as I nodded slowly.

"I should have cut it off when she told everyone we were moving to California for her job without even talking to me first. It was the start of the end. I had zero ties there; everyone important to me was on the opposite side of the country. The longer we stayed, the more distant Sarah and I grew. By the end, we were more roommates than an engaged couple.

"And then, when the plane landed and I got to baggage claim and saw you and Emma waiting—I'd never felt so relieved. Just seeing the two of you standing there holding up that stupid sign—"

"Ding-dong, the witch is dead," I said in a sing-song voice, laughing at the memory.

Jason chuckled. "And you. Your hair was bright blue—"

"Yeah, not my finest moment," I mumbled, pushing an errant piece of wavy hair behind my ear.

As I looked back over to Jason, his eyes met mine, a new intensity crackling across the space between us.

When he spoke again, his voice was lower. "Which is wild because I never thought the color blue looked as beautiful as it did when I saw you that afternoon. You know, I've thought about the night I came back home a lot over the years—probably more than I should be admitting."

"And then at the lake, when Emma left to sleep it off and it was just you and me? You would smile, and man, that smile." His eyes flicked down to my lips before meeting my gaze again. "It's like, suddenly, everything just felt right again."

I froze as I tried to process Jason's words. "Jason..." I said, voice barely above a whisper. I shifted to sit on my knees, trying to find the right words.

Jason moved across the dock. Everything froze as he knelt next to me, tenderly taking hold of my hand, grazing my fingers with his thumb.

"I should have told you then," he murmured.

His eyes flicked down to my lips as his other hand gently cradled my cheek. My eyes closed, and I felt his breath ghosting across my skin, the heat from his chest nearly touching mine.

"Oh! Shit. Sorry!" a voice yelped.

I jumped, nearly falling back into the post as Jason shot to his feet.

"Fuck, Emma, maybe announce yourself first?" he sputtered.

Emma raised her eyebrows, deliberately making a show of looking around. "You...do realize we are in the middle of motherfucking nature?" She gestured to the camp behind her. "Honestly, you probably should be paying more attention to your surroundings—like right now." She gestured to me, still on my ass where I'd fallen backward, unable to do more than stare dumbly at the bickering siblings. "For the love of anything still holy, help her up, dumbass."

"Shit," Jason muttered under his breath, extending a hand to help me up, wrapping his arm around my waist as I rose. His hands shifted to my hips, prompting me to face him as he spoke quietly. "Maybe we can continue our conversation later? Again?" A hopeful look crossed his face, the blues in his eyes so cool they almost looked silver in the night.

I nodded, finally able to force a response. "Yeah-yes, sure."

Emma cleared her throat loudly. "Jayce, why don't you grab a spot for us inside one of the cars? Russell and Sam already claimed the truck bed, before you get any ideas."

Jason glared at his sister. Noticing the tightness in his stance, I touched his arm, pulling his attention back.

"Hey, it's okay," I said quietly. "I'll walk with Em and we'll talk later."

"Okay." He gave in, squeezing my hips once more before he reluctantly let go and started walking toward camp.

Emma grabbed his arm before he could pass her, pushing a finger against his chest. "And don't think I won't be speaking to you at some point, as well," she warned.

"Whatever," Jason muttered.

As Jason turned to walk away, I saw the soft glow of his blue tattoo underneath his white shirt. I made a mental note to bring up the 'heightened emotions' theory, later. Preferably in the light of day once I could form cohesive thoughts again.

I slowly approached Emma's side as Jason gained distance. My heart still pounded in my chest as I swallowed, trying to restore some moisture to my dry throat.

Once I reached her side, Emma snapped her attention to me, grabbing my hands.

"Holy shit," she gasped, eyes wide. "What did I just walk in on? Oh, by the way, you're also glowing so you're going to have to tell me everything. Walk slowly and talk fast." Emma linked her arm through mine as we walked at a snail's pace.

I told Emma everything Jason had said, right down to the last word. I didn't see the point in keeping anything from her, especially considering she'd caught the end of it anyway. I couldn't help the twinge of anticipation that danced in my stomach. Though the timing couldn't be worse, I had literally dreamed of this moment for how long, now?

"It *would* take an apocalypse for that idiot to come to his senses," Emma muttered once I recapped everything.

I couldn't help the laugh that burst past my lips.

"Em!" I hissed, lowering my voice. "I'm pretty sure his respect for *our* friendship also played a large part." I raised an eyebrow, pointing a finger between us and daring her to object.

"Sure, fine. Whatever." Emma paused before rolling her eyes in exasperation. "Ugh, okay, you're probably right. I'll give that theory merit—Old Emma would one hundred percent be freaking out. Post-Alien Invasion Apocalypse Emma? I mean, she's still freaking out, but that bitch is *here* for it. You two could totally beat out Russell and Sam for Best New Dystopian Couple of the Year." She batted her eyelashes, mock sweetness coating her last words.

I rolled my eyes at her. "Okay, let's not get ahead of ourselves. This isn't exactly the environment to start anything. Who knows how much time we'd even have?"

"Depressing, much?" Emma scoffed before her expression softened, her voice turning serious. "I get it, though." She stopped walking and turned to speak face-to-face. Grabbing my hands, she said, "To use your own words, who knows how much time we have?" She pursed her lips into a tight smile, lightly squeezing my hands before letting go.

I knew in a way, Emma was right. We never knew what the next day would bring. I couldn't help feeling like I was running in place, trying to move forward in a world that stopped eight months ago.

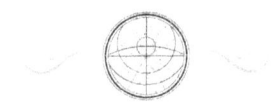

Half of our crew already settled into their chosen sleep spaces. The truck and SUV were parked parallel, facing opposite directions, with the driver's side doors open on each vehicle. The setup created a kind of boxed-in area between the cars. With all the windows down, it allowed for a cross-breeze so we wouldn't overheat, without leaving us completely open.

Russell and Sam were, just as Emma said, curled in each other's arms in the back of the truck. I couldn't help smiling as I heard the two softly whispering to each other, quiet laughter drifting over the sides of the bed.

"You should take the backseat, Lee," Emma suggested as we approached the passenger side of the truck. "I had a whole backseat to myself last night, plus I have the second shift for night-watch, anyway. You might as well take advantage of getting a longer sleep in a more comfortable spot."

"Oh, are you sure?" I asked Emma.

"Positive." She slapped my butt as she opened the door. "Take your spot before I change my mind, bitch."

I couldn't help rolling my eyes at her, even as a smile crossed my face. I wrapped my arms around her neck, pulling the tiny woman into a tight hug. "Love you, bitch," I said affectionately.

"Love you too, Lee," Emma replied with an uncharacteristically soft smile.

As we crawled into our seats, Emma scrunched her nose, giggling. "It's like the sleepovers we used to have as kids! Except in a car! And... there are *actually* monsters hiding in the shadows. Oh—" She scrunched her nose. "Definitely not as funny when I say that out loud. Anyway. Night!"

Jason laughed, shaking his head at his sister. "Alright, weirdo. Sleep well, Em." He turned to face me in the backseat, reaching back to squeeze my knee. "Night, Lee."

"Night," I murmured, squeezing his hand before he let go and faced forward again.

As I shifted, trying to find a comfortable position without falling off the seat, I felt a pair of eyes on me. As I looked out of the open car door, I realized Carter was in the driver's seat of the truck, facing the back seat of the SUV where I was laying. The open car doors created a kind of hallway between the vehicles, and the corner of his mouth quirked upwards when my eyes tracked across the narrow space to meet his own.

"I was going to say that's probably an upgrade from the bumpy truck bed last night, but now I'm not so sure." He smirked.

"Yeah, I might have to agree, there," I said in a soft voice. My cheeks warmed as I realized what I'd said and just how I'd woken up this morning.

The corner of Carter's mouth twitched in amusement. "Get some good sleep. By the way, you're with me in the woods again tomorrow."

"Oh," I breathed, not realizing the schedule was already set.

"See? I'm doing better with communication already." He smirked again. "There's hope for me, yet."

I laughed softly. "We'll see."

I curled on my side, folding an elbow under my head.

Somehow, I managed to fall asleep, mind swirling with words both spoken and yet unsaid.

THIRTY-TWO
CARTER

Mornings were spent foraging with Alina, teaching her about the local vegetation, testing her knowledge, and convincing her to learn how to hunt. The last part wasn't going well.

"Carter, I don't care how many cricket shish kabobs I have to make; you won't convince me to kill a small animal," Alina hissed as loud as she dared raise her voice.

Over the last few days, we'd established a modified system for communication and exploring that worked for us. While our time in the forest was a bit more conversational than I was used to, we were actually starting to make a decent team. I started looking forward to our routine each morning.

"And don't you dare smirk! I see the corner of your mouth starting to do that little...tilting thing." She put a hand on the curve of her hip, throwing a stern look my way—well, trying to, at least. She was barely holding back her smile.

I snickered, trying to keep my own sound on the quieter end of the spectrum. We were supposed to be camouflaged, blending in with the surroundings so I could teach her how to catch rabbits.

"What tilting thing? What does that mean?" I was barely holding back my own laughter. "Alina, I'm not sure you even know what you're arguing anymore."

Her face strained against the serious expression she was trying to maintain, but ultimately, her laugh won out. She doubled over, cackling.

I couldn't keep from grinning, either; her laughter was infectious.

She caught her breath, arms cradling her stomach. "Okay," she panted. "Okay, I'm good now. I'm good," she sputtered through the last few bursts of laughter.

I raised an eyebrow at her, still wearing a crooked smile on my face.

"Well, there you go, that's a start!" she said in a cheery voice, gesturing in my direction. "Half a smile! Now we just have to get the other half to follow." She grinned, the singular dimple on her left cheek highlighted by her wide smile.

I chuckled, shaking my head. "Next time, I'm leaving you back at camp."

"You wouldn't dare."

"Wouldn't I?"

"I...hope not?"

"Nah, you're right," I confessed. "It's too much fun beating you at your own games."

Alina scoffed, rolling her eyes, still light from her previous burst of laughter.

As we moved through the trees, the humidity grew thicker. The sky wasn't yet heavy with gray storm clouds, but it was only a matter of time. While I was looking forward to the inevitable break from the heat, if rain was coming, we'd have to find a spot farther from the lake to stay safe from lightning.

We knew there was a ranger station up one of the roads running past the campsites, but we hadn't ventured that far, yet. Most of our exploration was on foot since we couldn't waste gas taking the truck or SUV to a location that hadn't been vetted. Cap and Michelle happened upon a trail map yesterday that marked the distance between our campsite and the ranger station—three miles away. So, at least now we were able to seek it out with some more direction.

It made sense why we didn't hit the station in our exploration, yet. We had been very conservative with how far we pushed camp boundaries and exploring beyond that border, even when Alina and I were foraging. Today, though, Cap and I would hike to the ranger station.

"How much longer do you think we have?" Alina asked, breaking the silence.

"We can probably hit the persimmon tree before we have to double back."

Alina nodded. "How far do you and Cap have to go, again?"

"According to the sign, it's about three miles. Not so bad. Even if we take our time, it will likely only take an hour and a half max to get there with just the two of us."

"Why can't you just take a car then?" Alina asked.

"Well, for one, that would take a vehicle from the larger group. If the rest of you needed to make a break for it, it would be much harder and more dangerous to try and fit everyone and everything in one car. Second, we don't know what we will find there. Cars are loud, and if there are any hell-creatures, or even a bad group of humans, we don't want them hearing us before we see them."

"Right," Alina agreed softly.

After a few more quiet minutes, Alina asked, "How long do you think you two will be gone?"

"Worried you'll miss us too much?" I teased.

Alina rolled her eyes. "No." She paused. "Well, kind of, actually."

She was biting her bottom lip again, a habit that I realized after spending so much one-on-one time with her, meant she was imagining a world of different outcomes in her head.

"Hey," I said, grabbing her attention. We stopped walking. "Do you know why Cap and I are going?"

"Why?"

"Because we are the best at this—vetting locations, moving silently so nothing hears us coming—we might as well be our own special ops team at this point."

Alina smiled, but it was forced. She started to look down at the ground and I touched her arm to steal back her attention.

"Everything will be alright. I mean it."

"Promise?" she half-whispered.

I held out my pinky, and she stared at it for a moment before that soft laugh slipped from her lips. She locked her finger with mine, holding it there, waiting. I lifted our hands and we leaned in to kiss our thumbs at the same time, my eyes locked with hers.

"Promise," I murmured.

She studied me with those hazel eyes until she was satisfied with the truth she saw.

"Okay," she said.

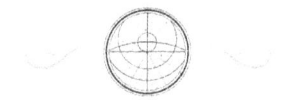

On our way back, we found a rabbit caught in one of the traps we'd set, and I was relieved we didn't have to put it out of its misery. As much as I thought everyone in the group should learn the basics of hunting and trapping, that didn't mean I enjoyed any part of it.

Once we returned, I looked for Cap and found them talking quietly with Michelle. Not wanting to interrupt, I waved so they knew I was back, then stepped off to the side so they could finish their conversation.

"I hate when you have to leave," Michelle said.

Even from this distance I could hear the waver in her voice. Michelle did a good job of putting on a brave face and positive outlook to keep the group's motivation high, but it was her unabashed vulnerability that made me realize just how strong she was.

"You know nothing could ever keep me from you for long," Cap replied, rubbing Michelle's arms as they pressed their forehead to hers. "And I always come back, don't I?"

"Well yeah, obviously," Michelle scoffed. "It doesn't mean it gets any easier. I'll still always count the seconds until you're back with me."

"I know," Cap murmured. "Me, too."

After Cap and Michelle finished their goodbye, Michelle walked with Cap to meet me.

"And you," Michelle said, squeezing me in a big hug. "Be careful. I know I don't have to tell you, but I still need to say it. Take care of each other out there, and make sure you check in every hour."

"Will do. Thanks, Michelle," I replied.

She squeezed me once more for good measure before turning around, no doubt still crying.

Though Cap had been sent on similar trips, often with me on their team, it seemed to get harder for Michelle to let them go each time. I didn't blame her. After a while, it was hard to look at any good luck and not wonder how much longer it would last.

"You ready?" Cap asked, slinging their bag over their shoulders.

I nodded and we walked towards the trails, waving goodbye to the others as we set out.

I looked back over my shoulder as we left and caught Alina's eyes still on us. She gave a half-hearted wave, not even bothering to mask the worry written all over her face.

I wondered if these goodbyes would ever start getting easier.

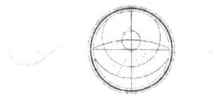

The trip through the forest was uneventful. Quiet.

We kept to the tree line as we approached the ranger station, surveying the area for any unwanted surprises. The squat log-cabin-style building was planted in the middle of a clear spot of land not too far off the hiking trail and didn't look big enough to have more than one or two rooms. There was a small porch out front, shaded by the overhanging roof. The door was wide open, not even a whisper of sound rolled across the stretch of grass.

We took the opportunity to rest just past the tree line as we scanned the area, making sure we didn't miss any red flags. I pulled a water bottle from my pack and drank slowly. The water was warm, but as the liquid rushed through my system, it still felt like I was being resurrected after melting in the heat on the way here.

Cap knelt by my side without a word, but our routine was solid; we didn't have to communicate out loud to understand what came next. The familiarity in how we worked together came with a pang of nostalgia I wasn't expecting. Just a few weeks ago, everything was so different.

Cap hadn't been with my small team the day of the attack when the explosion prevented us from making it to the city. They were supposed to come, but were struck with a migraine as we prepared to head out. If I didn't notice something was off, they wouldn't have said anything, either.

Once they finally admitted they were in pain, I walked them straight to Emma's section where she was in charge of medical supplies. When she saw how much they were struggling, she refused to let them leave until they took Ibuprofen and a bottle of water. On the way out, Emma shoved a small bag of persimmons into my hand, discreetly slipping me four more pills and instructing me to deliver them to Michelle.

"The potassium in the persimmons will help to restore electrolytes. They need to drink at least that entire bottle of water and eat the fruit as soon as they can stomach it. No working. Two every four hours for the rest."

I remembered the look she gave me as she handed me the pills; the trust that must have taken. The decision-makers of the group had been getting stricter with medical supplies, questioning why she used what she did to treat those who needed it. Say what you want about Emma's stubbornness and fire in any other situation—she fought them tooth and nail on a daily basis with a fierceness that left witnesses in shock. It was all so she could keep helping people.

"I don't care if Michelle has to tie Cap down and force-feed them—just tell her to make it happen. No one else gets that bag," she said.

So, I did just that. I caught up to Cap and walked with them back to Michelle, reiterated the instructions word for word, and left.

Cap's staying back meant they were in the exact place they needed to be to save what remained of our group.

According to Brian, he and Russell were rushing to help Dan, who was bleeding on the ground, when Cap and Michelle crossed their paths. Cap demanded one of them give up their shirt, and Russell passed his over without question so Cap could wrap Dan's leg and slow the bleed.

When I finally got back to camp, I heard Emma screaming for

help, a duffel bag of medical supplies on her back and an unconscious Sam in her arms. The others and I reached the women at the same time. Brian and Russell were supporting Dan, so Cap tugged the heavy duffel from Emma, who looked like she was about to collapse. They ordered me to take over carrying Sam, and there was no question what my mission was from there.

Cap kept us going in more ways than one. They knew our motivations, our strengths. They brought us together so we could carve a way forward, when it seemed like there was no way to win. We owed them more than we could ever repay, and they still gave without hesitation.

My mind drifted back towards the present as Cap signaled an 'all-clear' sign, and we moved quickly through the grass towards the ranger's station. I kept a close eye on the surrounding area as we jogged, just as I'd learned from Cap the first time we ever worked together. Grackles rasped and cawed their songs from just below the trees, a grating, almost mechanical sound, as they rustled through the brush.

We were nearly at the station when the grackle's discordant songs turned into a harsher, rapid-fire series of, *chuckchuckchuckchuckchuckscreeeeee.* Wings flurried, propelling the birds through the branches of the trees, shaking leaves, and snapping twigs as they exploded into the sky. Then a loud, frantic *screeeeeeeeeeeeeech* echoed from the underbrush.

Cap and I froze, trying to identify the location of whatever caused the chaos. We were still a good length away from the ranger's station, too far from the cover of the trees. My eyes frantically darted across the tree line, but I couldn't place the sound.

Aggressive grunting and snorting carried across the open space as something large barreled through the underbrush, crashing past smaller trees behind the ranger's station. The sound of screeching and squealing burst across the field in waves as the animal burst into view.

My blood ran cold, and for the first time in a long time, I didn't know what move to make.

"*Run!*" Cap whispered.

The mess of tusks and teeth slammed into bushes to break into the clearing, eager to give chase. My heart pounded and I grit my teeth as I ran.

It streaked towards us diagonally across the field, closing the distance to the ranger's station. The screeching reached ear-piercing levels, cutting through the animal's aggressive snorting and panting that came with each exhale from its lungs as it gnashed its teeth. Shaking its head violently from side to side as it charged, it was like it was trying to slice through the space that separated us.

"Up!" Cap yelled, and I followed their line of sight to the overhang that would take us to the roof of the ranger station.

Head down, I put everything I had into the last few feet, launching upwards to grip the overhang, struggling to keep my grip as I pulled myself up. Cap reached the top first, grabbing my arms as I scrambled, finally getting a knee up. The beast jumped, aiming to clamp its jaws around my leg that still dangled.

Thank whatever powers existed, I was faster.

We panted, shoving off our backpacks and scooting as far from the edge as we could get.

"Fuck," Cap cursed. "That was way too fucking close."

I nodded, still panting heavily as I leaned forward to peer below at the feral hog still slamming its body against the front porch posts, trying to shake us down.

THIRTY-THREE
ALINA

The last few days were...interesting, to say the least. Our group had fallen into an intense but functional routine as Jason and I were thrown into Bushcraft Boot Camp. I didn't hate it, though. In fact, I felt quite the opposite.

I really enjoyed foraging with Carter. There was a thrill every time we explored a new part of the forest, like stepping into another world. It was almost enough to forget what else was happening outside of the safe bubble we'd settled into.

Today, Jason and I were learning how to cook over a campfire, which was honestly more daunting than any of the other tasks so far. Brian was in the middle of teaching us how to make a fish broth with the minnows he and Dan regularly caught for 'Forest Soup,' aka whatever could be cooked together without tasting too weird.

Jason's arm brushed mine as we stood beside Brian, and my fingers reflexively went to the spot where we'd briefly touched. I was still trying to wrap my head around everything Jason and I talked about a few nights ago. Though I tried not to get distracted, the memory of that night kept slipping to the forefront of my mind—

It felt like I had just closed my eyes when Emma woke Jason and me to take over night watch. Dan and Emma gave us the rundown of responsibilities again, and then Jason and I were on our own.

We walked the perimeter quietly, gaining a sense of how things looked at night, and the regular sounds we could expect from the nocturnal forest dwellers we couldn't see. Once we found a good spot, I decided to break the ice.

"So, feelings," I said, not quite sure how to follow up my opening statement. Smooth, Alina, *I thought.*

Jason chuckled, shaking his head. "You always had a way with words, Lee."

I let out a soft breath of a laugh. "I have to be honest—my mind is kinda all over the place right now," I replied.

"Lee, I don't expect you to have a response, so please don't feel pressured to say anything if you aren't comfortable. I swear there are no hidden ultimatums, strings, stipulations, or motives with what I told you." Jason paused, nervously running a hand through his hair. "I just wanted you to know—you know, before it was too late."

Jason and I stared at each other for an extended breath as I took in his second bold statement of the night.

His blond hair was messily sticking up from our brief sleep in the car and I absentmindedly reached out to smooth it down. I hesitated, fingers still touching his hair, when I realized how close we'd gotten.

"Alina," Jason said. "It's still me. Nothing's changed."

He took my hand in his, holding it with the same affection I'd been overanalyzing all week; the same touch that soothed my nerves like a balm. He was right; he hadn't changed—but we *had.*

Jason and I were connected in a way no one else could understand. We were still trying to unravel theories about the tattoos and whether there were others like us out there. So much had happened in the last week and we weren't even close to finding answers.

It was easy to cling to Jason like a lifeline and forget everything else when it was just the two of us. But now, we were part of a group. Our lives were now endlessly twisted and entwined with the others'—a hopeless knot that I hoped would never separate, never fray.

I knew Jason was patiently waiting, hoping I'd give him a hint as to what was going on inside my head. Still, he gently rubbed his thumb against the back of my hand, letting me process.

"Should we move to the next spot?" Jason asked after we'd been sitting for a while.

We stood up and were about to start walking when I said, "Wait—before I lose the courage." I took a deep breath, slowly exhaling before I continued, "I'm sure it was obvious how hard I was crushing on you when we were in high school—maybe the years after high school, too...

"But...that night at the lake, you have no idea how badly I wanted—" I paused, feeling a lump growing in my throat, the corners of my eyes burning as I tried to keep my emotions in check. "You mean a lot to me, Jayce, so much more than I could ever express. And it's important to tell people how you feel, especially now..."

"I feel a 'but' coming," Jason said, patiently waiting for me to continue. "It's okay, Lee." He squeezed my hand.

I nodded, mapping out my next words carefully. "But—we've been through a lot. I don't want either of us to say something and then feel the need to backtrack once the adrenaline and shock of our multiple life-or-death situations wear off—or when the rush of endorphins from still being alive inevitably ends. If something is growing between us, I don't want it to just be a coping mechanism."

Jason nodded, swallowing hard and taking a moment to process before replying, "Trust me, Lee, you are anything but a coping mechanism. I'm not asking you to commit to anything other than what we already have. As long as I have you in my life, that's all I need. There's just one thing, though...Lee, I've been dying to kiss you for way too long. Can I?"

I nodded, staring into the sky-blue eyes that had infiltrated my dreams over the years.

Jason smiled, and the intensity from earlier returned to his eyes as they stared into mine. He cupped my jaw, his other hand resting on my waist. After taking a moment to study my face, he leaned in.

My heart raced. His lips were only a hair's breadth from mine and my eyes closed, feeling the buzz of anticipation. Finally, his lips softly brushed against mine.

A whisper of electricity tingled, hovering just over the surface of my skin like a static shock as he exhaled heavily. When his lips met mine again, *it was with more confidence. His hand moved to the back of my neck, tangling in my hair as the other slipped around my waist to palm the small of my back. He pulled me closer and I arched into him, the rest of the world disappearing as I melted into the moment. It was like he couldn't be close enough as he pressed his body against mine, eager to close what remained of the smallest space between us.*

My hands glided over his chest and broad shoulders, through his hair, fingers trailing down the back of his neck as I sank into his warmth. His tongue boldly ran against my bottom lip, and I couldn't help the shiver of anticipation that rolled down my spine.

Our tongues touched tentatively, grazing the other as we fell into a rhythm before he deepened the kiss. His stubble scraped my jaw as our mouths moved in desperation. As I wound my arms around his neck, pressing against him, a low groan rumbled from his throat and reverberated down to my core.

His mouth moved down, traveling along my jaw as I gripped his shoulders. As his teeth lightly scraped the skin over my racing pulse, a shiver trembled through my body.

His kissing slowed, growing tender as his lips brushed back up my neck, barely whispering over my jaw. He paused, his mouth so close I could feel the heat ghosting across my lips, before he pulled back, resting his forehead against mine, sighing heavily. His hands slid down to rest on my hips and he pulled away, exhaling shakily. "I'm sorry, Lee; I think I made a mistake."

My eyes shot to his.

He touched my cheek, staring deeply into my eyes before resting his forehead against mine again. "It's going to be really hard seeing you every day without wanting to kiss you again," he murmured, pressing his lips to my forehead before backing away, his arm falling heavily to his side. "We'll know when the time is right, if and when it comes."

As my mind returned to the present, I couldn't help but wonder if we would ever know anything for sure. Yet, even with the confessions out in the open, everything between us still felt the same. I expected at least a little awkwardness after our kiss—oh man, that *kiss*—and while that night hung over our heads every moment we were together, it still felt like...us. We still had the same kinds of conversations. Jason still managed to create excuses to be near me, never hesitating before wrapping an arm around my shoulders. Only now, every so often, his eyes would linger a second longer with that spark of heat. I can't say I wasn't tempted to explore things further; but the logical side of me couldn't dive in without knowing what was waiting for us on the other side. It looked so easy for Cap and Michelle, for Russell and Sam; but I didn't know how to make space for anything else with all of the unknowns that cluttered my mind.

I found myself looking towards the tree line, wishing my trip to the forest with Carter hadn't been cut short today. Carter and Cap left not too long ago, maybe just hitting an hour of the hour-and-a-half mark Carter estimated it'd take to get to the ranger station. Though I understood why only the two of them went, and that being on foot gave them a stealthier advantage, I still didn't like the idea of them being in a new place without the rest of us; no matter how close it was.

I thought back to the events that brought us here. Every time I thought about the creatures, pins-and-needles crept across my skin like tiny invisible insects pulling at the hair on my arms, trying to burrow inside.

"Are you alright, Alina?" Brian asked, and I snapped back to attention.

"Yeah, of course. I'm fine. Sorry, I just got a bit lost in my head," I replied, still trying to shake off the lingering prickly feeling.

"You're, ah, glowing," Brian replied.

I cursed under my breath. Not only was the tattoo a constant reminder of everything that happened, now I couldn't even keep my own feelings to myself.

"What about you?" Brian turned to Jason, who shook his head.

"I don't feel anything," he said, turning around and lifting his shirt for us to check his mark. No glow.

Just me, then. Coolcoolcool.

"Lee," Jason said carefully, "I know it's awkward to talk about, but—"

"No, I know. It's necessary." I sighed. "I was thinking about them

—the creatures. Remembering what it was like when we escaped. I guess my imagination was just a little too good."

"And physically?" Brian asked.

I shivered, trying to shake it off. "You know that pins-and-needles feeling? It's like that sensation, but just slightly less intense. I start to feel it in my chest, and it spreads to my arms and down my legs, until I feel it all over. It's like there's a magnet that's only tuned to the cells in my body. If it weren't for my skin keeping everything in place, I feel like I would burst into microscopic pieces trying to reach it."

"Well. Okay." Brian nodded. "Oddly poetic, but helpful. Jason, is that what you feel when it happens, too?"

Jason nodded. "Yeah, that was eerily accurate, but only when the creatures are close. When I get frustrated or whatever emotion makes it glow, I don't feel any different, physically."

"I'm going to go grab Emma so she can write this down," I said. I wasn't exactly eager to repeat the conversation, but I had to move if I was going to shake this feeling off.

We'd talked to Cap more in depth about our marks the day after we got to the state park, and agreed that it would be helpful to bring up the topic with the rest of the group. I was a bit overwhelmed at first, and felt like a subject in a test tube. However, the group was incredibly supportive and I was quickly put to ease as Emma jumped in first with an idea from her history as an RN.

We repurposed a notebook that Emma was already keeping for medical notes. Every time she treated someone at camp, she logged everything, just as she did when she worked at the hospital—date, any medicines taken, symptoms, and a bunch of other stuff I'd have never thought of...It was a lot, but it was effective.

Emma was sitting with Michelle in the truck bed when I found her. As I got closer, I realized that Michelle's eyes were red, cheeks flushed, and she was sniffling. Emma was rubbing Michelle's back, speaking in low comforting tones.

"Oh, sorry. I don't want to interrupt—" I said, as I realized I was intruding.

"No, no," Michelle sniffed, waving an arm out. "Come join us. It's fine."

"If you're sure?" I asked tentatively.

"Yes, get your ass in here," Emma said, patting the spot in front of them.

I climbed into the truck bed and sat cross-legged in front of them.

"Can I do anything?" I asked, brow furrowing in concern.

"I just worry when the group separates," Michelle said without any hesitation. "Seeing Cap leave never gets any easier."

"Oh," I breathed, a pang in my heart reminded me how similarly I'd felt this morning. "I get that. No matter how capable they are or how many times they've come back to you, I imagine it's always going to be a bit scary."

Michelle nodded, wiping a few stray tears from her cheeks. "I just have to let it out every so often. But they just checked in a short while ago and will be checking in again, soon enough. They'll be fine," she said, picking up the walkie-talkie to note the time in the top right corner of the tiny screen. "Now, what brings you over?" Michelle reached over to pat my knee.

"Well, my tattoo was glowing again—not in the scary way, though," I explained. Emma snapped to attention, and I saw the switch as her nursing instincts kicked in. Michelle sat patiently, listening with a focused sort of calm.

"Brian was teaching us how to cook over the fire," I continued, "and I guess I just spaced out. I started thinking about our last encounter with the creature, and it was like all of the feelings and sensations rushed back in. Hence...glowing." I tried to smile and make light of it, but I already knew my expression was more of a grimace.

"Let me get the notebook," Emma said, squeezing my shoulder as she hopped off the truck.

I sat with Michelle while Emma went to dig out the notebook from her backpack.

"What are you feeling right now?" Michelle asked, not in a demanding way, but with genuine concern. "Not physical symptoms, but in here." She tapped her heart.

I hesitated, feeling guilty for making myself the center of attention when she was hurting.

"Well?" Michelle asked, and I realized she wasn't going to just let the question go.

I took a deep breath before I spoke. "I feel...responsible. And I know that what happened wasn't something in my control, but I think that's at the root of it, too—*so much* is not in control. And that night, the night we ran—" I paused, blinking back tears. "I tried to lead it away because I couldn't bear the thought of it hurting anyone because of me. I fully came to terms with the fact that what I did was probably my last..." My breathing hitched, an invisible band tightening around my chest. "But if Carter and Jason could get inside, warn you, and everyone else could escape? It would have been worth it. I didn't care what happened to me."

Michelle nodded, waiting for the words to sink in. It was the first time I'd said any of it out loud, and the reality of what I'd done hit me in the chest.

After giving me a moment, she spoke again, "That's a lot to sit with. A lot of weight you're carrying."

I nodded, sniffing as one of the tears I'd been holding back slipped down my cheek. "I can't help it."

"Maybe not now, but with time and support? You are part of our group now, which means you have all of us to help carry anything you're too tired of holding. What you're feeling is valid. Your nervous system has been on overdrive since you woke up a week ago. It's okay to give in to the not-so-great feelings every once in a while, but it's equally as important to be able to come back after. Learning to cope with trauma and live with the grief of everything we've lost is a process without a timeline. It's normal to blame ourselves when we don't have control, but you are not responsible for anything that happened—not the invasion, abduction, tattoos, or hell-creatures. And what's more, I am so happy that you *are* here because our group is stronger for it." Michelle grabbed my hands, squeezing them.

"I...don't even know what to say," I replied through the tears that were freely flowing down my cheeks. I didn't realize how much I'd been holding in until it all spilled out. Already I felt lighter with the words out of my head.

"Yeah, Chelle has that effect on you, doesn't she?" Emma said from behind me. I turned around, surprised that I hadn't noticed her return before now. "She's right, babe," Emma continued. "None of this is your fault. And if anything I said contributed to you feeling like that, I'm so fucking sorry. You are one of the most compassionate humans I've ever met, so selfless you'd literally sacrifice yourself to a beast from hell so people you just met could escape. I swear though, if you ever do something like that again, I can't guarantee I won't kill you myself." Emma's expression settled into a soft smile as she hopped into the back of the truck again and wrapped her arms around me in a hug.

"Don't worry, you can't get rid of me that easily. I'd just come back as a ghost and haunt you for the rest of your life," I said, and both of us laughed.

"Well, how are you feeling now?" Michelle asked as Emma and I sat down once more.

"Like a weight has been lifted." I sighed, laughing nervously at the admission.

"Good." Michelle smiled.

Emma took over the conversation from there, asking questions about what I'd felt when Brian noticed the mark glowing.

"You know," Emma said thoughtfully, "when you were upset just now, there was no glowing."

"Huh." I frowned, processing that information. "So fear, anxiety, frustration, but not sadness or any of the happy emotions so far?"

Emma shrugged. "So far. Maybe it's tied to heart rate or adrenaline secretion. We'll just have to keep monitoring."

As we were getting up to leave the truck, static burst from the walkie-talkie.

"Base, come in," Cap's voice rang over the speaker.

"We're here. Everything alright? Over," Michelle responded.

"We're...okay. Over," Cap answered, but there was hesitation in their voice.

Clearly, Michelle heard it, too.

"But something happened. Don't beat around the bush, Copernicus. What's going on? Over," she fired back.

"Copernicus?" I questioned, looking at Emma.

"Chelle's busting out Cap's full name. She means business," Emma whispered back.

"So, we found the ranger station, ah, we're on top of it, actually."

We looked at each other in confusion as Cap continued to explain.

"There was, well—still is, actually—a feral hog. It chased after us from across the field and we were too far from any trees, so we...climbed onto the roof instead."

There was a moment of silence as we processed what Cap had just told us.

"Well...I wasn't expecting to hear that," Michelle responded. "But you're both alright?"

"Yes, we're alright. Just waiting it out before we go inside the station. We don't want it to see us and get angry again. Over."

Emma signaled for Michelle to hand over the walkie. Though Michelle hesitated, she passed it over to an eager-looking Emma.

"Hey, it's Emma. I just wanted to ask why you haven't turned that sucker into bacon yet?"

I choked back a laugh as Michelle glared at Emma, holding out her hand to take the device back.

"Feral hogs can break through doors, and we only have knives—too short range to take out what is, essentially, a murder-pig. Now, if you don't mind, we're going to continue waiting for said pig to find something better to do. We'll check in at the hour mark. Over," Cap answered.

"Stay safe, love. Over." Michelle ended the call, looking at the two of us, shaking her head at Emma and glaring once more as she said, "Bacon, Emma? Really?"

"Listen," Emma said, barely holding back laughter, "I'm hungry. I can't be held responsible for what I say when I'm so hungry."

Michelle rolled her eyes. "I was going to say I'd rather have pork chops."

THIRTY-FOUR
CARTER

"So...*are* we going to turn the murder-pig into bacon?" I asked Cap.

"If *you* want to get close enough to make it happen, then sure," they retorted.

After realizing we wouldn't get in its way again, the hog lost interest in us and decided to snuffle around the brush nearby. At least it was only one pig. Feral hogs usually stayed in groups, but every once in a while, there would be one on its own. The pigs had been a problem in Texas for years. Now that their already fast-growing populations were running unchecked? Just another danger to add to our growing list. Feral hogs were the very definition of waking up and choosing violence.

"So, should we play Twenty Questions or something until it wanders off completely?" I joked, leaning back against the roof. We were already soaked in sweat from when we were making our way through the trees. Now that the sun was beating down directly on top of us, along with the humidity from the rain clouds accumulating, the heat was even more stifling. I was not looking forward to the inevitable sunburn and dehydration we'd be subjected to if the hog didn't leave soon.

"That depends; which version were you thinking of?" Cap answered.

"There's more than one? I was talking about the one where you guess what object or animal or whatever the other person is thinking of. You can ask twenty 'yes or no' questions."

"Oh, wasn't there a version where you have to guess things that the other person has done that you haven't?" Cap asked, laying back and stretching out.

"You mean, Never Have I Ever?" I laughed.

"Yeah, that sounds way more fun than guessing random objects." Cap grinned.

"You serious?" I asked.

"Never have I ever traveled to another country," Cap said.

"Well, I haven't, either," I replied.

"Okay…so you ask one now."

I couldn't help laughing at the bizarreness of the two of us sitting on the roof of a log cabin, in the middle of a field, playing Never Have I Ever, while avoiding a feral pig.

"Alright," I said, thinking of what I could possibly ask. "Never have I ever…forgotten to return a library book."

Cap scoffed. "Come on, do you even know who you are talking to? Never have I ever worn socks with sandals."

"People really do that?" I asked, actually unsure.

Cap nodded solemnly. "Unfortunately, yes, they do."

We tried a few more questions before realizing how terrible we were at the game.

"Well, clearly, we are not the fun ones of the group," Cap said, pulling their backpack closer to dig out their water bottle.

"Hey, speak for yourself; I'm plenty fun." I smirked at Cap.

"You know," they said, "it's been nice hearing you joke again. I was worried about you—even before the attack."

"You…why?" I could feel the pressure building. Though it was coming from a place of care, the sudden interest everyone had with what was going on in my head was too much.

"Fuck," I said in exasperation. "First I get a speech from Sam about letting people in; then a fight with Emma for not talking about my feelings; now you're telling me you're worried about me, too? Has everyone just been talking about how much of a shitty robot I've been? What the fuck, Cap?"

"Not at all," Cap said, shaking their head. "I can't speak for the others, but what I'm saying only comes from a place of concern for a friend."

I nodded, staring out at the field as the muscle in my jaw ticked. My body heated like my blood was trying to boil me from the inside out and I itched to move.

Instead, I took a deep breath, letting it out slowly. As the edges of my vision went dark, I closed my eyes, taking another deep breath. Something touched my arm, and I realized Cap had bumped me, offering their water bottle as their eyes still faced forward.

"I have my own, thanks," I said gruffly.

"Not the point. Take it," Cap replied.

I accepted the water bottle and took a drink.

"Carter, I need to know how you're really doing," Cap said carefully. "I'm saying this as a friend, not because anyone asked me to, but because I care. Plus, that pig isn't moving anytime soon. If we don't talk, it will just get more awkward the longer we are sitting up here in silence."

I rolled my eyes, feeling the annoyance written all over my face. Still, because it was Cap, I nodded.

Cap took that as the invitation to continue, "I always admired how you worked, the way you carefully measure each situation before diving in. You remind me of a slightly younger me, which Michelle used to tease me about, by the way. *Of course, the first friend you make would be your brain-twin.*' She would say it every time I brought you up in conversation." A smile crossed Cap's face as they replayed the memory. "The last few weeks I could see you getting more closed off...but I didn't want to push. I wasn't sure where the boundary of our friendship was. After the attack, when just eight of us were left..." Cap trailed off. "It felt like you were so far away at times, you weren't even with us anymore, even when you were physically present."

I continued staring into the field, letting Cap's words sink in.

"When you and Brian brought Alina and Jason back and I saw how you reacted—I didn't understand why you were being so combative. And then lately you seemed to be doing better... but it never really goes away, does it? The anxiety?" They looked at me, waiting for a response.

"Who doesn't have anxiety these days?" I shifted uncomfortably, unsure how we went from a stupid question game to talking about my mental health.

"You've been struggling," Cap added.

"Who hasn't been struggling? Why does it suddenly matter what's going on with me? I'm fine. It's always been this way and I deal with it," I muttered.

"It doesn't make what you are going through any less valid, Carter. And maybe it's selfish, but I don't want to lose what little I have left, either. The next time you're feeling like that...talk to me. Please."

We made eye contact again, and reluctantly, I nodded. I thought back on the last few weeks and the intentional distance I'd created. Cap was right. It was one thing to keep a circle small; it was another to close yourself off entirely, which is exactly what I had been trying to do—at least until recently.

I clapped a hand on Cap's shoulder. "You're a good friend, Cap."

"I know," they said, smirking.

A laugh escaped as I shook my head.

"I don't know how you do it," I said. "It's hard enough not to lose your mind worrying about people you just met, let alone friends—and you have a partner, too. I can't comprehend how you've managed to carry the weight of that extra risk."

"The stakes might be higher now, but there's always a risk when love is involved. You're trusting the most important pieces of yourself in the hands of someone else. It can be hard, but it's what keeps me going. I think if we learned anything from the last eight months, we really have to make the most out of what we have. No matter what else is happening, if you can still manage to care, to love, to feel—you're holding on to the very core of what it means to be human. We feel it all and keep going to build towards a better future so others will have a chance, especially those we love."

"Goddammit, why do you have to be so smart?" I muttered jokingly.

"Oh, hey!" Cap exclaimed. "The pig's gone."

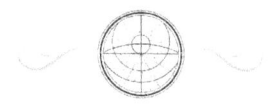

After ensuring that the feral hog was, in fact, gone, we carefully dropped down from the roof of the ranger station and did a full walk around the building. There really wasn't much we didn't already see from our spot on the roof, but if the murder-pig taught us anything, it was that we should always cover all the bases.

It's a good thing we did, too. Upon circling the building, we discovered a small generator. We couldn't try powering it on right then; those things were too loud even without a feral hog lurking. Still, it opened the realm of possibilities just a bit wider than it was before.

As expected, the ranger station consisted of two main rooms—a central office area and a smaller kitchen. Dust and dirt lightly coated the surfaces of the few pieces of furniture in the space—a desk, a few chairs, a filing cabinet, and a coffee table in the office area. Bookshelves lined the walls and were filled with field guides, books on wilderness first aid, and wildlife management resources. In the kitchen, there was a small table and two dining chairs squeezed against the wall across from a small sink and fridge, along with a camping stove. I almost fell to my knees when we opened the lone cabinet in the kitchen to find a tub of instant coffee still three-quarters of the way full and an unopened twenty-four pack of instant ramen in a cup. But the real prize was sitting in the corner between the kitchen and office, propped up on its own table—a high-frequency radio.

Thunder cracked outside and I rushed to the window to check for rain. Dark storm clouds filled the distant sky. They hadn't reached our area yet, but rain would find us before long.

Cap was already pulling out the walkie talkie to call the others.

"Base, come in."

THIRTY-FIVE
ALINA

The sudden shock of thunder made me jump. "You're glowing again! That's two for fear and/or anxiety in one day!" Emma said cheerily as she logged more notes in the notebook.

"You are...way too excited over this," Jason said, cocking an eyebrow at his sister.

Michelle laughed, patting my shoulder. "Congratulations, you have now become Emma's new hyper-fixation."

"I mean, that isn't too new." Jason laughed as Emma punched his shoulder, holding back a smile.

"She's mine forever. Everyone else can try and fight me for her, but I'm telling you now, you'll lose," Emma said, sticking out her tongue before turning back to her data.

We were packing up the camp, getting ready to meet Carter and Cap at the ranger station. I expected it would take a while to get everything ready, but it only took a few minutes. I shouldn't have been surprised—the night of the attack, everyone got out pretty quickly, and we'd kept our stuff ready to go since we arrived at the park. At this point, we were just waiting for Russell and Brian to return from checking our traps before heading out.

"Man, keeping track of all of that by hand? How are you going to sort through all that data, Red?" Dan asked, looking over Emma's shoulder.

"Ugh, I know," Emma groaned. "What I wouldn't give for a good spreadsheet."

"Right? Give me some VLOOKUPs," Dan answered.

"Or CONCATENATE?" Emma said, a wistful expression on her face.

"Don't get me started on CONCATENATE," Dan replied.

"This is probably the most bizarre exchange I've witnessed in a long time," Sam said, cringing.

"What can I say? My love for data is...*off the charts*," Emma said with a smirk.

"Red." Dan clutched his chest, reaching a hand towards her. "You *auto-complete* me."

Emma put her hand in Dan's, demure as a princess, as she batted her eyelashes. "You're my favorite *cell*-mate."

"The constant in my *formula*."

"We're a perfect *match*!"

"I think my brain just returned an *error*," Brian said, dropping the bag that held whatever they'd found. He and Russell had just returned, and were standing a few feet away with equally confused looks on their faces.

"Sorry, not sorry, everyone," Emma said. "Our feelings are formatted in bold. There's no return from here."

"Please," Sam pleaded, looking at Jason. "Make it stop."

"Am I having a stroke?" Russell asked, actually looking concerned.

"Alright, fine, I'll be the adult," Michelle said, shooing us away from the truck so she could close the gate. "Brian, you're driving the truck. Russell, you're driving the SUV. Let's get going."

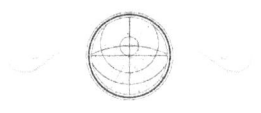

We arrived at the ranger station just in time. The heavy clouds were filled and ready to burst as we pulled up, and we'd just managed to get our stuff inside before the downpour started.

Michelle immediately wrapped Cap in a hug, and I could practically see the relief melt off of her. I couldn't help the smile that crossed my face as I watched for a moment longer. Movement beyond Cap's shoulder drew my attention just in time to catch Carter looking at the couple with a soft expression. As if he felt me looking, his eyes met mine, and an embarrassed half-smile pulled at the corner of his mouth.

He skirted around Cap and Michelle, to meet me where I stood.

"Told you," he said once he was in front of me.

My face scrunched in confusion. "Told me what?"

"That everything would all be alright. I keep my promises."

That crooked smile bloomed on his face and my stomach flipped as I remembered the conversation from this morning, the pinky swear. Mentally shaking away the sudden flutter, I rolled my eyes, letting a smile slowly spread across my lips.

We spent the rest of the afternoon cleaning the ranger station as best as possible with the station's limited cleaning supplies, knowing we'd have to sleep on the floor when night fell. Without blankets or cushions, we'd been using stray articles of clothing as pillows the last few days. I still had Brian's hoodie from our first night in the park. Just as Carter said, Brian was happy he could help in any form. He even insisted I keep the hoodie for a while, and the inconspicuous item of clothing became a sort of comfort item.

There wasn't much to unpack, as we always needed to have our stuff ready to go at a moment's notice. Russell and Dan organized the bags and supplies close to the door so at least we could find things quickly. After that, there was nothing to do but to get dinner ready. We unanimously voted to break into the pack of ramen cups that Carter found in the kitchen, and I swear, nothing ever tasted so heavenly.

The rain poured on, splashing the ground where small mud puddles had formed. The sound was a comforting white noise, influencing a calm that fell over our collective group. For a while, all that could be heard was the boiling water on the camping stove, rain pounding the roof as it poured in waterfalls off the edge, and the distant sound of rolling thunder.

Once we'd eaten, we'd fallen into casual conversation, much like the other nights in the park. Only this time, the small talk was dominated by Russell's questions about the feral hog.

"Yeah, but, like, why didn't you just jump on top of it and stab it?" Russell asked.

"How's about this—the next time you run into a feral pig, you try jumping on top of it and let me know how that goes," Carter replied.

"Okay, please don't do that," Cap looked at Russell pointedly. "Normally, hogs won't even bother approaching humans unless they smell food, are provoked, or something is encroaching on its territory. It's probably had the run of the place for a while with the station being empty and was trying to defend its space. The best thing you can do in that situation is either make sure you have accurate aim and shoot it, or get up someplace high. You do *not* want to mess with their tusks."

"Well, yeah, but theoretically, how awesome would it be to have some fresh pork in this ramen?" Russell replied.

Cap laughed. "Theoretically, yes, that would be great. But alas…"

"Why didn't you shoot it?" I asked curiously.

"The guns we had ran out of ammo," Carter answered. "Others were missing or ruined during the attack on camp. There's a few we still have, but until we find the right ammo, they are basically useless."

We moved inside shortly after that as the night grew darker with the day's end.

I was getting tired, so I wandered over to the line of bags at the door, looking for mine. The thought of curling up with Sam's book, snuggling my hoodie-pillow, and listening to the rain sounded like the best possible plan.

I caught Russell's attention as he grabbed his pack. "Hey, you helped organize these bags, right? I'm trying to find mine, but I'm not seeing it here. Would it be anywhere else in the cabin?"

"No, all the bags are right here. Damn," he said, kneeling to look closer. "Maybe it's still in the truck," Russell said, running a hand down his face.

I grimaced, looking out the window. "The doors are still unlocked, right?"

Russell nodded, peering out the window with a look of utter defeat. The rain was coming down heavier than a waterfall.

"Please don't make me," he all but whimpered.

I laughed. "Don't worry, I planned on doing it myself."

I started walking towards the door when Russell grabbed my attention again. "Hold up—take this," he said, passing me a flashlight.

"Thanks." I saluted him with the flashlight before slipping out the door.

Standing on the front porch, I watched the rain pour off the overhang, questioning how badly I actually needed the book and hoodie. The storm had picked up significantly and lightning sliced through the darkened sky, temporarily illuminating the field. A few seconds later, the crack of thunder boomed and I jumped, a tiny squeak escaping my mouth as I startled. I tried to ignore my heart pounding in my chest and stay in the present, even as my memory tried to pull me back into the thrift store the day of the explosions. All day, the loud sounds had been catching me off guard, temporarily stealing my breath; but it had been easier to recover with the others nearby.

"This is fine. It's fine. It's just a sound. You're not afraid of sounds," I muttered, trying to psych myself up as my hands shook. I took a breath, exhaling slowly as I clicked on the flashlight and prepared to run through the water.

Tilting my head, I burst forward, boots squelching against the ground as I sprinted to the truck.

"It's fine, it's fine, it's fine," I chanted under my breath, squinting to see through the rain as the flashlight's beam bounced ahead. The mud was so slick I nearly crashed into the truck, skidding to a stop in front of the vehicle.

Yanking open the door to the back seat, I searched the floor where I'd been sitting as rain pelted against my back. Nothing. I checked the front and cursed under my breath, hoping my bag was packed into the SUV instead and not genuinely missing.

Pushing the door closed, I darted to the other car. The only positive was that the air was still warm, so at least I wasn't wet and shivering. Still, I was beyond soaked. I cursed the fact that the SUV was parked so far from the truck, holding the flashlight under my armpit so I wouldn't drop it as I pulled the back door open.

There! I grinned triumphantly. The backpack was half-stuffed under the seat in front of it, and I had to tug the bag free. Heaving it onto my back, I'd just shut the door and grabbed my flashlight again when the light caught two glinting orbs shining in the middle of the field. My heart skipped a beat as I slowly lifted the flashlight to investigate the source of the shine.

In the light, a giant hog blinked, grunting and shaking its head from side to side to avoid the blinding spotlight. I started backing up slowly, scared even to breathe as I kept the light aimed at the pig's face, hoping it'd retreat or at least stay disoriented until I could escape—but to where?

I quickly considered my options—if I ran back towards the house, the hog could barrel through the door and hurt the others. I glanced at the truck instead and started inching back in that direction. I kept my light trained on the hog, attempting to keep it blind to my exact position. If I could make it over the truck bed, that would hopefully put me in the clear.

Whether its eyes adjusted to the light or it was too pissed to stand around any longer, the feral hog was done waiting. It squealed an ear-piercing sound as hooves propelled the large animal with shocking speed towards where I'd been standing by the SUV.

The spotlight left the pig's face as I turned and sprinted back towards the truck, losing traction from the mud packed between my boot treads. I took a chance to look behind me as the pig slid past the SUV, realizing that the source of the light had moved. It hesitated half of a second before spotting the beam. The hog changed direction, charging toward the light that bounced in front of me with each pounding step.

Fuck. The light! I turned off the flashlight, frantically trying to blink the afterimage spots away as my sight adjusted. If I had any luck left, the hog was just as disoriented. With white circles dotting my vision, I kept running towards the truck. I knew the animal was gaining on me and I grit my teeth, pushing myself to keep moving.

The truck was almost in reach, right in front of me, but my foot landed awkwardly—I crashed to the ground near the back wheel. The hog skidded past the truck, scrambling to change direction while I pushed myself up, slipping as I tried to regain my footing.

The hog squealed again, a guttural, angry sound that was impossibly close.

I got to my feet just in time to hear another kind of grunt, the smack of something heavy hitting the ground. I turned around in time to see Carter struggling to try and keep the animal pinned on its side.

"Go!" he yelled, and I grabbed the top of the truck bed, using the tire to push myself up. My foot slipped, but I was able to get an elbow over the rim and pulled myself over.

The pig screamed, a harsh, panicked screech, and I scrambled around in the back of the truck, rain pelting my back as I looked for anything I could use to try to help Carter.

Another yell. Different this time. I shot up in time to see Russell and Cap jump on the hog, Brian and Jason close behind. I fell to my knees in the back of the truck, unable to keep moving. I clutched my head, curling in on myself. I had no way to help. No weapons. It was my fault. I couldn't—

A final scream left the hog, followed by a wet gurgling sound from deep within its throat.

The truck shook as something thudded next to me. I stayed frozen, curled on the floor of the truck, gasping to try and keep the air in my lungs, only faintly registering the sound of footsteps approaching. Calloused hands gently touched my shoulders.

My chest tightened and every muscle seemed to contract at once. But the oxygen felt like it was sucked from my body as I choked on sobs that wouldn't come out.

I heard voices around me. Yelling. The truck shook again.
Lifting.

I was being carried.

Eyes scrunched tight as my chest heaved.

I couldn't breathe.

"*What the fuck happened? Is she hurt?*" I registered Emma's voice—like it was floating above me, existing in an entirely different space.

"*No, not like that, but—*" said the panicked voice belonging to the person carrying me.

"*The blood?*" Emma sputtered.

"*It's mine,*" the voice answered again.

Another voice called, so far away, "*Here—lay her down.*"

My head swam as the world spun impossibly fast and my body was lowered to the ground.

Numbness spread from my fingers to the tips of my toes and my throat felt fuzzy.

I couldn't—

THIRTY-SIX
ALINA

A SHARP, acrid smell filled my nose.

I coughed, gasping for breath as I rolled to my side and my eyes fluttered open.

"There she is," Cap said in an even tone, but I could hear the tension in their voice. "You're okay, Alina. Don't move too fast."

My pounding head was cradled in someone's lap—wet jeans that smelled like mud and rain from outside.

"Wha—How?" I rasped.

"We think you had a panic attack and passed out. You weren't out long, though," a voice above me murmured. Jason.

"That smell—what was—" My scratchy voice was no louder than a whisper. It felt like sandpaper was rubbing against my vocal cords.

"Smelling salts—I guess that stuff really does work," Jason tried to joke, but I could hear the nerves in his voice.

"Here, sip this slowly." Cap passed me a water bottle and Jason helped me sit up straighter.

"Is this alright?" Jason murmured, gently rubbing my arm.

Nodding, I leaned back against him, trying to focus on the way his fingers felt against my arm. I still felt woozy, but as I drank the water and the stinging in my throat eased, I started to feel more solid.

The soft glow of the emergency lanterns created just enough light to see who else was in the room. Michelle was off to the side talking in low serious tones with Brian and Dan. Movement caught my attention out of the corner of my eye, and I turned to see Russell pacing, chewing on a thumbnail, and looking distraught.

My heart started pounding again and I sat up, eyes darting around the room. Where was Emma? Why was Cap the one taking care of me with Jason? Where was—

"Carter?!" I asked frantically. "Where's Carter? I saw him—"

"It's okay. He's okay," Jason answered, brushing my hair behind my ear. I turned so I could see his face as he spoke to me. "He got a cut on his arm, but he's okay," Jason answered. "He's just in the kitchen getting stitched up by Emma. Sam is with him, too. No one else got hurt." Jason kissed the top of my head and I nodded, leaning into him and resting my head against his chest. I took a shaky breath; the sudden movement gave me the spins.

Russell paused his pacing, seeming torn with conflict as his gaze darted outside, to the kitchen, and then back to me. He closed his eyes for a second, running both of his hands through his wavy light brown hair as he took a deep breath. Quickly, he walked over, kneeling at our side.

"Lee, I'm so fucking sorry," he said, and I could hear the hitch in his voice. The tall, young man looked like a little kid as he knelt beside me, mud still flecked on his sun-kissed skin. His face was clouded in worry and remorse as he picked up one of my hands, squeezing. "I should have gone to get the stupid bag. This is my fucking fault. Everyone could have—you—Carter almost—"

"Woah," I said, placing my hand on Russell's to catch his attention. "Russell, hey, look at me. Did you summon the murder-pig?"

"What—no!" he exclaimed, and his wide, panicked eyes finally met mine. His pulse pounded wildly, visibly banging against the side of his neck. "But *I* should have gone. I shouldn't have let—"

"You didn't do anything wrong," I interrupted. "You are still getting to know me, so I'm going to fill you in on something my closest friends had to find out the hard way—I'm as stubborn as they come when I set my mind on something. You *couldn't* have convinced me not to do it myself. Plus, you gave me that flashlight, right?"

He nodded, and I could practically see the thoughts racing behind his eyes as he swallowed.

"That flashlight messed with the hog's vision and helped me escape. I was going to go out in the rain without anything until you made sure I took it, right?"

"It's just," Russell started, "after every-fucking-thing else—*our* home planet is trying off us, too?" Russell snapped, his nerves burning into anger. "When do we catch a break? When does it stop?" His voice broke as he covered his face with his hands, elbows resting on his knees.

"Yeah, it's pretty fucked up, isn't it?" I said with a sarcastic huff of a laugh. "Whoever is running this simulation must really fucking hate us. I mean, come on—who needs alien monsters when Mother Earth is set on taking us out herself?"

An incredulous laugh burst from Russell as he looked up, adding, "Right? Earth was like, 'Oh, you're gonna ignore climate change? Bet. Here's an alien invasion, besties. Not good enough? Okay, plot twist: murder-pig.' Fuckin' hell, man." He paused, his brow creasing in concern before asking, "You're really okay, though?"

"Yeah, I'm okay." I smiled, almost for real this time.

Though he didn't seem wholly settled, the look of panic on his face had subsided. He was coming back down. I leaned forward to hug Russell and he returned the embrace without hesitation, squeezing tight.

Letting go, Russell took a deep breath before telling me, "Thanks for helping me out of the spiral, Alina. You're a real one." He flashed a smile, just a bit weaker than his usual grin as he said, "I'm going to check on C-Dawg. Sam's with him and Red."

I froze, sitting up straighter as I remembered I hadn't seen Carter yet. "Wait. I'll come too," I said, shifting to try and get up. Jason wrapped his arm around my waist to help me stand.

I couldn't help feeling guilty for trying to leave. I opened my mouth to explain, "I—sorry, I just, I have to—"

"Lee," Jason murmured, squeezing my shoulder reassuringly. "It's fine. Whatever you need. Do you want me to walk you over there?" He gestured towards the kitchen and I nodded.

Jason kept his hand on the small of my back as we walked across the room. It was clear everyone else was still visibly shaken, still processing. For some reason, this seemed to hit us all a bit harder. Russell was right; it felt like a betrayal. It was one thing when it was the aliens or the hell-creatures coming after us...but this was our planet, *our* creatures. We kept facing a stream of obstacles and life-or-death situations, one right after another, and I couldn't help echoing Russell's sentiment—when would it stop?

As we approached the entryway to the kitchen, Sam walked out, protectively nestled under Russell's arm.

"Alina! Russell just told us you woke up. I was coming to check on you. How are you doing?" Sam asked.

"I'm...I'll be okay," I said, nodding toward the kitchen. "Is it alright if I go in there?"

"Yeah, totally," Sam said.

"I'll go hang back with the others so it isn't too crowded. It's a small space," Jason said, kissing my temple before dropping his arm. He walked with Russell and Sam back to join the others.

As I entered the kitchen, Carter moved to stand. He didn't get far, though—Emma pressed her palm to his chest to stop him, shooting a stern look in his direction. "Nuh-uh. No moving until these stitches are done. Sit. Stay," she commanded, pointing a finger at his face with a look that screamed, 'try me.'

She peered over her shoulder and relief melted the hard expression from her face. "Lee, I want nothing more than to run over and give you the biggest hug, but I have to finish this idiot's stitches. Want to hang in here with us for a bit?"

I nodded, walking over, feeling the pressure of tears in the back of my tired eyes.

"Hey," I said, trying to force a smile.

"Hey, yourself," Carter answered, looking me over, concern still etched across his face. As I grew closer, his expression relaxed and he took a deep breath.

I tried to ignore the quiver in my lip as I spoke again, "I saw you before I—I must have passed out. I'm so sorry you had to—"

Carter reached out with the arm Emma wasn't stitching and grabbed my hand, pulling me closer. He squeezed my fingers, prompting me to look him in the eye.

"Hey, it's okay. We're all fine. Everyone's still here," Carter said in a soft voice, holding back a wince as Emma worked on his arm.

Emma's hands paused, but she didn't look up, staying focused on her task. Carter held my hand for a second longer, stroking the back with his thumb before letting go.

"Did you...really tackle a feral hog?" I asked, remembering what I saw before panic took over.

"Ah, yeah, I did," Carter replied, wincing again as Emma tightened the last stitch before tying the knot.

"Alright. You're done. Stay there while I get more water to clean up that blood," Emma said, pulling off her gloves and vigorously rubbing her hands with hand sanitizer.

Emma turned, her shoulders losing all the tension she'd been holding as she hugged me. She pulled back, but kept her hands on my shoulders as she locked her fierce, blue eyes on mine.

"Alina. Marie. Ríos. This is *not Scooby Doo*. Please stop acting as bait for every fucking monster we come across, or so help me, I will tie you up and keep you in the back of the truck where you can't get into trouble anymore. Got it?" She raised an eyebrow, waiting for me to agree to her terms.

"Okay, yeah. No more monster hunting," I replied, stifling a laugh at the very 'Emma' statement.

"Seriously, though. That was scary. You're really ok?" she asked.

I nodded. "Yeah...I'm fine."

She paused as if she were debating whether to say the next part. "Your mark...it was different this time. It was glowing so bright it actually lit up the area enough to see what was happening, even from inside. And then you must have passed out and—" She took a deep breath. "Lee, when you passed out, the glowing just...burnt out. It faded so fast, I thought...It was terrifying." Emma shook her head, rubbing her arms. "But that's something to dig into later." She paused, looking towards the other room. "Alright, I'm getting more water. I'll be back."

After Emma left the room, Carter gestured to the seat beside him, asking, "Stay a while?"

I sat, leaning an elbow on the table, and it was then that I noticed the blood on the front of my shirt. I frowned, pulling the sticky fabric away from my skin. It didn't hurt, even when I pressed the area.

"Yeah, sorry about that," Carter said, and my eyes snapped up.

I looked at his arm, then back to his face. "Yours?" I asked, confused.

"Yeah, from carrying you inside," he said, shifting in his seat.

"You were bleeding enough to need stitches and you still carried *me* inside?"

"Yeah, and he wouldn't let anyone near you until I checked you out," Emma said from the doorway. I moved to give her back the seat, but she waved me off.

Emma had Carter turn to face the table so she could reach his arm better from the other side before sanitizing her hands again and cleaning the stitches.

"I mean, I just had a cut. Alina was unconscious and we didn't know why the glow faded so quickly. I'd say that takes priority," Carter defended, gripping his knee with his free hand and wincing as Emma cleaned the blood from his injured arm. I reached over, taking his palm and pulling his hand into my lap.

"Squeeze if it hurts," I said with a weak smile.

Carter turned to me, and I thought I saw the corner of his lip curve into a slight smile as he laced his fingers in mine and squeezed lightly. I glanced down at our hands, realizing this was the first opportunity I was able to actually study Carter's tattoos up close. The intricate design started on the back of his hand, growing into a collage of images on his forearm—a compass, galaxies, mountains, a bird with a third eye...there were so many individual pieces. Still, they all wove together like a tapestry across his skin. Words in Spanish were written in bold cursive, interspersed between the images, as well. I wondered what the tattoos on his shoulders and his ribs looked like…whether the injury on his other arm was carved too deep to repair his art.

"That wasn't just a cut," Emma said, returning my attention to their faces. She gave Carter a stern look before saying, "That motherfucker sliced you good."

Emma spread a generous amount of antibacterial ointment across his stitches despite his protesting to save it for someone else. He squeezed my hand as she taped gauze around his arm.

"Alright. You're set. Be gentle with that arm because I don't want to have to fix any popped stitches. If it gets wet, the gauze has to come off. Rinse off your hands as best you can and use the hand sanitizer before going anywhere near that wound. Look out for redness, swelling, warmth, and pus, and if you start feeling feverish, tell me *immediately*. If I find out you have any symptoms and have been keeping quiet, I *will* step on your balls."

"Geeze, alright," Carter exclaimed before turning to me and stage-whispering, "Please tell me this isn't how she spoke to real patients?"

I laughed. "No, Em's really good at her job. Very professional. Usually."

"I just don't take shit from you, Carter." Emma smiled sweetly before pointing a finger at us. "Speaking of patients, stay here. I'm grabbing some leftover nopales for both of you."

I blinked. "Well I heard about an apple a day keeping the doctor away, but I had no idea that cacti could be just as effective."

Emma groaned, "I am not even going to reward that terrible joke by acknowledging it further. I'll be back."

I laughed as Emma left the room.

"You doing alright? For real?" Carter asked, drawing my attention back to him.

"I…yeah, no, I think I'm okay. A little shaken up, but I'm coming back down."

"Well, you aren't glowing, so that's a good sign," he added.

"And what a fun party trick that is. I'm like a walking, talking mood ring," I muttered.

"If you think about it, that party trick makes you one of our best defenses," Carter interjected.

I stifled a laugh, raising an eyebrow at him. "And how exactly did you come to that conclusion?"

"It also tells you when the hell-creatures are close. Once we figure out how to read the signs, it'll give us a heads-up so we can hopefully escape quicker. You're...a protector. Way more valuable than a party trick."

My shoulders relaxed as I studied his face. His bronze skin was still streaked with mud and blood, except for the spot on his arm that Emma had cleaned and dressed. Though purple bruises were already visible and he wore a tired expression, there was a shine to his deep brown eyes, a warmth that put me at ease.

The corner of Carter's mouth ticked, curving slightly as he wrinkled his brow. "What?"

"Oh!" I exclaimed, my neck growing warm as I realized that I was staring. "Sorry, I guess I spaced out for a bit."

"Alright," Emma said as she breezed into the room, unceremoniously dumping the nopales onto the table before us. "All of them. Eat. Now."

"Yes, nurse Emma," I responded, smiling at her as she sauntered back to the door.

Emma turned to throw me a wink. As she reached the doorway, a devious smile curved across her lips. She pointed at something under the table. "Oh, by the way—you know you're still holding hands, right?" She raised her eyebrows, a teasing smile on her face as she left the room.

Carter and I looked down at our hands, still twined together on my knee. It was only when the absentminded brushing of his thumb against mine stopped, I realized—we'd never let go.

THIRTY-SEVEN
CARTER

Dan and I sat on the front porch, keeping watch while the others slept. The rain was still coming down, but not as aggressively as before. The sky over the horizon was already clearing, which meant the storm was likely to pass soon. That's the thing about rainstorms around here—as quickly as they began, they ended. As I looked across the area, my eyes kept getting stuck on the spot where we'd killed the feral pig.

I shifted and a twinge of pain shot down my forearm where the hog's tusks had sliced me open. Grimacing, I cursed the damn thing again. It's a miracle none of us were hurt worse.

Once Alina joined Emma and me in the kitchen, Cap took Brian and Jason to work on the hog. As much as the timing sucked, we knew that we couldn't let it go to waste. Between the heat and the moisture, it was essential to work fast so the meat didn't spoil. At least the rain helped wash away the messier parts.

Field dressing the hog and constructing a smoker took much of the evening into the night. Under normal circumstances, it would have been difficult. The rain made it that much more brutal. At one point, everyone except Alina, Emma, and I were outside fighting against the rain to construct the cone-shaped smoker in the dark, using mud, rocks, green wood, and the tarp we usually used to collect water or shelter from the rain. As I stared at it now, smoke clouded from the top like a chimney, and the smell of smoking meat wafted in my direction. Hopefully that wouldn't attract anything else; hell knows we needed a break. I knew we'd have to check on the smoker soon to ensure the fire didn't burn out entirely or grow too high—it was a delicate balance.

"You alright, C?" Dan asked, his voice low.

I nodded, wincing again as I moved my arm. "Not excited for how long it's going to take to heal this thing, but I'm alright."

"Figures, my leg would finally start feeling better as your arm got torn to shit." Dan chuckled sarcastically. "Nature sure has a way of fucking with us. I wonder what fresh new hell tomorrow will bring."

"Don't be too optimistic, or people will accuse you of being me." I raised an eyebrow mockingly.

Dan shrugged. "Eh, there are worse things to be compared to."

"Thanks, kid," I said, bumping his shoulder lightly with my fist. "So, what do you think of this whole radio situation?"

Cap and I briefly informed the group about the generator and high-frequency radio after Alina and I were allowed to leave the kitchen. Still, we had to put a pin in the larger conversation to focus on the more pressing issues. Aside from the fact that none of us knew how to operate that kind of radio, the amount of time we'd have to figure it out would be thin. We needed to be conscious of the noise created by the generator and keep in mind that the fuel to run it wouldn't last forever. To increase our chances of reaching someone, we'd have to use our time wisely. While the obvious intention of using the radio would be to reach someone, what we'd do if we found anyone on the other end was still up for discussion.

"I don't mind if we eventually find other people, but not gonna lie —I kinda want to keep what we have for now. Aside from the pig, it's been pretty chill the last few days. I wouldn't mind sticking around a while," Dan replied. He lazily pulled out his pocket knife and dug the tip into the porch's wooden planks.

"I can relate to that. But you know we have to take advantage of resources when we find them. Who knows how long we'll have to act on the opportunity? Still, I wouldn't mind staying, either. You know how well I do with change," I joked.

"You seem like you've been doing alright lately," Dan said without looking up, continuing to carve out the beginning of a letter. "At least since we got here, you've just been vibing. Brian keeps going off about it."

I snorted a laugh. "Listen kid, you're going to have to translate for me. What does that mean?"

Dan smirked, still staring at his carving, "Ever since he saw your cuddle sesh with Alina, he's convinced y'all are endgame. He's lowkey obsessed."

I blinked, taken aback. "What are you talking about? Cuddling?"

"Yeah, the first night. You two were curled up together in the back of the truck when he woke Alina up to take Sam's place. He said she was all embarrassed and shit." Dan paused his activity to look at me with a smirk. "So, what's the tea, C?" Dan put down his knife, steepling his fingers in front of his chin, resting his elbows on his knees as he leaned forward.

I frowned, unsure why this was the first time I was aware that Alina and I had ever been that close. Thinking back to that night, the last thing I could recall was Alina's nightmare waking me up. I remembered holding her hand to comfort her, but nothing more than that. Still, I woke up alone, so only Alina, Sam, or Brian could confirm for sure. A thought struck me—"But why would Brian talk to *you* about it?"

Dan shrugged as he flicked open the knife to dig back into his carving. "Why would it matter that he did?"

"Well, that implies there was something *worth* talking about."

"That it does," Dan casually agreed, still not lifting his focus. His mischievous smirk didn't give anything away, either.

I studied him as he dug the tip of the knife into the wood with a relaxed kind of focus.

"Are you fucking with me?" I asked.

"Do you think I'm fucking with you? Or the better question is, what do you *want* that answer to be?" He stood up suddenly, dusting his hands off on his shorts. "Time to check the pig," he declared. I moved to follow, but he held up a hand, saying, "Nah, you stay, I got it."

Dan walked away, chuckling, while I sat on the porch, more lost than ever.

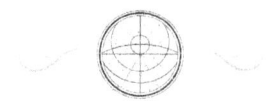

By the time morning came, I was even more restless. Between my throbbing arm, the confusing conversation with Dan, and the phantom sounds I kept hearing throughout the night, I couldn't begin to imagine what functioning would look like for the rest of the day.

I hated that I couldn't stop thinking about what Dan said. Alina and I spent the majority of the last few days together and nothing seemed different. Maybe I was blowing this all out of proportion. Dan was probably just trying to fuck with me. But...why? It didn't make sense, which bothered me even more.

By the time the first rays of daylight trickled through the window, I decided I needed to know what really happened. I looked towards the front door—Sam and Russell were finishing the last shift keeping watch on the porch. I could trust Sam; she'd tell me what actually happened.

But first, coffee.

I gathered the camping stove and everything else that we'd need to make coffee, setting everything by the front door. "Morning," I said as I stepped outside. "Russell—want to grab some of this?" I gestured to the items sitting by the door.

"Wait—stop, is that coffee?" Sam exclaimed, her wide eyes darting between me and the tub of instant coffee on the floor.

"It sure is." I grinned.

"I think I'm going to cry," Sam said, her eyes actually shimmering with tears.

Perfect.

"So, now that I'm your favorite person, I wondered if we could talk."

"Yeah, fam, of course," Russell answered as he set up the camping stove to boil the water. "What's up? What can we help with?"

Of course.

I meant to direct the question to Sam only, but with Russell so eager, I knew I couldn't exclude him from the conversation. All that would do is bring up even more questions. I sighed, sitting on the porch.

"So I was on watch with Dan last night," I started.

"Nice," Russell said, nodding his approval. "Dan's the GOAT."

Great start. I held back an eye roll.

"Yeah...confusing as shit, but he's a sweetheart," I deadpanned.

"But you didn't come out here to talk about Dan, I'm assuming?" Sam asked with a raised eyebrow, taking back the reins.

"No—he mentioned something about you and Brian seeing me..." I trailed off, suddenly unsure whether I wanted to continue the conversation.

"Dude, the suspense is killing me. What did Sam and Brian see? Was it something...dirty?" Russell lowered his voice on the last word, glancing behind him to ensure no one was there to overhear. "I swear, everything stays in the vault." He crossed his heart for good measure.

An amused smirk crept across Sam's face, and she was no doubt reveling in the awkward turn the conversation took.

"Yes, Carter, please continue." Sam giggled.

Why did I think this was a good idea?

I exhaled in frustration before continuing, "He said you and Brian saw me cuddling with Alina when we were sleeping in the truck that first night."

"Oh, that?" Sam scrunched her brow. "Yeah, it was right before I swapped with Alina for watch. It was actually really sweet. You looked so peaceful; we didn't want to wake you."

"That's nice, thank you for that; going back to the other thing— can you tell me *exactly* what you saw?" I studied Sam's face, trying to gauge what my reaction should be. Her answer was so nonchalant; I had no idea whether I was making a big deal out of nothing or if I should be asking more questions.

"Do you want me to paint a picture? Because I can try, but Dan is the artist of the group," Sam teased.

"Come on, kid," I pleaded, intentionally not meeting her playful tone.

Her face grew serious and she sat up straight. "Wait—is something wrong?"

"No!" I answered too fast. Dammit, this was not going the way I thought it would. So much for simple answers. "No," I said, more even-keeled. "I just thought it was odd that Dan knew when I didn't. No one mentioned it until he told me this morning. You're awake and you were there, so I figured—you know what, forget it. It's not a big deal, anyway." I stood to go back inside, but Russell jumped up, stepping in front of me before I could get there.

"Wait, C, are you catching feelings?" Russell asked, a genuine smile pulling at his mouth.

"Okay, I'm going inside," I replied.

"No, Carter," Sam protested, joining Russell's side. "I'm sorry. I didn't mean to scare you off. Let's sit." She gestured to the spot I'd just been sitting. "I'll be serious, I promise."

"Fine," I muttered.

"Navigating this shit can be chaotic, for real. We're here for you, big guy," Russell said, clapping me on the shoulder before he and Sam sat next to me.

"I'm going to pretend you didn't call me that," I muttered.

"Okay! Reel it in, guys," Sam interrupted, giving me a warning look. "Like I said, it was sweet, innocent. Your fingers were laced as you held hands, and your forearms were pressed together, kinda like this—" She paused to twine her arm with Russell's, interlacing their fingers. She rested her cheek against their closed hands. "And you were just sorta snuggling her hand." She unraveled their arms and looked at me expectantly.

"Oh," I replied, unsure of what exactly I was feeling. "Thanks for clearing that up. I'm going to go check the smoker now."

"Woah, hold-up," Russell said. "That's it?"

"Uh, yeah," I answered.

"Carter," Sam said, all joking, gone from her tone as she tilted her head. "You didn't answer Russell's question from before."

"Because there's no point," I answered. "Thanks again." I got up and walked away before they could say anything else.

THIRTY-EIGHT
ALINA

When I finally woke, it felt like I had a hangover. Such was the aftermath of a full-blown panic attack followed by tossing and turning all night. As I sat up and looked around the room, I realized I was the last to rise, as the cabin was quiet and empty aside from one other. Emma sat beside me, sipping a cup of steaming brown liquid.

"Morning, sunshine," Emma said, giving me a wide smile. "There's hot water on the camping stove outside. I think it's still hot enough for the instant coffee, but if not, it'll be a quick boil."

I jolted upright. "There's coffee? What the heck—why didn't you wake me earlier?"

"Because you needed the sleep, girl." She gave me a challenging look. "Go get a cup and come back. You're on bed rest today. Or...floor rest? Maybe chair rest." She paused. "Whatever, you get it. You're resting."

"What? Why? It's not like I'm sick," I asked, unsure if I should be offended.

"No, but you need a mental health day. Nurse's orders," Emma said matter-of-factly, and I knew there was no arguing against it.

I nodded and a smile curved across my lips. "So, if I'm on rest, doesn't that mean someone else should make my coffee? Someone oh, so good at taking care of others? Someone generous, and kind, who loves her best friend more than anything?" I batted my eyelashes at her as she rolled her eyes.

She braced herself to stand as Jason walked through the doorway. Smirking, she leaned back, calling across the room sweetly, "Jason, hi! Would you mind making Alina a cup of coffee? Thank you!"

"Yeah, sure," Jason said, flashing a smile at me before heading into the kitchen to grab a cup to bring outside.

I glared at her, though I shouldn't have been surprised. "Really, Em?"

"What? He fit the description."

"I'd whack you with a pillow if I had one," I replied, bumping her shoulder with mine. "Also, I have to pee, so I'm getting up anyway, I guess."

Emma stood with me and I gave her a look.

"I swear I'm not being clingy." She held up her hands defensively. "Michelle lectured us about being better with the buddy system, and I'd rather avoid another talk."

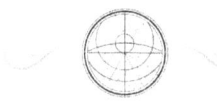

Once I took care of myself, I followed Emma to the porch. The rain stopped overnight, and the fresh, dewy smell of morning engulfed me like a hug. These mornings always seemed to inspire a comforting kind of nostalgia; I wanted to wrap myself in it. I stretched my arms above my head, breathing deeply. Maybe a day of rest wouldn't be so bad.

I grabbed the book Sam let me borrow, bringing it outside to read. The book opened to the page I'd bookmarked with a stray piece of paper, and I smiled, looking forward to diving into a different universe. I let myself fall into the words, slipping between the pages until I barely noticed the world around me.

By midday, Cap called us to the porch to have a meeting. After our quiet morning, I felt a sleepy kind of ease. Maybe Emma was right; I just needed to turn off for a bit to reset.

"I don't want to push us too hard today," Cap said, addressing the group. "We all could use some extra rest. We're good on water. The meat is still smoking. I think it would be a good idea to focus on figuring out the high-frequency radio, though. What do y'all think? Does that sound okay?" They waited for anyone to object, but the group seemed to be in tired agreement.

"Sam, how confident do you feel after reading the manual?" Cap asked.

The night before, Sam stayed up reading the radio's manual until she couldn't keep her eyes open any longer, determined to learn how to use the device.

"Eh, so-so," she answered. "It looks like the radio has an automatic scanning function that tries to find active frequencies, but there was also a note about how manual adjustment might be necessary. I feel like this is kind of a 'figure it out as you go' type of task."

Cap nodded. "I don't have much experience with high-frequency radios, but my dad kept a simpler version in the garage when I was younger. Let's work together to figure out the best way to piece the information together. Once we feel a bit more confident, we can talk about actually powering it on."

Sam nodded. "Sure. Sounds like a plan."

"What's our goal, though?" Carter asked from across the circle. "I know we have to take advantage of resources when we find them; but what do we need from another group that we can't take care of ourselves?"

It was the first time I'd seen Carter all morning. I couldn't believe we hadn't at least checked in with each other, especially after last night. I studied his stoic face as he stood with one hand in his pocket. He always seemed to be the picture of indifference on the outside, but after spending so much time with him, I knew there was so much more beneath the hard exterior. He looked tired, and every once in a while, I noticed a twinge in his expression, likely from the pain he still felt from his wound. The injured arm rested stiffly at his side, and I could tell he was trying to move it as little as possible.

"Well," Cap started, "I think it would still be worth trying to connect with others. The radio is a way we can vet people before meeting in person. Plus, someone else might know some relatively safer areas where we can actually settle in longer-term. They might have new pieces of information we can use to piece together more of the unknowns."

"Yeah, plus it's been kinda creepy not seeing any other humans in over a week," Emma added, crossing her arms. "I also really want to know how many people like Lee and Jayce are out there, and if they have the same...symptoms." Her eyes darted to me quickly before looking back at Cap. "If we can compare experiences, it might help us understand more about what the glow means."

"I definitely agree on that part," I added.

"Can I be real with y'all?" Dan asked.

"Of course," Cap answered.

Dan paused, gathering his thoughts. "What if we chill here for a while longer? Just us." A few moments of silence followed before Dan continued, his words measured, "The pig thing sucked, but before that, it felt like we were starting to get into a good rhythm. I don't think I'm ready to give that up."

"I have to admit," Michelle said, "I've been thinking the same."

"Me, too," Jason agreed.

Cap nodded, taking in everyone's comments. "I understand, especially after the chaos we've experienced. I'm worried about long-term sustainability, though. We've been comfortable with how our tasks have been divided so far—but what if it gets to be too much? If people get sick or injured? Take last night for example—we're lucky Alina was alright and Carter wasn't hurt worse. We've had *just* enough people to split our most important tasks—but I want to avoid risks down the line, too. We don't have to completely merge with another group for that to happen, but those connections would give us options, and hopefully make us stronger."

"I agree," Brian added. "We've come across way more groups who were helpful than people who weren't. Who's to say that the next group wouldn't be looking for the same things we are? I think it's a smart move."

"Same," Sam said, nodding.

"Do we need to figure out such specific steps right now?" I was nervous to share my thoughts, but once I got started I couldn't stop. "I think we should take advantage of having access to the radio while we can—especially not knowing what might happen next. I can't lie, it'd be nice to know Jason and I aren't the only formerly-abducted wandering around, too." I paused, remembering Gabriela, Jean, and Ben. We still had no idea whether there were more people like us out there. "Plus, we don't know whether it'll even work. Why don't we see what we can do with the radio first, and then circle back tonight after we've all had some time to think on the rest?"

After talking a bit more, we decided to table the points brought up until later tonight. I'd seen the group in action a few times now when it came to planning and decision-making, but this was the first time I truly felt like I was a part of that process. I looked around the circle at the people I'd come to know in the last week. With all the time we spent together and everything we'd faced so far, it felt like I'd known them so much longer. There wasn't a single person in the circle that I wouldn't trust with my life; last night had only solidified that as fact.

As the group dispersed, I jogged over to Carter so I could catch him before he disappeared again.

"Hey, you," I greeted him with a smile, happy I finally got a chance to speak with him. "Where've you been all morning? It felt a little weird not starting the day together."

The corner of his mouth tipped in his signature almost half-smile. "I've been around. It looked like you were deep into that book, so I figured you'd appreciate some quiet."

"Oh, so you saw me, but you *chose* not to come say hi? I see how it is."

"Listen, if you're anything like Sam when it comes to reading, I didn't want to risk my life by interrupting. It was self-preservation."

I laughed, a lightness filling my chest.

I was glad our tense first encounter didn't stop us from finding a comfortable kind of companionship. I'd have never expected someone so intense to become such a source of security. Being with Carter and having these normal conversations didn't feel like it was just a distraction from everything we were trying to forget; instead, it reminded me that the world was bigger than the small pieces we'd come to know.

"Do you think we would have gotten to know each other if we met before all this?" I asked suddenly, tilting my head as I studied his face.

He thought for a moment, and a real smile crossed his face as he answered, "I'd hope so."

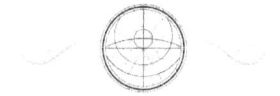

We stayed around the ranger station while Sam and Cap read the manual for the high-frequency radio and familiarized themselves with the buttons and dials. Brian found a deck of cards and roped Michelle, Dan, Russell, and Emma into a game I was almost sure he made up on the spot.

I'd curled up with Sam's book again in a quieter corner of the office. The smell of smoking meat wafted in through the open door, and I wasn't sure how to feel about it. My stomach flipped, and nausea churned in my gut.

"Hey, you're looking kinda green. Everything okay?" Jason asked as he came over to sit with me.

"I was just thinking about what the…meat…looked like. Like, does it have a face, still?" I asked, wincing.

Jason chuckled, wrapping an arm around my shoulders. "No faces, don't worry." His fingers traced soft circles on my arm and I relaxed against him. "So, what do you think about…everything?" he asked.

I sighed, leaning my head against Jason's shoulder. "I don't even know. Once I start to accept the last thing that happened, something else pops up to throw me through a loop all over again."

"Yeah, I get what you mean," Jason answered, sounding far away.

"What I can't get over, is how so much has happened so quickly. It hasn't even been two full weeks yet. If you and I are overwhelmed, I can't imagine how everyone else feels. Eight months of this? Or worse than this?" I thought out loud.

"Yeah..." Jason answered. "I've been wondering the same." Jason glanced across the room to where the others were playing cards.

"I think last night was the most sleep I've gotten since we escaped, and I'm still exhausted," I declared, failing to stifle a yawn.

"So rest," Jason said, his voice soft. His lips brushed gently against my forehead, not quite a kiss. I settled into his familiarity and comfort, relieved for the opportunity to turn everything off and slip back into sleep.

THIRTY-NINE
CARTER

I STOOD with Cap and Sam as they compared the manual to the radio in front of them. They took turns reciting each function until they felt comfortable doing it without the manual. Who knew whether the studying would help once the thing was on, but they both seemed to build confidence in understanding how something worked before diving in.

I stole a glance across the room; Alina was curled against Jason, her brow furrowed in her sleep. She twitched every so often, and I wondered whether she was having another nightmare. Jason lifted his head from where it rested against Alina's and caught my eye. He nodded a hello, wearing a tired but friendly smile. As curious as I was about the radio, I couldn't listen to Sam and Cap recite the steps again without feeling stuck in a loop. I stretched, realizing how stiff my muscles felt from standing in one place for too long. My arm throbbed with the movement, and I tried to push the sensation to the back of my mind. The others were still playing a card game, but the energy was too high for where I was at.

Before I knew it, I found myself crossing the room to where Jason and Alina were.

"Hey," Jason greeted me quietly as I lowered to the floor a few feet away.

I nodded hello, looking at Alina as she slept in his arms. "How's she doing?" I murmured.

Jason rested his cheek against her head for a second before answering. "I'm not sure, honestly. I mean physically, yeah, she seems fine," he spoke softly, barely above a whisper. "The rest? I don't know. I think she is still feeling the nerves from last night."

I nodded, realizing that I had nothing else to say.

"How are you doing, man?" Jason asked. "Your arm?"

Even as I sat there doing nothing, the wound still throbbed underneath the gauze. I knew if I asked Emma for Ibuprofen or something, she'd give it without hesitation. Still, I sat with the pain, knowing I could take it for a while longer.

"Hurts, but what can you do?" I shrugged.

"You moved so fast, I barely knew what was happening before you were tackling that thing. Thank you. For, you know." He hugged her closer, shifting to get more comfortable.

A muscle in my jaw ticked. "Yeah, I wasn't thinking. I just saw her and knew—"

Alina tensed in her sleep, a whimper escaping her lips.

"It looks like she's having a nightmare," I thought out loud, eyes still on her.

"Maybe; she's been pretty restless," he murmured.

I swallowed. "Try holding her hand. It might help her, having something physical to hold onto." I stood and walked out of the ranger station before I could see whether my advice actually helped.

I wandered outside, leaning back against the building just outside the door. We'd all agreed to stick to the buddy system if anyone went beyond the porch, so even though I could have used a longer walk, this would have to do for now. After a few minutes, Michelle stepped outside.

"Oh, hi, Carter," she called in her usual cheery voice with just a hint of exhaustion.

"Hey," I answered.

"Restless?" she asked.

"What?" I blinked, realizing my focus had drifted off again.

"You don't know what to do with your time?" she clarified.

"Oh." I rubbed the back of my neck. "Yeah, I guess so. I feel like I should be doing something, but I can't decide what."

"Same. But every time I'm about to relax, I just end up thinking that I can sit like a bump on a log when I'm dead—oh! That was morbid, wasn't it?"

Michelle laughed and I shook my head, chuckling. I could never figure out whether her humor was intentional, but it always had the same effect. Her one-off statements had a way of catching everyone off-guard, bringing levity back into any situation. For a group that tended to cope with trauma by finding ways to laugh through it, it just worked.

"Anyway," she continued, "has there been any luck figuring out that radio yet?"

I sighed. "While they insist they aren't ready to try turning it on, I've heard them recite each step so many times that I could probably repeat the instructions word for word without even trying."

"Yeah, that sounds like my Cap." Michelle smiled like she was wrapped in an invisible hug. "I'll go in there in a few and tell them to get this show on the road. The anticipation is killing me."

Michelle never had to go inside to move things along, though. Not too much later, Sam came outside to let us know it was time to power on the generator.

I took Michelle with me, as per safety protocol, and she waited while I checked the generator over one more time. The generator ran off of propane, and if the gauge was accurate, we had about seventy-five percent of the tank to work with. The plan was to switch through the radio for thirty minutes every few hours to see if we could connect with anyone. It took four pulls of the starter-chord, but the engine roared to life, scaring the grackles out of the brush.

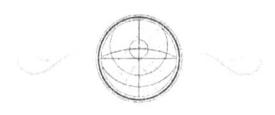

The radio ended up working way quicker than we expected. After only three sessions, Cap and Sam managed to catch a new sound underneath the radio static. Sam was explaining to the rest of us how to tune the frequencies, and Jason heard it first—the rasping voice was easy to miss underneath the buzz of white noise, but it was there. Another person.

My heart pounded as everyone else crowded around the radio, staring in anticipation as Cap adjusted the settings, moving fractions of a centimeter at a time. The room was frozen in rapt silence, no one moving as the voice slowly grew clearer. The garbled words repeated at the same cadence and intonations a few times over as the message became coherent, and, finally, we realized what we were hearing.

It was a recording.

"It worked!" Sam gasped.

"Everyone, quiet!" Cap called to the room as the message repeated.

"Attention: This is Skyview240. Please listen carefully to this recorded message. The beings left our skies and returned those who were taken. Now we must forge our way forward. For anyone looking for a place to belong; for anyone who can't find their way; for anyone wishing for a greater tomorrow—join us. Join us in seeking a greater purpose as we rebuild the path forward, ascending the human race to our greatest destiny yet. We can and will thrive once again. We have safety, shelter, food, water, and protection at the community, and all are welcome."

Sam jotted down the address mentioned at the end of the recording as we all listened to the message on a loop. After a few more minutes, Cap switched the radio off, leaving the room without a word. The generator turned off, and there was a ringing in my ears from the sudden lack of sound. No one spoke as we waited for them to return, processing what we'd just heard.

When Cap joined us again, it was a few more minutes before someone broke the silence.

"So, community," Russell said.

"I'm still stuck on the 'ascending the human race' bit," Jason muttered.

"It did sound a bit off," Michelle added nervously.

"Could it be a language barrier? Or maybe a class thing? Like they're trying to appeal to a specific group of people?" Sam asked.

"Do we want to go there if we aren't the kinda people they want to appeal to?" Dan added.

Cap and I exchanged a look from across the circle. Though the outcome made the project a success, not knowing *what* waited on the other end created more issues to work through. If we took it at face value, it sounded like everything a person could ever hope for. On the other hand, it also sounded like a cult.

I weighed the options in my head, thinking about what decision I would make if I were alone. The fact that there was a fully recorded message broadcasting across the airwaves when the ships hadn't even left that long ago didn't sit right. Then again, if they had the knowledge to do so, they could have been planning for this very situation for months. Then there was the question about what they were trying to build—was this an already established group that had been together a while who were looking to grow their numbers? A newer group looking for allies? Or something else? The offer of protection also sat like a rock in my stomach. Anyone presuming they could guarantee safety had to be living with deliberate ignorance or cocky arrogance of the world we all lived in now.

"Okay, so the community's location points to a residential neighborhood," Dan said as Cap identified the location on one of the station's maps. "It still feels off. I'm not convinced it's a good idea to actually go there," Dan finished.

"What would convince you? What would someone have to say or do for you to be convinced?" Brian asked, clearly frustrated with the conversation not moving forward.

"B, come on. I'm not saying we shouldn't do anything. I just don't want anyone else getting hurt," Dan answered calmly, staring directly at Brian.

"Whatever," Brian scoffed, pulling off his glasses and rubbing at the lenses with his shirt.

"Woah, okay," Sam jumped in. "Let's take it back a step. Both of you are making good points. Dan, you're right—we don't have a way to find out for sure what their intentions are. And Brian, you're also right—we won't know unless we actually go there and see what these people are like."

"Couldn't have said it better myself," Cap added. "Sam, I want to hear more about what you think."

"Well..." Sam paused, gathering her thoughts. "Thinking about Brian's question—what *would* someone have to do to prove that they were trustworthy? Honestly, I don't think there is a surefire way outside of personally knowing the person, like with Jason and Alina. We have to go with what we see, what we hear, body language..."

"Yeah," I agreed, standing up straighter as I processed what Sam had just said. "We need to be able to see them when they think no one else is watching—catch them when they are at their most natural."

"Okay, now we're getting somewhere," Michelle said, her excitement returned.

"So, what does that mean? Are we going to spy on them?" Alina asked.

"That's exactly what it means," I answered, glancing at her.

"We'll have to create a contingency plan in case we are caught. With this message out, they will be expecting people to find them. How will *we* prove that we don't have ill intentions? How will we ensure our own safety? They'll be questioning us just as much as we are questioning them," Cap added.

"We should have a safe word," Russell called out. "So like, if it's too sus, we can throw a word or phrase into the conversation and abort the mission."

"Smart, Russ," Cap said, and Russell beamed under the recognition. "And with this line, the second anyone uses it, we are out. We have to trust each other's judgment."

"I got it!" Emma shouted. "The perfect line, '*I could really go for some pig.*' Because let's be real, I don't think anyone would mind not seeing another one of those suckers again." Emma smirked, clearly proud of herself.

"It's...kind of perfect, actually," Jason said.

Alina shifted uncomfortably next to them, but she nodded all the same.

"Alright, so are we all in agreement? '*I could really go for some pig*' as our bad vibes bail-out phrase?" Brian asked the group.

We all nodded, and the rest of the plan started coming together. The route was mapped and we planned for multiple scenarios in case things went south. It was really the only way we could prepare without knowing what we'd be walking into. Hopefully, we'd be able to quickly determine whether this was a group worth approaching, or whether we should continue on to the next town instead. Every plan had to start somewhere, I guess.

That night, we all ate together on the front porch, trying to keep the mood light. I tried not to think about the feral hog that became our dinner, knowing that this was the most solid meal we'd had in a long time. I just hoped it wouldn't be the last.

FORTY
CARTER

THAT NIGHT, I was on watch with Brian. The night was still young as we sat outside on the porch. With the smoker down and the skies clear, it felt like a new start. I anticipated Brian striking up a conversation, but he was oddly quiet. When I guessed an hour had almost passed and he still wasn't talking, I knew something was up. What to do about it, was another story.

"So, nice night," I said, unsure where to start.

"Yeah," Brian answered, eyes fixed straight ahead.

I tried to think of a way to ease into my next question, but when no ideas came, I realized I was just going to have to be blunt.

"What's wrong?" I asked.

Brian froze for half a second, so quick that I'd have missed it if I hadn't been staring at him and waiting for him to answer. He stayed quiet and I waited, letting the silence grow. While I might have been comfortable with silence, I knew Brian would cave.

Finally, he sighed. "Just feels like I have no idea what I am doing anymore."

I didn't reply, waiting for him to continue, giving him the space to find his words.

"I love our group. Sometimes, I think, too much. I want to fix it all, find answers, but how can I do that for anyone else when I don't even know how to do it for myself?"

"What are you trying to fix for yourself?" I asked. "I might not be the best person to give advice, but I could try."

Brian finally turned to look at me, studying me for an extended moment before nodding his head, turning to lean his back on the porch's front post so he could face me. I mirrored his position and waited patiently.

"You know that feeling when you're surrounded by people, but you still feel alone? I was stuck there for a long, long time. I want to know people, really know and understand them, and make sure that I am always the one person anyone can turn to. Dependable, constant, trustworthy, just...worthy. My former therapist called it 'people pleasing,' but I always hated that term. What's wrong with wanting the people around you to be happy?

"I had a tight-knit group of friends at college, but half the time, I felt like I was just the one they resorted to when no one else was around—when they made a mistake anyone else would tear them apart for; when they were scared of how they'd be perceived for their actions; when they were fighting with someone else and needed to fill the space. Outside of that? I might as well not have existed. It didn't stop me from caring, but I didn't know how to fix it—how to find *my* person.

"It's been different here. For the first time I can remember, I really feel like I'm a part of something. I mean, this right here, you asking me how I am? That means more to me than you can ever imagine. Then Michelle is always there, making sure I'm eating and remembering to drink water. Cap shows their love through teaching. Emma might be brash, but she has threatened more people on my behalf than I'm sure I'm aware of—however unnecessary it may have been at the time. She's actually given me some really solid advice that's helped me through...well, things. Even Alina and Jason, it's wild how quickly it felt like they'd always been a part of this, us. Russell and Sam are the first to go looking for me if they don't know where I am, even if I've only been gone five minutes. And Dan, well, Dan's

Dan." Brian sighed. He tilted his head to the side to look at the stars, trying to hide the fact that tears threatened to fall.

"It sounds to me like you got what you've always wanted, then," I replied. "I might not be as vocal as the others, but I admire you, really. No matter what, you're always able to see the good in people, pull out the positives, even with all the crap we've been dealing with. I've never been able to do that. You make us better."

Brian removed his glasses, rubbing the back of his fist against his eyes.

"Yeah, Dan said something similar earlier." His jaw flexed, and he swiped at his eyes once more before putting his glasses back on and staring down at the ground.

"So, what's really going on, then?" I asked.

Brian looked back at me, a sad smile on his face. "I'm just so fucking scared." He took a shuddering breath. "I'm scared of losing people—more people. I'm scared that things are coming that we won't be able to beat. That I'll misjudge someone or something, and it'll hurt someone else. That we won't have enough resources as a smaller group and we'll end up starving, or worse. There's just so much."

Brian's composure broke, and he pulled his knees to his chest, heaving quiet sobs against his folded arms. An invisible string pulled at my chest, opening an empty space in my ribs to absorb the pain pouring from him as I shifted to sit at his side. I gripped his shoulder, showing him I was still there.

"I get it," I said quietly.

I didn't say anything as everything Brian held inside was released, never once moving my hand—the little comfort I knew how to offer. He slumped down, spent from the outpouring of emotion.

"Thanks," he said, turning to make eye contact. "Really, Carter. Thank you."

"Everything alright?" a voice said from the door.

We both turned, seeing Dan slipping outside, quietly shutting the door to the ranger station.

"No, but the only way out is through, right?" Brian answered honestly.

"Can I sit for a while, too?" Dan asked.

Brian nodded, and we adjusted so Brian was sitting in the middle of us. Dan draped an arm across Brian's shoulders and Brian leaned against him, resting his head on Dan's shoulder.

The three of us didn't speak for the rest of our watch. Emma and Dan were due to take over next. Even when I went inside to grab Emma to take over, Brian stayed out there, never moving from his spot on the front porch next to Dan.

Emma paused at the door, biting her lip. As she turned, I saw a sad look on her face that was gone a moment later. She quietly rushed back to where she had been resting, digging in her backpack for something, grinning in success when she found it. She turned to me, waving goodnight as she walked back to the door, a bag of Sour Patch Kids in her hand.

When she reached the porch, she dropped the bag of candy in Brian's lap, sitting on his other side. Emma wrapped her arms around them both, and a new vigil began.

FORTY-ONE
ALINA

I WAS reluctant to say goodbye to the state park, the forest, and the quiet calm I had grown so quickly accustomed to. My heart sank as we drove away, watching the trees blur together outside the truck's window as we traveled toward the community we'd learned about on the radio.

Our destination was just over thirty miles away and our planned route took us through a more desolate area. Jason was at the wheel with Carter in the passenger seat while Emma, Sam, and I sat together in the back. In the SUV, Cap was driving with Michelle, Russell, Brian, and Dan, straight ahead of us.

It seemed there were only fields, trees, hay bales, and more fields the further down the road we drove. It starkly contrasted the cluttered highways we'd experienced before leaving Austin. Shivering, I tried to brush away the thought that maybe we were the only people left in the world. That message had to come from somewhere though, so I guessed we'd soon find out who else was out there.

Out of nowhere, the SUV swerved in front of us, careening into the field adjacent to the road. Sam grabbed my hand from where she sat in the middle seat, clutching it tight. Jason reacted instantly, driving us as close as possible before slamming on the brakes and throwing the car into park. He and Carter were out of the front seat in a flash, rushing to the aid of the other vehicle.

"Go, go, go, go, go!" Sam urged us to open the doors, scrambling out of the truck and running ahead.

Sam ran straight to Russell, a choked sob escaping her mouth as she clung to him. My eyes darted to the rest of the group. Emma was checking in with each person to ensure they weren't hurt, and aside from looking shaken, it didn't appear anyone suffered any injury. The SUV on the other hand...

Carter and Jason looked at the damage, talking in hushed tones before deciding to walk back to me. Carter's eyes were glued to mine as he approached. "You sure you're alright? We stopped fast," he asked, as he analyzed the expression on my face.

"Yeah," I said, "I was mostly worried about everyone else, but it looks like they're okay for the most part."

Carter studied me a moment longer until he was satisfied that I was telling the truth. He moved to my side to scan our group again, his arm just touching mine.

Jason squeezed my shoulder on the other side, looking at me with concern.

"You might be physically okay, but your tattoo says you may be feeling otherwise," Jason replied.

I cursed under my breath, trying to look over my shoulder, knowing that I wouldn't be able to see it, no matter how hard I tried.

"Yours is glowing, too. Right through your shirt," Carter said, his expression neutral as he looked at Jason. "Everyone is a bit anxious right now. It's a normal reaction."

Jason paused, seeming to reflect on that thought for a moment before nodding. He gave me a tight smile before turning to Carter. "You're right," he said, then to me. "Sorry, Lee. I didn't mean to overstep."

"It's fine, Jayce," I reassured him, "I understand why you're worried, but really, I'm okay."

I folded my arms across my chest and shifted so I was standing in front of them. "What happened to the SUV?"

"Looks like nails or something sharp took out two tires," Carter answered, frowning at the vehicle. Carter turned suddenly, walking back towards the road. Jason and I followed, as Carter scuffed the toe of his boot against the dirt road.

"What are you doing?" I asked.

"He's checking the road," Jason answered for him. "Good thinking."

Jason walked further down, crouching to look closer. "Over here, but be careful, even on the grass. There's a bunch of sharp debris scattered here."

Jason stood up as Carter and I approached saying, "I don't want to sound paranoid, but—"

"I agree," Carter said before Jason could finish. "It doesn't look right."

"What do we do?" I questioned, knowing that this mission was turning into bad luck way quicker than I could have anticipated.

"We need to talk to the others," Carter said, gesturing to the area where the group had formed a small circle.

We made our way back and my heart beat faster with each step. We agreed that we should at least check out this community, even if it was to rule out connecting with them. Losing one of our vehicles put us at an immediate disadvantage, and I wasn't sure what would happen from here.

"Alright, here's the deal. We are about five miles out from this community's location. That debris took out two tires, so the SUV isn't an option anymore. Carter, how is the gas on the truck?" Cap asked.

"Lower than I'd like. We'll need to change our target to the next town on the map to fill up and find a car to replace the SUV. Even if we decided to turn around now, the truck would be near empty by the time we got back to the state park, and that's with the addition of the remaining gas siphoned from the SUV."

My stomach churned as we weighed our options, but there was only one logical choice. We had to get to the next town, fill up the truck, and get another car before we even attempted to look for the community.

After siphoning the gas out of the SUV, we began packing the truck. It would be a tight fit, but I knew we'd make it work. Just as we were talking through seating arrangements, a sound in the distance caught my attention.

"Wait, does anyone else hear that?" I asked.

The group fell silent as they listened, and in the sudden stillness, even the light breeze from the field was audible as it rustled through the trees.

Jason nodded. "Yeah, a motor."

"I don't hear anything," Dan added.

"Same here," Michelle said.

"Wait—" Sam tilted her head. "I hear it now."

"That's definitely a motor," Carter said grimly.

We looked at each other, knowing we were stuck. It was too close.

"Michelle, Alina, Sam, Emma, squeeze into the back seat of the truck," Cap ordered. "Emma and Sam in the middle; y'all are the smallest. Russell, you're driving. Carter, in the passenger seat—you're freshly injured, don't argue. Russell, put the truck in drive, but keep your foot on the break until I say so. Everyone else, in the back. We are a tired, desperate group of travelers looking for support. Tell just enough truth to keep looking honest and avoid inconsistencies in our motivation. We don't want to give any reason to think we are a threat or that they need to pursue us if we need to break away. Keep the supplies secured, but if anything falls out, consider it gone. People are the priority; items are replaceable. Now. Get in."

Dan pulled the tailgate closed just as the vehicle came into view and slowed to a stop on the opposite side of the road. My heart pounded as the window rolled down. Emma grabbed my hand, squeezing.

"Well hi, there!" a woman called out from the driver's seat. "Listen, I'm not here to cause no trouble." Her southern accent was thick as she called out the driver's side window.

"What are y'all doin' there on the side of the road?" She eyed the skid marks and the SUV with its tires sinking lower on one side.

"Tires blew," Cap answered.

"Were y'all headed somewhere? How many of y'all are there?"

Her face was obscured, but I guessed her to be on the younger side of twenty, based on her tone. I stretched in the backseat to try and see if anyone else was in the car with her.

"Two others. I think I see guns," Russell said under his breath.

"Yeah, I see them," Carter answered.

"We heard a broadcast," Cap answered.

"*Ohmahgawd*!" the woman exclaimed, turning to her car-riding companions. "They heard it, too!"

"Was that you?" Cap asked.

"Yes, that was our community! *The* Community, as it's called, actually. Y'all are the second batch of travelers we've gotten in the last week with that message! You know what? Our fuel run can wait. I'll lead y'all back myself. If you'd like to drive a bit safer, we can take two of y'all, maybe three, in the car with us?"

"Very kind of you to offer, but we will stay together," Cap answered.

"I completely understand. Alright then, let's git goin'!" The woman rolled up the window and pulled a U-turn.

Cap tapped on the car's hood, letting Russell know he was good to follow.

"Where was she going to get fuel?" Carter asked under his breath, knowing we'd just come from that same direction and there was nothing for miles. The closest town was in the opposite direction. Emma and I looked at each other, and her grip on my hand tightened.

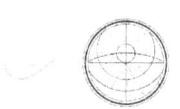

None of us trusted the woman's story, yet we still followed. I tried to find comfort in knowing we planned for scenarios like this, hoping it was enough. I held Emma's hand, trying not to let fear take over completely as my heart pounded.

"Lee," Emma said, voice shaking. "I can see your glow reflected in the window."

Carter turned around, hearing Emma's declaration. I could see she responded, voice quivering. She turned back to look at us once more, eyes darting behind us before saying, "They're pretty serious about responsibilities here, so I gotta...Hopefully, I'll see y'all later to catch up," she said, giving a subtle wave with two fingers before walking away, her face grim.

"We will see!" Willa responded in a sing-song voice. "Why don't I take y'all to my place for a bit so you can sit back and rest up?"

"That would be nice," Cap answered.

I reminded myself this was part of the plan—play along, don't act too suspicious, find a safe way out, then run.

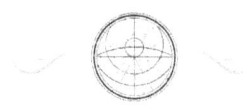

I kept my arm tight around Alina as we followed Willa into one of the houses. Brian and Dan stood on either side of Jason just ahead of us while Emma continued walking at Alina's side. I caught Emma's attention over Alina's head, and her blue eyes sparked as they met mine; her fear turned into something fierce. She didn't have to say a word for me to know she'd go down swinging if she had to. Good. So would I.

"Welcome to mi casa!" Willa chirped as she ushered us inside.

We walked into the house and a chill rolled across my skin. Alina gasped, looking around, and I saw goosebumps rise on the back of Brian's neck in front of me.

"Oh y'all feel that, don't ya?" Willa giggled. "I know y'all had cars, but when did you last feel central AC? It's a cool seventy-one degrees in here." Willa hugged her arms across her chest, pretending to shiver as she shimmied her shoulders, laughing. "Y'all are gettin' the special treatment here today. Now, who wants some sweet tea?"

"Water will do just fine, thank you," Cap answered for the group.

"You got it!" She clapped her hands, yelling, "Sander! Sander where are you? We have guests."

A blond teen with a pinched nose and gaunt-looking face entered the room, glaring at Willa.

"Y'all, meet my brother Sander. Don't mind his sour-puss.

already formed a tight circle around Jason, Alina, and Gabriela, but we were clearly outnumbered as more folks from The Community gathered, casually watching from their front lawns.

"We'll be late. You know how important timeliness is," the second man added.

Though the men tried to look casual, the stiffening of one's jaw and clench of the other's fists gave away the tension they held.

"Oh, sorry, we must have missed your names," Sam asked in her most polite tone, clearly stalling.

The first man's eyes darted between her and the inner circle where Gabriela was still holding Alina's arm.

He forced a smile, barely hiding the snarl underneath as he said, his voice just as even and calm as before, "I'm Dennis; that's Jim. Gabriela, clock is ticking."

Jim stepped forward as Russell moved in front of Sam, putting himself between her and Jim. The fact that he bothered to answer at all—they didn't want to scare us away, pretending this was still a normal introduction. But why?

"So, like, what's with the rush?" Russell asked, running a hand through his wavy hair and flashing a smile. "Let them catch up for a bit. You know how rare it is for people to reunite with loved ones."

I had to give him credit for his control. Russell's body language was relaxed, but I saw the muscles in his shoulders tensing, even from where I stood. It was clear he didn't trust them, but he picked up on the need to buy more time for the girl.

"Oh, there will be plenty of time for that later!" Willa chirped. "Or, Gabriela, your two friends could go *with* you to help Dr. Don. What do you think, Gabriela? Or should we escort them somewhere more comfortable so they can rest up a bit? It's rather hot out, and I bet they're plenty thirsty."

Gabriela dove up to wrap her arms around Alina's neck in one more hug, tilting her head and barely moving her lips. Whatever she said, it was too low for me to hear it. The girl let go and then turned to leave the circle.

"Sorry, Willa. I've just missed them so much. I couldn't help it,"

FORTY-TWO

CARTER

THE GIRL BARRELED into Alina's arms and Alina clutched her tight. "You're alive. Holy fuck, you're alive," Alina gasped.

As they hugged, Jason whipped around, staring at the young girl in shock for a moment before gesturing for Emma to move to the side. Emma released her hold on Alina, making space for her brother as he pretended to join the hug. Jason's voice was barely audible as he whispered, "Danger?" into the girl's ear. I would have missed it if I hadn't been so close.

Fear radiated from the young girl who clung to Alina, and her face was so pale I thought she might pass out. For someone so young, so scared, I could only imagine what pushed her to take the chance and run with armed guards watching.

Gabriela nodded slightly, just enough to confirm our suspicions. She stepped back, still keeping a hand on Alina's arm as she looked at the two of them, trying to communicate something without words.

I clenched my fist, feeling the sting of the fresh wound on my arm. The cut throbbed as my muscles tensed, but I had to channel the nervous energy somewhere so I could stay focused—in control. Our plan went so wrong. So, so wrong.

"Come along, Gabriela," a man's voice called. Too close. We'd back when the ships first appeared in the sky. He led us here and built up a safe place for us to wait things out. We've been takin' in people as we've found 'em hidin' out and around. Since the power came back, we've been shoutin' out our message to anyone who can hear it. Took a few days to figure out how to get everythin' up and runnin' again, but once we did, it was cake!"

I felt eyes on me from behind, and as I peeked over my shoulder, I saw three men behind us. A gasp escaped, and no sooner did the breath leave my lungs than one of them called out, "Marked Ones. Two of 'em."

The man pointed to Jason and I, and Carter hugged me closer to his side. Emma shifted, wrapping her arm tightly around my waist and reaching forward to grab her brother's hand.

"Oh, don't be scared—I sure ain't! We're just so lucky now, aren't we? Y'all are more special than you know. Come on, now, what are y'all's names? Let's get to know each other a bit."

I was still debating whether I should reply when I heard someone yelling from one of the houses behind her.

"Alina! Jason!"

My heart skipped a beat at the sound of that young voice.

That *familiar* young voice.

The girl ran towards the street, her long blonde hair blowing behind her as she ran away from the people who had exited the building with her. Though she was trying to keep her face neutral, I'd seen enough of her terror to recognize it in her eyes.

"Gabriela?" I breathed.

"Oh, y'all know each other?" Willa cooed, the tiniest hint of annoyance underlying her words, but she recovered quickly. "It must be a sign from God, then!" She clasped her hands in front of her chest as Gabriela ran to us.

"How do you know the girl?" Carter asked me under his breath.

"She escaped with us."

most peaceful dreams of all your favorite places with your favorite people."

"I think this is the street," Russell murmured as we turned.

I opened my eyes, and they locked with Carter's in the front seat.

"Try and hold onto that feeling," Carter finished. "I got you."

"Promise?" I whispered.

We drove down a long street before we hit what I assumed was The Community. No one spoke as we followed the other car past a barricade with armed guards. The men standing guard didn't so much as blink in our direction.

If they weren't there to vet newcomers, what exactly were they guarding?

We followed the car to the end of a cul-de-sac before Russell reluctantly turned off the engine, pocketing the keys as we all piled out.

As I left the car, Carter was there. Without hesitation, he lowered his head so close to mine that his exhale tickled the shell of my ear as he murmured, "Always." He glanced down at me once more before pulling me closer, blocking what he could of my tattoo with the arm he wrapped around my shoulders.

We joined our people, sticking to the back. Emma immediately locked herself to my other side, taking hold of my hand as we approached The Community's representatives.

The woman tilted her head, her blonde hair falling over one shoulder in a perfect wave. "I do wanna warn you—my men with the guns? They won't hesitate if they think y'all are gonna pull any funny business, so I recommend no one makes any sudden movements." She giggled, wrinkling her tiny nose. Her tinkling laugh sent a chill down my spine. "Just wanted to make that clear, hm?"

"Crystal," Cap answered.

"*Ohmahgawd*, where are my manners?" The woman giggled again. The thin blonde couldn't have been more than twenty-five. She looked oddly clean and styled for being so far into the aftermath of the invasion. Her aesthetic, combined with the plastic smile stamped on her face, was creeping me the fuck out.

"I'm Willa. My daddy is the one who started The Community way the worry on his face clearly from where I sat behind the driver's seat.

"We don't know how The Community will react. Alina, you have to try and push it back," Emma said in the slow but even tone she used with patients when she was trying to keep them calm.

"I'm not sure I can," I half-whispered.

Carter paused for a second, thinking. After a moment, he asked, "Do you trust me?"

I took a deep breath, nodding.

"Close your eyes and listen to my voice," he said.

I followed his instructions and the rest of the car went silent.

I could feel Emma's nails running up and down my arm, something my mom used to do to soothe me as a kid. My heart clenched at the memory, but I knew I had to push my emotions in the opposite direction.

"Just do the best you can, alright?" Carter said in a gentle voice.

I swallowed, nodding again.

"You're in the forest, surrounded by trees," Carter started. "It's cool out—one of those false fall mornings where you can get away with jeans or a hoodie, but not both at the same time or you'll get too warm. There's a breeze, and you take a deep breath, hold it, then let it out."

I breathed deeply, thinking of how the air smelled on our forest mornings with dew still on the grass and leaves. It was always so easy to forget about everything else when we were deep in the trees.

"That's it, another deep breath."

I breathed in again, running through a list of the plants we used as landmarks. Held my breath, and imagined what ripe fruit we might have found if we were there this morning. Released the air, and thought of the small animals we'd see in the brush.

"It's working," Emma whispered, still running her nails up and down my arm.

"You find a nice dry patch of grass, and you sit. The birds are singing, and you see rabbits playing in the bushes. You're so relaxed, you could fall asleep. And if you did fall asleep, you would have the

Teenagers." She tried to shrug nonchalantly, but her smile was tight, unable to hide the fact that she was not satisfied with his reluctant hospitality.

The kid rolled his eyes, taking in the group. He glared at his sister before beckoning us to follow him into the kitchen.

The house was large on the inside, with a winding staircase in the foyer. We followed Sander around the stairs and down a short hallway that led into a full kitchen. The fixtures looked new, and I noticed the time blinking on the microwave above the stove. How were they powering a whole house?

"Solar panels," Sander muttered, noticing me staring at the microwave.

He took out ten bottles of water from what must have been a pantry and set them on the counter. He looked at us out of the corner of his eye as he walked out of the room, holding up a peace sign at the last second.

"Why don't y'all wait here for a while? Get comfy, and feel free to help yourself to any snacks in the kitchen. I have to run down and see how Gabriela is gettin' on. She seemed a bit out of it, poor girl." Willa stuck out her lip in a mock pout before that plastic smile stamped across her face once again. "If you need anythin' else, just holler! A few of my men are by the front door and in the backyard, so don't be frightened. Y'all can explore anythin' you like down here, but don't go upstairs, please. A lady needs her privacy."

"Of course," Cap agreed. "Thank you again."

"What about our bags? Our supplies?" Brian asked.

"Don't worry about that. We're settin' up a suitable place for y'all to crash. Someone will bring all your stuff over," she answered.

By 'bring our stuff over,' I'm sure she meant 'dig through our belongings to ensure anything dangerous or of value miraculously disappeared.'

Willa flashed one last smile as she turned on her heel and quickly walked to the front of the house. We stood in the kitchen, listening for the slam of the door. Once we heard the lock click, Cap walked to the window, peering through the blinds.

"Three," they said, voice low.

They turned to face us. "I'm sure we all could go for a nice pig dinner right now, but let's try and control our appetite. We're hungry, but we don't want to get sick from eating too fast. Understand? Let's start with one snack at a time."

Cap was speaking in code, knowing there was a strong chance someone would be listening in. We'd briefly talked about the possibility at the ranger station when we were going over scenarios we might run into, but I didn't expect us to actually resort to communicating this way. I'd never been more thankful for Cap's preparedness.

The message was loud and clear—we needed to get the fuck out, and we needed to be safe about it.

Cap continued, "We can't trust someone who doesn't trust us, so let's see how much they are willing to reveal."

"Oh!" Alina yelped suddenly, and I snapped my attention to her. "Sorry, I thought a...spider ran across my foot. It was just a regular *bug*, though." She looked at Cap, cupping her ear, and we both realized what she was trying to communicate simultaneously. A bug. Somehow, they were listening in. That must have been what Gabriela whispered to her before leaving.

Alina pointed to her eyes, shaking her head, and Cap nodded firmly. Cap mimicked Alina's signals to communicate the message to the rest of the group.

"I hope Gabriela is feeling okay," Alina said, looking directly at Cap. "Maybe they will let her stay with us for a while? After all, she quickly felt like family to me after we first met."

"We can certainly ask," Cap said, nodding so Alina knew they were following.

If we could get the kid, we'd try.

"Alright, I won't hold y'all back anymore; grab a snack, and let's find a place to rest until Willa returns," Cap said.

Though fruit and jerky were set out on plates on the counter, Cap pointed to the food and shook their head so we knew not to touch it. Instead, they grabbed a sealed bag of chips from the pantry. It may have been overkill, but I trusted that Cap was trying to keep us safe in any way they knew how—including making sure we didn't eat something that could have been compromised. We were playing the part of cautious but desperate travelers, but we couldn't let our guard down.

All I wanted to do was grab my people and run. Still, it was more important to fully understand what we were dealing with before making rash decisions that could backfire.

Alina stayed glued to my side as we walked around the ground floor. After the way Willa looked at her, I knew The Community couldn't be trusted. That woman was way too excited about the marks, yet our group still knew very little about them. I would have been less suspicious if she were to react with horror than that uncanny valley positivity and excitement she practically oozed.

The ground floor was one giant loop. Darker squares of paint checkered the walls in the hallways and I noticed the same pattern again in the living room. It looked like picture frames once hung around the house, but where were they now? Considering Willa said her 'daddy' started The Community, I had to wonder by what means this neighborhood was established.

I led Alina to the couch, keeping my arm across her shoulders as we sat in the middle of the big U-shaped sectional. Emma took Alina's other side, with Jason next to his sister. Sam sat beside me, and I caught her eye. She forced a tight smile, nodding to let me know she was okay so far.

Russell's leg was bouncing rapidly as he adjusted his position on the couch. The nerves were getting to him, and I didn't blame him for not being able to hold it back any longer. Thankfully, our plan from here on out didn't rely on us *not* being nervous—especially since they already knew about Jason and Alina's tattoos. Russell pulled Sam closer to him, hugging her and whispering something in her ear.

I looked to where Dan and Brian were sitting beside Jason on the other end of the sectional. Brian took his glasses off and was rubbing the bridge of his nose, clearly stressed. Dan didn't give anything away, but I knew from the stiffness in his jaw that he was mentally preparing for the worst.

Cap and Michelle sat on an ottoman in front of us, and I could see Cap trying to control their breathing as they rubbed Michelle's back.

Michelle wrung her hands in her lap, glancing at the doorway every so often to check whether we were still alone.

My arm throbbed, and I adjusted my position to change the amount of pressure I was putting on the wound. We were as ready as we could be, given the situation. All we had to do was wait for the right time to make a move.

FORTY-THREE
ALINA

"*THERE'S AUDIO, no video. Two's safe,*" Gabriela's words played over and over in my head as I sat on the couch, trying to process everything that had happened. The entire mission had been turned around on us, and we were the ones being monitored. Surveilled. We knew there were risks before we left the ranger station. Still, planning for a theoretical situation and living the actual situation are very different experiences.

I shivered remembering how the man called out, "*Marked Ones.*" I took a deep, shuddering breath, trying to find my calm. I did not doubt that my mark was glowing big, bright, and blue—not that it mattered anymore.

They knew.

Carter hadn't once let go, just as he promised. I tried to focus on the weight of his arm around my shoulders, his calloused fingers brushing against my arm to remind me he was still there. I looked at Emma on my other side. The fear that radiated from her in the car had been forged into a fierce determination. She sat preternaturally still, one hand gripping mine, the other clasped with her brother's. Jason was next to her, and I noticed his mark glowing brightly through his shirt; at least I knew I wasn't alone there.

His gaze met mine with an intensity I couldn't place, and his words from the night of confessions repeated in my head, "*I should have told you then...We'll know when the time is right, if and when it comes.*" A sad smile ghosted across his face, moving so quickly I thought I might have imagined it.

Would we ever find out now?

"Why are y'all so quiet in here?" Willa's voice burst from the entryway, and I jumped, the spike in adrenaline causing a burst in my heart rate.

"Oh, I will never tire of seein' a Marked One's glow!"

I turned around to find Willa's eyes locked on the spot between my shoulder blades, an unnaturally wide grin on her face. I felt deeply exposed, and the hair on my arms stood on end.

"Stop looking at her like that," Carter growled.

"Well, aren't *you* a protective one," Willa said, looking him up and down like a predator eyeing their prey.

"Listen," Cap interrupted, standing in an attempt to draw Willa's attention away from us. "To be transparent, we are all just a bit on edge with the armed guards and lack of information about your... community. Maybe you could shed some light on why you keep this place so protected?"

"Oh, well, that's easy," Willa answered, waving a hand. "Y'all are still around, so you know what it's been like out there. Not everyone can be trusted. We've had one too many visitors who were less than friendly."

"And your interest in our friends?" Cap asked.

"Alina and Jason, ya mean?" Willa's eyes glittered, and I remembered how Gabriela had called to us when she ran over. I hated the way our names sounded on Willa's tongue.

"Yes," Cap answered.

"Well, how could we *not* be interested? If they're anythin' like our little Gabriela, and judging by the familiarity we saw earlier, I have a feeling they are." She turned to look between Jason and me, circling the couch to stand before us, locking us in her sights. "The Beings took you, kept you for a reason. A purpose larger than any of us could ever understand. The answers you must hold, waiting to be unlocked. Don't tell me y'all haven't thought about it yourselves?"

"Of course we have," Jason answered. "But the way you're talking, it seems like you think we are something we're not. The marks on our backs have been nothing but a glorified mood ring that glows when too much adrenaline is pumping through our system."

"Surely that's not all y'all have noticed?" Willa asked, a skeptical look crossing her face.

"That's it," I answered, trying to keep my voice even, confident. "Half of the people in our facility didn't even make it out of the pods alive. If there was something more they were trying to do with us, their experiment must have failed."

"Hm," Willa hummed, studying me. "Well, you wouldn't be the first we've found that didn't fully ascend," she muttered before catching herself. The plastic smile snapped back, and she laughed, scrunching her nose. "Anyway, all this science talk is givin' me a headache. Listen. We set up a place for y'all a few houses down, one of the empty ones. Some of y'all might have to double up, but from the look of things, y'all won't mind." She winked at Russell and Sam, looked Jason up and down, and a new burst of adrenaline pumped through my body, wicked hot. "Sander will be by to drop off some extra food and goodies later. No guards posted outside, promise! There's just one last thing." She smirked. "I'm gonna need the rest of y'all's names if we're going to really get to know each other!" Her grin widened.

"Well, as you know, that's Alina and Jason; I'm Cap," Cap said, pointing to themselves, "This is Michelle, Brian, Dan, Emma, Carter, Sam, and Russell."

I was surprised Cap shared everyone's real names, but then again, names didn't hold the information they once used to when anyone could be looked up on the internet.

"Well, it's lovely to meet y'all," Willa beamed.

I might have started doubting my initial impression if it hadn't been for Gabriela's warning. The woman seemed to ooze hospitality, but there was something about how she spoke, the words she chose, and that too-wide smile that made it feel...off. I couldn't figure out what her end goal was. Clearly, she was trying to sell us on the idea of The Community, but why? If she wanted me, or Jason, or any of us for whatever reason, she had the manpower to take us. She seemed to be trying to win over the rest of the group just as hard. There had to be something more.

Willa led us down the street to the empty house, and as promised, our bags were right in the foyer when we walked inside. The truck was still up the block where we'd left it, another small reassurance.

"If y'all need anythin', y'all know where to find me." Willa winked before shutting the door and leaving us to take in the new surroundings.

"So, everyone else is still craving pig, right?" Russell asked, cautiously looking at the rest of us.

"If I could, I'd eat pig for the rest of my life," Emma muttered.

"Let's take a look through our supplies and get situated. Then we'll talk about our…meal for later," Michelle suggested.

Emma made a beeline for her bag, pulling out the notebook where she'd been logging Jason's and my symptoms. She flipped to the back where the newer notes were, scanning the page before handing it to Russell, demanding, "Tell me what you see on the page."

Russell studied the page, frowning in confusion. "Ah, no offense, Red, but I can't figure out what this chicken scratch says." He pointed at a word on the page. "That doesn't even look like a word. Are you using glyphs or something?" He handed the book to Sam, who also shook her head before handing it back to Emma.

"Well, darn. Guess I won't be…logging the points for…homemade scrabble later. You're all safe from my notes." Emma scrunched her brow in annoyance, struggling to find relevant references for our coded talk. "You get me, right?"

"Yes. Good thinking," Michelle replied. She nodded towards the notebook. "Your handwriting is only legible if we're looking through your eyes."

"Yes," Emma said, clearly relieved.

"Actually, can I see that, Em?" I asked her, reaching for the notebook. She nodded, handing it to me. I pulled the pen from its spot in the middle of the book, flipping to an empty page. I quickly scrawled a note, hoping that the others would get the gist of it—

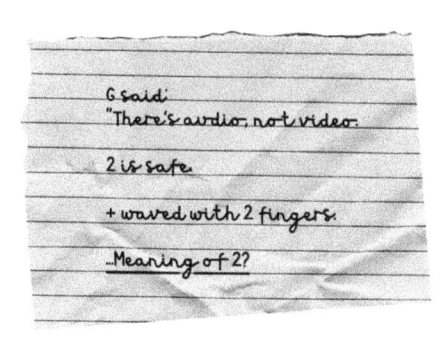

> G said:
> "There's audio, not video.
> 2 is safe.
> + waved with 2 fingers.
> Meaning of 2?

I held the notebook out so the others could read it. Carter reached for the notebook next, and I let him take it to respond—

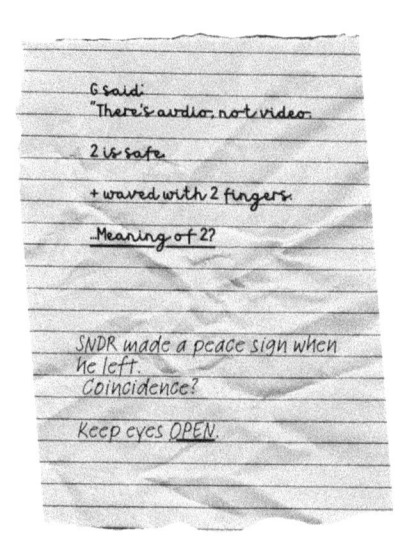

> G said:
> "There's audio, not video.
> 2 is safe.
> + waved with 2 fingers.
> Meaning of 2?
>
> SNDR made a peace sign when he left.
> Coincidence?
>
> Keep eyes OPEN.

He passed the notebook around so the others could read, and they nodded in agreement, one by one.

So now, we just had to wait.

FORTY-FOUR
CARTER

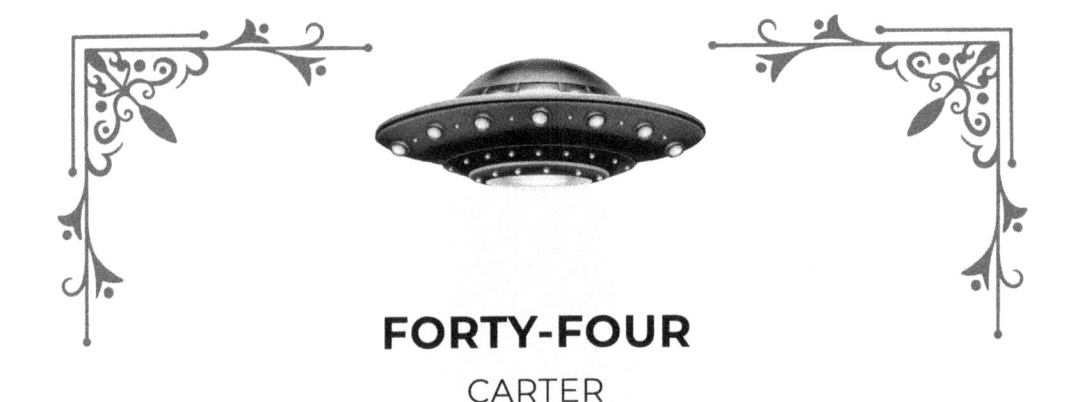

We explored the house in groups of three or four, mapping out the new location and looking for signs of what was being used to listen in on us. I walked with Alina, Emma, and Jason as we scoped out the upstairs floor. There were three bedrooms—two neutral colored ones with king-sized beds, and a bright pink room with a full-sized bed. Like the other house, there were darker squares on the walls where framed photos had likely hung. Dressers and closets were emptied of personal items, and I assumed that meant this neighborhood had been cleared out entirely as The Community moved in.

That in-and-of itself wasn't unusual. We stayed in plenty of abandoned houses while navigating the invasion's aftermath. I could even understand clearing out some of the former occupant's personal items so the place felt less like a mausoleum. Still, the emptiness was deeply unsettling. Each blank space was like a reminder that there were others who came before us and were wiped away—like a crime scene painted over.

Though we looked in the air vents and any other hidden crevices we could find, we didn't see any hints of surveillance devices. We made our way back downstairs. As we reached the foyer, Jason tapped me on the shoulder, pulling me to the side before we could follow Alina and Emma into the living room.

"I'm just going to steal Carter for something quick," he called to the others. Emma nodded, taking Alina's hand and pulling her into the living room.

"What's up?" I asked, watching Alina leave with Emma as my nerves heightened.

"Your arm," he said, voice low as he looked down at my injured arm. "It's bleeding. I didn't want Alina or Emma to see and freak out."

"Shit," I cursed. Bright red blood was soaking through the gauze. The sting had become secondary to everything else—I didn't even notice that I might have busted it back open.

"Come on, I can help." Jason led me to the bags in the foyer and grabbed Emma's medical supplies. He glanced toward the living room once more before rushing me to the kitchen.

Jason set the bag on the counter, taking out an almost empty roll of medical tape, hand sanitizer, antibacterial ointment, and a few unopened packs of gauze. Jason was about to pull out a sterile pair of gloves when I stopped him.

"No—we only use those for serious injuries like stitches or… worse. Just use the hand sanitizer. It's fine," I let him know.

"Alright." Jason nodded. "Well, I can definitely help you clean and rebandage, but just to warn you, I won't be able to redo any stitches if you popped them badly. I'll only tell Em if we have to, though." Jason put the pack of gloves back in the kit. "Can I?" Jason gestured to my arm.

I rested my arm on the counter beside the supplies as Jason sanitized his hands. He looked at my arm, taking a deep breath as he honed in on the wound. Jason moved carefully, gently peeling back the gauze and tape that held the bandage in place. I hissed as the gauze stuck to the wound.

"Fuck. Sorry, man, I know this part sucks," Jason said.

"Goddamn stupid fucking devil pig." I winced as the gauze finally released.

"I know we might not be *best* friends but isn't that a little harsh?" Jason joked.

I huffed a laugh, caught off guard by his humor.

"I really didn't like you those first few days, you know," Jason said.

"Really? Couldn't tell."

A quick smile crossed his face as he grabbed a new piece of gauze.

"Alright, I gotta put some pressure on it to help stop the bleeding."

I grit my teeth as he pressed down on the open wound with the new gauze, slowly applying pressure to stop the flow of blood. Clenching the fist on my uninjured side I said, "I didn't like you much at first, either."

Jason chuckled, still applying pressure on the part of the wound that was bleeding. "Lee changed that, didn't she?"

I let his words sink in before answering.

"Kind of," I replied. "Getting to know her helped, but you did a lot to prove yourself, too. You took action, went out of your way to help, adapted quickly, and didn't give up or complain when shit got hard. Even that first night downtown, you had my back without question—hating me and all."

"Yeah, not going to lie, part of me definitely thought you were going to use me as monster bait and run."

"Well, that was the backup plan," I deadpanned. There was some truth to my statement, but I wouldn't be admitting that part. "How's it looking? Is Emma going to step on my balls?"

"What?" Jason barked another laugh.

"That was her threat if I popped a stitch."

"Of course it was." Jason shook his head, still laughing. "I think you'll be safe. The stitches are still intact. You probably just banged it on something or irritated it in some way. Bleeding's slowed down. I'll finish cleaning this up and then you'll be good, man."

"Thanks," I said.

"Anytime," Jason replied.

I helped Jason store the medical supplies after he rebandaged my arm, making sure the space was clean. Once everything was put away, I looked back towards the living room where everyone else was waiting. Nerves rolled in my stomach, and I found myself trying to find a reason not to go back into the room with the others.

"You also trying to avoid the inevitable?" Jason asked, nodding towards the other room.

I didn't answer. Jason must have read the expression on my face, because he just nodded, a tight smile of understanding on his face.

"We'll figure it out," Jason said.

Though we had a rocky start, the truth was, I didn't think I could have disliked Jason even if I tried. He had proven to be a good person in the short time I'd known him—loyal, willing to sacrifice for the group, going out of his way to look out for others.

I nodded, about to leave the room before Jason stopped me once more. His voice was so low I could barely make out his words. "I'll do whatever I can, but if they're coming for both of us, get Lee out."

He pulled back and a look of solemn resignation crossed his face.

I nodded, holding out my hand, and he took it without hesitation, giving a firm shake to seal the understanding.

As we turned to walk back towards the living room, a knock at the door stopped us in our tracks.

FORTY-FIVE
ALINA

THE KNOCK on the door was quick and abrupt, just two short knocks. That for sure couldn't have been coincidence.

Jason and Carter were at the door before anyone could get up. As expected, it was Sander. He stepped inside carrying a large cardboard box.

He put down the box, then asked Jason, "Is this everyone?" Sander's voice was low, with a slight rasp to it. It was a stark contrast to his sister's quick-paced, high toned trill.

Jason gestured towards the living room, and the lanky teen shoved his hands in the pockets of his cargo shorts, trudging into the room. He seemed to wear a permanent scowl, which seemed at odds with the freckles scattered playfully across his pale nose and cheeks. I guessed him to be around sixteen or seventeen.

He crossed his arms across the plain black tee he wore, taking each of us in. We looked at him expectantly as he took a moment to gather his thoughts.

"Fuck it," he said and very deliberately cast a look in my direction. "Did y'all see this?" he asked, holding up a peace sign again.

I held up two fingers and nodded.

This was what Gabriela meant by *two is safe*? Willa's brother?

I hadn't known Gabriela long, but there was no faking the panic on her face. Whatever was happening here, she was trying to warn us. And apparently, Sander was helping.

"Everythin' y'all need should be in the box, but if y'all find yourselves *missin'* anythin'—" He held up two fingers again. "In the mornin' is the best time. Understand?" He held up two fingers again to drive the point home before repeating, "In the mornin'."

I held up two fingers. "In the morning, got it. And the...rest is in the box?"

"That's what I said," Sander said in his apathetic tone. "I threw in some extras for y'all. Ya know, to help with the *adjustment*."

"Thank you," I murmured, wondering what we were about to find.

Sander nodded. "Alright, I'm out. I have stuff to take care of."

He gave me a pointed look as he walked past us, around the couch, and out the door without another word.

Carter locked the door behind the teen, and Jason picked up the box, carrying it to the center of the room.

Even if I hadn't trusted the signal, what I saw in the box was enough to convince me to go along with the plan.

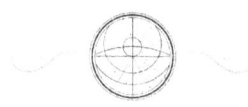

The top layer was covered with food packs, a few hand towels, hand sanitizer, electrolyte packs, a bottle of Ibuprofen, and other random toiletries. Underneath it, though, was the real package.

There was a roll of duct tape with 'tattoo' written across the outside layer in Sharpie. It was easy enough to surmise what the tape was for—to cover our tattoos so the light wouldn't give us away. There were a few worn leatherbound notebooks and a note—

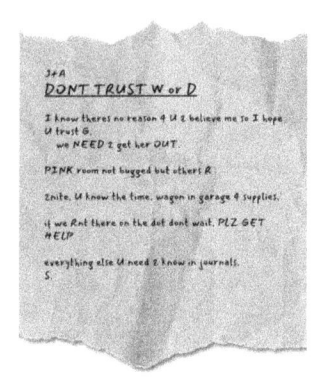

> J+A
> **DONT TRUST W or D**
>
> I know theres no reason 4 U 2 believe me so I hope U trust G.
>   we NEED 2 get her OUT.
>
> PINK room not bugged but others R.
>
> 2nite. U know the time. wagon in garage 4 supplies.
>
> if we Rnt there on the dot dont wait. PLZ GET HELP
>
> everything else U need 2 know in journals.
> S.

We passed around the note, unsure how to react. I certainly didn't trust Willa; apparently, neither did her brother. With how she'd been talking about Jason's and my tattoos, I had a feeling that whatever 'responsibilities' Gabriela had to take care of earlier wasn't a typical teenage chore. I shivered, imagining all the possibilities.

Once we all were able to read the note, Cap stood and held one thumb up and one thumb down, pointing back to us. The vote was unanimous.

Once two in the morning hit, we were getting the hell out.

FORTY-SIX
CARTER

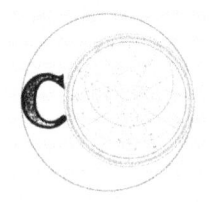

We talked our way through making dinner to keep up appearances for whoever was listening in. Still, we didn't bother hiding our opinions on how fucking weird everything was at The Community. It wasn't a secret that we didn't trust the situation when we arrived; it would have looked suspicious to drop all skepticism completely. We were still working the 'desperate traveler' angle, hoping it was believable enough for them. Hopefully, they'd continue to give us space to adjust to our new 'community.' I was half-surprised when our welcome committee left us to settle in without another surprise visit, and completely shocked when we realized they left us our knives. Considering they were still listening in, it made sense why they'd supposedly let their guard down. What better way to build trust than to let your newcomers think they're unsupervised—that you're just interested in taking care of them with supplies and a roof over their head?

Once it started getting dark, we talked for the audio surveillance about unpacking our bags and going to bed early, then silently shut ourselves in the pink room to build the plan.

"Well, I'm never trusting the word 'community' again," Emma whispered once the door was shut and a blanket was shoved in the gap.

"How the fuck did we end up finding a group of actual body snatchers on our first close encounter with another camp? Our luck fucking sucks," Russell muttered.

"Enough with the body snatchers, dude! We went over this," Dan hissed in response.

"Focus," Michelle snapped, her voice firm but quiet.

We taped a blanket over the window using the duct tape, and turned on our camping lights so we wouldn't have to sit in the dark. Sander's note was in front of us, and Brian was flipping through the journals, trying to understand what exactly we were up against.

"It reads like a science-fiction novel where the narrator is trying to be the main character," he muttered as he closed the book, scrubbing his hands down his face. "It's going to take a while to make sense of these notes."

"Let's recap what we agree on so far and figure out exactly what to do next," Cap whispered. "We are choosing to trust Gabriela because she is in danger and needs help. We are choosing to trust Sander because Gabriela told us to. The Community has some kind of obsession with the glowing mark, which is more than unsettling. From how Gabriela was being treated, the mention of a doctor, and the journals Sander gave us, we can assume that The Community has ulterior motives regarding Alina and Jason, too."

"We have to assume that two kids aren't working completely alone, either," I added. "Whatever this is, it has to be bigger than just a kid wanting to get a new friend out of a bad situation. We have to assume at least one other person is helping them—especially if they think we'll get past the armed guards out front."

"And that's another thing—what about the guns?" Sam swallowed hard. "How do we protect ourselves against that if…"

"I don't know," Cap said.

We sat in silence for a moment, letting those words settle.

"How do we keep Jason and Lee safe, too?" Emma whispered, a dark look on her face.

I noticed that Jason had been distancing himself since our conversation. He caught my eye across the room, and his mouth pressed into a thin line. I knew what he was trying to communicate without him even using words. He was still set on sacrificing himself if he had to. I knew better than trying to argue with someone whose mind was set—which meant I had to try even harder to make sure *both* of them made it out.

Emma had already double-layered tape over both marks to ensure they were fully concealed. Since the incident with the hog, clothing hadn't been enough to cover the glow. Whether it was because their emotions were running higher or their bodies were adapting, we still didn't know.

Once our plan for the night was mapped out, Cap told us to rest as best we could. It was clear no one would be able to relax for long, but we had to try to at least to conserve energy. Jason leaned against his backpack in the corner and Emma rested her head on his thigh with her eyes closed. The siblings hadn't spoken much since earlier this afternoon, though I could say the same for everyone else, too. Whether it was to avoid saying something that shouldn't be overheard or because no one knew what to say, the group was abnormally quiet.

The Twenty-Somethings were sitting on the bed, quietly whispering between each other. Sam was curled in Russell's lap, silently crying on and off. Dan and Brian tried to keep a conversation going, but it was clear they were all too anxious to be invested. It reminded me of the days after the camp attack when we were trying to figure out how the group would fit together again.

I looked over to where Alina was sitting with Cap and Michelle. She was no longer part of their conversation, and instead sat with her knees curled to her chest with a faraway look in her eyes.

"Hey," I whispered, and her eyes darted towards me. She stood without hesitation, crossing the room to sit at my side.

"Hey, yourself," she whispered back, trying to force a smile. I could see tears shimmering in her eyes and how hard she fought to keep them back.

"Remember when we had to hide from an armadillo?" I asked her as the memory suddenly popped into my head.

She breathed a laugh. "We're about to walk through armed

guards to escape a bunch of creeps who want to make us join their sketchy community, and you're thinking about an armadillo?"

"When you replay your life's greatest moments, if there isn't an armadillo encounter, did you really experience life to the fullest?"

"Carter, that is the worst attempt at a joke I have ever heard." Alina laughed softly.

"And yet, you're laughing, so I think I win that game." I couldn't help the slow smile that grew as I saw Alina's eyes brighten. I knew that nothing I could say would make her feel better about the situation, but I could at least try and help her escape for a little while. "What were you before all of this? What was your job?" I asked her.

"Oh, wow. Work. I was in marketing. What did you do?"

"Chief Security Officer for a start-up. It might sound impressive, but I was the only person on the Security Operations team, so I'm pretty sure the title was mostly just for show."

"Well, I'd for sure be impressed if you told me that at a bar," Alina joked.

I sat back to rest against the wall, tilting my head slightly so I could still look at her. She mirrored my position and I studied her face, finding myself at a loss for words. Even in the dim light, her dark, tan skin still reflected warmth—as if she had just come in from the sun. She always seemed to have this radiance that burst from the core of who she was. It was so much a part of her that I knew if I could just keep that light going, everything would be okay.

"Carter?" she whispered, and I could practically feel the thoughts racing through her mind.

I held out my hand and she laced her fingers in mine.

There was no way I was letting her leave my side.

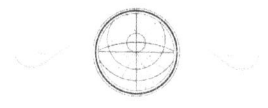

At 1:50 a.m., we crept downstairs towards the back of the house. It was so quiet I could hear the pounding of my own heart. Earlier, we'd moved the stroller-wagon full of supplies to the back door so it would be ready to go. Now we just had to make it happen.

There was a chance we'd have to abandon the wagon, so we tried to be as strategic as possible with packing. Brian and Russell picked the wagon off the ground as we eased the door open, carefully walking it through the doorway to stay as quiet as possible. True to her word, Willa didn't have guards outside our house. She was probably confident that her surveillance, the armed guards at the front gate, and our ignorance or desperation would be enough to keep us in place. Fuck that.

We walked as quickly as we dared towards the truck, and I kept Alina close to my side, her hand held tight in mine. Dan took over pushing the wagon so Russell and Brian could flank Jason, who was just in front of us. Jason tried to argue against walking too close to Alina, saying it was too risky for them to be near each other if we got caught. Luckily, the others refused to let him move from their protective circle.

The only sounds were the wheels of the wagon crunching against the ground and our soft footsteps. I hoped the subtle sounds weren't as deafening as they seemed amidst the quiet. It was dark without streetlights, and we could only hope that it was enough to conceal us from anyone who happened to look outside in the middle of the night. We slowed down as we approached the guard station, knowing that this was the moment of truth.

Two people were leaning against the barricade, their guns only visible when the metal caught a glint of moonlight through the shadows. My arm was killing me, but I still kept a tight hold on my knife in the hand that wasn't holding Alina's. It wasn't a great defense against guns, but it was better than nothing. These people were too tall and broad to be Gabriela or Sander, and I could only hope they were on our side as that constricting band of anxiety tightened around my chest.

Two smaller figures ran from across the street straight towards the guard station. As they grew closer, the guards stood alert, raising their guns at the quickly approaching figures.

"It's us," a voice hissed, and the guards lowered their guns, recognizing Sander clutching Gabriela's hand at the same moment I did.

"Come on," one of the guards called, their voice barely above a whisper. He handed two backpacks to Sander, as the other passed one to Gabriela. The four of them jogged over to meet us just as we reached the truck. Russell, Dan, Brian, and Jason were already loading the bags and wagon into the truck bed, and I pulled Alina to the back passenger door.

She stared back at me, her eyes wide with fear as she stepped up into the truck, holding my hand until the last second. I didn't want to let go, but we needed to keep moving. Before her hand completely slipped from mine, I caught her pinky finger, looping it with my own.

"I got you," I murmured, unable to look away from those hazel eyes. "I promise."

I gently kissed the back of her hand, feeling her soft skin just graze against my lips before I finally let go. Her lips parted, and I held her gaze until the door shut.

Snapping back into action, I checked the back to make sure Jason was in his place. He had taken to watching over Gabriela and Sander, and was crouched down low next to them. Good. The last thing I needed to worry about was him trying to sacrifice himself for anyone else. Russell opened the driver's side sticking the key in the ignition, but leaving the engine off as he popped the truck into neutral. The plan was to push the truck as far as we could before turning it on and risking someone hearing the engine. With my arm, I was banned from pushing the truck, so instead, I climbed into the front passenger seat, lowering the window so I could keep an eye on the others.

"There's more of us this time. What if I can't keep the truck steady enough?" Russell muttered, not even trying to hide the way his voice wavered.

"I believe in you, kid; you can do this," I told him. He nodded, looking forward again, a hardened look of determination on his face.

The guards helped push us down the road, and Russell jumped into the driver's seat as the car picked up momentum so he could steer the vehicle better. We were almost at the entrance to the neighborhood when the guards told us they needed to turn back.

"Don't come back, Sander." I heard one of them say. "Get help if you can, but don't you come back for anything. You and that girl get far from here and warn whoever else you can."

The other guard jogged to the driver's side door, quickly repeating directions for Russell to follow as the truck stopped for the others to get in. Emma, Sam, and Michelle piled into the backseat again, as the others climbed into the back of the truck, ducking low. No one said a word as Russell started the engine. The sound was like a roar in the quiet of night, and I hoped to any deity that still existed that we weren't heard.

FORTY-SEVEN
ALINA

Russell drove slowly as we turned out of the neighborhood, looking in the sideview mirror every few seconds to ensure we weren't being followed. Once we had enough distance, he stepped on the gas, pushing the truck as fast as we could go without threatening to lose our group in the back.

The windows were open, and the air that crept like a mist into the car was heavy with moisture. Already, I could feel my sweat mixing with the humidity on my skin as we sat crushed together in the back seat, unable to turn the air conditioning on in order to conserve gas.

Every once in a while, Carter would turn slightly to glance at me in the back seat as if he needed to ensure I was still there. Something had changed in the last few days, and the pull I felt towards him tightened, undeniable now.

Emma had her head turned, staring out the small window in the back of the cab that looked out towards the truck's bed, keeping an eye on her brother. She gripped my hand like a vice, a pledge to keep us together at all costs.

I still watched over him, as well. Jason and I made it through so much already, somehow finding our way back to Emma in the process. Then, we were welcomed by a group of people who quickly claimed permanent places inside my heart. Though the danger never really left, it felt like as long as we were together, we could make it through even the worst parts.

My entire life, I believed that humans were inherently good. I truly felt that, especially with such a threat to our species, as a society, we would ultimately unite and fight together. I knew there would always be bad in the world, but I also thought that human empathy and compassion would be what allowed us to recover. Yet, the first community we encountered was so deceptive and predatory, how would I be able to trust anyone else again? No matter what The Community's end goal was, nothing could justify keeping a young girl prisoner, or conspiring to capture others.

Ultimately, humans were still fighting to keep our spot as apex predators on this planet—and now? That fight was going so well that our own species became the greatest threat to humanity's survival. The irony sat bitterly on the tip of my tongue.

"Gas is low," Russell said, his voice wary.

We'd already passed through the next town, unable to stop since it was in such close proximity to The Community. At this point, I knew I wasn't the only one doubting whether we should have taken the risk earlier on and just stopped. The back roads we followed led us through abandoned farmland and open fields, and we hadn't seen any other opportunity to refuel. Eventually, we would have to pull over or risk our journey ending before we were ready.

"Hold on, back up here, slowly," Carter instructed Russell in an even tone.

Russell slowly rolled to a stop before reversing until we backed up to a long dirt road that I hadn't noticed passing.

"Can the rest of you stay in here a sec? I want to ask Cap about stopping here. It looks like it might be a ranch or an abandoned farm. Might have a car or something we can siphon gas from on the property."

"Good idea, Carter," Michelle said, her voice sounding tired and worn.

Carter opened the door and walked around back to talk to the others. The majority of the group was in agreement that we should pull off at the ranch. My nerves were buzzing, and my stomach churned with uncertainty. I hated the idea of standing still, worried that if we stopped moving, they'd find us. But, to keep moving, we needed to refuel. We were beyond exhausted, so to stay safe, we also needed to rest. It was the right choice.

Carter got back into the passenger seat, shutting the door as he turned to look at the four of us in the back seat. His eyes lingered on mine as he asked, "You all doing okay back there?"

"I hate this," Sam said, her voice barely above a whisper. She had been quietly crying most of the drive, nerves shot from everything that had happened during the day.

"We'll be okay. We just need a break," Michelle said.

I nodded, leaning my head against Emma's shoulder. Emma didn't say a word, but squeezed my hand and rested her head against mine.

Russell turned onto the dirt road, flicking the high beams on to light the way. The truck jostled on the uneven terrain, but Russell kept the pace slow for the others in the back.

"There—pull around the barn." Carter pointed to a large structure that seemed to hulk over the field in the dark.

"What about the house up there?" Russell questioned.

"Let's start here," Carter answered. "We can keep the truck closer to the entrance to the barn while still keeping it hidden from the road."

Russell turned off the dirt road, parking the truck behind the barn.

Everyone slowly hopped down from the truck, and we gathered in a circle.

Cap called everyone's attention. "First, I want to introduce myself to our newcomers. My name is Cap, my pronouns are they/them. I tend to lead these discussions, but we make our decisions as a group. In our camp, everyone's voice matters, no matter how long you've been here, how old you are, or how you identify. We'll go through more in-depth introductions once we are able to let our guard down a bit more, though."

Cap gave the teens a warm smile, which they both returned.

Sander's shoulders visibly relaxed as Cap continued and Gabriela loosened her hold on Sander's arm.

"We are dangerously low on gas, and it's harder to navigate accurately in the dark. We're going to need to stay here until daylight when we can safely set ourselves up to drive again. I don't like the idea of stopping so soon, but Russell did a good job taking the less obvious roads. Hopefully, that will keep them from finding our trail for a bit. If they even decide to pursue."

"They will," Sander said grimly. "They're gonna be pissed Gab got away, and even more pissed y'all escaped before they could indoctrinate."

"Okay, kid," Emma said, clearly beyond the point of caring about niceties. "You're going to have to give us more than that—what exactly is this group your sister started?"

"She didn't start it," Sander answered, scowling. "Dad did. The Community wasn't meant to be this way, though—it was a good place when it started. We really tried rescuing and helping people. But when Dr. Don showed up..." Sander trailed off, trying to find the right words before speaking again. "When Dr. Don showed up, things started changin' quick.

"Accidents started happenin', and the people who used to make decisions, anyone who disagreed with Don, one-by-one they started dyin' or disappearin'—includin' my dad. All of a sudden, talk about 'The Ascended' was spreadin', and Dr. Don was makin' all of these predictions sayin' that the ships would leave, and explosions would fill the sky. He said the electricity would come back, and the captured would be returned—ascended to the next stage of human evolution. He also said that The Beings would leave guardians to watch over the planet until they returned again and that we needed the ascended to harness those guardians' power.

"And then, all of those things started happening. The Community was half-scared, half-convinced he was a new revelation from God.

"I begged Willa to leave, but by that point, she was completely brainwashed. I didn't wanna leave without her—she was my only family left. Then I found others who didn't believe, they were organizin' to fight back. So, we started workin' together, plannin'.

333

After the ships disappeared, a scoutin' group brought us Gab." He turned to the girl who still held his arm.

Gabriela cleared her throat, her voice still shaking with nerves. "Ben was killed in the explosions, and one of those creatures got Jean," Gabriela said quietly, looking at Jason and me. "I was alone, and then a car pulled up and told me they could help me. It was either that or stay on my own. I was so hungry and thirsty. So tired." Gabriela took a shuddering breath before continuing. "As soon as Dr. Don saw my mark, they all but locked me up. They had two guards on me all the time. At first they said it was for safety, The Community's and my own. The doctor made me go to his house for testing, and that's where I met Sander. He helped me. Said the others had gone too far and that rebels were working on a way to get us out and protect other people from The Community...but I didn't think...I thought I'd be..." Gabriela choked on a sob and turned to bury her face in Sander's shoulder.

That poor girl. She had been through so much more than I could even fathom, and my heart ached, knowing that if we hadn't been separated, I could have helped her.

"I am so, so sorry for everything you have been through," Cap said, and I could see the pain on their face after hearing the kids' stories. "Thank you for trusting us with that information. I hope you'll tell us more after we all get some rest so we can figure out a way to help. You won't be forced to stay with us, but I do hope that you will consider it. As long as you follow the rules that keep us safe and contribute to the group, that's *all* that will be asked of you."

Sander nodded, and his shoulders slumped. As exhaustion spread across his face, he looked even younger than before. What he must have seen...at least he was with us now. Hopefully we could keep him safe—keep them both safe.

Cap turned to the rest of us, making sure we were ready to continue.

"So, here's what I'm thinking. Let's stay here in the barn tonight. We'll close off the other side, so there will only be one entrance to guard. In the morning, we can check out that house and see if there are any other vehicles on the property. We only have a few more hours until sunrise, so we should make the most of this break. I want everyone to stay in the barn close together unless you need to go outside to relieve yourself. No one goes anywhere without a buddy. I don't care how close you are to the barn door, if you step foot outside, you need a partner. And keep your weapons on you."

"Oh!" Gabriela called, "Sander! The backpack."

Sander perked up, his face breaking from the stiff expression he'd been holding as he remembered the bags the guards gave to him.

"They gave us guns," Sander said, looking at Cap, then shifting to the rest of us. "I'd like to keep one if y'all don't mind, but y'all can have the others as a sign of good faith."

"Thank you, Sander," Cap replied.

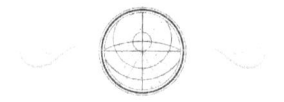

We kept our bags and supplies in the truck, only taking some food and water into the barn. I'd also grabbed Brian's hoodie, needing something to hold onto. Then there were the guns. As promised, Sander kept one of the guns. The rest went to the others who were most experienced using one—Cap, Carter, Dan, and Michelle.

Empty stalls lined the walls and the ground was covered with hay. The space still smelled kind of like a petting zoo, but judging by the open barn doors and stalls, the animals had clearly vacated their home a while ago. Saddle blankets and other riding tack were neatly stacked by the back door or hung on the wall, and Michelle gathered the blankets for us to cushion the ground while we rested.

We settled into the space, lying back against the blankets in a way that reminded me of the naptime circles you'd see at preschools or daycares. Carter and Russell insisted on taking the first hour of watch and were sat by the door to the barn, just inside. Soon, the sound of rustling hay drifted into an echo of deep breathing as the others fell asleep. I could never figure out how some of them could fall asleep so easily, no matter the situation.

I wanted so badly to rest, but my brain refused to let go of the intrusive thoughts that ran like a highlight reel of the worst possible things that could happen next.

I sat up after I realized sleep wouldn't come anytime soon, and looked around the space. Carter and Russell were talking quietly by the barn door, barely visible in the dim light that tricked in from the moon. Carter's head turned my way, and there was a flutter in my stomach as I thought about what he'd said as we left The Community. Before I knew it, I was walking over to the barn's entrance.

"You can't rest either, I take it?" Carter asked as I approached, standing up to speak with me.

"I wish," I said, hugging Brian's hoodie to my chest.

Russell yawned, his eyes heavy and ready to close. The adrenaline crash was hitting him hard, and I had a feeling he might benefit from an hour of rest more than I would.

"Hey, Russ, do you want to swap?" I asked him.

"Nah, I'm good." He yawned again. "Fuck, maybe. I don't know."

"Go on, kid," Carter said with a half-smile.

Russell nodded, pushing up to his feet and shuffling over to the rest of the group. I watched as he squeezed in between Brian and Sam, curling around his girlfriend and burying his face in her neck. The tension practically melted off of him as he relaxed into the space next to her, and my heart squeezed.

I turned to look at Carter, seeing that his gaze was still fixed on Russell and Sam, a real smile on his lips.

"Oh, hey, Carter," I said, grabbing his attention. "You just have something on your face right here." I pointed to the corner of my mouth, and his hand went up to the same spot on his face.

"What is it?" he asked.

"Just a real, genuine smile. And I'm pretty sure it was because of Russell, so that makes it even better," I teased.

He tried to glare in my direction, but his smile broke through again. "Ah, fuck," he muttered. "It's from shock, I swear. Or delirium. One of those things."

"Right, of course," I said with a tired laugh. "It couldn't be that you think Russell and Sam are *actually* the sweetest thing ever?" I looked back at the couple. "It's one of the things that keeps me going, honestly. Gives me faith that good things can still happen," I murmured.

"I think I get that," Carter said, and I turned to find his gaze fixed on me.

"I didn't get to say thank you, by the way."

"For what?"

"For keeping me grounded; helping me make it through everything without having a complete breakdown today. I've been kidnapped by aliens, experimented on, chased by eight-legged creatures, and charged at by a feral hog—yet today was probably the scariest yet. Maybe it was just the build-up and overflow of it all. I don't know. But—" I hesitated, meeting his eyes. The deep brown of his irises looked almost black against the canvas of night. As he looked back at me, I remembered what it felt like to have his arm holding me close, his fingers laced through mine.

As terrified as I had been, I also felt safe in a way I hadn't ever known before. As he held me, protected me, Carter managed to pull at the fragments of strength I didn't even know I had left, helping me to stand so *I* could face whatever came next. He made me feel like I could get through it, not because someone else was holding me up, but because I already had what I needed to get to the other side.

"But?" he asked, prompting me to continue.

I shook my head, bringing myself back to the present moment, "Just—thank you."

He reached out with his right hand, the side without the injury, and slipped his fingers underneath mine, teasing the pads of my fingertips with his.

A tingle that started at the base of my spine swirled up, through my chest, reaching out to the places where our fingers touched. He pulled his hand back, turning it to slide his fingers between mine, slowly, testing the way we connected without panic and fear driving us together. Our fingers clasped, the blank canvas of my skin pressing against the art that covered his as he pressed his palm to mine.

After a moment, his voice barely above a whisper, he said, "You never have to thank me for that."

I glanced up at him as his thumb teased slow circles against mine, but he was still staring at the spot where our hands connected, an expression on his face I couldn't quite define. He shifted, gesturing to the ground and we sat just beside the narrow sliver of light from the moon. I moved closer as he rested our clasped hands against his knee, his uninjured arm pressed against mine.

And it was something so simple, so innocent—but in that moment, it was everything I needed and more.

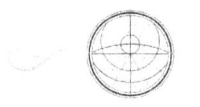

Michelle and Emma approached after a while, yawning as they woke up from their short rest.

"Alright, you two need to go get rest," Michelle said, tapping Carter's leg with her foot.

"Yeah, you're probably right," Carter answered as we both stood.

"Wait, before we take over—Michelle, do you have to pee? I have to pee," Emma asked.

Michelle scoffed. "Really? That's how you ask? I know we're in a barn, but we don't have to act like we grew up in one. No. I don't have to pee."

"I'll go with you, Em" I said, laughing. Carter let go of my hand as Emma smirked and looped her arm through mine.

Though it was still dark out, the beginning signs of morning were starting to peek out from the horizon as we quickly walked behind the truck. Orange started blending into the dusky gray that always hit just before dawn and birds were already chirping in the trees.

"Man, I wish we never left the goddamn forest," Emma muttered as she squatted behind the truck.

I leaned against the hood as I looked back at the barn's door, sighing. "Same. What a day."

"Well," Emma said, "at least that day is over. Fuck, I keep trying to think back to whether things were this insane when the invaders were still here, but—"

Emma went silent as a soft thud hit the grass next to the truck.

"But?" I asked, turning around.

A sharp pinch jabbed into my neck and spots flashed before my eyes, a buzzing feeling spreading across my body as I tried to lift a heavy hand to my neck. The edges of my vision clouded, and my legs went numb.

I tried taking a step forward, but my knees gave out and I crumpled to the ground. Pins and needles engulfed my skin as a heat spread across my neck, down to my chest.

My eyes were so heavy, too heavy to keep open any longer.

Spots danced on the backs of my eyelids, fading into static before—

Darkness.

FORTY-EIGHT
CARTER

"Alina! Alinaaaaaaaaa! Alinaaaaaaaaaaaa!"

The shrill scream snapped me to attention like a hook snaring me through the gut. Michelle jumped as we both looked towards the door.

"Emma?" I heard Michelle call as she stepped forward.

"Wait," Cap yelled, running to Michelle's side, grabbing her arm before she could move any further. "Don't go out there."

I ignored Cap who was preoccupied with Michelle, moving towards the barn door just as Emma tore inside. It had barely been more than a few minutes. What could have possibly happened in that short amount of time? Still, Emma stumbled in, full body sobs heaving from her small frame as she tried to form words. The blood in my veins froze, as I realized Emma was by herself.

She grabbed my arm, nails digging into my skin as she sobbed. Her blue eyes were wide as pools, and a bruise was starting to bloom on her temple. "You...have to...find...her," Emma gasped through the sobs that wracked her frame. It was then the weight of the situation hit me.

I abandoned Emma where she folded in on herself, hearing but not comprehending the other voices in the room as I shouldered my way outside.

The rising sun's morning rays were blinding in the distance as I scanned the field next to the barn that seemed to go on for miles—

Nothing.

Nothing.

Nothing.

There was fucking nothing.

Nausea rolled in my stomach as a buzzing hum filled my head, absorbing all other sounds. Pushing my hands against my temples, I squeezed my eyes shut, trying to will myself out of this reality.

Air filled my lungs, but I couldn't breathe.

Hands gripped my shoulders, but I barely felt their hold.

There was no sign of her.

Nothing.

No.

No.

FORTY-NINE

This is not the end.

THANK YOU!

Thank you for reading book one of the
Afterglow Rising Trilogy!
Don't forget to leave a star rating and written review on Amazon and/or GoodReads!
The invasion continues in 2025.

Rate on GoodReads

Rate on Amazon

ACKNOWLEDGMENTS

Oh my gosh, I cannot believe I actually wrote a whole book.

The *Afterglow Rising Trilogy* would not be here today if it weren't for some very significant people in my life, so I have to spill my thanks before wrapping this novel up in a cute little bow for publishing.

First, my Hot Toxic Trauma Bible Study group—

Jenna, Lauren, Suz, and Caroline, it is literally thanks to the unhinged stream of conscious ideas born in our group chat that this book even exists. Though the story has strayed from glowing appendages and turned into something wildly different—it is because of your sincere feedback, constructive notes, tarot card pulls, horoscope readings, and endless support that *Afterglow: Rising From the Ashes* is the epic story it is today. Thank you for pushing me to run with it, and for being there every step of the way. I love you guys so much.

Also, a second call-out to Jenna for diving in so deep. Jenna, your notes, spreadsheets, and character trackers were next level, and I love you so much for dedicating so much effort towards *Afterglow*. Not only did you read every single freaking version of this book, you have been the best hype-person I could ever imagine. Our 'what-if' talks contributed to so many ideas that made it into the trilogy, and I cannot wait to bring the rest of the story to life!!! Here's to many more rogue marketing road trips across Texas, sister novels, Buc-ees pit stops, coordinated outfits, and alllllllllllllll the things.

Mel, you wonderful human. You were so on board with *Afterglow* from day one, and your texts played a significant role in building the confidence I needed to make it through to the end! Thank you for believing in me, sharing authentic Austin, TX knowledge, and for believing in the story.

Loren Lee, Chris Walters and R. A. Hunter, my lovely hilarious indie author writing buddies,

You three were such a huge part of my writing process. From the writing sprints and body-doubling, to panic chats on Instagram, to the general support and encouragement y'all offer on a regular basis—I love youuuuu.

Have to shout out my beta reader team as well—thank you for dedicating your time to read *Afterglow* in its early stages and for your feedback/notes! It takes an exceptional eye to see through the rough draft and pick up on the quality of the story beneath, and y'all did that. Your support means more than you know.

And of course, to my wonderful ARC team, thank you for being the first to read *Afterglow*. One day I'll come up with a fun team name. It means so much that some of y'all stepped outside of your normal genres to give *Afterglow* a try, and I loved every single enthusiastic reaction text that was sent my way! I promise, Book two is coming soon. I won't leave y'all hanging for too long!

A special thank you to my copy editor, Hannah G. Scheffer-Wentz of English Proper Editing Services. I love the work that you dedicate to supporting indie authors, especially those of us working on our debut novels. Your comments absolutely gave me life. Working with you made me feel so much more confident about releasing *Afterglow* into the world, and I'm endlessly thankful to have found you!

Okay, time for the mushy part.

Mom, thank you for being the best alpha reader I could have asked for. Seriously, being able to say, "Look at what I did, mom!!!" and seeing you just as enthusiastic and excited as when I wrote my first words back when I was a tiny human—it's everything. All of the library trips, reading programs, and bedtime stories with you forged my love of literature and all its forms. I love you so much, and your support means more to me than I can ever express. I believe in me because you believed in me first.

My kiddos, L and E, at five and three years old, you don't fully grasp what exactly I've been doing. Nevertheless, you've been mom's biggest cheerleaders. I'd say a good 40% of this novel was written on my phone as I lay on the floor of your bedroom curled in fetal position waiting for you to fall asleep. I love you, I love you, I love you, I love you, I love you. And I hope by the time you are able to read this, you'll be sleeping much better than you are right now.

And last, but certainly not least, Mike, my husband, my Bob... from day one you have been an endless stream of support, and I am so lucky to have you as a partner. You went above and beyond to make sure I had the time, space, and mental capacity to complete this book. Thank you for listening to me read every version of every chapter out loud, and for hyping up my book to everyone you crossed paths with. Our conversations led to so many pivotal moments in the story...like the battery conversation. For the record, I am still Team: Don't Question It...It's Aliens. IT'S ALIENS!!!!

And to you, lovely, sweet, angel-baby of a human reading this book, thank you for taking a chance on a debut author, and for checking out *Afterglow*! I hope you hang out for the rest of the trilogy, as well as the other books I have a-brewin' in my noggin.

In the words of *The Terminator*, 'I'll be back.'

Love y'all

🤍—Stacey

SIGN UP FOR STACEY'S NEWSLETTER!

To stay up to date on all upcoming releases, sneak peaks, giveaways, contests, and more, don't forget to sign up for Stacey LP's newsletter! Please scan the below QR code, or visit:
www.authorstaceylp.com
to sign up!

ABOUT THE AUTHOR

Stacey LP was born and raised on Long Island in NY, and currently resides in Texas.

After a major plot twist where she lost her full-time job of almost a decade in a mass layoff, Stacey's friends urged her to pursue her dream of writing a book of her own…and thus, an author was born.

Stacey writes in the sci-fi and fantasy genres, frequently weaving love stories into each plot. When she isn't writing (or reading), Stacey enjoys spending time with her husband, children, two cats, and goofball of a dog…or going to pop punk shows. #elderemo4ever

Stacey has an MA in English Literature from SUNY New Paltz and is proud (aka relieved) to finally use her degree for more than just a punchline.

You can find Stacey on Instagram, Tik Tok, and Threads at:
@authorstaceylp

ALSO BY STACEY LP

AFTERGLOW RISING TRILOGY:

Afterglow: Rising From the Ashes (11/15/24)

Book Two: Coming in 2025...

Stay up to date by following Stacey on GoodReads and Amazon:

Milton Keynes UK
Ingram Content Group UK Ltd.
UKHW021851231124
451423UK00002B/347

9 781965 557013